DESIGN FOR DYING

A Lillian Frost and Edith Head Novel

RENEE PATRICK

A TOM DOHERTY ASSOCIATES BOOK • NEW YORK

This is a work of fiction. All of the characters, organizations, and events portrayed in this novel are either products of the author's imagination or are used fictitiously.

DESIGN FOR DYING

A Forge Book
Published by Tom Doherty Associates
175 Fifth Avenue
New York, NY 10010

www.tor-forge.com

The Library of Congress Cataloging-in-Publication Data
is available upon request.

ISBN 978-0-7653-8185-9 (trade paperback)
ISBN 978-1-4668-8458-8 (e-book)

Our books may be purchased in bulk for promotional, educational, or business use. Please contact your local bookseller or the Macmillan Corporate and Premium Sales Department at 1-800-221-7945, extension 5442, or by e-mail at MacmillanSpecialMarkets@macmillan.com.

First Edition: April 2016
First Trade Paperback Edition: March 2017

Printed in the United States of America

0 9 8 7 6 5 4 3

Praise for *Design for Dying*

"*Design for Dying* reads like a dream, one in which classic Hollywood does a dance with old-school crime fiction. It's spiced with famous faces and features a beguiling newcomer, Lillian Frost, who's destined to be a star in her own right. They don't make 'em like this anymore—so it's a good thing Renee Patrick is here to write 'em."
—Eddie Muller, Shamus Award–winning author of *The Distance* and host of Turner Classic Movies, *Summer of Darkness*

"A complex environment for sleuthing replete with possibilities and an exciting sense of the glamorous, gossipy, and creative world of cinema's golden age. The warm working relationship that develops between Lillian and Edith will leave readers eager to see more of their adventures."
—*Publishers Weekly*

"Cue the applause! This stylish and cinematic take on vintage Hollywood will delight movie buffs—and mystery-lovers—with its star-studded cast and clever whodunnit. Straight from the silver screen, it's smart, authentic, and irresistible."
—Hank Phillippi Ryan, award-winning author of *What You See*

"A champagne-flavored frolic of a first mystery set during Hollywood's golden age. This is sure to delight fans of old Hollywood and Turner Classic Movies."
—*Library Journal*

"Paced like a gunshot and sheer fun to read. A smart, wicked gem of a book."
—David Corbett, award-winning author of *The Mercy of the Night*

"Scandal, intrigue, and clothing descriptions to die for abound as salesgirl Lillian Frost joins forces with legendary Hollywood costume designer Edith Head in this sparkling debut. If you love historical mysteries crackling with wit and seamlessly interlaced with period detail, you'll want to try *Design for Dying* on for size; it's guaranteed to be a perfect fit."
—Ashley Weaver, author of *Murder at the Brightwell*

Also by Renee Patrick

Dangerous to Know

To Muriel LeFave, who inspired Lillian Frost
and who loved a mystery

Acknowledgments

The movies are widely known as a collaborative art while writing a novel tends to be viewed as a solitary pursuit. The two halves of Renee Patrick have already shot holes in that theory. An abundance of people contributed to this book, all without the benefit of a craft services table.

We'd still be cooling our heels at Schwab's waiting for our big break if it weren't for our tireless agent, Lisa Gallagher, the epitome of elegance, even in a bicycle helmet. Editor extraordinaire Kristin Sevick took a look at a rough cut and didn't flinch, helping us find the story we wanted to tell. Our gratitude to Tom Doherty, Bess Cozby, Justine Gardner, and everyone at Tor/Forge. Artist Gerad Taylor created a cover we wanted to plaster on marquees across town.

We received a welcome dose of validation when an early version of the manuscript won a 2013 William F. Deeck-Malice Domestic Grant for Unpublished Writers. We are indebted to Harriette Sackler and the grants committee, and to the entire Malice Domestic community—particularly previous grant recipients—who welcomed us with open arms.

Eddie Muller is the godfather of this book. His work with the Film Noir Foundation, the Noir City film festivals, and Turner Classic Movies has not only saved individual films from disappearing but has also preserved moviegoing as a social experience. Knowing him sent us tumbling down this rabbit hole, and Eddie has been an invaluable resource every step of the way.

Our first readers came through big. Ray Banks sent an epic encouraging e-mail that got us through many a dark night of the soul; David Corbett kindly introduced us to the right person; and Christa Faust, G. M. Ford, and Skye Moody offered advice and, even better, support.

Any research into the life of Edith Head begins with her own books, *The Dress Doctor* (cowritten by Jane Kesner Ardmore) and *How to Dress for Success*, with Joe Hyams. Edith inspired three different biographers, each approaching her life from a unique perspective. Paddy Calistro based *Edith Head's Hollywood* on hours of taped interviews for Edith's uncompleted autobiography, with Edith credited as coauthor. David Chierichetti drew on his background as a costumer and his friendship with Edith for his book *Edith Head: The Life and Times of Hollywood's Celebrated Costume Designer*, while Jay Jorgensen places the emphasis on her handiwork in his lavishly illustrated *Edith Head: The Fifty-Year Career of Hollywood's Greatest Costume Designer.* Many thanks to Ms. Calistro and Mr. Chierichetti for being gracious enough to answer our questions.

Edith willed her papers to the Academy of Motion Picture Arts and Sciences. The staff at the Academy's Margaret Herrick Library made it a pleasure to review Edith's personal correspondence—while sitting at a table from Edith's house. Marilyn Moss contributed a critical research assist.

For a perspective on Edith's legacy, as well as the art of costume design itself, our thanks to Deborah Nadoolman Landis, the founding director and chair of UCLA's David C. Copley Center for the Study of Costume Design, and her associate Natasha Rubin. The dedicated team of archivists at Paramount Pictures rolled out the red carpet for us. To walk in Edith's footsteps was a thrill. We will never be able to repay Andrea

Kalas, Randall Thropp, Geraldine Pace, and Jaci Rohr for their time, their enthusiasm, and their willingness to let us hijack a little of the studio's history. It's worth underscoring that all these talented, busy people happily assisted two novices out of a shared respect for Edith Head and her work.

We plotted many story twists, drowned every heartbreak, and celebrated each milestone at Seattle's Zig Zag Café. Throughout, the staff talked about the book as if its seeing the light of day were a foregone conclusion. And as always, they pour a lovely cocktail.

Vince thanks Bob Sobhani and the entire team at Magnet Management, as well as the readers of VinceKeenan.com. Rosemarie thanks her colleagues at Fred Hutchinson Cancer Research Center, and the vintage fashion and classic film online communities.

We'd both like to acknowledge our parents, who never forced their movie-obsessed children to go outside and play.

In writing *Design for Dying,* we strove to honor the Hollywood history that inspired us, but on occasion we adjusted time lines and geography. All mistakes are our own, and when in doubt, we printed the legend.

What chance has a woman got?

—Barbara Stanwyck, *Baby Face*, 1933

DESIGN FOR DYING

Los Angeles Register *November 6, 1937*

'ALLEY ANGEL' SLAIN IN HOLLYWOOD

Mystery Woman in Fashion Finery

LOS ANGELES, NOV. 5 (AP) - The body of an unidentified woman was found in an alley behind a butcher shop in Hollywood today. The woman had been shot several times, according to police sources. More baffling to authorities, the woman was dressed in attire more suited to a movie colony premiere than the humble environs where she was discovered.

The body, draped in a silk gown and numerous shimmering stones, was found in the early hours of November 5 by an employee of the shop. "She looked like an angel," said Spyros Makadoulis, age 41. "Like she'd fallen from heaven itself."

1

THE HEM OF the dress was drenched in blood. I could only hope no one would notice.

"If a romantic afternoon listening to the Philharmonic at the Hollywood Bowl is in your plans, try this stunning gray worsted suit that will ensure his eyes are on YOU, not the stage. A nipped-in waist and mauve accents bring out the natural beauty that any lover—music lover, that is—will appreciate."

A graceful model strolled a platform in front of fifty Los Angeles ladies of leisure. Tremayne's fall fashion show brought them to the department store to lunch, browse, and with any luck, spend thousands. Every shopgirl had been pressed into service in the backstage frenzy of last-minute alterations. Some of us were better at it than others. Still bleeding from where a needle had pierced me, I pushed the next beauty forward and dragged myself clear of traffic.

"Or perhaps modern music is more your style. Then it's dinner and dancing at the Cocoanut Grove. Wearing this gown of midnight-blue satin you'll captivate any dance partner. Bell sleeves sway sensuously as you glide across the floor. And be sure to put your best foot forward in a pair of silver sandals."

Pure corn, but the patter played. The audience oohed appreciatively as the gorgeous strawberry blonde pirouetted. Even I couldn't see where my blood had stained the gown. With a curtsy to her imaginary partner, the model stepped behind the curtain and fell into a chair next to where I was sucking the pad of my thumb.

"Good luck dancing in these. It's like wearing mousetraps." The strawberry blonde, my fellow Tremayne's employee Priscilla Louden, pried the offending shoes off her feet. I peered through a slit in the curtain as the announcer started her spiel.

"Back home after your fantasy evening, keep the romantic mood alive with an alluring gown and robe in blushing rose. A marabou collar adds just the right soft touch. Is that matching marabou on the pumps? Mais oui."

The statuesque brunette on display pressed her cheek into the feathers as if lost in memory. For one terrible moment I thought she was going to sneeze.

Priscilla, having changed into a simple blue dress, joined me at the curtain as the well-heeled matrons applauded politely. "Did it go over?"

"We won't know until they open their pocketbooks. Where's Mr. Valentine? We pull out all the stops and he misses the show."

The proceedings over, we started for the sales floor. Georgie, a stock boy, chased us down.

"Mr. Valentine needs to see you, Lil."

"Now? And it's Lillian."

"Right this minute. I've got Frank Buck orders to bring you back alive." He eyed Priscilla up and down. "Does your beautiful friend need company?"

"Aren't you a cute kid?" Priscilla said.

"Kid? I'm plenty grown already." Georgie puffed up his gangly physique, but all it did was awaken his cowlick.

"Any chance you'd tell Mr. Valentine you couldn't find me?"

"For fifty cents."

"See you later," I told Priscilla.

• • •

EN ROUTE TO his office I pondered the possible meanings of a summons from Mr. Valentine. Heart sinking, I deduced it had to be the hat display.

Mr. Valentine ran Tremayne's second floor—millinery, foundation garments, and other mysteries of womanhood—like a retail Mussolini. He groomed every display, negligees arranged by shade, girdles by suction power, priciest hats out front. Two days earlier I'd seized the initiative, moving an inexpensive black toque to a position of prominence because it was a dead ringer for one Katherine Hepburn wore in *Stage Door.* It had been a hot seller ever since.

You can't argue with numbers, I'd tell Mr. Valentine, using one of his pet phrases in my defense. I built up a good head of steam as I charged across the floor, but I knew the outcome would be as predictable as a Gene Autry western. I'd state my case, then surrender gracefully. Jobs were tough to come by. I'd rather eat than be right.

I pushed open the door to the stockroom that doubled as Mr. Valentine's office, and any fight left in me drained away. For one thing, the boss looked more somber than angry, jowls drooping over his florid pink shirt. For another, he wasn't alone. With him were two men who didn't seem the type to frequent Ladies' Lingerie.

"Miss Frost. Thank you for coming. I'm sorry to call you back here."

A thank-you *and* an apology? This did not bode well.

Mr. Valentine mopped his brow with a monogrammed handkerchief, which he then waved toward his visitors. "These gentlemen are from the Los Angeles Police Department. They would like to talk to you." Spent, he dropped his considerable frame into a chair pushed against the shelves of hatboxes.

The taller of the two men stepped forward. The fedora held at his side had swept his hair back into a sleek dark brown V.

Beneath it blue eyes coolly appraised me. "Miss Frost, I'm Detective Morrow. This is Detective Hansen."

His reedy partner, resting his haunches on a step stool, nodded in my direction. He then returned his gaze to the boxes of brassieres opposite him, seemingly staggered by what they represented.

"What can I do for you?" I'd once stolen a licorice wheel on a dare, but that was back in New York when I was eight. It seemed unlikely that Mrs. Fishbein at the candy store had the resources to track me down sixteen years later and three thousand miles away.

"I believe you know Ruby Carroll," Detective Morrow said.

Ruby. The person I knew in Los Angeles most likely to land in trouble.

"Yes," I said. "We used to room together."

The stockroom door swung inward and Miss Baker, an older saleslady with posture worthy of West Point, entered clutching an order slip. She stopped short at the sight of Hansen, then turned and noticed the rest of the party.

"Not right now, Miss Baker," Mr. Valentine said.

"I only need to see if we have the Mesdames Choice No-Bones Corset, large." With desperation she added, "It's for Doris Pangborne."

Mr. Valentine made a shooing gesture with his pocket square. Poor Miss Baker about-faced and went to meet her fate. Asking Doris Pangborne to wait was like trying to flag down the *Super Chief*, futile and life-threatening.

Detective Morrow turned to Mr. Valentine. "Any chance you could let Miss Frost sit down, maybe keep people out?"

"Certainly." Mr. Valentine hoisted himself out of the chair and held it for me, then fixed the door with a vigilant Rin Tin Tin stare.

"You can watch better from the other side," Hansen said, his voice a dry twang. He ushered Mr. Valentine out of the room then resumed his perch on the step stool.

"When was the last time you spoke to Ruby?" Detective Morrow prompted.

"It's been at least six months. I catch a glimpse of her sometimes when I visit the girls at Mrs. Lindros's place."

"Six months. You two didn't stay close."

"We weren't exactly friends by the time I left."

Hansen leaned forward. "What were you then?"

"I couldn't say. We had a fight before I moved out."

"A fight?"

"Not twelve rounds or anything. We argued."

"About what?"

"The typical things girls argue about. Odds and ends going missing, leaving the place a mess. With the two of us in that tiny room, I'm surprised we put up with each other as long as we did."

"Close quarters. I understand." Detective Morrow smiled as he said it, and I felt absurdly grateful.

"Can you tell me what this is about? Is Ruby in some kind of trouble?"

Detective Morrow glanced at the floor. He was about to speak when Hansen piped up. "She's dead. That's a kind of trouble."

I saw the dirty look Detective Morrow fired at his partner, then the storeroom swam a little. *I'm crying,* I thought. Then I heard Ruby's voice in my head. *Good thing you didn't wear mascara, mermaid. It'll be easier to fix your face later.*

The next thing I knew Detective Morrow was kneeling beside me, offering his handkerchief. "I'm sorry, Miss Frost. Take all the time you need."

"What happened to her?"

"She was found in an alley not far from Mrs. Lindros's boardinghouse. She'd been shot."

"Shot? She—she wasn't the Alley Angel, was she?"

Hansen was standing over me now, too. "Why do you think that?"

"I read about it in yesterday's newspaper. I know the store where the body was found. I still live in the neighborhood. I thought, 'I hope that's not anyone I know.' I even thought . . ."

Detective Morrow finished the sentence when I faltered. "That it could have been you." After a pause he said, "Yes, Miss Frost. I'm afraid that was Ruby Carroll."

There'd be no stopping the tears this time. I dabbed them away and held out Detective Morrow's handkerchief. Instead of taking it, he pressed it against my punctured thumb. "Keep it. You shared a room with Ruby. We're hoping you can tell us about her."

I nodded several times too many, still struggling to accept what Detective Morrow had told me.

Stay calm, mermaid. Look 'em in the eye and tell 'em what they want to hear. It's the only way to get by in this town.

I shouldn't have been surprised it was Ruby's advice that came back to me. She wouldn't have been jolted by news like this. At the boardinghouse we liked to pretend we were tough. You have to when you're facing the world on your own. But Ruby didn't need to fake it. She'd earned her wisdom the hard way. She was the McCoy.

And now she was gone.

2

HOLLYWOOD IS LOUSY with beauty queens. Ruby taught me that. Every girl convinced she's the next Jean Harlow comes to town with a sash buried in her suitcase proclaiming her Miss Apple Blossom or Harvest Princess.

Ruby's secret sash declared her Miss Johnnycake of Smithville, Ohio. Or maybe it was Indiana. Ruby didn't dwell on specifics. It was a small town without a smidgen of glitter, and she was desperate to escape it. Along with a six-month supply of cornmeal, she won a train ticket to Los Angeles and a screen test.

As for me, I was Miss Astoria Park of 1936, crowned the day the city christened the swimming pool. My bone-dry red velvet bathing suit won me a screen test of my own. I didn't have stars in my eyes, though. What I did have was a love of the movies and an appreciation for the labor it took to make them. Both came courtesy of my uncle Danny, who toiled for years as a set painter at the Paramount Studios in Astoria. He'd bring me to work with him occasionally, telling me to church mouse in a corner. I'd drink in the hubbub behind the scenes then marvel at the transformation that occurred when the cameras rolled. Actors would take their places, and the flats that Uncle Danny and his boisterous pals had erected and painted would become a banker's office or a police station before my eyes. In the soft flicker of light at the Prospect Theater in Flushing, I'd thrill whenever Danny leaned over and whispered, *I did that bit there, pet.* Thanks to Danny, hard work and magic were indistinguishable for me.

Uncle Danny and Aunt Joyce had raised me after my mother died when I was three and my father stepped out for cigarettes and never came back. Danny, front row center the day of my Miss Astoria Park triumph, insisted I take the trip west. The Astoria Studios had closed in 1932 and he'd been painting houses ever since. "You should see where they're going to make movies from now on, love," he'd said. I boarded the train with the inexpensive grip he'd bought for me. Inside was a loaf of Aunt Joyce's soda bread. I made it last all the way to Omaha.

On my big day I arrived at the Lodestar Pictures casting office and learned it's always someone else's big day, too. Name a type of girl and she was there waiting. Curvy blondes, fiery redheads, sultry brunettes. All of them dressed to the nines, brimming with confidence, and gorgeous.

Unnerved by the competition, I sank into a chair next to a petite blonde with eyebrows so thin they seemed to have been sketched in as placeholders. They loomed over an angular face that could be dismissed as sharp. Huge brown eyes anchored it, though, and the square neckline of her dress set it off beautifully. She knew how to exploit what she had.

"Join the party," she said as I sat down. "Some crowd, huh? The cream of the crop fresh off the farm."

"I didn't come from a farm. I came from a swimming pool."

The blonde offered me a cockeyed grin my comment didn't deserve. "As long as you made it, sweetie. I'm Ruby, by the way. Ruby Carroll."

"Lillian Frost. Glad to know you."

"Lillian Frost," she repeated with a sideways look. "Lucky you. You won't have to change your name. It's your first test, isn't it? Stand up, give us a look at you."

At five foot eight I towered over her. I was wearing what was supposed to be my lucky suit, a navy blue number with crisp white trim and a matching hat bought specially for the trip.

"You've got a nice shape, mermaid," Ruby said. "Must be all the swimming."

I couldn't bring myself to tell her that I wasn't capable of a dead man's float, that I hadn't bought the bathing suit responsible for my trip to Hollywood to get it wet. Instead I blushed and thanked her.

For the next two hours I listened to Ruby hold forth on the subject of crashing the movies. I was so spellbound I almost didn't hear the heavyset woman with a pince-nez and a clipboard calling me to my shot at stardom. Ruby told me to break a leg. I should have taken her literally.

Standing still and smiling for the camera I could manage. I even sashayed back and forth without falling down. The acting was what tripped me up. The scene I had to read was from some misbegotten costume drama. One line—"The chancellor shall hear of your impertinence"—still haunts my sleep. The director, a fellow New York refugee half in his cups, walked me through the speech a few times, but I wasn't very good and we both knew it. I could only hope the film was reduced to ukulele picks in short order. Maybe the descendants of King Kamehameha would have better luck with Madame Renault than I did.

I was in no rush to return to the dicey boardinghouse on Yucca Street where I'd paid a month's room and board, so I waited for Ruby. She wouldn't tell me how her test went. "You've got to put it behind you and think about the next one," she said, then suggested dinner out to celebrate my maiden Hollywood effort. I wound up with the check and didn't mind.

"At least this test was bona fide," she said. "One guy I saw had some racket going. I was such a rube, I didn't catch on until I was alone with him in his office. He makes movies for a 'special market,' he says. Takes the pictures himself. Kept the Brownie in the corner right next to the clothes hanger for my dress. I scrammed pretty quick. Started learning the ropes as his door was closing."

"How'd you land this test at Lodestar?" I asked.

"You might as well start learning, too, mermaid. In this town, it's who you know. Which is why I'm always glad to know anybody."

THE SCREEN TEST didn't pan out. At the end of my allotted month to be discovered, Ruby asked me to share her room at Mrs. Lindros's boardinghouse. By then I'd grown accustomed to navigating Los Angeles by streetcar and bus, as well as to the city's near-constant sunshine. I traded in my return ticket. New York would be waiting when I finally tired of California's weather.

I soon fell in with the other girls, several of whom had already tried rooming with Ruby, and initially had a ball. Casting calls, late-night gab sessions, trips to the beach on the Western Avenue streetcar. Ruby ruled the roost, the queen bee who deigned to share her secrets with us. What sob story to tell Mrs. Lindros when you were late with the rent, how daubing Vaseline on your eyelashes before bed made them grow more lustrous. Once I overheard her consoling a weepy housemate who feared she'd "gotten in trouble" by giving her a doctor's name. "He can take care of it if it comes to that," she'd said. "I've seen him a time or two myself." Being around Ruby was exhausting and exhilarating. We sought her approval even as we feared her judgment.

Her romantic entanglements with a procession of men claiming to hold sway at one studio or another were a reliable source of entertainment. "No more swimming for me, mermaid," she'd say as she dolled herself up before the cracked mirror in our room. "My ship has come in." She always wound up back in the water soon enough. Ruby would simply reapply her war paint and target her next prospective meal ticket.

A gift-wrapping position at Tremayne's Department Store during the Christmas season led to a permanent job offer. I accepted, with vague plans of someday being promoted to buyer. I didn't weep for my stillborn acting career. You can't give up a dream you never really had.

My newfound sense of responsibility blew a chill into my relationship with Ruby. I couldn't help her anymore, even if only by faring worse than she was. I was merely a warm body taking up the other forty percent of the room.

Ruby had made a science of persevering. She landed a few chorus or background parts thanks mainly to her dancing. Our Miss Johnnycake could cut a mean rug. In the meantime she had the typical stints as waitress, stenographer, switchboard operator. For a few days, she'd give the position her all. Then she'd start slipping out early for auditions or sneaking in late because she'd been gallivanting with her current beau until 2:00 A.M. Sooner or later, usually sooner, she'd be out of a job.

About two months after I moved in with her, Ruby met Tommy Carpa. Too Much Tommy, we called him, everything about him excessive. His stocky frame, his profusion of black hair forever tumbling into his hooded eyes, his cashmere overcoats and extravagant gestures. He owned a second-rate nightclub called the Midnight Room and kept unsavory company. He never claimed to have pull at any studio. Ruby didn't care. Tommy gave her entrée to swanky Hollywood parties.

I didn't like Tommy, and made the tactical error of telling Ruby so. She called me jealous. Maybe she was right. Maybe I wouldn't have objected to being squired around town by a sharpie in an almost-new Packard. But I still didn't trust the guy.

Tommy was the first substantial rift between us. The next one was personal, portable, and irreparable.

THE BROOCH WAS a simple piece, nothing special. Two intertwined gold circles set with garnets. Paulette Goddard would have turned up her perfect nose at it.

But for me, it had worth beyond measure.

My uncle Danny presented the brooch to me on my sixteenth birthday. We were sitting at the kitchen table after dinner. I was itching to leave for my friend Peggy's house but Uncle Danny asked me to wait. From his bedroom he retrieved a scuffed jewelry box.

"Before your mother passed, she gave this to me for safekeeping. She said to give it to you when you became a young lady." His face held its usual smile, but his eyes were fogged with memory. "I think you've become a fine young lady indeed."

I opened the box, the lid snapping as if new. The brooch felt weighted and warm in my hand, like it had been recently worn. All at once my mother was there with us, a presence in the tiny kitchen that smelled of ham steaks and turnips.

I fetched a pale blue scarf and tied it around my neck. With his thick fingers, Uncle Danny pinned on the brooch. "Very elegant," he said, and at that moment I didn't feel like a girl anymore. I never made it to Peggy's house that night. I sat drinking milk and eating graham crackers while Uncle Danny told me stories about his spirited sister Maureen. The mother I remembered only as a jolly laugh, a snatch of lullaby, a whiff of lavender.

I never wore the brooch, but after moving to Los Angeles I would take it out and gather my few recollections of my mother. On one of those long, lonely nights I didn't hear Ruby coming down the hall. Staggering tipsily to her bed, she caught an eyeful of the brooch. "Where'd you get that bauble?"

"Just a family heirloom. Not much of one at that." Feeling silly, I tucked the brooch back in my drawer under some clothes.

A week later I was putting away some freshly washed stockings when I felt ritually for the box and discovered it wasn't there. I tore our room apart searching. I looked in jacket pockets, inside shoes, the unlikeliest places. Then I went through all of Ruby's things. The brooch was gone.

Devastated, I waited up until Ruby tottered home. She bristled at my touching her possessions, said she didn't even remember the brooch, and fell asleep. She stuck to that story over oatmeal the next morning, swearing up and down that she hadn't taken it, hurt that I thought she could have.

I knew she was lying. Ruby had picked up a few tricks in her acting classes, but she couldn't fool me. She'd borrowed the brooch without permission then decided she liked it. Or maybe she dropped it while fumbling with Tommy in the backseat of his car. That was what upset me the most, not the possibility that the only memento from a woman I had never known was lost forever but that it had disappeared in so cavalier a fashion. I wouldn't let the matter rest, finally telling Ruby I'd forgive her if she'd misplaced it as long as she admitted she'd taken it.

"What do you keep going on about it for?" she said, exasperated. "Maybe *you* misplaced it. Maybe somebody else who lives in this dump helped themselves to it. I don't want to hear about it anymore."

Uncle Danny once told me you couldn't truly hate someone unless you'd liked them first. You had to let them under your skin.

I avoided Ruby as much as possible after that, giving her the silent treatment whenever I couldn't. When I heard about the open apartment nearby I jumped on it, the salary I'd been squirreling away now a godsend. I never said anything to Ruby, but my packing had to be a dead giveaway. On my last morning in the boardinghouse we sat at opposite ends of the breakfast table without a word to each other.

Friendships in Hollywood never last, Ruby once advised me. Another valuable lesson. At least she'd given me fair warning.

3

"SHE SOUNDS LIKE some piece of work, this Ruby." Morrow holstered his notebook inside his jacket.

"She wasn't all bad."

"Coming between a girl and her mother's memory? Did other girls in the house have items go missing?"

"The ones who'd roomed with Ruby before me had the same problem." I frowned. "A little advance notice would have been appreciated."

"You're a stout judge of character if you didn't care for Tommy Carpa."

"You know him?"

Morrow nodded. "Guy's an operator."

Hansen clucked from the other side of the room, evidently favoring stronger language.

"First time we've heard his name in connection to Miss Carroll," Morrow said. "No one at the boardinghouse mentioned him."

"He may be out of the picture by now. I didn't keep up with Ruby's social calendar."

"Right. Six months since you last saw her." Morrow eyed Hansen. "Figure a call on Tommy is in order?"

"Tonight," Hansen said. "When his club's open and his high-hat pals are in attendance." He chuckled, the sound like a match strike near dry brush.

"The newspaper said Ruby was wearing an evening gown and a lot of jewelry."

"They laid it on a bit thick to play up the Alley Angel angle," Morrow said. "The jewelry was paste, costume stuff. Now the dress was something. Looked pricey to me, but what do I know? You work in a department store. Maybe you'd have an idea."

"I can tell you Ruby never had her share of the rent on time. The gown could have been a gift from an admirer. She did tend to collect men friends."

"Maybe the Shark bought the duds for her," Hansen said.

I turned to him. "The Shark?"

"Carpa. Fair-sized fish fancies himself a bigger one. Still a minnow swimming in Mickey Cohen's wake, but growing bigger all the time."

The gambit was a long shot, but I played it anyway. "Perhaps if I saw the gown, I could tell you something about it."

"You'd be willing to do that?" Morrow asked.

"If there's any chance I could give you an idea of when and where Ruby got it."

Morrow nodded thoughtfully. "Sure. And while you're at it, you could take a gander at Ruby's jewelry. Look for that pilfered brooch of yours."

I felt my skin flush. "You saw right through me."

"Yes, Miss Frost. Truth be told, it wasn't that mighty a challenge." Now, though, he seemed to be weighing the idea's merits. "It couldn't hurt to have you look at the dress. And at the station I could scrounge up enough chairs for everybody."

We made quite the procession heading toward the escalators, the curious faces of the other salesgirls staring after us. My notoriety had spread across the second floor, and I was the center of attention. For an instant, I felt like Ruby.

• • •

THE POLICE STATION did not live up to my expectations. No gaggle of wisecracking reporters, nary an immigrant mother begging to visit her son before he went up the river. The movies had deceived me again.

Hansen lingered in the parking lot to crack knuckles with another detective. Morrow escorted me inside, shouldering a door marked ROBBERY HOMICIDE DIVISION. The masculine aroma beyond, a potent combination of sweat, smoke, and hair tonic, nearly KO'd me. Shirtsleeved men raised their heads as we walked by. Behind me I heard, "Nice going, Gene. Got one for me?"

Morrow sat me down next to a desk that, compared to the others we'd passed, was immaculate. He placed a folder in front of me.

"What's this?" I already knew the answer. Photographs of Ruby in the alley behind Keshek's Meat Market, lifeless in black and white.

"You said you could identify Ruby's clothes."

"Yes, but I thought you'd show me the clothes themselves."

"Either you recognize them or you don't," Hansen said, the bad penny turning up again.

"With a picture there's no way to see the fabric's color, examine the . . . the warp and weft." That sounded almost believable, even to me.

Morrow gave me a skeptical look and then walked Hansen over to a bank of file cabinets, out of earshot. I occupied myself with an inventory of his desk. One smudged ashtray, empty if not clean. A second ashtray containing a battered baseball, the sole indication of a life beyond this office. No photographs of a new bride posing by the sleeping car in her going-away suit, or a fresh-faced kid with a soapbox derby trophy. And no reason for me to be cataloguing clues about Detective Morrow's marital status.

I got the impression the partners were disagreeing. Maybe it was the way Hansen kept shaking his head and scowling before finally stalking off.

Morrow returned. "Detective Hansen is retrieving the clothes from Evidence. He doubts the trip will be worth it." He slipped the file of photos back into his desk. "I think we should adjourn to an interview room. The clothes may be more upsetting to you than the photographs would have been."

My new surroundings made the stockroom at Tremayne's look like a suite at the Beverly Wilshire. A dim overhead bulb spilled weak light over two chairs and a table that had recently hosted a mumblety-peg tournament. Hansen skulked in with a cardboard box. Morrow opened it while Hansen stood sentry in the corner.

"One pair of sandals." Morrow deposited the shoes on the table.

"Silver kid high-heeled sandals with rhinestone buckles," I said.

Morrow scarcely faltered. "One white evening gown."

"White silk, with tulle overlay trimmed in fur." I glimpsed a dark stain on the dress and averted my gaze, studying the rest of the garment. It was gorgeous, intricately designed. I could envision Ruby wearing it with startling ease. She would have looked like a million bucks that night. She would have looked like a movie star.

"Your expert opinion, Miss Frost?" Morrow asked.

"It's a stunner, all right. Certainly not cheap. Is there a label in it?"

"It was cut off. Do you recognize the dress?"

"That's the queer part. I do and I don't. I feel like I've seen it, but not on Ruby."

"Maybe on a hanger at the store."

"Tremayne's doesn't carry anything like this."

"How can you be sure?" Hansen addressed the table, not me. "You don't work in Dresses. We found you in . . . the other department."

His spasm of manners was slightly endearing. "I know our stock. I have to."

"All of it?" Morrow looked dubious. "And where else would you have seen it? You spending your evenings at the Trocadero?"

He made a valid point, but I couldn't shake the certainty that the ivory gown was familiar. The explanation flickered maddeningly at the edge of my thoughts.

Morrow placed his hands on the cardboard box like a teacher at a lectern. "Tell me again, when did you start at Tremayne's?"

"Last Christmas."

"Gift-wrapping," Hansen said, finding the notion amusing.

"And that led to your current position? In . . . the other department?"

"Yes." We were no longer discussing the clothes. My stomach soured. This wasn't going the way I'd hoped.

"At least the job allowed you to find your own place. You live alone, is that right? Dangerous out there for a girl on her own."

I gestured at the bloodstain on Ruby's gown without looking at it. "It would appear so."

"Getting back to this dress from Tremayne's—"

"I never said that. This dress is not—I don't think it's from Tremayne's."

Morrow raised a calming hand. "For the sake of argument, let's assume it is. And Ruby was in her usual dire financial straits. If she wanted this dress, how could she get it from the store?"

"Steal it," Hansen fairly spat.

"Wouldn't be easy," Morrow said. "Not with all those salesladies watching. Wouldn't you agree, Miss Frost?"

I may have blinked in response. I hadn't been whipped around so fast since riding the Thunderbolt at Coney Island.

"She'd need help," Morrow continued. "Someone allowed to handle the merchandise."

"A booster in sheep's clothing," Hansen said. "Taking home a paycheck and whatever catches her eye."

"Hold on." My voice was back, bringing my indignation with it. "Are you accusing me of . . . of stealing clothes? For Ruby? Why would I do that? We weren't friends anymore."

"Big falling out." Hansen, damn him, was still directing his comments at the scarred tabletop. "Hadn't spoken in six months."

"Unless it wasn't quite that long." From his jacket pocket, Morrow removed an envelope. From that envelope, he extracted a scrap of newspaper. Even before he laid it on the table I spotted the curlicued "T" of *Tremayne's*, the elegantly elongated "Y." "We found this in Ruby's dresser. Do you see why it would strike us as interesting?"

The advertisement, from eight weeks earlier, trumpeted the store's new fall gowns in the Parisian style. Directly beneath the date was "Lillian, 2nd floor" in Ruby's schoolgirl script. I could picture the pink nib of her tongue protruding as she concentrated on her penmanship.

The detectives' visit to the store made perfect sense now, their willingness to have me inspect Ruby's last possessions even more so. They'd known I was lying.

Look 'em in the eye, mermaid.

I did. "We had lunch."

"When?"

I pointed at the advertisement. "Shortly after that ran."

"Why not tell us that before?"

"Because I like my job. I want to keep it."

"Miss Frost, I don't care about your job. I want to know about Ruby."

"But now you won't believe me." I scanned his face for a sign I was mistaken and came up empty.

"I'll decide when I hear what you have to say." He crossed his arms. "Tell me about this lunch."

Ruby had gotten me into this mess. To get out of it, I did the one thing she'd been incapable of doing. I came clean.

4

ON THAT TUESDAY—already I was thinking of it as the Tuesday in question—I was tidying up the hat display after a particularly brutal matron had dervished through it when I heard a familiar voice.

"Excuse me, miss? I'm looking for something in straw for the donkey I left double-parked downstairs. Maybe one with holes for his ears?"

I sighed and faced Ruby. My first thought was how good she looked. She'd abandoned the dye bottle, her blond hair back to its natural lustrous russet. She wore a deep red silk dress, the shade suiting her darker locks and contrasting with her ivory skin. Very dramatic. Very Ruby.

"You were interested in dressing an ass?" I asked sweetly.

"That, and making silk purses out of sows' ears. I've made a lot of mistakes lately, mermaid. The worst was letting things with you end the way they did. I need a sensible friend, someone to let me know when I'm about to screw up again. I thought I'd tell you the position is still open."

A well-rehearsed speech, and she'd hit her marks. Now a lopsided smile. "We should catch up. How about lunch?"

"All right. My break's at twelve forty-five."

"But that's an hour from now. You can't slip away before then?"

"Were you listening to yourself during that sensible friend speech a minute ago?"

At a quarter to one I presented myself at the Tremayne's cafeteria. Ruby broke away from a conversation with Mr. Simkins from Haberdashery. "That fellow's a bit overbearing. Wouldn't want him measuring my inseam. I'll blow you lunch, mermaid. Anything you like, on me."

"A cup of tea's fine." Ruby kicked up a squawk, but I held firm. I'd brought in some leftover breakfast sausages wrapped in waxed paper and I couldn't abide letting food go to waste.

Ruby ordered the ham-and-egg platter—"Still a growing girl"—and settled in at a table by the window, the afternoon sun striking her porcelain face like God's own key light.

"You look good," I told her with great reluctance. "If I had hair that color I never would have changed it."

"That platinum look's finished now that Jean Harlow's dead. I'd hate to remind anyone of Baby. What if I run into William Powell?"

"If you were going to compliment my looks in return, this would be the time."

"Come on, mermaid. You're always well turned out. Unlike the rest of us, you don't need constant reassurance about it."

"Shows what you know. So what have you been up to?"

"Whatever keeps the wolf from the door. I hired on at Paramount, did you hear?"

I sipped my scalding, just-arrived tea to buy myself a moment. "You don't say."

"Didn't your famous uncle Donny lift a brush there?"

"Danny. I'm surprised the girls never mentioned that to me." In truth, I could readily understand it. The other boarders at Mrs. Lindros's house knew how I'd react to the news, well aware I longed to present myself at the studio's Bronson Gate and be clutched to Paramount's breast as a member of the extended family. I wasn't necessarily jealous of Ruby when it came to

Tommy Carpa, but I was positively green-eyed now. "How'd you wind up there?"

"Friend of a friend. It's all who you know. One call and I was in Wardrobe, helping the stars into their gowns. Of course, I'm not there anymore."

"You were fired from Paramount?"

"Hardly, mermaid. I quit. The grind got in the way of my real work. Clomping around behind some studio stooge's 'discovery' who can't keep time." Ruby sighed grandly. "Lately I've been giving some thought to the theater. The stage is where real acting is done."

"You were born to play Lady Macbeth."

"Don't be catty. I've had loads of time to reflect on my career since I gave Tommy the heave-ho."

I perked up. "You did? Why?"

"Everything you ever said about him turned out to be true. In spades. He's a louse and a bum. A four-flusher and a terrible dancer." Ruby pressed her lips bloodless. "You warned me about him and I didn't listen. Could have spared myself a boatload of heartache if I'd paid attention to my one true friend."

For the next half hour, as Ruby devoured ham and eggs to the accompaniment of my growling stomach, she brought me up to speed on the doings among Mrs. Lindros's current class and alumni. With the last of the yolk soaked up, she pushed away her plate. Still packing away the chow and never gaining a pound. "This is some store," she said.

"Thanks. I worked hard on it."

"Doesn't that designer Irene have a boutique here?"

"No. She's at Bullock's on Wilshire."

"Irene does all of Claudette Colbert's clothes. I saw her once, at a party Tommy took me to. Claudette. She was so tiny and beautiful I just wanted to claw her face and throw myself in front of a bus." From Ruby there could be no higher praise. She paused. I felt the calculation in it. "There's some choice stuff here. What's the policy like?"

"The policy?"

"You know. On returns."

She winked, and I knew I was in trouble.

"It's fairly strict. You need a receipt. Ideally witnessed by a priest."

"Too bad. I don't have any receipts handy. Or priests, for that matter." She leaned across the table. "Would they notice if something had been borrowed and brought back in near-mint condition?"

She wanted me to steal clothes. For her.

My face burned. Instinct told me to storm away from the table, to milk the moment for every drop of drama. Instead I cocked my head and gazed out the window as if contemplating her suggestion.

"It might be possible. We *do* carry a lot of lovely merchandise here. But you know what I've never seen is anything like that brooch I used to have. The one that went missing. I've looked for a replacement, but I can't find one."

Ruby was a better actress than I'd given her credit for, because what she said next sounded completely natural. "That's a shame. It's funny, I was thinking about that brooch the other day. Remember Elizabeth, that Spanish-looking girl who used to sit in our room with us sometimes? Maybe she took it. She ditched on her last bill and left Mrs. Lindros holding the bag. And I mean literally. Her suitcase is in the basement. I could go through it if you want, see if the brooch is there."

"You'd do that?"

"Absolutely. I'll check that bag and a few other spots you might have missed. If I find anything, I'll bring it to our next lunch. Maybe by then you'll have sized up the store detectives."

I smiled. "Won't that be a fun afternoon."

We said our good-byes and I bustled to the stockroom to feast on my leftovers. They tasted divine, not least because Ruby hadn't paid for them.

MORROW LISTENED WITHOUT rolling his eyes once. I took that as a good sign. Then Hansen snorted. "So you *did* steal this dress for Ruby."

"I didn't steal anything. I wanted Ruby to think I would, so she'd return my mother's brooch. But she didn't come back after that. I never saw or spoke to Ruby again."

"If you didn't take anything, why keep the lunch a secret?"

"I don't want to jeopardize my job at Tremayne's. If Mr. Valentine found out I'd even pretended to think about stealing, he'd replace me in a minute. I felt guilty enough as it was."

"You felt guilty for *not* stealing?" Hansen looked like he'd pulled a muscle in his head.

"The sisters at St. Mary's are very thorough," I said.

Morrow smiled. "A Catholic girl. I should have known."

"The nuns took care of whatever master criminal instincts I may have possessed," I said, and that's when it hit me. I almost yelped.

I pointed at the evidence box. "Is there a wrap hiding in there? More tulle and fur?"

Morrow lifted a sheer cape with a fur trim. The garment looked insubstantial in his hands. "That's an uncommonly good guess," he said.

"I knew that outfit looked familiar."

"Then you did see Ruby wearing it."

"No. Someone else. Gertrude Michael, on screen at the Rivoli in New York."

Hansen stirred. "In what picture?"

"*The Return of Sophie Lang.*"

"Right. The wife liked that one." He turned to Morrow. "It's about this dame who's a jewel thief. There was another one out a few weeks ago, *Sophie Lang Goes West*. The wife didn't care for it as much."

"I saw that one, too. Ruby and I talked about the Sophie Lang movies all the time. She read in a fan magazine that she and Gertrude Michael were the same size."

"Hold the phone," Morrow said. "You're suggesting this is the dress some actress wore in a movie? Maybe it just looks like it. Don't stores do that? 'Wear the same styles as the stars,' all that bunk?" He waved his hand over the clothes, dismissing them.

"First, it's not only the dress. The entire outfit was in the movie. Second, it's too elaborate to be mass-produced. I'd need a lady's maid, a set of instructions, and a running start to put it on. Third, the fabric on a look-alike would be cheaper. I'm pretty sure that fur trim is real. Ruby didn't pick that up downtown on Dollar Day. That's a costume from a movie."

"And how would Ruby get her hands on it?"

"Ruby worked at Paramount for a while. In Wardrobe. If Paramount makes the Sophie Lang movies . . ."

Morrow eyed me, then Hansen. Then, saints be praised, he pulled his notepad from his jacket. "What's that fella's name, handles security over there?"

"Barney Groff," Hansen said.

"Pal of yours, right?"

"We have a professional acquaintanceship."

"That occasionally meets over a card table. Okay, Miss Frost, we'll ask about Ruby's stint at the studio."

"Didn't you say something about jewelry? I might recognize that from the movie, too." Intriguing as Ruby's possible Paramount pilferage was, I was more concerned with a smaller-scaled theft.

Morrow reached back into the box and extracted a large policy envelope. He slid the contents onto the table, where they glittered against the scarred wood.

The onyx drop earrings I'd seen before. I couldn't say the same for the allegedly gold necklace set with large squares of purported topaz, each gaudy slab gleaming like a pat of butter in a hot skillet. The cocktail ring was also new, a faux sapphire encircled by equally bogus diamonds, all of them sparkling desperately. The pieces didn't work together much less complement the Sophie Lang gown. Accessories had always been Ruby's fashion Achilles' heel. *Less is more, mermaid? What does that mean?*

More importantly, there was no sign of my brooch.

"There's nothing else?"

"Just her purse." Morrow turned the box over and a white silk moiré clutch landed on the table.

With a soft metallic *clank*.

I didn't think. I reached for the purse and flipped it over. My brooch was pinned to the flap, a splash of red against the pale fabric.

"Don't touch the evidence," Morrow said sharply.

"But that's my brooch." I pointed at it.

Hansen picked up the bag. "Now why should we believe that?"

"Because it's the truth."

He attempted to unpin the brooch from the bag. The sight of his fingers clawing at it made my throat close. I wheeled toward Morrow. "I told you. She took it from me."

"Can you prove it's yours?"

"Prove it? I never wore it. I didn't want to lose it."

Hansen had removed the brooch and held it closer to the anemic light. Which revealed more red on the white purse. A constellation of wine drops.

My most prized possession, used to hide a stain. Damn you, Ruby. How could you?

Appearances count, mermaid. Never let yourself be seen at less than your best.

"I'm sorry," Morrow said. "For all we know the jewelry was taken from Paramount, too."

"But the brooch wasn't. It's *mine.*" I was tempted to snatch the pin from Hansen's grubby fist and make a break for the door. Instead I slammed my palm on the table. It didn't sound as loud as I'd hoped and stung more than I'd expected, but it got their attention.

"The pieces themselves are proof. Earrings in the moderne style. And cocktail rings are all the rage now. But a brooch set with garnets? Those went out with hoop skirts. That pin is practically Victorian. That's because it's a family heirloom. *My* family heirloom."

"When it's no longer needed as evidence," Morrow said, "there's a procedure for you to claim it."

"Assuming the family don't take it first," Hansen added.

"Ruby's family?"

"They're on their way from Ohio," Morrow said.

"The brooch doesn't belong to them. And Paramount will know it's not from their wardrobe department."

"I'll let you know what we find out. You have my word."

"Or you could take me with you to the studio."

Morrow's eyes twitched, one after the other like a railroad crossing signal. "It's been a long day, Miss Frost. Wouldn't you rather get home?"

"Not if I can be there when Paramount Pictures tells you that brooch is not their property."

"I still won't be able to give it to you."

"I don't care. I'll know it's one step closer to being mine again."

"Miss Frost. I understand how you feel—"

"Do you? Because unless you had the only thing your mother left you stolen, I don't think you do." Tears welled up. I steadfastly ignored them. "*Please,* Detective."

I sensed Morrow's resolve cracking. He'd had a long day, too.

"You're not giving weight to this malarkey?" Hansen palmed his three-o'clock shadow. "C'mon, Gene. Enough is enough."

Frantic, I blurted out, "Don't you want to question Gertrude Michael?"

"I hear she's a lush." Hansen turned to his partner. "If I start blubbering, will I get whatever I want from you? The dress was stolen from Tremayne's, not Paramount. I guarantee it. Double or nothing if you walk in with this girl and her cockamamie story, Barney Groff laughs you off the lot."

I was considering the consequences of telling a detective to go wash his neck when Morrow spoke.

"I'll phone your pal Groff. You get to work on turning up Tommy Carpa." He tipped his hat onto his head. "Let's go, Miss Frost. Before I change my mind."

5

THE TINGLE BEGAN as we tooled within view of the wrought-iron Bronson Gate. It thrummed in my every nerve once we were on the Paramount lot itself. Stepping out of Detective Morrow's car, I couldn't shake the wholly undeserved feeling that I was home. It seemed perfectly normal to spy a Marie Antoinette with a skyscraper wig loitering outside a building branded WARDROBE DEPT. while her ladies-in-waiting finished their smokes. Her Highness winked at Morrow as he held the door for me.

A sparrow of a receptionist directed us toward a small office, its walls rainbowed with sketches and fabric swatches. Twin drafting tables faced each other in the room's center. Perched before one of them was a pert brunette grimacing at her handiwork.

"Good afternoon. We're looking for . . ." Morrow consulted his notebook. "Edith Head?"

"Not me. I'm Adele Balkan." Happy to be distracted from whatever was vexing her, she hopped off her stool. "Are you with the police? Edith's doing a fitting and asked me to take you in."

We followed her down a lengthy hall to a door marked TRAVIS BANTON. Beyond it lay a well-appointed outer office. Its sole occupant was a secretary blessed with striking silver hair held in place by matching antique barrettes. Her skin had the continental glow that came from a steady diet of fresh vegetables and kept secrets. She nodded as Adele led us to one of two doors.

The salon felt equal parts Park Avenue club and Hollywood hideaway, making it the most perfect room in the world. Walls painted soothing terra-cotta shades, French baroque furniture. Past the Japanese screen depicting a grove of cherry trees, though, it became apparent the tranquility was merely decorative; the fitting area, dominated by an illuminated three-panel mirror, pulsed with activity. A woman stood on a low pedestal, her back to us, head down. A seamstress knelt at her feet as if in supplication while a second crouched nearby, pincushion at the ready. A photographer circled the scene backward, possessed of complete faith that no obstacle would bestrew his path.

All this frenzy over a white petticoated dress that seemed downright dowdy.

The action was clearly being staged for the benefit of one woman. She wore a shirtwaist dress the color of fresh buttermilk, a pattern of pale green leaves scattered across the fabric. Her petite frame should have been overwhelmed by the print but something about her bearing balanced it perfectly. Before Adele could signal her, the woman was striding toward us. Her dark hair was cut into a bob, sharp bangs in a ruler-straight line above eyes that moved past lively to ferocious. Thick, heavy-rimmed glasses only magnified their intensity as they took in the evidence box in Morrow's hands. As her gaze swept over me I had the sense of my measure being taken, both ruthlessly and accurately. I straightened my spine, and could have sworn the woman nodded in approval.

"You must be Detective Morrow. I'm Edith Head."

Morrow shook her outstretched hand and introduced me. Edith looked me up and down—mostly up, as I had a good six inches on her. The eye-of-the-storm stillness she radiated was daunting. "The young lady with the memory for fashion. A pleasure."

At that instant, the photographer snapped a picture. He was half turned in our direction, the explosion of light from the flashbulb catching me off guard. As I blinked away stars Edith glared at the shutterbug, his hands aloft in apology. The woman in crinolines atop the pedestal peeked over her shoulder at us. One hazy gander at her face was all I needed. "That's Gracie Allen," I said gracelessly in response to Edith's greeting.

"Indeed it is. Would you care to say hello? When I mentioned you'd be arriving, Miss Allen said she'd never met a real detective before."

Edith nodded at the two seamstresses. "Thank you, Martha, Inez." The photographer was already slinking out of the room. Adele trailed them out and closed the salon's door, leaving us mere feet from Gracie Allen, studying herself in the mirror with a doubtful expression.

"What do you think, Gracie? Will the new hem keep it from sweeping up the chalk dust?"

"The scene's set in a schoolroom," Gracie explained in that familiar voice like the tinkling of bells. "I'm some kind of a student, and not a good one. Aren't you in stitches? Edie here has been for ages. I play my own ancestor. Who was apparently a milkmaid." She put her hand on the designer's shoulder. "No offense, Edith. It's charming."

"As charming as the year 1738 will allow."

"I think you look lovely," I said.

"Aren't you sweet. Or possibly blind. Either way, you're a dear."

The salon's door opened, admitting a man in a black tailored suit who carried himself like someone entitled to open any door he encountered. Gracie also spotted him. "More guests? I couldn't have an audience for that pink dress I wear in the love scene?"

Edith excused herself to greet the newcomer, leaving us with Gracie's full attention. "I'm going to need to see a badge, Officer."

"Detective. Yes, ma'am." Morrow was still fumbling for his identification when Edith returned.

"Travis Banton, our lead designer, isn't using his office today. Why don't you wait there while Miss Allen and I finish?" Morrow managed to flash his shield at the actress. She clapped her hands with delight.

The gent in the sepulchral suit preceded us into the outer office, breezing past the secretary and stepping through the suite's other door. Morrow, a faint smile on his lips, drifted after him. I played when-in-Rome and went along for the ride.

The walls of Travis Banton's office were light burled wood polished to a high sheen. The man made himself at home behind a massive oak desk, plucking a cigarette from a red lacquered box. His slicked-back hair and thin mustache aimed for sophistication but only emphasized he had the flat, pie-plate eyes of a carnival huckster. "Barney Groff, head of Paramount security. Our mutual pal Roy Hansen gave me a courtesy call."

"That's Roy. Courteous to a fault."

"I thought I'd sit in on your meeting with Miss Head. Make sure you get what you need. I'm sorry you came all this way to talk to an assistant and not the man himself." His cigarette traced an arc encompassing the entire office. "We spring for all this space and he's never here."

"I'm sure Miss Head will be able to help."

"Yeah. She already acts like she runs the place." The glowing end of his cigarette pointed at me. "I see you brought your own audience."

"This young woman suggested a connection between Ruby Carroll and Paramount Pictures. Her—"

"I know who Miss Frost is." Groff must have received a comprehensive report from his good friend Roy, considering I hadn't been introduced. "What I don't know is why she's here. What gives?"

"Do I get to tell you how to make pictures?"

Groff smiled instinctively, a perpetual smoother of the ways. "Fair enough. You must know your business as well as I know mine."

Conversation over, Groff sat at Banton's desk and smoked. Morrow stood before him, smiling pleasantly at a point just over Groff's head. I passed the time picturing Carole Lombard swanning around the room in a golden gown. Then I fitted myself into the dress. Miss Lombard looked better.

When Edith Head stepped into the office, she immediately took charge. "Shall we begin, Mr. Groff? I'm curious to see what our visitors have brought."

Groff puffed a smoke ring at the ceiling. "Carry on, Miss Head. Pretend it's your office."

Edith ignored his tone and approached the desk. She shifted a chrome-and-oxblood leather correspondence tray, leaving enough room for Lucky Lindy to touch down. Morrow opened the box and laid out the cape and shoes Ruby had been wearing. He saved the dress for last, taking pains to fold the fabric in order to conceal the bloodstain.

But Edith would have none of it. "May I?" When Morrow nodded, she straightened the material, blanching at the splash of red, its undeniability. She composed herself by flicking away phantom threads. "Oh, my. Yes, these are ours."

"You're certain?" Morrow asked. "There's no chance of this being a copy?"

"No, Detective. I designed this gown myself. You say poor Miss Carroll was found wearing it? Then she must have stolen it somehow."

"Where was this dress kept?" Morrow asked.

"In our storage room on the third floor."

"Which apparently anyone had access to." Groff's voice was remote, as if he were at the end of a long-distance line.

"Any Wardrobe employee. We regularly need to fetch items from storage."

Morrow interjected. "Would you have needed this gown?"

"We reuse wardrobe for publicity photographs and other films. Typically that involves remaking the costumes slightly."

"All those pretty actresses cost a pretty penny, so we cut a few corners," Groff said drily. "No need to draw the curtain so far back, Miss Head. You'll give away our secrets."

I could practically see Edith biting her tongue. "In any event, we wouldn't have done that with this gown. It's too distinctive, and the picture too recent."

"*The Return of Sophie Lang*?" I asked.

"That's right. I'm astonished you remembered it."

"How could I forget it? It's so striking, with the cape that ties underneath the dress collar. I'd never seen anything like that before."

Edith permitted herself a small smile, which she immediately covered with her hand. "Thank you, Lillian. I was quite pleased with how it turned out." She inspected the dress's seams and hem. "What amazes me is Ruby didn't have to change the length. She could have been a stand-in for Gertrude Michael."

"Ruby had read they were both the same size," I said.

"Our costumes customarily have tags naming the actresses who wore them. Ruby could have looked for something of Miss Michael's knowing she could wear it without alteration."

"Meaning she browsed our storage room like a clearance sale

at Bullock's and came out with something extra for herself," Groff said to his buffed fingernails. "Hardly an advertisement for your department, Miss Head."

"I'm sure you mean Mr. Banton's department."

Groff's hands took in the ether currently unoccupied by Mr. Banton. "Which is, on the frequent occasions when your mentor is indisposed, your responsibility."

"Do you remember Ruby from her time at Paramount, Miss Head?" Morrow asked. "What was your impression of her?"

"That she wouldn't be here long. In Wardrobe, I should say." Her eyes strayed back to the sullied dress. "We ask the girls to do whatever needs doing. Answering phones, running errands. Picking up pins off the floor, I call it. Ruby, I'm sad to say, couldn't be bothered."

Groff took over. "Ruby Carroll was in Paramount's employ less than three weeks. In that time she missed four days. That was unacceptable, and she was let go."

"Ruby was fired?" It was an odd time to feel vindicated, but I knew Ruby would never have quit.

"Yes. For absenteeism, not theft. We didn't know about that."

"So many girls would love a job here, Detective. There's no point in keeping someone unreliable," Edith said.

Groff slapped his thighs and stood up. "Anything else for Miss Head to look over?"

Before I could blurt out a single panicked word about my brooch, Morrow stepped in front of me. "Is jewelry stored with the costumes?"

"Yes. Once filming is finished we sort the accessories by type and historical period so we can access them for future productions. Was Ruby wearing jewelry as well?"

Morrow reached inside his jacket for the envelope. Edith produced a square of felt to lay on the desk. As Morrow spread out the jewelry, Edith raised a dismayed eyebrow. "Ruby was wearing *all* this with the gown?"

"Yes. Are they from the studio?"

"I can't say for certain. I can guarantee they weren't worn in the Sophie Lang film. The gown was designed to make its own statement. The earrings are a touch muted while the necklace and ring strike me as, perhaps, excessive."

"What about that red piece?" I waved what I hoped was a seemingly indifferent hand over my brooch.

"When we found it, it was pinned to this." Morrow took the clutch from the box and showed it to Edith.

"Clever. Ruby added charm to an inexpensive bag and hid a stain as well. If only she'd shown such ingenuity when she was here."

"Do you recognize that piece?" Morrow asked.

"No. It's not even the correct time period for this costume. Sophie Lang is a modern heroine. This brooch is . . ." She examined the clasp. "I'd say Victorian. Last century, certainly. It is lovely in its way, though, isn't it?"

I had to restrain myself from hugging her.

Morrow noticed my elated look. "The very argument Miss Frost made."

"It's obvious Lillian has an eye for these things."

Groff rapped Banton's desk with his knuckles. "So the Alley Angel shuffled her coil off while wearing clothes swiped from us. An unfortunate coincidence we can keep amongst friends, I think. There's no cause to drag Paramount into this."

"Your concern for your former employees is touching," Morrow said.

"I'm known for my tender heart. Just trying to keep Mr. Zukor's machine well oiled is all. Now if you folks don't have any more business related to the studio, maybe we can let Miss Head get back to work."

The lady herself spoke up. "I'll show our guests out, Mr. Groff. Thank you for coming."

"We'll have to have a talk about security around here with Mr. Richardson. Someday when Travis sees fit to roll in." He nodded at Morrow and didn't acknowledge me at all as he sauntered out.

Edith poured the necklace back into the envelope. "I'll check our jewelry collection to see if anything has been stolen."

"Jewelry already has been stolen. Ruby took that brooch from me. It was my mother's."

"Your mother's brooch." Edith cradled it in her hand. "You poor dear."

"I'm hoping to get it back someday," I said.

"Someday?"

"There are procedures for Miss Frost to reclaim her property," Morrow said.

"It should only take twenty years."

"Miss Frost." Morrow gave me a severe look.

Edith repacked the evidence box and laid the jewelry envelope on top. She walked us into the reception area. "I'll also organize a search to see if other costumes are missing, particularly those worn by Gertrude Michael. Shall we coordinate our efforts, Detective?"

While they made plans, I wandered back into Travis Banton's salon. Bereft of activity, it was as hushed as a chapel. I stepped onto the pedestal where Gracie Allen had stood and gave myself the once-over. My lucky navy blue suit, the one I'd been wearing when I met Ruby, had seen better days. As for what lay under the clothes, my final assessment: tall, slim, somewhat underendowed in the curves department.

"You're in rare company," Edith said from behind me. "Only the biggest names use this room. I fit Mae West for *She Done Him Wrong* on that very spot."

"I loved that movie. My aunt Joyce and the rest of the Rosary Society didn't, but I did."

"Miss West certainly is forthright. It's why she's a joy to work with. Did you know she has two versions of each costume made? One for standing and another a bit looser she can sit down in. That's the secret to her elegance. Never a wrinkle."

"I wish I could take advantage of that trick."

"Who wouldn't?" Edith lowered her voice. "I'm sorry you had to hear me speak ill of your friend, Lillian. And for your loss."

"You didn't say anything that surprised me. And I'm not sure what the detective told you, but Ruby and I weren't close anymore. I, I haven't really suffered a loss."

"Yes, you have." She peered up at me, her eyes holding me in place. "A rather difficult one, because there was unfinished business between the two of you. Much left unsaid."

She retreated a step, looking almost comically prim. "Do you know what would flatter you? Off with that jacket and raise your arms a bit." She laid my jacket on a sofa, untucked my blouse from the high-waisted skirt and pinched the fabric above my hips. "If you let the blouse or sweater, a lightweight sweater only mind you, drape over your waist and add a belt, you'll show off your figure to better advantage."

I checked the mirror. I was still no Mae West, but my curves did appear more bountiful.

"Remember, there's no reason not to look your best at all times."

"That's what got Ruby into trouble."

"True. I'll amend my point. Always look your best up to the limits of larceny. Words to live by."

6

MRS. LINDROS'S BOARDINGHOUSE was a rambling Victorian pile on a Hollywood side street. Divided into apartments after the '29 crash then subdivided three years later, its exterior had been repainted piecemeal using whatever color was on sale at Lundigan's. The crazy quilt of garish and institutional shades put the structure somewhere between landmark and eyesore. And it was where, for six pleasant months and two chilly weeks, I'd lived with Ruby.

I was in no mood to spend the evening alone staring at the walls of my apartment. Taking the long approach to Mrs. Lindros's allowed me to avoid the alley where Ruby had met her fate—and to confirm my worst suspicions. Cars cluttered the block. Slouching men smoked cigarettes down to nubs while hawkeyeing the front door. The fraternity of the press out in force now that Ruby had been identified as the Alley Angel.

I veered to the parallel street, having no interest in being the buzzards' latest serving of carrion. A shortcut across the Gustafsons' neighboring property would let me slip to the house unnoticed.

Or so I thought until I spotted the sleek roadster in the drive, midnight blue against a wall of dingy lime. A figure reclined behind the wheel, the brim of his Panama hat resting on a pair of sunglasses. His hand hung over the car's door as if awaiting the return of a faithful hound. I inched past quietly, glancing at the man's hand. The dangling digits were freshly manicured.

But the knuckles were swollen and scarred, as if he'd thrown a punch or two in the not-so-distant past.

"Sneaking in late or early, sweetheart?"

The man roused himself minimally, nudging the hat's brim with a finger. I wasn't worth sitting all the way up for. His honeyed voice was charged with insinuation. "I'd hate to see you land in trouble with Mother."

"Just avoiding the reporters. Hello, Laurence. I haven't seen you since the wedding."

Laurence Minot perked up, lowering the sunglasses enough for me to see additional cuts and bruises. A few scrapes near his temple, a near-miss black eye he sported like the wrong color necktie. Even without the battle scars, his face had the charismatic ugliness of a bulldog's. "Yes, of course. How have you been?" The space he left for my name, which he clearly couldn't remember, was large enough to drive his car through.

Deliverance came in the person of his wife, Lodestar Pictures' newest ingénue Diana Galway. When she'd done her time with us at the boardinghouse she'd been plain old Diane O'Roarke. At least they'd kept her Irish. "Lillian! You've come to pay your respects, too."

"Yes, and to see how everyone is holding up." Diana cantered toward me on high heels, arms wide. What hardhearted soul could not respond in kind? Diana then stopped short, forcing me to cover the last few inches on my own. A little trick ensuring she was the one embraced. As usual, I fell for it.

"You look great," I said in blatant understatement. Always a beauty, Diana had spent time in dry dock getting the studio overhaul since signing her contract. Once thick eyebrows now perfectly shaped, brown hair turned a glossy chestnut and, if I wasn't mistaken, a well-padded brassiere under her printed crepe de chine frock. Lodestar had refurbished the SS *Galway*, cracked a bottle of champagne over her bow, and put her out to exotic ports of call.

"I'm a mess. The instant I heard about Ruby I had Laurence run me over from the lot." She turned to the chastened man sitting ramrod straight behind the wheel, sunglasses still in place.

"Yes, dear. Lillian and I were catching up." Laurence spoke with a borrowed aristocratic accent, part of the worldly image he'd constructed for himself; word was at birth, his name was spelled with a homely "W." He'd started as a theater director with a flair for stagecraft. Now he was Lodestar's master of the middling musical with titles like *Larks A'Plenty* and *Pioneer Panic* to his credit. More importantly, he was Diana's husband of less than a year. I'd met him at their wedding, a gin-soaked shindig at which I had obviously made no impression. Ruby and I, along with some other girls from Diana's soon-to-be-forgotten past, had been corralled at a back table in a drafty hotel restaurant for the reception, where we ran down the rumors on the groom. Drinker? Heavy. Womanizer? Incorrigible. I wondered if we should have added brawler to his tally of vices.

"It's such a shock," Diana said. "Ruby and I were to have lunch this week."

"Ruby so enjoyed your lunches." Even more, she relished parroting Diana's litany of complaints about her new life in luxury's lap. I hated Ruby for running down her alleged friend in this way, and I hated myself more for hanging on her every word when she did. At least Ruby got a free meal out of it.

"Perhaps you and I should get together, Lillian. I'd like that. And with Ruby gone . . ." I mustered a yes or three, and we exchanged telephone numbers. With an air kiss and a nod from Laurence, the Minots were off.

I found Mrs. Lindros muttering over what remained of her

zinnias, the press hordes having laid waste to her flower beds. She wrapped her meaty arms around me while firing a black gaze at the remaining reporters. "Jackals," she said grimly, then pushed me toward the house.

The familiar chintz curtains and tattered sofa greeted me in the parlor, the upright piano waiting contentedly in the corner. My stay at Mrs. Lindros's ended badly, but I had fond memories of the place as well.

"Hello, stranger." Kay Dambach strolled into the room. Dimples showing off plump cheeks, dark curls bouncing. She wiped her hands on her apron before giving me a hug. "You've heard the news. Did you and Ruby ever make up?"

I finessed the answer. "We had lunch a few weeks ago."

"Good. I'm glad. You hungry? I just made a coffee cake." I took off like Floyd Bennett and beat her to the kitchen.

Kay was a marvelous cook, helping Mrs. Lindros for a break on her rent. Her ambition was to become a writer, and she labored in obscurity as a gal Friday at *Modern Movie* magazine while awaiting her chance to prove she was the next Dorothy Parker. Dottie, I would wager, could not work Kay's magic with streusel. I inhaled the cake and chased it with a cup of coffee.

"I saw Diana on my way in," I said.

"The new and improved model. Lodestar does good work. She still can't sing, though."

"What gives with Laurence? Looked like he'd stepped in the ring with Jimmy Braddock."

Kay pulled the plate of cake away from me so she'd have my full attention. "Specifics, if you please." She detected a potential story. I gave her the one of my eventful day instead.

"Paramount sent over photos of Edith Head," she said. "They want us to do a story on her. Girl designer to the stars or some such."

"From what I saw she practically runs the place."

"Somebody has to. Travis Banton's not around enough. The studio's been loaning him out a lot lately. You know what that means." Kay pantomimed taking a slug from a bottle. "Banton's a genius. But what good's a genius if he's never at his drafting table? Word is he's on his way out. Paramount won't renew his contract. And when he goes, Edith goes."

I pressed my fork into the last of the crumbs on my plate. "That's a pity. I liked Edith. She gave me a personal wardrobe consultation. A tip, anyway."

"What is it?"

"I'm not telling until I experiment and see if anyone notices. Any chance of a second piece of cake?"

"After you stop putting off what you came here for."

Kay knew me too well. "Is Vi around?"

"In her room," Kay said. "She's been up there a lot since Ruby was killed. You know how close those two had gotten. Get her to come down. The cake should still be here."

I FELT THE tug on the second-story landing. My old floor. I walked to the door of the room I'd shared with Ruby. Knocking on it felt supremely odd. I was used to simply throwing it wide.

There was no answer. I stepped inside.

Ruby apparently hadn't had a roommate when she died. The cramped space was filled with only her clutter. A dressing gown tossed over a chair, an overflowing ashtray. The closet was half full of her clothes, a familiar assortment of blouses, day dresses and skirts plus a pair of slacks for around the house. Ruby, proud of her dancer's legs, didn't care for women's trousers. *You know why Garbo wears them, don't you? To hide those gunboats below her ankles.*

I sat on my old bed. How many nights had Ruby and I lain here in the dark, sharing stories, tales of Uncle Danny, secret codes Ruby had invented during her childhood? On the other side of the wall behind me was the lemon tree in the garden, its fragrance filling the room. Ruby had always referred to it as hers.

"You can't even see it from in here," I'd complain. "The window's in the wrong place."

"Or the tree is. Doesn't matter, mermaid. I know it's out there, like the glorious future that's waiting for me. You, too." I didn't mind being an afterthought. It was her fantasy.

I rested my head on the pillow and sought comfort in the pattern of water stains on the ceiling, feeling years older than the girl who had done the same thing months before.

PUTTING TINY AND delicate Violet Webb in the attic room that once sheltered two household maids was akin to placing an angel atop a Christmas tree. Vi had come to Hollywood by way of Seattle, where she'd played Peter Pan in a musical production written by her vocal coach. I pegged her as more the Tinker Bell type, all golden hair and faraway eyes.

A scratchy baritone rendition of "Stardust" greeted me at the summit of the narrow stairs. Vi, always ready to belt out a tune, was letting others sing for her. She opened the door to my knock, blinked as if waking from a dream, then held me tight.

"I was going to call you," she said.

"Now you don't have to. See? I saved you a nickel."

The song ended and Vi turned off the phonograph. She wiped her eyes. "I was just thinking about that day Ruby called you mermaid and it gave me the idea we should go to the beach."

"You know what I remember about that day? The handsome fellow who followed you around all afternoon."

"Edward! He wore me out with his stories. At least we got

something from him." She went to her bureau and her face fell anew.

"What's wrong?"

"That picture Edward took of the three of us at the beach. I forgot I gave it to a policeman. He stopped me outside and said he needed a picture of Ruby. It was the only one I had." She stared mournfully at the spot where the photograph had been, framed by scraps of yellowing tape.

"How did Ruby seem lately?"

"Strange. One day last month we were planning to go to Warners for a call. When it was time to leave, she was in the parlor reading a magazine, not even dressed! She wasn't going, said she was beyond that. Can you imagine? Beyond Warner Brothers?" Her eyes widened in cartoonish amazement. "A few days later I found her in the garden staring at Mrs. Lindros's roses. I could see she'd been crying, but she wouldn't say why."

"Crying? I never once saw Ruby cry."

"It wasn't in her nature. She was so stubborn. 'I'm not stopping until everyone knows my name.'" Vi's voice couldn't do justice to Ruby's timbre, but she nailed the intensity. More impressively she captured some of Ruby's spirit in the set of her shoulders, the casual toss of her head. "I wish I could be like that and not get down in the dumps when things don't pan out. Which is a lot. Maybe I should be like you and get a regular job."

"You forget that as an actress I'm a terrific salesgirl. You're too talented to give up. And you're still pulling down good money at the Midnight Room." Ruby had strong-armed Tommy Carpa into giving Vi a cocktail waitress spot at his club back when she and Tommy were still an item. "How's your boss?"

"Tommy took the news about Ruby real bad. After she threw him over he made like he didn't care and had forgotten all about her. But every couple of nights he'd track me down on the floor and ask what she was up to. 'How's Ruby? She seeing anybody?'"

"Did Ruby ask about Tommy?"

"Not as much as Tommy asked after her, but sometimes. It got confusing, like I was carrying messages they weren't actually sending. I'm not Western Union."

"The detectives thought it was odd nobody had mentioned Tommy's name."

"Why would anybody? Tommy and Ruby hadn't been going together for months."

"He was still pining for her. You're not a little suspicious?"

"Of Tommy? Everybody thinks he's some kind of tough guy. A gangster. But it's not true."

Right, I thought. *And the cops call him Tommy the Shark because he was born with too many teeth.*

Vi's fingers worried a tissue. "You told the detectives about Tommy, then?"

"They're interested in anyone who knew Ruby."

"They should talk to her new friends while they're at it."

"What new friends?"

"Armando something or other. And Natalie. Ruby said he was rolling in it and Natalie was the most elegant lady she'd ever seen."

"Did you tell Detective Morrow about them?"

"I told one of the detectives everything I could remember. Which wasn't much. Ruby never even mentioned their last names. But she was seeing a lot of them lately."

I could tell Vi was tired of talking about Ruby, so I babbled about work, my trip to Paramount and my subsequent encounter with Edith Head. I pitched hard for her to come have cake with me and Kay.

"Maybe later."

I kissed the crown of her head. As I shut the door the phonograph started up again. "Smoke Gets in Your Eyes" drifted down the stairs behind me as my mind turned over the question I couldn't bring myself to put to Vi: *Did Ruby ever mention me?*

"VI JUST NEEDS time," Kay said as I demolished a second piece of cake. "It can't help seeing Tommy every night. You know she secretly loved being caught in the middle of their twisted little romance."

"Tell me, Scoop, what do you hear about these new flush friends of Ruby's?"

"Not a thing. I got tired of Ruby, flitting around like she was already a movie star. I paid no mind to her stories even when Vi repeated them. What friends are these?"

"Vi mentioned Armando and Natalie. He's rich, she's beautiful, the three of them are the best of pals. It could be Ruby stole that gown from Paramount so she could take a spin in their social circle."

Kay's brow furrowed as her fearsome brain set to work. "I doubt they're movie people. I'd recognize the names. Armando sounds south of the border. There are so many South Americans around with pesos to spare. Tell you what, I'll ask around the *Modern Movie* office, thumb through the clippings."

"Great. Anything you find I can pass on to the detectives."

"The good-looking one, I hope."

"I hadn't noticed either one, to be honest."

"Really?" Kay fanned herself. "Because one of them sent me. Quite a specimen, that Detective Hansen."

"Hansen?" I sprayed Kay with her own coffee cake. "Have you gone goofy? Morrow's the handsome one. As well as smarter and better mannered."

"So you did notice him, to be honest. No shame in admitting

it. And maybe he noticed you, seeing as he let you tag along to Paramount. I'd better turn up something on Armando and Natalie so you have a reason to talk to Detective Morrow again."

"Enough with the matchmaking."

"Somebody's got to look out for you. You're too busy looking out for everyone else. Stop eyeing the cake. You've had enough for one night."

"Fine. I'll be back first thing in the morning."

DINNER WAS AN apple, penance for my double dose of Kay's handiwork. Then I made my way to my own personal matchbox. There wasn't much to my flat but what there was was all mine, from the drab white walls to the blue coverlet on the bed. A breeze nuzzled the lace curtains as I changed into my nightgown and robe. I sank into the only decent piece of furniture, an overstuffed armchair where I could read or, more frequently, nap.

Through drooping eyelids I glimpsed my lucky navy suit, sagging over the settee where I'd left it. It had served me in good stead for too many months to deserve such treatment. Visions of Edith Head's reproving face spurred me to my feet.

As I draped the jacket on a hanger, something shifted in one of the pockets. I knew what was in my hand before I opened it. I recognized the object's shape, its warmth against my skin. I smelled lavender on the air.

My mother's brooch.

For an instant I felt light-headed, fearing I'd slipped into a fugue state at Paramount and stolen my property back.

Then my mind flashed on Edith asking for the jacket, carefully laying it on the couch in Banton's salon. She must have taken that opportunity to drop the brooch into my pocket.

Now I had an assignment for tomorrow. I had to thank Edith, as if words would be sufficient to acknowledge what she'd done.

But first to let my uncle Danny know I'd at long last made the pilgrimage to Paramount's new home. I fixed myself a cup of tea and dashed off a letter, the brooch gleaming on my pink chenille robe.

Los Angeles Register *November 7, 1937*

LORNA WHITCOMB'S
EYES ON HOLLYWOOD

. . . Constance Bennett told pals she'd figured out what her husband Marquis Henri de la Falaise was planning to gift her for her birthday. Turns out it wasn't the sparkling stones she'd predicted, but two of the cutest French poodles in town. Hope the lovely Constance doesn't try wearing *them* to the premiere of her next film! . . . The blond beauty beaming at the beach on page one of this very paper turns out to be an aspiring actress struck down too soon. Hollywood hopeful Ruby Carroll had scored several small dancing parts and even worked at Paramount for that genius of glamour Travis Banton and his stern wardrobe mistress Edith Head. But poor Ruby lost her step amid the traps and snares of moviedom. No doubt several of our silver screen sirens are contemplating her fresh face this morning and whispering "There but for the whim of Dame Fortune go I" . . . Some wags are wondering if those fire engines Fox amassed for the filming of *In Old Chicago* could be used next summer to cool off sure-to-be overheated Los Angeles residents. What say you, Mr. Zanuck?

7

TIME TO TEST Edith Head's advice. I let my tan sweater hang over the matching knit skirt, cinching it with a narrow belt. In my own biased opinion, I looked pretty good. But my ego demanded unsolicited compliments. Any more than the usual number—zero—and I'd declare victory.

The early bird may catch the worm, but she can forget about finding a seat on the streetcar. The man in front of me couldn't be bothered to rise and let a lady take the weight off. He was lost in the *Register*'s morning edition. Glancing down, I found myself staring into Ruby's eyes.

ALLEY ANGEL IDENTIFIED, the headline blared. RUBY CARROLL WAS HOLLYWOOD HOPEFUL. She'd finally made the front page.

Which disappeared when the man folded his paper to get at the boxing column. Two blocks later he started for the exit.

"Pardon me," I said. "Are you done with that paper?"

"I could be, for a smile."

Despite the ungodly hour I gave him his money's worth, teeth included at no extra charge.

"Take it and maybe I'll see you again sometime." He winked, which I credited to Edith's fashion tip.

Snagging his seat I opened the paper for a good look at the page one photo. Ruby knelt on a towel at the beach in a halter-top bathing suit, blond hair blowing away from her freshly scrubbed face. She looked like an advertisement for California health and beauty.

I recognized Ruby's swimsuit—the salesgirl had called it poppy, Ruby insisted it was orange—and the towel, shanghaied from Mrs. Lindros's linen closet. I also knew the girl on Ruby's left, though the only part of her remaining in the cropped photograph was her knee. It was Vi.

Making the hand on the towel to Ruby's right mine.

Poor, trusting Vi. She thought she'd given the photo of our beach jaunt to a detective, but it had been a reporter with a slick line.

Aside from the disclosure of Ruby's name and the "exclusive" photo, the *Register*'s story was a hash of old news, spiced up with idle speculation about the Alley Angel's morals. The rest of the ride to Tremayne's seemed longer than usual.

MR. VALENTINE STOOD at the entrance to Ladies' Wear, his goldenrod necktie so bright I was tempted to slip my sunglasses on again. "Miss Frost. Good to have you back after your ordeal."

"I'm sorry for any inconvenience."

"The way those detectives questioned you, I thought you were a suspect." He forced an amiable chuckle. So did I.

Next stop hat department, Mr. Valentine nipping at my heels like a terrier. "I read the story in this morning's paper," he said solicitously. "That was your friend, the blond girl? Tragic, just tragic. I thought Lorna put it beautifully in her column. Felled by 'the traps and snares of moviedom.'" He cupped his hand as he spoke as if clutching Yorick's skull.

"She certainly has a way with words." Ruby had always hated Lorna Whitcomb, branding her a "withered-face crab who bombed out as a chorus girl."

I started primping the hat displays, grooming every feather like a vain parakeet. Still Mr. Valentine lingered, reluctant to leave his flesh and blood link to the big news story of the day. He might have tarried all morning if the store's assistant manager hadn't come to retrieve him. He took his leave for Tremayne's loftier climes. Abruptly, he turned back. "By the way, that's a lovely outfit. Very smart."

Two compliments. Something else to mention to Edith now that I had a moment to call her.

HEARING EDITH'S UNMISTAKABLE crisp tone brought my mother's brooch to mind, making me absurdly emotional all over again.

"Lillian, a pleasure to hear from you. I hope you're well."

"I'm wonderful, thanks to you."

"I'm sure I don't know what you mean."

"I'm sure you do. Consider me in your debt forever."

"Let's say I'm happy to help a fellow working girl and leave it at that." She made a noise that sounded like a suppressed yawn. "Forgive me. I burned the candle at both ends last night searching our storage room."

"How much else did Ruby take?"

Her pause indicated I'd surmised correctly. "What makes you ask that?"

"Ruby came to the department store where I work to sound me out about stealing clothes. That implies taking the Sophie Lang gown wasn't a spur of the moment impulse. I also learned she'd been moving in some rarefied air lately." I told her about Armando and Natalie.

"I knew you were a resourceful young woman as soon as we met," Edith said. "You put me in mind of myself, in fact. Several women's costumes *are* missing. Ruby didn't necessarily take them . . . but they're in her size."

"Detective Morrow will be interested to hear that."

"Yes. Provided he does hear it."

"I don't understand."

"I issued a full report to our security chief Mr. Groff. He was, as you might imagine, displeased. Particularly with Ruby's brief history at Paramount being bruited in the newspapers this morning."

"I read the *Register* on my way to work."

"Then you likely saw Lorna Whitcomb's dig at me. Horrible woman. She still blames me for the costumes she wore when she was under contract here for seven minutes a millennia ago."

"Are you saying Mr. Groff doesn't intend to inform the police about the missing clothes?"

"He left me with that distinct impression. He wants to spare the studio additional negative publicity. Unless the clothes are found and conclusively tied to Ruby, I fear he won't report them."

I had an inkling Edith wasn't relaying this palace intrigue to make idle chitchat. Her hands were tied, but mine weren't. And I knew Ruby and her habits. Edith had stealthily given me my marching orders: Look for the stolen wardrobe and get cracking on repaying that debt. Apparently I wasn't the only resourceful person on this phone call.

WE MADE PLANS to speak later. Edith rang off to attend to the day's fittings while I spent the better part of the next hour wrangling two dowagers intent on buying twin turbans. I had my back turned, trying to restore order to my station, when I heard the voice.

"Hello, Lillian," it said, playing with each syllable like a piece of French candy.

Gooseflesh raised, I turned and spied a man I'd hoped never to encounter again.

Tommy Carpa wore a chocolate-brown topcoat with a velvet collar that made him look more like a young banker than a club owner of questionable repute. His nose was bent at an angle, the result of a childhood accident. That misleading hint of brutality lent his features a character they didn't deserve. He was flanked by two ambulatory monoliths in identical pinstripe suits. At least I assumed they were ambulatory; I hadn't seen either of them move. I tried to speak only to discover I'd gone cotton-mouthed.

Tommy set his homburg down next to a basket of beaded hair combs on the counter. "Any guesses why I'm here?"

"Probably not to jazz up that hat with a peacock feather."

"You've been telling tales out of school. Blackening my name to the law."

"Your name wasn't in such good shape to begin with."

His Too Much Tommy curl of dark hair spilled into his face. It made Tommy resemble an overgrown child, prone to tantrums and mulishness. He pushed the hair back, then his fingers batted the basket of combs. "I spent last night with a couple bulls fishing for leads. I'm never gonna get the stink of that police station out of this coat."

"Did you want a new one? Menswear is on three."

"I don't shop here. Soon as they kicked me loose I came to you. Because you're the one told them about me and Ruby."

"Why do you think it was me? Plenty of people knew you two were an item."

"Yeah, *were* an item. Ruby forgot about me. You didn't. Those cops grilled me like they found the pistol in my hand. What did you tell them? And I mean exactly."

"That you and Ruby used to go together. That's all."

"And that you don't like me. You never liked me." He brushed at his lapel. "It's okay, Lillian. You can admit it."

"I have no opinion of you one way or the other." But he was

right. Slow-cooling spite against Tommy had been a factor in my pointing the police in his direction.

Tommy plucked a comb from the basket and considered the beads adorning it. "Next question. What do the cops have?"

"Not enough to hold you, so what difference does it make?" He wouldn't dare pull any moves in the store, I reassured myself, so I could chance a little bravado.

"They couldn't hold me because I didn't kill Ruby. I'd like to know who did, though. And find him before the cops do. A few minutes ahead of them, that'd be enough. So I'll ask again. What do they have?"

"How would I know?"

In response Tommy stared at me, content to wait me out. One of his bulky compatriots tried to stifle a belch. I needed them gone before Mr. Valentine showed up. "Ruby was going out a lot. With rich new friends."

"Who, Armand and Natalie? Forget about them."

Armand, he'd said. Not Armando the way Vi had remembered the name. "You know them?" I asked.

Tommy laughed, a mirthless little bark. "Yeah, I know 'em. Those two aren't involved. And they're long gone, the both of them. What else you got?"

"Nothing."

"Nothing? No tidbits from that costume broad?" Morrow would never have told Tommy about our trip to Paramount. Only one person could have let that slip. Vi, feeling sorry for her jilted boss.

Tommy tapped the comb against the glass, his face softening into a concerned parish priest look. "What do you have against me, Lillian? Didn't me and Ruby show you a good time when we took you out?"

"Sure. Dragging me to nightclubs because some 'businessman'

pal of yours wanted to dance with a 'nice girl.' The trouble with those guys, when they think you're a nice girl they try twice as hard to put a hand up your skirt."

"So you don't like me and my friends. You don't have to. This is America. But I want to do the right thing here. For Ruby's sake."

"I think we can safely say Ruby's past caring."

"Jesus, that's some way to talk. You two were friends."

"For a little while. But you and I aren't friends. You're the guy who got Ruby hooked on the high life. And look where she ended up."

Tommy reared back as if I'd slapped him, that goddamned forelock falling into his eyes again. "We had some laughs, Ruby and me. We could have kept on having them if she hadn't given me the air. Remember that. She walked away from me."

"That may have been the one smart thing she did."

I expected him to scowl at me. Instead he gazed at the decorative comb he'd lifted out of the basket as if it contained the answer he needed. Then he dropped it into his coat pocket. Brazenly stealing it right in front of me, knowing I wouldn't challenge him. And he was right.

"I can live with you not helping me," he said. "But you're not helping the cops, either. Keep your trap shut from now on."

"For Ruby's sake?"

He looked at me, his eyes lifeless and dull, and I knew why they called him the Shark, knew it in a deep place inside of me that had grown unfathomably cold.

"No. For yours. For the sake of things could get uncomfortable for you if you don't. I know where you work. I know where you live, all by yourself."

"You wouldn't hurt me." It sounded more like a question than I had intended.

"You. Your friends. I even know people who know people back in New York. That's where you're from, right? Uncle Danny? Aunt Joyce?"

Content with the effect his words had on me, he took his time fitting his hat on his head, pausing to inspect his reflection in the nearby gilt-edged mirror. He stepped aside to let a customer pass, the very picture of gentlemanliness. I didn't start breathing again until he and his thugs were on the escalator. And even then, I kept the breaths shallow.

8

A CAR DOOR slammed behind me. So much for the shortcut sparing me the reporters still barnacling Mrs. Lindros's house.

"You live in the Lindros shack, sweetheart?" He was a tall man with hair like cut straw. His features clustered in the center of his face as if conspiring against his ears. He gestured at the house's kaleidoscopic walls. "What's with the paint job? Guess you don't mind. You don't have to look at it."

"I don't have any comment for the press."

"Not even for Beckett of the *Register?*" The sunlight did his cheap suit no favors. The fabric seemed to change color as he inched closer. "Give, sister. Tell me something about this Carroll dame."

"Sure. She didn't think much of men who lingered on sidewalks." I sidestepped him and continued toward the house.

"That's not what I heard." Beckett kept pace. "How 'bout her pal Natalie Szabo? Ever heard of her?"

Szabo. At least I'd gotten Natalie's surname out of the exchange. I walked faster. New York fast. "Here's my statement," I hollered over my shoulder at him. "Blow it out your ear."

"I've already got that quote," Beckett yelled back as he gave up the chase. "From multiple sources."

Mrs. Lindros was replanting her desecrated flower beds. I didn't interrupt her. Nothing was going to sway me from my multiple missions, not even the divine scent of cinnamon wafting from the kitchen.

Vi was in her attic room, doing her nails with the door ajar. When I knocked she started like a little girl caught rooting in her mother's makeup bag, blond hair flying. "Lillian! I didn't even hear you come up the stairs."

"I ran into your friend Tommy Carpa today."

"He's not my friend. He's my boss." She added the finishing touches to her pinky. "Did you see him at the police station? They picked him up at the club last night. It was some ruckus."

"No. He came to Tremayne's for a little midday threatening. That I-know-where-you-live stuff doesn't play as well over the phone."

"Threaten you? Tommy would never do that."

"Would and did. Somehow he knew I was the person who gave his name to the police."

"Maybe the detectives told him."

"They want to get information from him, not hand it over. Plus Tommy knew all about my trip to Paramount and meeting Edith Head."

Vi waved her hands. I thought she was drying the polish until she burst into tears. The instinct to rush to her side and comfort her was so overpowering I clutched the doorjamb to remain in place.

"You're right," she said. "I'm sorry. It's just . . . you should have seen him last night. He was so upset. He said the police wouldn't care because Ruby was a nobody. I wanted him to know that wasn't so. I started telling him about you and I guess everything came out." The swing shift arrived at the waterworks, and Vi started crying harder. "I try to help and I make things worse."

I felt my death grip on the door frame loosening, so I dug in my fingernails. Vi in dolorous waif mode was difficult to resist. I wondered if she knew it, if Ruby had advised her to play that card. *Fellas can't say no to a frail, angel, especially a weepy one. Give 'em a show.*

"Don't worry about it." I drained all nuance from my voice. "I understand."

"He's obsessed with Ruby."

"He certainly is. He said he's going to find her killer before the police do."

"Why?"

I gave her a moment to work it out. She frowned. "Oh, no. He shouldn't do that."

"Pass that suggestion on to Tommy. He seems to listen to you."

"Only when he wants something."

"That should tell you the kind of man he is. Watch what you say to him. You could be getting people hurt. And by people, I mean me."

"I'm sorry, Lillian. I'll keep my mouth shut, I promise. I'd shake on it, but my nails are still wet."

"Your word's good enough. I saw Ruby's photo in the paper."

Vi's face crumpled. "I feel so foolish. How could I have thought that man was a detective? Him and his cheap suit."

Cheap suit? "Tall fellow, hair like a haystack? Loitering near the shortcut?"

"Yes! Do you know him?"

I dabbed Vi's eyes with a tissue. "I've made his acquaintance."

THE AROMA OF cinnamon was still strong when I found Kay in the kitchen. "Remember Ruby's friend Natalie?" I said. "I may know her last name."

"Big deal. Jimmie Fidler had it in his column four weeks ago." Kay fished a notebook from her apron pocket and theatrically cleared her throat. "'Who was that lovely lady on the arm of Argentine Armand Troncosa, he of the prancing polo ponies?

None other than Princess Natalya Szabo of Hungary, who rumor has it is open to screen offers.' Told you I'd track them down. I asked around about Troncosa. A regular playboy, took a house in Whitley Heights. Facts about Natalie are more scarce. Woman of mystery, regal bearing, some looker, the usual."

"Tommy knows them. He told me to forget about them."

"Then that's the last thing you should do. Tommy knows them?" A feverish gleam stole into Kay's eyes. "Gangsters, royalty, and a murder. This caper gets juicier by the minute. I may ride this story all the way to Hearst's office. At least until Paramount hushes the whole thing up."

"That wouldn't happen."

"Come on, Lillian. Wise up. Paramount is Adolph Zukor's domain and nobody in Hollywood is more sensitive to scandal than ol' Creepy. He's already dealt with Fatty Arbuckle's trial and Wallace Reid wasting away in a sanitarium on morphine. Plus William Desmond Taylor's killer is still walking around, drawing a Paramount salary for all we know. Zukor's not about to let Ruby drag his studio's name through the mud."

At that moment, a tall drink of well water appeared in the back doorway. His rugged manner was undercut by a sweet grin. "Ladies," he said. "Forgive me if I'm a little spooked. Miz Lindros mistook me for one of those press fellers and threatened to shoot me."

"She actually has a gun, Ready," I said.

"Oh, I know. I helped her load it once." Hank "Ready" Blaylock had been involved with Kay for over a year. Ready had reliable work as a stuntman and rider in westerns, plus a fine car and an easy disposition. What he didn't have was any interest in the fairer sex. He wanted to avoid questions as he worked his way up the Hollywood ladder. Kay, fixated on her career, needed an escort to various show business events. Their romance of convenience suited them both perfectly.

"What brings you here, gorgeous?" I asked him.

"Kay made snickerdoodles. Word's out all over town."

"I'm practicing for Christmas," she said. "Shall we dig in?"

"You go ahead. I have to check something."

"It must be important if you're saying no to cookies."

"Who's saying no? I'm saying 'in a minute.'"

My objective was to find the clothes Edith said were missing from Paramount. I'd searched Ruby's half-empty closet again on my way down from Vi's room and turned up no trace of ill-gotten gain. But Ruby's words at our final lunch buzzed in my mind. I headed for the basement stairs. Mrs. Lindros still hadn't installed a light switch. The hall lamp illuminated the top steps, but below them was inky blackness. I took a breath and told myself only kids are afraid of the dark, then hurtled downstairs with a hand outstretched to grab the string dangling from the single bulb in the ceiling before Frankenstein's monster could grab me.

Mrs. Lindros had sectioned off a basement corner for boxes and suitcases left behind by girls who'd moved back home or ditched on their bills. Stooping and squinting I checked labels, pausing for the occasional sneezing fit. None of the abandoned luggage bore Ruby's name. One valise had a large paper tag reading ELIZABETH BUONO. Elizabeth, the "Spanish-looking" girl whom Ruby, the last time I saw her, had shamelessly suggested might have stolen my brooch. Elizabeth was Italian and from Fall River, Massachusetts. I wondered where she was, and took a moment to wish her well.

According to Ruby, Elizabeth had been gone for months. I ran my finger across the top of Elizabeth's suitcase. No dust at all.

I hauled the case upstairs without bruising my shins too badly. The racket brought Kay and Ready to the door. "Kind sir?"

Ready relieved me of the suitcase. "Ruby's?" Kay asked. "Let's take it to my room."

Ready, after checking for Mrs. Lindros and her trusty blunderbuss, lay the suitcase on Kay's mattress.

"Behold the most excitement this bed has ever seen," Kay said with a grin.

The latch was locked. I plucked a hairpin from Kay's head. "Shield your eyes, gang. No point in being accessories."

"These New York girls." Ready chuckled. "All of 'em lawbreakers."

The lock yielded with a *click* after a few seconds' effort. I raised the lid of the suitcase.

"What's in it?" Kay pushed Ready out of the way.

"Enough wardrobe to stage our own version of *Grand Hotel*." The case was stuffed with clothes. Shimmering silver lamé lay on top. I lifted up a gown, cut on the bias, with a neckline so low it was hard to tell the front from the back.

"Oh my," Kay said.

"I'll say," Ready seconded.

I sorted through the contents, garments Ruby couldn't afford to buy but had been bold enough to steal. Sophie Lang would have been proud. There were some good shoes along with several pairs of shabby ones polished to a high shine. I opened a small bag and a jumble of jewelry cascaded out. Pieces in a host of styles and all ostentatious, like the topaz tinsel she'd been wearing when she died. The counterfeit emerald bedecking one necklace gleamed with an almost resentful ferocity.

"Property of Paramount Pictures?" Kay asked.

"There's one person who could tell us for sure."

"Edith Head?"

"Good thing you know her," Ready said. "Could we mosey downstairs now, before Miz Lindros catches me up here and has me drawn and quartered?"

9

BY POOR RICHARD'S reckoning, given the hour I should have been healthy, wealthy, and wise. Instead I had the makings of a small headache, a sou or two to my name, and the foolish notion I could raise Edith Head while the cock crowed.

Some foolish notions pay off. Edith was already manning her post at Paramount when I called. With minimal preamble I briskly inventoried the contents of Ruby's stashed suitcase.

Edith made a faint clucking sound of the worst-suspicions-confirmed variety. "Could you possibly bring the items to the studio at once?"

I was due at Tremayne's in little more than an hour. I had to be sober and responsible. Edith, a fellow working girl, would understand.

"I'll be there as soon as I can," said a voice uncannily like my own. "Just let me figure out the streetcar route."

"Never mind that. I'll send a car for you."

After finalizing arrangements, I telephoned Tremayne's. Of course Mr. Valentine was at the store early. We salesgirls assumed he walked the floors at night turning out the lights, then donned a pair of Tremayne's City Squire brand pajamas and slipped beneath the starched covers of one of the demonstration beds on five.

I told him Detective Morrow wanted to ask me a few more questions, which I imagined would be the case after I delivered Ruby's bounty to Paramount. I was merely reversing the sequence of events. Telling a lie so white it was more the ghost of one, as Uncle Danny would say. Then again, a man who required a taxonomy of untruths might not have been the best role model.

I PURPLED MY calves lugging Ruby's suitcase of stolen wonders downstairs. I wished I'd had the sense to wear slacks, Ruby's anti-pants prejudice be damned.

A maroon Buick glided to a stop as I dragged the valise to the curb. A liveried chauffeur confirmed my identity and tucked the suitcase into the car's trunk. He grunted once with exertion for my benefit. I decided being whisked through crowded streets like a pasha made it worth my sworn oath to Mr. Valentine to work late sorting a shipment of undergarments.

The Paramount gates had lost none of their magic. I shivered as I passed through them for the second time in three days. The driver pulled up in front of the Wardrobe building. Edith stood by the front door. "Faster than the streetcar and more civilized," she declared. She instructed the driver, who had hoisted the suitcase out of the trunk, to follow her.

To my delight she marched us back to Travis Banton's salon, my new favorite place. A clothing rack waited alongside the three-panel mirror. The chauffeur placed the suitcase atop the sofa, touched the brim of his cap, and withdrew.

Edith eyed the case. "We're fortunate it wasn't locked."

"Who said it wasn't locked?"

I got only a quarter-raise of a single eyebrow in response. We had work to do.

We started with the silver lamé gown. Edith arranged it on a hanger and hooked it over the top of the mirror, sprinkling light throughout the room. We excavated the suitcase in silence, me removing items and Edith hanging them up, putting the matching shoes under each outfit. A glance into the jewelry bag merited a full raise of both her eyebrows. Once we finished, Edith stepped back to take it all in.

"I can't thank you enough, Lillian."

"Are they from the studio?"

"Every last piece save some of the shoes. Look here." From the garment rack she pulled out a suit in luscious burgundy, then held it next to its double from the case. "The script calls for the leading lady to be thrown into a swimming pool. We made multiple suits for multiple takes. The film hasn't started production yet." She took off her glasses, bouncing them against her palm. "You understand why this is so worrisome."

I waited for inspiration to strike. Alas, inspiration was still waiting for the streetcar. "Not entirely," I admitted.

Edith stretched out her arm to indicate the costumes adorning the mirrors. "All the pieces you discovered are from our active wardrobes, for films currently shooting or just finished. Meaning they were made *after* Ruby was let go. If they were in her possession—"

A light dawned. "She had an accomplice."

"Exactly. Someone with access to Wardrobe who's still in the employ of Paramount Pictures."

"Mr. Groff isn't going to care for that bulletin."

"I'm none too thrilled about it myself. We'd better alert the police as well." Edith scrutinized me over the top of her glasses. "Don't be surprised if Detective Morrow isn't pleased that you came to me before him."

"Where else was I going to go? We had to find out if the clothes were stolen first." The prospect of arousing Detective Morrow's wrath hadn't occurred to me. My palms began to sweat.

"I'm sure we'll be able to convince him you did the right thing," Edith said. "Besides, I talked you into it. I can be quite persuasive, you know. It's a requirement for this job. And perhaps we can deliver even more to the good detective. I took the liberty of making inquiries about Ruby and her time here. She didn't make many friends, from what I gather."

"That doesn't come as a shock."

"One name I did hear was Kenneth Nolan. A studio photographer, so he can come and go from storage as he pleases. He and Ruby were seen having coffee a few times. You've already met him."

"I have?"

"Yes, on your last visit. Mr. Nolan was the photographer during Gracie Allen's fitting. He wasn't scheduled to be, yet there he was."

"You think he heard the police were coming to meet with you and he wanted to know why."

"I think he did more than that. He accidentally took a photograph of you and Detective Morrow. I don't believe his finger slipped. I believe Mr. Nolan wanted a record of who was interested in Ruby. Pure speculation on my part, of course."

Something in her tone of voice caught my attention. "But it doesn't have to be."

"Mr. Nolan's boss John Engstead is a friend of mine. John took the only photos of me I can bear to look at. He managed to coax out my inner coquette. A trick requiring great patience." She glanced at her reflection and shuddered. "I arranged with John that our photographer be available today. While I telephone Detective Morrow, you fetch Mr. Nolan. I'd like him to explain how Paramount property that is my responsibility ended up in the real world."

EDITH DREW A map of the lot on the back of a discarded sketch. I stayed true to its course, faltering only when my path crossed that of a balding man immaculately attired in shades of brown, barking orders at a horde of people marching exactly three paces behind him. His voice, what God would sound like if he were your accountant, was familiar from *Lux Radio Theater.* I stepped aside to allow Cecil B. DeMille and his personal army by to storm the studio commissary.

At John Engstead's studio I knocked on the door and heard a faint "It's open" in reply. Entering the large, mostly bare space I noticed a length of wall, complete with fireplace and mantel, trundling across the floor. Only the fingertips clutching either side betrayed that it wasn't moving under its own power.

"Kenneth Nolan?" I asked.

"*Un momentito,*" the wall said. It sounded bored.

Several *momentitos* later the young man who'd taken photos of Gracie Allen and of me emerged from behind the faux wall. He was not very tall and moderately handsome, with black hair and brown eyes that fell just short of piercing. He recognized me at once, then pretended he didn't.

"I'm Ken Nolan." His handshake was a moist disappointment. "What can I do for you?"

"Edith Head would like to see you in Wardrobe with your camera."

"And what does Edith Head want with me and my camera?"

I rolled my eyes, placing a hand on my hip so I resembled a peeved teapot. "As if I'd know. Nobody tells me anything."

"A feeling with which I am all too familiar." He snatched a rag from the floor and buffed his two-tone wingtips. "Didn't I see you there the other day?"

"Yes. I'm working with Edith." Technically, not a lie. Score one for me and the nuns.

Ken seemed to buy it. "And are you enjoying that?"

"Who wouldn't? She's such a talented designer."

"Edith wishes she were a designer. She's one step up from a pattern cutter."

"Have you watched any of the films she's worked on? The gowns are spectacular."

"Then they're Travis Banton's. That's who she'd like to be, but she's just a journeyman. Journeywoman. Is that a word?"

I waited by the door as Ken shut off the lights and snagged his camera bag. As long as he was coming along, I wouldn't argue with him.

But Ken couldn't help testing my patience. "Don't get me wrong. Edith Head is a perfectly nice woman. But she's too conservative. She lacks the temperament of a true artist like Travis. If it wasn't for his indulgence, Edith would be lucky to be working at a department store. Hey, slow down!"

10

WE TRAVERSED THE lot without incident. Edith waited in the shade outside the Wardrobe building as we approached, a dark-haired man at her side.

"Oh, marvelous," Ken said. "This guy and his antics."

The man must have been telling a whale of a tale, because Edith rocked back and forth laughing. He leaped up and imitated an airplane, swooping in a circle then sputtering into a crash dive that landed him in his seat with a jolt. "So as parties go," the man said, "it wasn't bad."

Edith caught her breath and made the introductions. "May I present Preston Sturges." Mr. Sturges rose to take my hand, clicking his heels together. Or trying to; his woven kidskin loafers looked soft enough to sleep on. His wide shoulders filled out a well-tailored jacket with huge checks. A trim mustache balanced jauntily over a wide grin. "Preston is a writer, but if you ask me he'd make a marvelous actor."

"You know it's the director's chair or bust. Any job that comes with its own furniture is the one for me."

Ken declared himself a great admirer of Mr. Sturges's work, thus confirming his status as a fink. Mr. Sturges looked accustomed to such praise.

"Come by the café some evening, Edie. Bring Charles. Lovely dinner, on the house."

"You won't be open long making offers like that."

"Part of the plan to build name recognition for Snyder's.

Someday that spot will be a Hollywood landmark. I'll leave you to your business." He exited with an elaborate courtier's bow.

Edith executed a precise turn toward Ken. "Mr. Nolan. Thank you for coming."

In Edith's presence, Ken brimmed with bonhomie. "Happy to, Miss Head. I hope my photographs did justice to that lovely Gracie Allen ensemble you designed."

"Your usual fine work. Please, come this way."

"This way" didn't lead to Banton's office but to a third floor room marked WARDROBE STORAGE. Edith made a production of gaining entry, fussing with her keys. Ken, in turn, found reasons to adjust every dial on his camera. Then the door opened, and I lost track of the next several seconds.

The cavernous space beyond was nothing less than an enchanted closet, bursting with racks of clothes. A profusion of colors from riotous reds to vivacious violets peeked out from muslin dust covers, artifacts from movies already produced, released, and mostly forgotten. Cupboards against the walls held hats, shoes, and accessories. I moved in a dumbstruck haze. What woman would not go weak before such a sartorial bonanza? Certainly not Ruby.

Edith, on her home turf, wasn't dazzled. "You've heard the sad news about Ruby Carroll," she said to Ken.

He paused like a contestant on a quiz program. "A terrible thing."

"I understand you two were friends."

Now Ken took the pause of a man tapping the ice beneath his feet to test how thin it was. "Hardly. She wasn't here long enough for us to become friends. Where should I set up?"

"The photographs can wait. Then you did know her. How did you meet?"

More fidgeting with his camera. "In the commissary. She

heard I was a photographer and said she needed new pictures."

"New photos for her brunette phase?" I asked, thinking of the more natural look Ruby had sported at Tremayne's.

"That's right. She said she didn't have any." Ken turned to me. "You weren't working here then. How do you know Ruby, exactly?"

Edith wouldn't allow the conversation to deviate from the course she'd set. "Did you take any photographs of her?"

"No. As I said, she left the studio soon after."

"That's unfortunate. You do impressive work. I've always thought so."

Ken, confused by the kudos, coughed out a thank-you.

"Speaking of which, you may set up right where you are." Edith pushed one of the wardrobe racks forward, the rattle of its wheels loud. Hanging from the rod were the contents of Ruby's suitcase, the clothes Ken, for whatever reason, had stolen for her. He stared at the evidence of his misdeeds, swallowed hard, and faced Edith.

"Will we have any mannequins today?" he asked.

"They won't be necessary. We're not photographing these garments as wardrobe. Sadly, this is a police matter. Ruby . . . borrowed costumes from storage."

"Borrowed?"

"To put it one way," I said.

Ken shrugged, helpless as a foundling. "I'm afraid I'm a bit at sea here, Miss Head."

"Then permit me to throw you a lifeline. All these items from Paramount productions were found in Ruby's possession."

"In her . . . Ruby was a thief?" Ken did everything to convey shock short of clutching his throat. At least I wasn't the only lousy actor in the room.

"With an accomplice, no less. These articles were stolen

after Ruby was let go by the studio. Someone with access to this room was aiding her in her crime before she was murdered. It's most upsetting. Mr. Groff is on the warpath over it."

Ken nodded cagily, no doubt aware that his next words could determine his fate.

Which is why he seemed surprised when Edith didn't let him utter them.

"But the identity of the accomplice isn't our primary concern," she said airily. "Our interest is *why* Ruby borrowed the clothes, if her actions could in any way harm the reputation of Paramount Pictures. It's why I asked if you knew Ruby. We're desperate for any insight into her behavior."

"Of course," Ken said slowly, not daring to believe what he was hearing.

"Anything you might remember would be held in the strictest confidence." Edith touched Ken's arm. "Although I would certainly let Mr. Engstead know you'd been kind enough to cooperate. John is such a dear friend, my closest at the studio. I'd very much like to put in a good word for you with him. Could do wonders."

Simply by setting the scene—sending me to retrieve him, displaying the stolen clothes—Edith had accused Ken without a word. Now she offered a pardon before handing down his sentence. I was in awe.

"I only knew Ruby a little." Ken looked longingly at the door, then slumped as he chose not to use it. "But it seemed to me . . . she really knew the angles, that girl."

"Indeed. Which angles in particular?"

Ken licked his lips. "The idea—"

The creak of the opening door clammed him up. Detective Morrow walked in, shadowed by Hansen. And here I'd lived to the Biblical age of one score and four believing you should be happy when the police arrived.

"Ladies," Morrow said. "Are we interrupting?"

"Not at all, gentlemen," Edith said. "If you'd care to wait in my office—"

"No, Miss Head." Morrow worked to sand the edge off his voice. "We tried that."

Hansen targeted his ire at me. "Get a load of who's back again, for no good reason. I warned you not to bring her here, Gene. She's flypapered to this thing now." Hansen then eyeballed Ken and asked for his name. When he heard it, his face clouded. "I was about to come looking for you. Let's parley outside."

Edith stepped forward but Hansen already had Ken by the elbow and was guiding him out of reach. Ken glanced over his shoulder at us, a drowning man watching a boat sail past.

"Before you start, Detective," Edith told Morrow as the door closed, "let me suggest you are missing the point."

"Actually, Miss Head, I'm pretty sure the point's jabbing me in an uncomfortable spot right about now." Morrow crumpled the brim of his fedora in his hand. It's never a good sign, my uncle Danny counseled, when a man mistreats his hat. "You send us to your office while you're here questioning either a potential witness or a potential suspect."

"I was asking Mr. Nolan about the theft of Paramount wardrobe, which falls under my purview. What's more, Mr. Nolan was about to reveal Ruby's agenda."

"He can reveal it to Hansen."

"But he won't. That's the problem. He'll deny any involvement, because all the police can do is send him to jail."

Morrow smiled darkly. "Traditionally, that prospect loosens tongues."

"You can only hurt him, Detective. I could have helped him. Given him a leg up at the studio, which is what he wants. He would have told me the truth if you hadn't intervened."

Morrow's poor brim suffered further. "So we sic studio security on him."

"Again, Mr. Groff can only threaten to fire him or fire him. We're all stick and no carrot now. I'm quite disappointed."

Morrow was flustered, so naturally I decided to pile on. "Edith was only—"

The sight of the detective's back as he turned to examine the clothes silenced me. His own suit sagged on his frame as if he'd slept in it. "As for you, Miss Frost. You find a suitcase full of clothes stolen by a murder victim and instead of contacting the police, you call a movie studio."

"We needed to confirm they were stolen." My face grew hot.

"Don't berate Lillian, Detective," Edith said. "I insisted she see me. If she'd informed you about the suitcase, when would you have alerted me?"

"We'd have come by." Morrow was beginning to resemble a boy summoned to the principal's office.

"Undoubtedly. But tomorrow at the earliest. Thanks to Lillian you're talking to Ruby's accomplice now, even if he'll no longer admit anything."

I tried not to glow with pride. I failed.

"So this is the third degree," Morrow said. "No one wonder everyone grouses about it."

Edith chuckled. "Perhaps we can move on to what we've learned. We assumed Ruby stole that dress from *The Return of Sophie Lang* on impulse. Now we find she'd taken additional items. There's more to this than a single night's frolic."

"We know Ruby was fraternizing with some tony types," I said.

Morrow nodded. "Armand and Natalie. We heard."

"Armand's last name is Troncosa. He's from Argentina. Big money. Natalie Szabo is a Hungarian princess who might deign to crash the movies."

I could hear muslin settling while Morrow stared at me. Finally he took out his notebook. "Explain."

He didn't write anything down as I did so. "You haven't found Armand and Natalie. You've found *an* Armand and Natalie. Nothing ties them into Ruby."

"A reporter at Mrs. Lindros's asked me about Natalie by name."

"So? Reporters get bum leads, too. I need something substantial before I bother these people."

"Detective, I'd be inclined to listen to Lillian," Edith said. "She did find Ruby's suitcase."

Morrow snapped his notebook shut, besieged on all sides. "About that suitcase. What do we have, four or five outfits? Doesn't seem like enough for Ruby to traffic in high society."

"It would suffice for a while," Edith said. "Ruby chose well. The afternoon dress is appropriate for a number of occasions. A luncheon in the city, a daytime concert. The suit, of course, could also be worn to any of those functions."

"Isn't the embroidered accent on the lapel a bit . . . dramatic?" I ventured.

"Quite right. I'd say an opera. Not opening night."

"Yes, it's a trifle gauche for that," Morrow said.

Edith pretended not to hear him. "It would be at home in any audience, though. The theater, a prize fight."

"A prize fight?" Morrow asked.

"As an example," Edith said.

"Of its versatility," I added.

Morrow shook his head. "Clearly you ladies aren't at the Olympic on Tuesday nights. How durable are these costumes? Won't they fall apart after Ruby wears them once or twice?"

The temperature plunged precipitously as Edith drew herself up. "Fall apart?" She plucked one of the burgundy suits from the rack and turned the skirt inside out. "Examine this seam,

Detective. Closely. What do you see? Quality. Attention to detail. Our seamstresses are the best in the business." She slipped on the jacket and flipped up the collar. "Velvet, should the director ask the actress to turn the collar up. Real pockets, in case—" She'd tucked her hands into those pockets as she spoke. We watched as she pulled something out of the left one.

"What have we here?" She held up an oversized jigsaw puzzle piece. It was about three inches across, sky blue with what looked like bricks on one side. "It appears I've found a piece of the puzzle. Or at least *a* puzzle."

"Could be part of a building," I said.

Morrow nodded. "Congratulations, Miss Frost. You've broken this case wide open."

Edith turned the puzzle piece over. "There's writing on the back. 'Twelve-slash-eleven, seven thirty.' It doesn't say A.M. or P.M."

"December eleventh," Morrow said. "Over a month away."

"If that was Ruby's I guarantee it's not A.M.," I said. "I rarely saw her out of bed before noon."

Morrow produced an envelope. "If you'd place that in here," he said to Edith.

"Oh, dear. Will I have to be fingerprinted for elimination purposes? I'll be sure to wear something dark."

The door protested again and Paramount's house Napoleon Barney Groff strutted in, trailed by two timid young women looking as baffled as new arrivals at Ellis Island. "Sorry for the delay, Gene. Paramount's a big shop. My work is never done." He looked at me. "I see someone booked our featured performer for a return engagement. Even though there was no popular demand." Groff's eyes lingered long enough to banish me to extra-girl status—and to permit Morrow to spirit away the envelope containing the puzzle piece. Groff angled his head toward the Ruby Carroll collection. "So these clothes are ours, too."

"Yes, Mr. Groff," Edith said. "From films that had recently finished shooting."

"But now they're back. Problem solved. Terrific." Groff, I couldn't help noticing, did not look at Edith as he spoke. He nodded at the two women, who took off toward the clothes as if they'd heard a starter's pistol. "I drafted a few wardrobe girls to start tidying up."

One of the women snatched the bag of jewelry while the other lunged at the burgundy suit. Edith looked on in dismay. "Surely there's no need to move so quickly."

Groff kept his words clipped and his tone arctic. "What there's no need to do is extend police involvement in a studio matter resolved to Paramount's satisfaction. Are other clothes missing?"

Edith watched the first girl distribute the articles from the jewelry bag into drawers with all deliberate speed. "None I can account for, no."

"Was anything of consequence in the clothes?"

Behind her glasses, Edith's eyes flicked to Morrow. He discreetly tapped the breast pocket where he'd slipped the puzzle piece. "That's not for me to say."

"Precisely. And we've identified the responsible party. What was his name? The photographer?"

"Kenneth Nolan." Edith and Morrow said it simultaneously. Edith took a step back, deferring to him.

"My partner is talking to him now."

"Your partner cut him loose, and I handled the rest. Nolan is no longer in the employ of Paramount Pictures."

"Did he confess?" Morrow asked.

"Does it matter? The studio's role in this sad affair is at an end. We have our property back, the culprits no longer work here. You're free to concentrate on more important matters. You should know, Gene, I put a call in to Chief Davis this morning, telling him how impressed Mr. Zukor was by your diligence and discretion. We haven't seen headlines screaming 'Alley Angel Plays Devil at Paramount.' That hasn't gone unappreciated."

Morrow grimaced, passing it off as a grin. "It's why I do the job."

"In the unlikely event you do require additional cooperation, contact me direct. No need for you to waste time going through our Wardrobe Department." He couldn't even bring himself to pronounce Edith's name. She'd undermined Groff's authority by summoning Morrow herself. It wasn't only the jewelry he was putting in its proper place.

Edith would have none of it. "Given that poor young girl's murder, Mr. Groff, I'm happy to assist—"

Groff was already making for the exit. "If you'll excuse me, I've got other fires to put out." An awkward silence followed in his wake, broken only by the clatter of hangers as the wardrobe women undid Ruby's crime.

Morrow finally chuckled. "I almost have to admire that guy. Bet anything I hear from one of Chief Davis's glad-handers, strongly suggesting I keep Paramount out of the limelight. I should track down Hansen before he starts pestering Claudette Colbert. Can I give you a ride somewhere, Miss Frost?"

"Home, I suppose. I can't face customers just yet. Maybe after lunch."

"Nonsense," Edith said. "If you're expected at work, you've got to go."

As I said my farewell to her, she pressed a piece of paper into my palm. On it she'd written the information that had been on the puzzle piece: *12/11, 7:30*.

"Just in case," Edith said.

"Just in case what?"

Her owlish eyes blinked at me. "Well, I don't know."

"Oh, right," I said. "Just in case."

11

I WAS HALFWAY up the stairs to my apartment when Mrs. Quigley's voice boomed out of her perpetually half-open door. "Lillian! Is that you?"

My landlady had a trove of memories from a checkered show business career and a collection of late husbands, one of whom had bequeathed her a small building on the fringes of Hollywood that she kept in a state of faded glamour matching her own. Her inability to admit she was hard of hearing meant every conversation felt like a play in which I'd blundered onstage knowing only half my lines.

"Yes, Mrs. Q." I stopped at the threshold to her apartment. As usual, I smelled rosewater and the stew that seemed to be forever simmering in the event a platoon of starving soldiers turned up.

Mrs. Q was certainly dressed to receive them in an ivory and gold housecoat. I placed her age somewhere between fifty and the Pearly Gates. "The phone's been ringing off the hook for you! I've been popping out like a jack-in-the-box to answer it."

"I'm sorry about that. How many calls did I get?"

"Two!" A fairly high number, both for me and for Mrs. Quigley's in general. Life could be very sedate in a building without actresses. "It was the same woman both times," Mrs. Quigley went on. "She wouldn't leave her name, just said she'd call back. My land! I haven't had this much exercise since my Ziegfeld days."

In the lobby, I beelined for the phone. The mystery caller was likely Kay; I'd promised to tell her what Edith said about the suitcase. I dialed the *Modern Movie* offices and got her at once. "You don't know you're allowed to leave messages?"

"What are you talking about?"

"Didn't you call this morning?"

"Will this conversation consist entirely of questions? No, I didn't call. I was waiting for you to telephone me. Spill."

I summarized my Paramount excursion. "Wow," Kay said. "You cost a man his livelihood and it's not even lunchtime."

"That's all I could think about on the way home."

"You Catholics and your crushing guilt. If this Ken stole clothes for Ruby, he deserves to be tossed out on his ear. I'll take your mind off his woes. I got a peek at the full dossier on Armand Troncosa. Information remains thin on Natalie because she just came over from the Continent, whereas lover boy Armand has been hobnobbing here for months. The Troncosas are rich, obviously. Money from real estate, mining interests, cattle. Ranches on the pampas full of gauchos like Gilbert Roland."

"Gilbert Roland is Mexican."

"He is? Are you sure?"

"I read it in your magazine."

"Then he must be. The Troncosas are also important politically, very lovey-dovey with the generalissimo. I assume Argentina has a generalissimo. These places typically do. By all accounts Armand is the clan's black sheep. Something of a hothead. The juicy rumor is he killed someone he shouldn't have back home. A member of another prominent family. Possibly in a duel, if you can imagine. The Troncosas pulled strings and whisked him out of the country until the whole business blows over."

"How long does it take a blood feud to blow over? This dossier sounds like pure hearsay."

"You want to quibble over details? If there's a shred of truth in it, Armand's a likely suspect in Ruby's murder."

Assuming, per Detective Morrow's caution, that he was the *right* Armand. "What does Armand do, exactly?" I asked.

"He's a playboy. They don't *do* anything. His main interest, as Jimmie Fidler mentioned, is polo. You may recall Argentina took the gold medal at the Olympics last year."

"I cheered at every game."

"I believe they're called matches, kiddo. Armand reminds people of his countrymen's triumph at every opportunity. He was in Berlin for the whole show. His goal is to make polo popular in these United States, and I wish him luck with that."

"If he puts numbers on the horses and sells red hots in the stands, I'll take a flier on it. Too bad your impressive work is for naught. Detective Morrow thinks we're barking up the wrong Argentine. Even Edith couldn't convince him."

"Nuts. I'm staring at Armand's address in Whitley Heights."

The idea was out of my mouth before I could consider the wisdom of it. "What say we take a look at this Armand character ourselves? We won't do anything foolish. I know you're curious. You could try spinning this into a story you can—"

"Honey, why are you tying up the line with this palaver when I could be calling Ready right now?"

WHEN THE SILENT screen was king, many of its stars dwelled close to the firmament in Whitley Heights. The glamorously precarious neighborhood, perched on the hillside overlooking Hollywood Boulevard, had been the first celebrity enclave in Los Angeles. The houses on its narrow, winding streets had a

Mediterranean flavor, all red slate roofs and broad windows. They offered seclusion a stone's throw from the studios. The big names had since decamped for the more extravagant pastures of Beverly Hills, but once upon a time everyone who mattered lived up here. Charlie Chaplin, Harold Lloyd, Rudolph Valentino.

"A few famous faces are still around," I nattered from the backseat of Ready's car. "Francis X. Bushman never left."

"I think we just drove past him delivering the mail," Kay said.

"Beautiful up this way," Ready said. "I heard tell the big parties were thrown by Eugene O'Brien."

Kay snorted. "How do you two remember these people? Makes me think less of this Armand that he's getting a nosebleed in the boonies."

Ready kept the car tooling toward the heavens. The edges of the roads were lined with iron posts linked by chains, decorative reminders that should you lose purchase, the plunge to Grauman's Chinese Theatre was a long one. The hillside was gaudy with flora, bougainvillea and wisteria in abundance. I feared I'd get drunk on the scent of orange blossoms.

"Hollywood Bowl coming up." Ready swung the car around a hairpin curve and the stadium appeared below us, waiting to fill up with music and light. "Seats aren't the best, but you can hear the concerts from here."

"Troncosa's place ahoy." Kay indicated a villa shaded by olive trees and protected by a wrought-iron gate. Ready slowed as much as he dared. The house felt shuttered even from the street. Around the side we passed a garage and a wooden door like a chapel's entrance set in a white stone wall. Both were closed. Ready kept the car in motion.

"Not being skilled in detection as you ladies are, I'm unsure how to proceed. I'm guessing you don't want to knock on the man's door. And it's not like we can stop and have a scout."

We passed one of the staircases connecting the hillside's four levels. "Let me out at the top of those stairs," I said. "I'll walk past the house and give it a closer look. You can pick me up on the way back down."

"The ol' tourist gambit," Kay said. "Never fails."

Within seconds the sound of Ready's car faded, leaving me with only hummingbirds for accompaniment. I trod carefully down a flight of stairs that, like all of Whitley Heights, was picturesque and criminally vertiginous. On reaching its base I offered a word of thanks to Saint Elmo, patron of those who worked at altitude. Also of women undergoing childbirth, but I was saving that card for a later date.

At Troncosa's gate I stopped to adjust the strap on my sandal. The house remained eerily still. No newspapers on the porch, no uncollected milk bottles, every window closed. Nary a sign of life.

On I strolled, just a gal from out of town enjoying the sunshine. The scene at the side of the house was also unchanged. I crossed the street and lingered at the summit of the staircase leading down. Hibiscus and cedar scented the breeze as I gazed at the sign touting the Hollywoodland development, the letters shimmering in the distance a promise beckoning you onward. The neighborhood was both bewitching and benighted, the Garden of Eden after the serpent had set up shop.

Behind me, the garage door opened. I took my time turning around.

The car in Troncosa's garage was a Pierce-Arrow brougham in either blue or gray, the shadows masking its shade. Whereas the man who buffed its hood looked burnished, like something left in the sun until its true color had been revealed. His thick eyebrows were colonies under the protection of the motherland of jet-black hair atop his head. He moved with the preoccupied purpose of someone mentally sorting a list of errands.

If only I'd bothered to cook up a plan for the wholly likely eventuality of someone exiting the house.

I walked toward the garage. With each step, my hips drifted farther from their moorings. I found myself chewing a phantom piece of gum.

"How ya doin'?" I squeaked. "This Armand Troncosa's house?"

Dear God. In voice and manner I had become Louise Halloran, the good-time girl who'd lived down the hall from us in Flushing. Perhaps I had stumbled onto one of the secrets of acting. I couldn't create a character out of whole cloth, but impressions were a cakewalk.

The man squinted at me. He didn't speak with an accent, his voice more lightly dusted with Latin inflections. "Yes. May I help you?"

"Are you Armand?"

"Alas, I am not." The man slouched against the car, amused. The errands could wait.

I pouted in disappointment. "Is the man of the house here?"

"You wish to sell him brushes, perhaps? Armand is abroad at the moment. May I ask your name?"

"Lil," I said. I realized what I was doing: playing a brassier, dimmer version of myself, the me who would have stayed Ruby's friend. "Your turn."

"Esteban Riordan, at your service."

"That's a funny kind of a handle." Life really was simpler when you could say whatever you wanted.

Esteban, fortunately, did not take offense. "Equal parts Spanish and Irish. My family moved to Argentina decades ago."

"I love Argentina. They won the gold medal in polo at the Olympics last year, y'know."

"I do indeed." Esteban puffed with pride. "My brother Luis is a member of the team. An alternate, but still."

"Really? I wish polo was more popular. You never hear about any of the matches. So are you and Armand friends?"

"The closest. I also work for him. I'm his unofficial major-domo, you might say."

No acting required here. "Major . . . domo?"

"I tend to the small aspects of Armand's life so he may focus on the larger ones, like bringing polo the audience it deserves. And you, Lil? How do you know Armand?"

I had to proceed with caution. I desperately wanted to confirm Armand and by extension Natalie were Ruby's new highbred companions, but without compromising Detective Morrow's efforts. I wondered what Louise Halloran would do. Came the answer: *Play demure. As broadly as possible.* I batted my eyes and kicked at the oil stain on the driveway. "See, I don't really know him. My friend Ruby does, and she said I should make his acquaintance. Do you know my friend Ruby?"

The name had no effect on Esteban whatsoever. "Armand has met so many people it's difficult to keep them straight. She has been to the house, your friend?"

"That's right. She met Armand through her friend Natalie. Do you know Natalie?"

Some unruly emotion—possibly fear—flickered across Esteban's face only to vanish beneath an implacable mask, like a skim of ice forming over an ominous dark shape in the water. He volleyed my question back. "Do *you* know Natalie?"

"I—no, but—"

"But your friend does. Ruby. Has Ruby seen Natalie? Does she know where Natalie is? Who Natalie is with?"

Stumped for a safe answer, I stared at him. Esteban eliminated the distance between us. "Please. You must tell me."

"I, I can't. I don't know."

Esteban placed his hand on my upper arm as if he were

clinging to me. "Unless . . . has Natalie sent you to test Armand's affections? Has she?"

I was flummoxed. Any semblance of Louise Halloran was lost to me now.

Esteban saw the car before I did. Ready brought it to a halt and opened his door. I slipped Esteban's grasp and darted around him. "That's my ride. Excuse me."

Ready waited until I was in the car before getting back in himself. Esteban stepped into the street to watch us go.

"You all right, Lillian?" Ready asked.

"Is that Armand?" Kay demanded.

"I'm fine. That wasn't Armand. It was his majordomo. Sort of a butler."

"No, it's not," Kay said. "It's the head of the household. Butler is a completely different job."

"Is it?" Ready peered at her. "Then what's a valet?"

"We'll look it up later. The question is, did we find our Armand?"

"I'm sure of it," I said. "I just can't prove it yet."

"Still? Did you learn *anything*?"

"Yes. Armand and Natalie are both travelling, and not together. In fact, they may no longer be a couple."

"Doesn't that make Armand an interesting figure," Kay said.

"I thought so." I turned to Ready. "Home, James."

"You don't want to go to work?" he teased.

"You'll never make majordomo with that attitude," I said.

12

THE STRAINS OF "A Pretty Girl Is Like a Melody" thundered into the hallway. Time for Mrs. Quigley's afternoon exercises. My landlady walked the length of her parlor like she was balancing a pail of nitroglycerine on her head. A trouper through and through, Mrs. Q religiously practiced her Ziegfeld walk should she and Billie Dove be needed in the Follies once more.

She pirouetted to face me. I flinched as if the nitro were about to go, then again when I saw the rag-doll circles of rouge she'd applied to her cheeks.

"Lillian! Your caller tried twice more and still won't leave so much as her name! You know I loathe interrupting my routine."

Did I. "Sorry, Mrs. Q. What does this woman sound like?"

"Very breathless, very intense," Mrs. Quigley said, evincing both qualities herself. Who else in my orbit possessed a flair for the dramatic and my telephone number?

"ISN'T IT FUNNY you should call?" Diana Galway trilled down the line. "I was just thinking about you."

Her greeting didn't indicate whether Lodestar Pictures' promising new discovery and Ruby's steady lunch partner had been dialing me like mad all day. I'd planned on telephoning Diana anyway. She was the sole entry in my slender address book who might know Armand and Natalie. A little voice chirped that I was overdue at work, but I was in no mood to tote that barge for Tremayne's now.

"I'm still simply shattered about Ruby," Diana said without prompting. "It was such a help to go to Mrs. Lindros's and see some of the girls again. The poor things. I wonder where they find the strength to pound the pavement every day. To struggle."

"You did it, too. You're giving them hope."

"Yes, but I had an ace in the hole. I *knew* better things were in store. On my fifteenth birthday, a fortune-teller told me there was a bright star in my future." She paused expectantly, but I had no idea what she was talking about. She fed me my cue again. "A bright star . . ."

"Oh, Lodestar. I get it. Say, that's a good story. You should tell that to one of the magazines."

"I did. It'll be in the next *Photoplay.* It's so sad Ruby won't get a chance to see it."

"I spent the morning with the detective investigating the case."

"Did you?" Baiting actresses was almost too easy. Diana presumably feared her reputation might be tarnished by the Alley Angel Affair. The prospect of inside information proved irresistible. "I could use a friendly ear. I don't suppose you could come over."

"Sure. What streetcar line are you on?"

"We're in Beverly Hills, dear. Take a taxi. I'll pay for it."

I was being driven everywhere today. A girl had better not get used to this.

THE MINOTS, APPROPRIATELY, lived in a house out of a movie. Set back on the property, curved drive depositing visitors before squat marble columns. It merited a whistle from my cabdriver, at any rate.

The maid who answered the door sported a crooked nose and a shapeless uniform that made her look like a bag of bruised potatoes. Even the lascivious Laurence Minot wouldn't be tempted. Perhaps Diana was smarter than I thought.

As I trailed the maid down the hall something reminded me of Sunday mass with Aunt Joyce. Incense, that was it. The scent became overwhelming once she showed me into a small room. Diana sat on one of several tufted red silk pillows on the floor. She wore a blue kimono, legs crossed beneath her. The incense burned in a porcelain Buddha, smiling to himself on a table off to the side. He probably thought the pillows were a hoot, too.

"I've taken up the ancient Eastern custom of meditation," Diana announced, eyes squeezed shut as if warding off a migraine.

"How do you like it?"

"I hear Myrna Loy finds it relaxing but I can't sit still for that long. I do love the clothes, though." She untangled her legs and stood up. The robe's blue silk was shot through with golden threads, the deep cobalt making the blue of her eyes pop.

"I don't mean to be rude, but could you put a damper on the incense? I keep expecting an altar boy to wander in."

"It is a bit much, isn't it? Frankly, it doesn't help." She lifted the Buddha off his base and snuffed out the joss stick. "And I was so hoping to center myself today. I've been so distraught about Ruby I haven't been able to study my lines." She flung a hand at a script pup-tented on the floor. "I play a waitress in this one."

"Weren't you a waitress in the last one?"

"Yes, but this time I'm a waitress with a *secret*. You said you talked to the police about Ruby. Has . . . my name come up?"

"Not yet."

"Good." Disappointment feuded with relief in her voice, some part of her craving publicity of any stripe.

"You and Ruby were still close, weren't you?"

"Like sisters. She was always there to listen whenever I had a problem. She knew an awful lot about men."

"Or a lot about awful men."

"Lillian!" Diana giggled girlishly. She did everything girlishly. That's what Lodestar was paying her for. "Ruby would give me the best advice. Who am I going to turn to now? Who can I share my worries with, my fears?"

"What could you possibly have to be afraid of?"

"The things that always concern a woman." She paused, then lowered her voice. "A married woman."

"Laurence?"

"I know it sounds ridiculous, but at times I think he might be stepping out on me. You see, he's something of a flirt."

Unable to maintain a compassionate pan, I turned to the Buddha. The smoldering fat man's smile calmed me. Maybe there was a payoff to this meditation racket. *Something of a flirt?* Laurence Minot sprinkled come-ons by reflex. He made Chaplin look chaste. Ruby insisted she'd seen him make a play for a woman at his own wedding reception—a woman he'd already been married to. And that had been less than a year ago. Technically, the Minots were still newlyweds.

"Ruby always told me I was being silly. Her opinion was husbands who flirt never cheat. It's the ones who pretend not to notice other women who stray."

"That's an intriguing theory."

"Theory? So you think she could have been wrong?" Diana's mouth retracted to its tiniest size in dismay.

I'd forgotten I was auditioning for the coveted role of shoulder to cry on. "No, Ruby was right. Don't listen to me. I'm only a window-shopper when it comes to matters of the heart. May I ask, how did Ruby dress when you two got together?"

"In the dark, it seemed to me. Grabbing the same old rags from her closet."

"I heard she'd picked up new friends. Society types. You might know them. Armand Troncosa and Natalie Szabo? He's from Argentina, she's some kind of princess out of—"

Diana's laugh cut me off. "Society types? I'd hardly know about them. I have a job just like you. Not exactly, but you understand. On the days we're shooting I'm out of bed so early I might as well be a farmer. Can't say I've heard of either of them. This Natalie is a princess, you say?"

"From Hungary."

"Wants into pictures, I suppose."

"If Jimmie Fidler is to be believed."

"Oh, I always believe Jimmie." Diana imbued the words with the sincerity of a sworn oath. She started pacing, punting pillows out of her path as she walked. "Princesses. Gold diggers, more like. Coming over here with titles and stealing our jobs and our men, all the while asking us to feel sorry for them. 'Pity me, I've lost my throne.' Got your just desserts, more likely."

If Diana's empathetic grasp of geopolitics were any indication, the meditation room was not having the desired effect. The lady certainly seemed to be protesting too much. I suggested we talk about her upcoming picture. Or to be precise, Diana talked while I didn't smother her with a cushion. Her stories revolved around starlets out to sabotage her, writers whose lines were unspeakable, directors who ignored her brilliant suggestions, and photographers determined to make her look like Methuselah's maiden aunt. While contemplating which pillow would work best for suffocation detail, it occurred to me that I had assumed Ruby's responsibilities, listening to Diana natter about problems I'd surrender my eyeteeth to have.

"And after that I volunteered to do my own makeup if they couldn't find a competent professional."

I offered yet another variation on "You poor thing."

"You're so sensible, Lillian, not seduced by this mad Hollywood whirl. Money, clothes, parties. You and I know it's all so much stardust."

"Still, a sprinkle of it now and again would be nice."

"Speaking of makeup, I should get my beauty rest."

"Yes, and it will take me a while to get home."

"Gracious, I had completely forgotten. Let me give you cab fare." She flitted from the room, returning with a wad of bills that wouldn't choke a horse but might cause minor equine digestive distress. "I have no idea how much things cost anymore. Is this enough to cover both ways?"

"Now *this* conversation sounds intriguing." Laurence Minot leered from the doorway. He wore a navy suit with the merest suggestion of a pinstripe. The bruises on his face were healing nicely, now several shades lighter than his jacket.

Diana absently kissed his cheek. "I insisted Lillian keep me company so I've offered to pay for her taxis."

"Permit me to run the lady home." He crooked an elbow at me. I looked to the Buddha in the hope he'd suggest a suitable excuse but he kept silent. The smug little bastard.

LAURENCE CHATTED ABOUT the weather and the movies as he chauffeured. The director of *Sing for Your Supper* strongly recommended *The Life of Emile Zola*, "Not that they'd let me near a picture of substance like that nowadays." Small talk depleted, he said, "You and my bride do a lot of reminiscing?"

"Diana is still grieving over Ruby."

At the mention of Ruby's name Laurence snorted. The sound of a bull in a ring, utterly bereft of pity.

"You didn't like Ruby?"

"I never gave her much thought. I only met her once, at our wedding. Ruby struck me as someone who'd been in Los Angeles too long. Started to view every encounter as an opportunity and every person who'd achieved some success as an enemy. I don't think she cared for my wife very much."

I wanted to disagree. Too bad I couldn't.

"I have to say I didn't like Diana spending time with her," he continued. "Ruby was a bad influence."

"What makes you say that?"

"She was involved with a gangster. That hood Tommy Carpa. Diana dragged me to his dive of a club once to gawk at him. She'd come home aboil with news about Ruby's latest set-to with him. Sturm und Drang with hackneyed dialogue. I used to dread hearing about those lunches."

"Ruby had come up in the world lately. She'd been socializing with a better class of people. Maybe you know them. Armand Troncosa and Natalie Szabo?"

"Hmm? Sure, we've seen them around. He's been on the Hollywood circuit a while. She's new to it, I think. And Ruby was friends with them, you say? Wonder how that happened."

We stopped at a red light and Laurence considered me, a bit too avidly for my liking. "You've crossed my mind more than once since the other day. You don't act anymore, is that right?"

"Yes. To the acclaim of millions."

"If you don't mind my saying, that's a shame. You have a quality. You project a particular charisma."

"Congratulations. You're the first person to see it."

"That's because it's very contemporary. It might not show up onscreen without a capable man behind the camera." The light changed. The car rolled forward, Laurence continuing to subject me to intense scrutiny. "Would you be interested in a screen test? Under my humble tutelage?"

Words that girls travel clear across the country to hear, and I wanted no part of them. "Thanks but no thanks. My greasepaint days are over. I'm married to my work."

"When you change your mind, I can set up a test at Lodestar with a single phone call." Not *if*, I noted, but when. Laurence was cocksure but didn't press the matter further, undoubtedly tired after a full eight hours of pursuing chorus girls.

I barely held up my end of the conversation for the duration of the trip. I was too busy mulling over why Diana had lied about knowing Armand and Natalie, and what compelled Laurence's transparent attempt at ingratiation by reviving my film career. Whatever the explanation, something was rotten in the state of the Minot union. Ruby had predicted it at the reception.

After bidding Laurence a hasty farewell, I let myself into my building. Mrs. Quigley had closed her door for the night but she'd left Miss Sarah Bernhardt, her elegant sable-brown Burmese, patrolling the lobby. Miss Sarah brushed against my ankle, saying hello.

"I could use a friendly ear," I told the cat. "I don't suppose you could come over. Take a taxi. I'll pay for it."

Miss Sarah seemed indifferent to the offer, which I took as assent. I scooped her up and carried her to my apartment. Miss Sarah dozed off, and I followed her lead. No sense letting a fine idea go to waste.

13

THE PHONE'S RING cut straight through my none-too-deep slumber. Even asleep, I'd been waiting for the call.

The dawn light was still in rehearsals. I staggered downstairs, almost stumbling over a spry Miss Sarah. Mrs. Quigley stirred in her chambers. I hollered that I'd take care of it. I snatched the receiver, uttered a bleary "Hello."

After a brief silence I heard, "I am calling for Lillian Frost?" The accented female voice cooed each word, placing the tiniest emphasis on the wrong syllables.

"This is Lillian."

"Success at last." I realized if Miss Sarah could speak, she'd sound exactly like this woman. "You are most difficult to reach."

"Who's calling, please?"

"I am Natalya Szabo. Please call me Natalie. I am American now."

Any trace of grogginess dissipated. I was bucket-of-ice-water-over-the-head awake. I inched closer to the phone so her words would have less distance to travel. "I've heard your name. Why are you calling?"

"Because you knew dear Ruby. You were her friend." Natalie pushed forth a velvet sigh. "Hearing her name makes me sad. I've been sad for days, thinking about her."

"Do you know what exactly happened to her?"

"What do any of us know? I can only say dear Ruby made

some regrettable decisions. We all do. We women are creatures of the heart, aren't we?"

It was too early for riddles. "I've been looking for you. I was at Armand Troncosa's yesterday."

"Ah, Armand. Silly brute." Her words were laced with pity. She followed them with another decadent sigh, suited to eating chocolate-covered cherries in a bubble bath. "I feel as if I know you, dear Lillian, because Ruby spoke so highly of you. She told me more than once you were her one true friend. The only person she could trust. I hope I may trust you also."

"Of course. What can I do?"

"I know it is only a matter of time before the police seek me out. Perhaps they are already looking. I wish for you to tell them I know nothing."

"Actually, I was going to ask you to help them."

"This I cannot do, dear Lillian. For many reasons. I wish to cause problems for no one. All I want is . . . to fade away."

She implied so much turmoil in her last words I suspected the worst. "You're not going back to Hungary, are you?"

Her laugh could launch a thousand dueling scars. "You need have no fears for me. Now that I've learned how America expects me to behave, I like it here. And I intend to stay. Where no one can find me. After what was done to Ruby . . . our family has suffered enough."

It took me a moment to parse her request. "Your family . . . are you and Ruby related?"

I heard a startled intake of breath, as if Natalie feared she had revealed too much. At that instant, an operator cut in. "Excuse me. Please deposit—"

Natalie slammed the phone down. The operator nasally repeated hello several times before breaking the connection.

I slowly replaced the receiver, then felt the wood of the table the phone rested on, brushed my thumb against the faded pad of paper alongside it. Physical sensations to confirm I hadn't dreamed the entire conversation.

Behind me, Mrs. Quigley cleared her throat. "Was that the woman who's been harassing us? May I assume these intrusions will cease?"

"Absolutely, Mrs. Q. Excuse me." My fingers fumbled at the phone's dial. Detective Morrow needed to be informed. He had to know Natalie had contacted me. More importantly, he had to know I'd been right. About Natalie and Armand, about everything.

Except Ruby. I had to face the possibility I'd been wrong about her.

You were her one true friend, Natalie told me. Ruby had used those exact words the last time I saw her, in Tremayne's cafeteria. I assumed she'd said them to butter me up, to convince me to steal for her. But what if she'd meant them?

NATURALLY, THE GENT I'd eyebatted out of his newspaper two days ago was catching the same streetcar in. I managed to keep several other commuters between us. After leaving a message for Detective Morrow I'd dressed quickly and headed to work. I'd present myself at Tremayne's just after sunup, sort those panties I should have dealt with last night before the first matrons hit the sales floor, and be back in Mr. Valentine's good graces by lunchtime. Hard right into the employee's entrance, straight to the time clock—

And there was Mr. Valentine, talking to one of the store's other bigwigs. Wearing a magenta tie so garish you almost didn't notice the dark pouches beneath his eyes.

Not faltering, I flashed my best smile. Mr. Valentine did not respond in kind. The hollow *thunk* of the time clock punctured my mood as well as my card.

The situation did not improve at the lingerie counter when I tripped over a box. I landed on my hands and knees, nose pressed to cardboard, the words YOLANDA INTIMATES swimming before my eyes. At least I'd found the panties Mr. Valentine wanted sorted and put away.

Smoothing my skirt, I stood up. And locked eyes with a man whose smirk indicated he'd seen my pratfall and was waiting for my next number. His cheap suit didn't look any better indoors.

"Hello, Ginger," Beckett said. "You looking for a Fred?"

"You're that reporter who tricked my friend into giving you her only photograph of Ruby. I'm not talking to you."

"Reporter? I'm no reporter."

"When I spoke to you, you told me you were a reporter."

"Actually, you assumed it and I was happy to play along." He nosed around Yolanda's intimates. "The way you let people believe you're on the Paramount payroll."

He had me there. "Who are you then?"

"Winton Beckett. Call me Win, kitten, because that's what I do. I'm a private investigator."

"And what do you want to talk to me about, Mr. Beckett?"

"Your friend Ruby Carroll, what else? She fascinates me. You fascinate me."

"I have that effect on people. But you'll have to leave. Tremayne's isn't open yet. How did you even get in here?"

"One of your house dicks owes me a favor. What say we both leave? I'll buy you a steak and we can talk."

"It's not even eight in the morning. And I've told the police everything I know."

"Then I'll buy you a cup of joe and you can answer one question for me."

"Let's hear it."

"What do you know about Natalie Szabo?"

My Catholic poker face gave me away, because Beckett stepped toward the counter. "Yeah, you know her name. You're the inquisitive sort. Natalie flew the coop. I need to find her."

I wasn't about to share that his missing princess had phoned that very morning. I pivoted away from him and started sorting the undies. Beckett lolled at the edge of my vision like a fly that couldn't figure out how to leave a room. But I'd show him. I'd ignore him like he'd never been ignored before. I'd—

"Tell me something."

"Anything, kitten."

"If you're not a reporter, why trick Vi into giving you her photo of Ruby? And how'd it end up in the paper?"

"I'm sorry about fooling the blonde. She seems like a sweet kid. But I needed the snapshot for my files. And publicity never hurts in my racket. I'm the one who's gonna get to the bottom of this Ruby business. Now you tell me something. Have you heard from Natalie?"

"Everything I know I told the police. Bother them."

"You mean Gene Morrow, right?" Beckett braced an elbow on the counter and pushed back the brim of his hat. "You might as well tell your aunt Fanny. Gene's not gonna make any headway on this thing. Too stolid. A constipated thinker. And Paramount's got him bottled up. You want something done about your friend, you need an independent operator like yours truly."

I dropped some empty boxes into the trash. "I trust Gene. But you? You I could do without."

"You trust those broad shoulders, maybe. Think he might develop a yen for you. Believe me, kitten, it's not in the cards. I used to be on the force. I know Gene's history. It's sordid, is what it is."

"*Used* to be on the force?"

He shrugged. "Little difference of opinion with Chief

Davis. What's wrong with a guy has a little style?" He shot his cuffs. His shirt was somehow uglier than his jacket.

"Isn't there a sale at the five-and-dime you should be at? Hang around a minute longer and I'll call the store detective."

"Will a real one do?" Gene strolled around a display of housecoats as if he'd been dozing behind it. I was surprised, forgetting that I'd told him in my message I'd be at the store. "How are you, Win? Buying something to wear around the house?"

"If it ain't Bulldog Morrow. I was just telling Miss Frost here all about you." Beckett straightened up to talk to him. "Sharing memories of bygone days."

"Is this man bothering you, Miss Frost?" Gene didn't look at me, lavishing all his concentration on Beckett.

"Considering the store's not open yet, I'd say yes."

"Why you hanging around here, Win?"

"Unmentionables for a lady friend."

"He was asking about Ruby," I said. "He was outside her place the other day, pretending to be a reporter."

"I explained that, kitten." Beckett shrugged at Gene, helpless before his own charisma. "Dames. Am I right, Gene? You know a thing or two about women."

"Learn anything you'd like to share with the authorities?"

"You want me to do your job for you? I don't get paid by the city anymore."

"Who *is* paying you? Why the interest in Ruby Carroll?"

"Can't tell you that."

"A trip downtown might change your tune."

"You're going to arrest me for what? Running an errand?" Beckett turned to me, brandishing teeth fit to chew through wiring. "Some intimates, if you please. Pick whatever colors you'd wear, sweetheart."

"We're not open yet," I said through a clenched jaw.

Gene laid a heavy hand on Beckett's shoulder. Beckett brushed it off. "Run me in if you want," he said. "I got a lawyer who can make your life miserable."

"You don't need a lawyer for that." Gene turned to me. "I stopped by because of your message. Whatever you called about will have to wait, Lillian."

"First-name basis, huh?" Beckett spat. "Bet the widow doesn't care for that."

I spoke swiftly and softly into Gene's ear. "Natalie Szabo telephoned me this morning. Beckett's searching for her."

"I'll see what I can pry out of him." Gene gave Beckett a shove. "Let's get going. I want to meet this lawyer of yours."

"He'll enjoy meeting you, too." Beckett grinned at me. "Three pairs of your finest scanties, doll. Wrap 'em up pretty. I'll pick 'em up later."

I watched them march toward the escalator still firing barbs at each other, and wondered exactly when I'd started thinking of Detective Morrow as Gene.

"MISS FROST, A word?" Thus ended my hope Mr. Valentine hadn't witnessed the performance.

He gestured broadly, at either the lingerie counter or the entire Southern California watershed. "What's this?"

"I was putting away the undies. Sorry, undergarments."

"And leaving boxes everywhere?"

"I was interrupted."

"Yes, I couldn't help but notice. Not exactly the kind of display Tremayne's is known for." He moved an empty box toward the trash, then frowned and lifted another out of the bin. "This package isn't empty."

Rats. A pair of beige bloomers was balled in the corner of the carton.

"I would have realized when I checked."

"*If* you checked." He paused. I steeled myself for the final blow.

"Miss Frost. I know you've had a trying experience. But I'm disappointed in your performance of late. Not returning to duty as you promised, bringing unsavory types into the store."

I wanted to object, but I knew arguing wouldn't aid my cause. Tugging the forelock was the order of the day. "You're right, sir. I can't apologize enough."

"I see you're contrite. But will that show in your actions?" He mused a moment. "Tomorrow is your day off."

"Yes. If you want me to come in, I will."

"I have another suggestion. Take the rest of today and tomorrow to settle your assorted melodramas. Clear your head. Then come back ready to work."

"I will, sir. Thank you, sir. That's very kind."

"Understand your first misstep after that will have you looking for another job."

Okay, maybe not so kind. I bowed, scraped, grabbed my purse, and skedaddled. A Frost seldom has to be told anything twice.

14

"AT LEAST I can say I spent some of my free time working," I told Vi as we left the theater.

"That was work?" My phone call had brought a morose Vi downtown in time for a matinee of the Technicolor extravaganza *Vogues of 1938*. The cloud over her blond head hadn't quite lifted, but a little light had filtered through.

"I knew I'd like it when the girls rolled out the titles on huge bolts of fabric. Tremayne's has a tie-up deal with the studio. We're going to sell hats from the movie."

"Even that green number with the veil?"

"Swing by when the shipment comes in and try it on."

We paused before a shoe store window. A pair of emerald dancing slippers with ribbon laces beckoned to me. To resist their siren song I turned to Vi and saw her gazing forlornly into the street. "The picture didn't take? What's wrong?"

"Rough morning. Ruby's family showed up. Her mother and uncle. Mrs. Lindros asked me to tend to them."

Ruby's family. Which could also be Natalie's family. "You poor thing. How did it go?"

"It wasn't easy. But they were sweet. Ruby's real name was Roza, did you know that? Roza Karolyi. I think I'm saying it right."

"I knew Ruby wasn't her right name, and she grew up speaking another language. Karolyi. So her people are what?"

"Hungarian. I don't think I ever met one before. There aren't many in Seattle. My father calls them hunkies." She looked abashed as she said it. Meanwhile I labored to tamp down my excitement. Everything Vi said was consistent with Natalie's furtive phone call. *Our family.*

"Ruby's mother spoke some English," Vi said. "Her uncle . . . I don't know. He didn't say much. They gathered Ruby's things from her room. Her mother said the girls could go through the clothes and take what they wanted."

I couldn't help picturing the frenzy in Mrs. Lindros's house had the contents of Ruby's suitcase been included in that offer.

"Did they say how long they would be here, or if they have other relatives in the area?"

"They're going straight home. And they weren't exactly chatty. Her mother talked a little about Ruby. 'Roza, such a pretty girl. So beautiful on the screen.'" Vi's accent was more Italian than Central European, but I got the general idea. "The worst part was when she reached into her carpetbag and pulled out a photo. 'Roza send to me. Her first Hollywood picture.' It was practically a publicity still. Ruby looked fantastic in it. I can't imagine how she could have afforded a picture like that."

"She had her ways," I said, thinking of a certain Paramount photographer. "What was Ruby wearing in the photo?"

"The most beautiful suit, with lots of pretty business on the lapel. I never saw it before."

Something told me I had.

"In the letter Ruby sent with the picture, she said she'd signed a contract and would be starting a movie soon. With Clark Gable! Her uncle was standing against the wall while we were talking. I figured he couldn't understand a word. But when he heard 'Clark Gable,' his face lit up. He came over and tapped the picture. 'Roza, Clark Gable,' he said. Couldn't have been more proud."

"How awful."

"I don't know how I kept from bawling until they were gone." Vi clutched my hand. "Do you know how often I've come close to writing my family I'm about to duet with Dick Powell? I need to get out of this business before I end up like Ruby."

"Don't get gloomy now. It's a waste of a twenty-five-cent movie ticket. I'll march you back in to see the picture again."

"I'm fine. It was nice to get out of the house after that."

"Happy to help. How's Tommy?"

"I wouldn't know. I've steered clear of him, like I promised."

"Good for you. Where to now? My day's free."

"I should go home. I have to work at the club tonight."

"I thought you had the day off. I was going to offer you your choice. Late lunch or early dinner, on me."

"I really should go. Thanks again for the movie." Eyeing a streetcar, Vi ran off, leaving me with my green temptation in the shoe store window.

"SHIRKING YOUR OWN job and inciting others to do likewise. I don't know you anymore." Kay chuckled. We sat behind two schooners of beer in a tavern around the corner from *Modern Movie* headquarters. She'd snagged her purse before I finished asking if she could leave work early.

Kay dug into a dish of peanuts. "Ruby kith and kin to a princess. Is it possible you bunked with a crowned head of Europe and didn't know it?"

"She always acted like blue blood ran through her veins. At the very least we know both Ruby and Natalie are Hungarian."

"I can see it. A family reunited in America under the palm trees. Natalie invites her—what, cousin?—to some soirees."

"What's Ruby to do, say no?"

"Not our Ruby. She's going, by hook or by crook. In this case crook." Kay chased a fistful of peanuts with a ladylike sip of beer. "Hollywood's a democratic town. You can brazen your way anywhere provided you know the lingo."

"And have the right clothes."

"Which Ruby certainly had. Not to mention the nerve. Sending that photograph to her mother?"

"I'm glad she did it. At least her mother has a keepsake."

"You think that Paramount photographer took the picture, don't you?"

"Yes, I do. Someone needs to talk to him about that. And Gene has to ask Ruby's family about Natalie."

"So he's Gene now."

"That's the man's name."

"And a fine one it is. I like that you're using it. I just wonder if he's aware of this state of affairs."

The street door opened, saving me from having to reply. Late afternoon sunlight silhouetted a lanky figure.

"You're not one of those cowpokes who starts a fight every time he ambles into a saloon, are you?" I asked.

"No, ma'am." Ready gave Kay a squeeze. "Not 'less they ask for it."

I lobbied for a second round, but Kay put her foot down. "I've got to help Mrs. Lindros feed her hungry brood. Want to stay for supper?"

"Either I fill up on peanuts or take Vi's place at the table."

"Where's Vi going to be?"

"She said she's working."

"Tonight?" Kay shrugged, then turned to Ready. "Bring your chariot hither. Drive two ladies home."

"Us, too," I said.

I WAS ANSWERING one of Ready's detailed questions about the fashions in *Vogues of 1938* when he turned onto Mrs. Lindros's street and dropped the brake to the floor.

"Don't go off half-cocked now, ladies," he said.

"At what?" Kay peered through the windshield at the green Packard parked outside our destination. A car I'd ridden in a time or two.

"Tommy Carpa has come calling." I bailed out, Ready running after me.

I beat him to the house. Tommy was perched on a wingback chair in the foyer, leafing through a month-old copy of *Liberty*. The smirk that started blooming on his face wilted at the sight of Ready filling the doorway behind me.

"What do you want?" I demanded.

"You don't live here, so I'm not answering." Tommy stood, nodded at Ready, and waited.

Kay charged in puffing with exertion and sized up the showdown. "What did I miss? Anybody throw a punch yet?"

A clatter arose on the stairs. Vi bounded down, wearing a pale yellow chiffon dress with green ovals the color of celery. The demure neckline had too many ruffles to be fashionable, but enough to make Vi happy. It looked like something a maiden aunt had run up for Vi's senior prom. "Sorry I took so long. I wanted to—" She caught sight of the tableau by the front door and blanched, knuckles whitening against the balustrade.

"No problem, doll," Tommy said. "Got a floor show here to entertain me."

"I do rope tricks," Ready said. "End by hog-tying a member of the audience. Always brings down the house."

I seized Vi's hand and tried to drag her down the stairs, but she remained planted where she was. Another tug and she surrendered, flouncing after me into the parlor.

"You said you had to work tonight. You lied to me after I bought you a ticket to the movies."

Keeping her voice low, she addressed a mole on my clavicle. "My plans changed."

I noticed a familiar pattern of beads in Vi's hair. She was

wearing the comb Tommy had stolen from the counter at Tremayne's. Seeing that he'd made a gift of it to her enraged me. I struggled to compose my thoughts.

"What exactly are you two doing?"

"Tommy and I are going out."

"After what he did? He threatened me, Vi."

"He says different."

"And you believe him and not me. Knowing even Ruby finally had enough of him."

Vi still wouldn't meet my eye. The beads on the comb caught the light, mocking me.

"What's on tap for this big night on the town? Oysters Rockefeller and stories about Ruby 'til sunup? Seems like a strange kind of date to me."

"You're not my mother, Lillian. And at least I'm having a date." She seemed shocked by her own words, glancing at me briefly in horror.

I must have been lightly stunned myself, because without thinking I snatched the comb from her hair, taking a few blond strands with it. Vi gasped.

"Did Tommy give this to you?" I waved the comb in her face. "Because he stole it from the store. Right in front of me."

"Keep it. I only wore it to be nice. It looks cheap." Still startled by what she was saying, she returned to the foyer.

Tommy offered Vi his arm. Ready glanced at me, then blocked the door. "Hold on. I believe you've got something to say to Lillian."

This time, Tommy's smirk blossomed fully. "I do, but Lillian doesn't want to hear it." He shouldered Ready aside, then guided Vi through the door with all the compassion of a slaughterhouse lineman. Vi never ventured a look my way.

Kay threw an arm around my shoulder. "Vi sounded almost like Ruby there, didn't she? You okay, sweetheart?"

"Yes. No. Give me a minute."

I walked down the hall, stopping by the house telephone near the kitchen. Vi's duplicity cut deep. It hurt to learn the girl I thought of as an impressionable little sister had only pretended to heed my advice. I could hear Kay and Ready murmuring to each other. Then Ruby piped up in my head.

You know what you do when life gets you down, mermaid? Whatever you feel like doing.

Pitching a nickel into the jar Mrs. Lindros kept on the hall table, I dialed the now familiar number for Paramount Pictures. Hearing Edith soothed me instantly.

"I hoped I'd be receiving an update today, Lillian. How have you been?"

"Busy. Do you have several moments?" She did, so she got a full report, including my abortive expedition to Armand Troncosa's house and Natalie's unexpected phone call. When I finished, she had me repeat the conversation with Natalie word for word.

"If only I hadn't asked if she and Ruby were related. It scared her off."

"Might I suggest another possibility? This Esteban Riordan at Mr. Troncosa's home indicated that Natalie was traveling, did he not? And am I also right in saying while Natalie hung up after you asked if she and Ruby were family, it was also after the operator cut in requesting more money to continue the call?"

I said nothing, floored by what she was suggesting.

"You understand my point," Edith said. "If you'd heard how much the operator wanted, that would have been some indication of how far Natalie had traveled. It wouldn't have given you a precise location—"

"But I'd know where to start looking. I never thought of that."

"I'm accustomed to dealing with expenses. Natalie's call to tell you she wouldn't assist the police almost assisted the police. And it certainly sounds like Mr. Nolan may have taken that photograph of Ruby. I wish Mr. Groff hadn't so cavalierly dismissed him. A regrettable missed opportunity."

I was fed up with being stymied. By Gene's prudence, Groff's machinations, the universe's indifference. I wanted to stir the pot. "It doesn't have to be," I said.

Edith paused. "I couldn't possibly speak with Mr. Nolan today. These costumes for Joan Bennett have to be ready by morning."

"Tell her I loved her in *Vogues of 1938*. And I wasn't thinking you would talk to him."

"There's no way I'd send you to see him alone."

"It sounds like you were prepared to see him solo, and I'm taller than you. Besides, I'll bring a cowboy with me."

That Edith never inquired what I meant by that was one of the reasons why I loved living in Los Angeles. "I happen to have Mr. Nolan's address," she said.

Information in hand, I yelled to Kay that I couldn't stay for dinner and needed to borrow her fiancé.

15

THE COMPANIONABLE SILENCE of the drive was broken only by Ready humming snatches of Beethoven's "Ode to Joy." Ready was a fascinating man, down to his nickname. Henry Blaylock had ridden out of Oklahoma in 1931 with the idea of seeing the ocean and no intention of joining the throng at Gower Gulch hoping to work in pictures. But his way with a horse came to the attention of a B producer at Columbia and the young cowhand found himself on the set of *Sagebrush Serenade.* The lead stuntman on the picture was Elmer Redding, known as Reddy, famed for his prowess with both beast and bottle. He and his leather kidneys were sleeping one off when a novice assistant director waded into the stuntmen, pointed at Hank, and inquired, "You Reddy?"

Hank, thinking he was being asked about his preparedness to shoot, replied, "You bet."

Thus did Hank debut as a stuntman in a dangerous stampede scene. He performed flawlessly, commandeering Reddy's moniker and several of his jobs in short order. Or so the legend goes. Ready, when asked, would neither confirm nor deny the tale. It was the only sensible course of action.

KEN NOLAN'S HOUSE in a down-at-heel stretch west of Hollywood had been blue like the neighborhood had been prosperous, a lifetime ago. The white shutters hanging askew from the front windows gave the place a cockeyed look, as if it couldn't believe the state it was in either.

"Behold there was a very stately palace before him," Ready muttered, "the name of which was not Beautiful."

"You got that right, bub. Maybe you should wait in the car. You might make him nervous."

"I plan to. This feller is going to know I'm here." He knocked on the door.

It flew wide. Ken emerged into the glare to glare. "You again. Here to gloat?"

"Not exactly."

"Then what do you want? And who the hell is that?"

"My driver."

"And bodyguard." Ready pitched his voice even lower than his usual rumble.

"A bodyguard? That's a tad excessive, don't you think?"

Ready took in Ken's slight frame and argyle sweater vest. "Upon reflection, yes."

"Don't I know you?" Ken surveyed Ready with interest. "A party at George's?"

"Could very well be," Ready answered. With a hint of the vamp, about the last thing I needed.

"It's too bright out here." Ken sighed. "You may as well come in."

"I'll have a smoke, if you don't mind." Ready left it unsaid that he'd be within hollering distance.

THE HOUSE'S TIDY front room was set up as a photography studio. A tripod and lamp huddled in a corner next to a large wooden cabinet. Ken gestured to a scarlet rococo love seat in the middle of the bare wood floor. "If you want to sit, it's that or the kitchen. Why are you and that redwood here? Didn't you and your pal Edith have enough fun at my expense?"

"We didn't finish our conversation. You were about to give us your impressions of Ruby when the detectives arrived."

"Was I? Funny, all I remember about yesterday is getting the sack. Wasn't even asked a question before the ax fell. John Engstead won't take my telephone calls."

If I didn't circumvent his self-pity, we'd never get anywhere. "You said you didn't take any photographs of Ruby. Does that include one of her all dolled up, getting the full glamour treatment?"

"No photographs means no photographs."

Time for a calculated risk. "Then another photographer has this love seat's twin sister. With this identical woodwork." I laid my arm along the settee's back, caressing the filigreed detailing.

Ken paled. "How . . . ? There was only one print. Ruby swore she sent it to her mother."

"Her mother is proud of it. Shows it to everyone. Tells them her daughter was almost a movie star."

"Ruby looked like one that day."

Finally.

"She showed up in that beautiful suit. She looked stunning. Or she did once I fixed her makeup. I asked why she didn't pay for a real photo session if she could afford clothes like that. That's when she told me how she got them. She promised she wouldn't use the photo to land auditions. That could get us both in trouble." Ken chuckled. "Truth is I admired her pluck. She hadn't been at the studio a week."

"Did she also promise she'd bring the suit back?"

"First thing in the morning. Which meant she had it overnight. She said it was a shame to leave such a lovely outfit hanging in the dark, so she was going to give it an evening on the town. She had enough money for one drink. I donated cash for a second." He pointed toward the front door. "I watched her sashay to the Red Car stop. It was chilly that night. She was freezing, but you'd never have known it."

"Then what?"

"She wound up in clover. She went to a hotel bar and fell in with a bunch of swells, drank all night on their dime. Never spent her own money. Never gave mine back, either."

"Sounds like fun."

"Doesn't it just. She returned the suit and liberated a gown for her next night out. This crowd had invited her to a party, and that led to another. And another."

"Until she was fired. And asked you to steal clothes for her."

No denial, only a trace of petulance. "Not steal. Borrow. It was only supposed to be borrowing. I said no initially, told Ruby she was crazy. She said she'd find some other way."

"Some other way" being me and Tremayne's extreme employee discount. I was Ruby's plan B. For some reason, the news hurt.

"What changed your mind?" I asked.

"Her relentlessness. She wore me down. It was easy for me to take items from storage and return them a day later."

"Then how did Ruby end up with a suitcase full of Paramount wardrobe?"

"She stopped bringing the clothes back. Just stopped. Told me to live with it. That was Ruby. She didn't hesitate to change the rules in the middle of the game."

"That sounds like her, all right."

"You knew Ruby. That's why you're here." When I nodded, Ken waved toward the kitchen. "Do you want a drink? I want a drink."

I accepted his offer. Ken handed me a glass with two fingers of what tasted like bourbon. His glass contained an entire hand's worth, and he carried the bottle with him.

"If Ruby stopped returning the clothes, why'd you keep helping her?"

His drink was half gone already. "Because I enjoyed living vicariously through her too much. Because I didn't have the brass to do what she did."

"And look what it cost her."

"Don't start the violins. If Ruby knew the price, she'd have paid it. She'd rather live high for a few weeks than low for a lifetime."

He had that right. I sipped my drink, the liquor burning a bright, clear trail down my throat.

"She'd come by every few days." Ken canted his head as if expecting the swirling dust motes to resolve into Ruby's form. "I'd give her the clothes. She'd tell me stories."

"Care to repeat a few of them? Who was she seeing?"

"I didn't press for names and addresses. Ruby wouldn't have given them, anyway. She mostly told me things like the proper technique for removing a gentleman's hand from her thigh politely so the champagne would keep flowing."

"No names at all? No Natalie Szabo?"

"Oh, you mean women's names. Come to think of it, there was a Natalie. Ruby said this Natalie could be her ticket out."

"Did she say how?"

"Something about lining her up for a studio contract."

"What did she tell these people about herself?"

"As little as possible. She let the clothes do the talking. Look the part and no one asks questions. You know how these people are." He glanced at me. "On second thought, maybe you don't."

"Just when I was beginning to like you," I said. Ken apologized by pouring me another inch of whiskey. It was, upon consideration, pretty good bourbon. "Stories were reason enough to risk your job?"

"I'm the frivolous type, can't you tell?" He smiled and contemplated his empty glass. "They were for a while. Then about three weeks ago I got caught in Wardrobe after hours and had to lie my way out of it. I told Ruby I was done. I wasn't going to 'borrow' anything else. She raised hell, but I found some backbone. Shortly after that, her friend came to see me."

"What friend?"

"The dreadful man who knew everything. Knew I was taking clothes. Knew Ruby wasn't returning them. I was surprised he didn't want some himself, considering the tat he was wearing."

My fingers tensed against my glass. "Who was he?"

"He didn't divulge a name. Said unless I kept providing Ruby with wardrobe, something untoward would happen to me. Making threats with a sleepy half smile, like he found the whole thing endlessly amusing. I wanted to—"

"Slap his big blond face?" *Beckett.*

"Sounds like you know him, too," Ken said. "You know Ruby, you know her confidante, you know George's friend on yonder doorstep. You keep interesting company."

A fervent hope sprouted in my breast, that Winton Beckett was still at the police station with Gene. "You did as Ruby's friend asked, then."

"It was made clear I didn't have much choice."

"You wouldn't happen to have a copy of that picture of Ruby, would you?"

"Why would I? A photo of Ruby wearing clothes stolen from Paramount would be a confession. I tossed the negative and never took another photo of her. Kind of wish I had, though. I could get a bundle from the papers. Thanks to your chum Miss Head, I need the money. Are we done? Because I'll finish off this bottle." He poured another round. Before long he wouldn't be bothering with the glass.

"What's your beef with Edith anyway?" I asked.

"She's trying to get Travis Banton ousted so she can poach his job. Owes the man her livelihood and she undermines him every chance she gets."

"I find that hard to believe."

"Everyone at the studio says it's true."

"From what I hear, she's keeping the department running while he's painting the town."

"Not like it matters to me. My Paramount days are done. And Edith's will be soon enough, thanks to Ruby's hijinks. Everybody's going to get theirs." Ken deposited himself rather gracelessly on the floor. "Damn Ruby. She was something, wasn't she?"

THE ALCOHOL HADN'T hit me as hard as I'd feared; I only needed to hold on to the wall with two hands. Ready led me to his car, reassuring me the vehicle was not yet in motion. I sat quietly until something made me feel nauseous. And it didn't come out of a bottle.

Winton Beckett in his trademark attire covered Ken's walk in two strides and pounded on the door as only an ex-cop can. He then pushed his way inside.

"You saw that, right?" I asked Ready.

"Feller wearing a jacket the color of an oil slick on a puddle?"

"We need to go back."

"Hold on. That shutterbug was one thing. Slim there is a whole other kettle of fish."

"Could you not mention fish right now?" We heard glass shattering. As if a liquor bottle had been heaved across a room in a cold fury.

Ready and I were halfway up the walk when Beckett lurched out the door, head snapping to and fro. Ken had obviously told him I'd just left. He saw me and flashed a grin to make mothers lock up their daughters. "Hello, kitten! You bring those delicates I asked for this morning?"

"Delivery's extra. I'm surprised to see you out on the street so soon."

"Like I told Gene, my mouthpiece is the finest under the sun."

Ken peered out of the doorway as Beckett eyeballed my escort. "You always travel with a watchdog? Maybe not a bad idea."

Ready stepped forward, and Beckett raised his hands like a hausfrau spotting a mouse. "Relax, Buck. I'm just advising the lady there are some circles she shouldn't move in alone. And they're not always the shady ones. A tip from your uncle Win."

"I'd ask what you're doing here but I already know."

"Ken can't keep his mouth shut. Especially when he's had a few. He's like a woman that way." There was that smile again, all rancid insouciance. I was amazed there wasn't a permanent impression of a palm print on his face. Ken, meanwhile, had retreated almost entirely behind the front door.

"I'll be telling Detective Morrow about our conversation."

"I figured as much." He leaned closer to me. Ready moved with him. "Easy, big fella. Give my regards to Tom Mix. It occurs to me I never gave you the skinny on Gene's love life."

Ready's shadow gave me boundless confidence. "Get on with it, then."

"Okay, kitten. He's already squiring a woman all over town."

"That's his right."

"Only the woman is the widow of his ex-partner. Who died in the line of duty while Brother Gene emerged unscathed. Funny how that worked out. Word is Gene and the widow were seeing each other long before bullets were exchanged. Some friends on the force have questions about that."

My stomach began to hurt.

"Some of those same friends also tell me Natalie gave you a jingle this morning. Let me guess. You're not going to say a word to me about it."

Far be it from me to disappoint him.

"That's okay. I'll find her anyway." Beckett turned toward the door. "Now if you'll excuse me, Ken and I have our regular pinochle game. Don't we, Ken?"

Ken inched into the sunlight and nodded.

"I'm up for a hand or two," Ready said. "Why not deal me in?"

Ken spoke quietly. "I appreciate your concern. It's better if you left."

"You heard him. I'll see you again, sweetheart, when I come to pick up my order." With a victory smirk, Beckett slithered up the front steps and through the door. It swung shut, the grim little house swallowing him whole.

16

HOBNOBBING WITH A Hollywood costume designer made surveying my closet's meager wares even more of a chore. I was happy to abandon the task mid-sulk when Mrs. Quigley summoned me to the phone.

Naturally, my caller was said Hollywood costume designer. I tightened the belt on my robe, certain Edith's powers extended to divining how I was dressed based solely on my voice. "Have I got a story for you," I said.

"It's entirely possible I've not only heard it but can add to it. Is there any chance you could come to the studio today?"

"As it happens, I'm at liberty. I don't suppose—"

"No car today, I'm afraid. Can you still make it over?"

"Wild horses couldn't keep me away. Although I could use one to get across town."

ANOTHER FORAY INTO darkest closet unearthed a cute blue knit skirt and sweater set. I sallied forth.

The security guard at the Paramount gate directed me to the commissary, where Edith had left word she'd be. She sat by a window in a slim gray dress, a maroon scarf providing a bloom of color at her throat. She leaned over a coffee cup toward a balding man who hung on her every word. What he lacked in hair he made up in joie de vivre, his casual attire hanging on his trim frame with unforced elegance. He stood when I reached the table.

"Bill, this is the girl I was telling you about. Lillian, this is Wiard Ihnen." She pronounced his surname *EE-nan*, with a long "E" and a short smile. "Call him Bill. He's a good friend and a brilliant art director. We met doing *Cradle Song* years ago. You've seen *Duck Soup*, of course. Bill's handiwork."

I fumbled for a suitable compliment and opted for the truth. "*Duck Soup* is one of my favorite pictures ever."

"Not for the art direction, I'll wager." Bill chuckled modestly. "Edith has been regaling me with your exploits. You two make quite the team."

"I'm happy to follow Edith's lead."

"As are we all. You astutely learned in short order what's taken me years to comprehend. Edo knows best. Always." The affection on his face as he gazed at her was shaded with worry. "Although I do question this latest undertaking. It could do you harm."

"What difference can it make?" Edith clucked. "You've surely heard my days here are numbered."

"That's not true and you know it. Travis could still pull himself together. Even if he doesn't, you're a valuable member of the team. Why antagonize the powers that be and jeopardize your place at the table?"

"Firstly, assisting a police investigation is not antagonizing anyone. It's simply the right thing to do. Second, I would not presuppose I've earned a place at any table other than the one we're at right now. If anything, my actions should only demonstrate my ability to oversee every aspect of the Wardrobe Department. Need I remind you, a thief would still be in the studio's employ were it not for my efforts."

"With some help from Lillian, of course." There was deviltry in Bill's eyes as he nodded at me. He clearly relished winding Edith up.

"Of course. I'd also like to think I'm doing Mr. Groff a favor."

"How do you figure that, Edo?"

"We already know there's more to this matter than Ruby's thievery. In his haste to do his job, Mr. Groff may be doing the studio a disservice. He sees a small fire and opts to smother it with a blanket. A childhood in the desert taught me that if done incorrectly, that will only spread the flames."

"As I've said, you know best." Bill turned to me again. "Just be careful about involving our young friend here."

"Nobody involved me. I'm here because I chose to be." Although as I said the words I couldn't help wondering how true they were. Had Edith cleverly exploited me? And if so, did I really mind?

Bill rapped the tabletop. "Sadly, I should take my leave now."

"You don't want to hear what Lillian's been up to?"

"I'd love to, but I have appointments. I expect a blow-by-blow later." To me he explained, "Edith's got a way with a story. I suspect she's working in the wrong department." They embraced, Bill bussing her cheek. He strolled off as if heading for a tennis court, a spring in his step.

Before I could order some java, Edith checked the time. "We'd better adjourn to my office."

She set a brisk pace, the extra height I had on her of little help. "I know all about your confab with Mr. Nolan last night," she said.

"Did my press agent call you?"

"Detective Morrow told me. After I alerted him that Kenneth might be, as they say, on the lam."

I stopped. Edith didn't, so I sprinted after her.

"Scuttlebutt out of John Engstead's office this morning," she announced once I'd caught up. "Kenneth turned up on the doorstep of several friends last night, grip packed and hand out. That sounded like a man making a run for it, so I contacted

Detective Morrow. He was somewhat aggrieved. He planned on visiting Kenneth after hearing about your encounter with him."

The previous evening's conversation with Gene had been brief and to the point, Gene having decided that lecturing me was a task that would make Sisyphus throw up his hands.

"Detective Morrow also seemed displeased you had put yourself in harm's way," Edith added.

"He didn't mention that to me."

"He hardly needs to when his regard for you is so evident."

His regard for me? I fell behind Edith again and scrambled to catch up.

The usual buzz of activity greeted us at the Wardrobe building. Edith paused at a workroom full of seamstresses and addressed one in fluent Spanish. We then continued to Travis Banton's suite. I recalled Ken's insistence that Edith was scheming to depose Banton, and speculated whether her reference to his domain as "my office" was a slip of the tongue.

She'd certainly made herself at home, a stack of sketches waiting, bright fabric swatches attached to each. "I'll never understand how you can work with these colors when the film will be in black and white."

"That's why I carry this." Edith held a square of dark glass against the clear lens of her eyeglasses. "To see how the costume will read on camera. Bit of a nuisance, though."

"You should have spectacles made of those."

"What a clever idea. I'll be doing my first color picture shortly. Flying aces in the Great War, so no ball gowns. We shall see how expressive a color brown can be." She sat behind Banton's desk, which somehow didn't dwarf her. "I commend you on getting Mr. Nolan to admit he'd taken the clothes. We were so close the other day. I knew it required a woman's touch."

"The bourbon didn't hurt, either."

"Tell me about this private detective. Could he have scared Mr. Nolan off?"

I pictured the photographer's reaction to Beckett the shady shamus. "I think Kenneth is in Ensenada this lovely morning, en route to points farther south."

Banton's elegant receptionist tapped on the door. "Excuse me, Miss Head? Your next appointment is on the way up."

"I should probably head home," I said.

"Could you stay longer? There's another matter I wanted to discuss."

We moved into Banton's salon. Edith surveyed the room. As she nodded in satisfaction, there was a knock on the door. "Is everyone decent?"

"I'm afraid so," Edith replied.

To my astonishment Bob Hope came bounding in, the Broadway and radio star preceded by his proboscis. "I really need to work on my timing. How are ya, Edie?"

"Splendid, Bob. And you?"

"I've been better. Played eighteen holes with Crosby at Lakeside and he thrashed me pretty good. He won't let up about it."

"That doesn't sound like Bing."

"Oh, he's not saying a word. That's how he needles you, by never bringing it up. Who do we have here?"

Edith told him my name and Hope darted toward me, eyes glittering on either side of his prominent nose, brows summiting his forehead as he assessed my assets. He took my hand in both of his, stroking it as if it were a nervous cat. "Lillian. A pleasure."

"Likewise, Mr. Hope."

"Call me Bob, please. And promise me you're going to help with the fitting. I'll warn you right now I'm ticklish." He came out with a girlish shudder that had me laughing.

"Actually, I'm just—"

"She's just crazy about the picture, Bob," Edith interjected. "I was telling Lillian all about it."

Hope continued caressing my cuticles. "Pretty excited about it myself. Can you believe Dorothy Lamour plays my girlfriend?"

"It *is* a comedy," Edith said.

"I'll do the jokes, if you don't mind. You handle the wardrobe."

I extracted my hand from Hope's. He was in no hurry to let it go. "Will you be designing Dorothy's costumes, too?"

"Yes. I've worked with her several times."

"So you did the sarong from *The Jungle Princess*?"

Edith fixed me with a steely gaze. "You're not going to critique its authenticity, are you? I don't need another person to point out an actual sarong would bare the breasts. I am well aware of that fact. But we're making motion pictures here."

"I asked her to put accuracy first," Hope said. "Begged her, in fact." He found a bonnet in the corner and tried it on. He pressed his hands together under his chin and tilted his head like a silent movie sweetheart. I couldn't help laughing again.

"I doubt that hat will go with your tuxedo," Edith said. "Speaking of which, we made a few minor adjustments to it. Let's make sure it still fits."

"Don't see why it wouldn't. I've been eating nothing but pineapple buttercream layer cakes since the last time I tried it on." He doffed his suit jacket, placed it on a hanger with a flourish, then reached for the belt on his trousers.

"Behind the screen if you please, Bob," Edith said.

"You're taking all the fun out of this." Hope winked at me then did as asked, humming under his breath. "New song for the picture. Don't know if I'm ever going to get it down."

Edith cleared her throat and spoke in a loud voice that rang out like a brass bell. "I've been giving some thought to that puzzle piece, Lillian."

I lowered my own voice when I replied. "Gene said the police haven't turned up anything on it yet."

She nodded, still playing to the rafters. "I keep wondering why Ruby would be carrying, of all things, a *jigsaw* puzzle piece. And in that particular suit."

"Me, too. It did seem a touch formal for a quiet night around the games table."

Bob Hope stepped from behind the screen looking dapper in a classic tuxedo, the ends of his bow tie trailing around his neck. "Did I hear you gals talking about jigsaw puzzles?"

"We came across a piece recently," Edith said, "but we have no idea where it could have come from."

Hope preened at his reflection in the mirror. "Dollars to doughnuts I can tell you what it is. Sort of a party invitation."

"What do you mean?" Edith asked.

"You ladies ever hear of Addison Rice?"

"Isn't he some kind of millionaire businessman?" I asked.

"Go ahead and stick a multi in front of that millionaire. He's flush. Throws huge parties, each with a nutty theme. For his last wingding he sent out puzzle pieces. You had to fit yours into the big picture before you could escape to the patio for a drink."

"You attended this party?" Edith asked.

"Sure. I let Dolores figure out where the piece went. She's good at those things. A few minutes later we were swilling champagne with the big names. And they had to swill it with me. Serves them right."

"When was this party, Bob?"

"Last Saturday."

Edith speared me with a look, our thoughts aligned. Ruby had been found dead the morning before that, an invitation in her possession. One on which she'd written a distant date in December.

"I must confess I'm not familiar with this Addison Rice," Edith said.

"I am." Not that I'd been reading the business pages. Addison Rice's parties regularly provided fodder for *Modern Movie*. "He made all his money in radio parts back east."

"Radio, huh? We've been working together for years and I didn't know it." Hope deftly knotted his tie and admired his efforts in the mirror. "His wife had to take the cure, spends her time at their place in Arizona. When he's not in the desert he's here entertaining the entertainers."

"Then these are show business parties?"

"You know us actors when it comes to a free meal. And drinks. But Addison's got an address book thicker than Jack Benny's wallet. He invites local movers and shakers, East Coast society friends looking to rub elbows, a few shadier folk. I wanna tell ya, ol' Addy likes to mix it up."

"I wonder if Ruby's friend Princess Natalie ever wound up on the guest list," I said.

"Princess Natalie? Now there's a charmer and no mistake."

Edith and I both whipped our heads around to stare Bob Hope down. "You *know* Princess Natalie?" Edith demanded.

Hope took a step back, raising his hands over his head like it was a stickup. I heard a seam rip, and Edith closed her eyes. "Let's not get too excited, ladies. I'm telling you right now you're going to have to sweat it out of me. If you're up for it. I met the princess at Addison's place, as a matter of fact. Said she was a big fan of my radio show. I had no idea it was on overseas. I should ask Woodbury Soap for more money."

Edith abruptly spun around to me. "Lillian, may I speak to you?"

"Was it something I said?" the comedian asked.

"Excuse us, Bob. We won't be a moment." Edith took my

arm, her fingers as gentle as grappling hooks, and led me out of the salon.

"Detective Morrow must be told about this Addison Rice," she said. "The issue is how seriously he'll take the information at this point. Which is why you should also talk to Mr. Rice."

"I should? I know ol' Addy likes to mix it up, but he won't find a stranger showing up on his doorstep inquiring about a dead girl very appealing. And why would he talk to me?"

"He won't be able to resist a lovely, inquisitive young woman curious about his fabled parties."

"Wait, are we still talking about me? I'll have you know I have a reputation as a terrible actress."

"You'll be marvelous."

"I've never been to a millionaire's estate before. Something tells me it's not on any streetcar line."

"You really should learn to drive if you're going to live in Los Angeles, Lillian. I could use a break from the studio. Let me finish with Bob and call Detective Morrow. Then I'll take you."

We returned to the dressing room, where I retrieved my bag. Bob Hope was lying on the chaise, flipping through *Collier's*. "This is the life, huh, Lillian? You're not leaving, are you?"

"I'm afraid so. Good luck on the picture, Mr. Hope. I'll be sure to see it."

"You don't even know what it's called. Neither do I. They're changing the title."

"It doesn't matter. I see them all."

"Hold on a minute." He jumped to his feet, placing his hand on my arm again. "We were just getting to know each other. I thought you were going to be my personal wardrobe girl. What's the rush?"

"I have a date with a millionaire," I said. "Multi."

17

I LEVELED THE accusation as we crossed the Paramount lot. "You used me as a prop."

"Whatever do you mean?" Edith chugged along at her usual clip. Calculating how to match her speed delayed my response.

"Not that I object. You wanted me here so you could mention the puzzle piece while Bob Hope was in the room."

"The notion it could be one of these offbeat invitations so popular right now had occurred to me. And I know Bob gets invited to everything."

"So you asked him without actually asking him."

"It would be inappropriate to inquire about his social life. And I didn't want him to suspect I had him try on that tuxedo for no reason."

"You didn't!"

"A woman must know how to wield what power she has. Remember that." We reached a crossroads. Edith spotted someone approaching from the right and uttered a faint, vaguely exasperated sigh.

"Edie!" a rich baritone boomed. "I was setting out to find you." The speaker was a tall man with a receding hairline and thinning pate. Vanity spurred him to compensate sartorially, his impeccably cut gray suit accented by a purple tie and red eyes.

Edith pressed her lips white and teased the corners upward. "I didn't realize you'd be stopping by."

"Neither did I. But the stream of life washes me up on your

doorstep yet again." He turned to me with a pleasant if foggy smile, not bothering to wait for an introduction. "Charles."

"Lillian." I shook his proffered hand and was wreathed in the scent of juniper. Charles, despite the hour, had been at the gin already.

"One of Edie's new sketch girls, Lillian?"

"Actually, we're about to run an errand and can't stop to talk. Just wait in my office." Edith strained to make the request sound less like an order.

"Say, is Travis around? Always happy to pop in and toast the events of the day."

"He is not, as you well know. Go say hello to Adele and I'll join you shortly."

Charles bowed formally and struck off toward the Wardrobe Department with the sad pride of an exiled prince returning to seek a hero's welcome. Edith didn't tarry to watch him go, and again I sprinted after her.

"Charlie's party starts early, judging by the aroma. Who is he, anyway?"

"Charles. My husband."

A white-hot knot formed in my stomach.

"Now. Regarding my behavior with Bob . . ."

How was I supposed to know Edith was married? Everyone at Paramount called her *Miss* Head. Okay, maybe Preston Sturges *had* dropped Charles's name. But Edith had never alluded to a spouse. She seemed completely self-sufficient, an island unto herself. I didn't see how my blunder could be solely my fault. Then I realized Edith was still talking.

"I admit I'm pushing rather hard on this front. But that's only because I fear Detective Morrow's efforts may be thwarted. And whatever Ruby did, my costumes played a role. In light of those circumstances, I don't view my actions as excessive." She glanced at me. "None of which obligates you to participate in what I'm proposing with Mr. Rice, which is rather . . . unorthodox."

If Edith wasn't going to comment on my unintentional bad-mouthing of her husband, I wasn't about to bring it up. I was all for keeping things professional. "Didn't your friend Bill say we made a good team? I *want* to help. Not just you, but Ruby. I keep thinking about what Natalie said, that Ruby called me her one true friend."

"'We women are creatures of the heart, aren't we?' Yes, I've been contemplating Natalie's words myself. Here we are."

Edith owned an eminently sensible gray sedan, which she drove like a bright red racing car. Two turns off the Paramount lot and I was hanging on for dear life. She pulled off Sunset onto a street spiraling into the hills. It was another glorious day, the sun beaming on automatic, the air so fragrant with oranges and promise it was practically moist. The trees overhanging the road were garlanded with tiny red blossoms. I felt like we were the only float in an impromptu parade, and I was too keyed up to enjoy it.

"Stop whimpering every time I make a turn, Lillian, and let's discuss your overture to Mr. Rice."

We'd formulated a plan by the time we reached a wrought-iron gate flanked by white stone pillars. An intercom was set into one. Edith told the box that Mr. Rice was expecting Miss Frost, and the gate swung open at once.

"Unbelievable," I said. "Why do I think you could finagle an audience with Pope Pius himself?"

A sweeping lawn eventually gave way to a mock Venetian palazzo. Possibly openly mocking; the eye-popping edifice of whitewashed stone had a demure flamboyance. Edith pursed her lips and refrained from judgment. She maneuvered the car around a fountain and stopped before a front door so large I expected it to lower like a drawbridge. "I'd wait for you but I have a wardrobe check on the extras in Dorothy Lamour's latest. We can't have any island natives wearing wristwatches. Will you be able to get home?"

"Either Detective Morrow will give me a ride or I'll move in. I'm sure they've got a spare wing."

THE HOUSE MAY have been faux-Italian but the butler was authentically English, as welcoming as the moors of his native scepter'd isle. Arched windows filled a foyer big enough for the Army–Navy game with a buttery glow.

With Jeeves's discreet departure a smartly dressed and hugely pregnant brunette appeared. She smiled so I'd know she'd already forgiven the monumental inconvenience I would undoubtedly prove to be. "Miss Frost? From *Modern Movie*?"

I'd heard enough of Kay's stories to feel I could plausibly pass myself off as a stringer for the magazine. I tested out a bored nod.

The brunette accepted it. "Gladys Somers, Addison Rice's social secretary. Mr. Rice will join us momentarily. Do you have any questions I can answer in the meantime?"

Brandishing a stenographer's notebook liberated from Paramount, I rummaged for a pen, crayon, or sharpened feather. A regular Nellie Bly I was. I unearthed a pencil with no eraser but plenty of teeth marks. "Some basic background on Mr. Rice should suffice."

"Addison Rice holds the patents on a number of advances in telephone and radio equipment over the past twenty years. He retired to California from Massachusetts to be closer to Arizona, where his wife Maude spends much of her time for her health."

"Mr. Rice has become quite the host. We've featured his

parties many times." My voice had become strangely patrician. So help me, I was acting again.

Mrs. Somers was good. You could scarcely see her fuming. "Mr. Rice does much more than that. He also makes his home available for various concerts and charity events."

As she recited chapter and verse on several dozen such soirees, my attention drifted to the garden where a man came toward us. He was either stout or portly, wealthy enough that a vocabulary had been devised to conceal his girth. Not that his blazingly white suit did the same. The orange tie he wore with it gave him the appearance of a roaming butterscotch sundae, his florid face the cherry on top. A trim mustache dozed under his nose.

"I do hope I haven't kept you waiting. Addison Rice." Against my better judgment I found myself admiring his seersucker suit. He should have looked foolish in it. He *did* look foolish in it. But he also seemed completely at ease. "Marvelous, the colors one can wear in California. I'd be laughed off Boylston Street in these clothes. Shall we move our conversation to the patio? No sense wasting a lovely day. We could have iced tea sent out."

"I don't want to take up too much of your time, Mr. Rice."

"Addison. Mr. Rice worked for a living, Addison is a man of leisure. You're all I have on my docket for the afternoon." He labored to keep his pronounced Boston accent in check. "I'm tickled a movie magazine would want to talk to a staid old businessman like me."

"Our readers want to know what America's premier fan of the movies thinks of pictures and Hollywood in general."

Addison fairly levitated at my words, and the butterflies that had been circling in my stomach all made flawless three-point landings. "'America's premier fan of the movies.' Oh, we'll most definitely be sitting outside."

• • •

THE WICKER CHAIRS were cushioned, the table shaded by a green canvas umbrella, the freshly brewed iced tea seasoned with mint and lemon. The phony correspondent was deliriously happy.

"Addison, what's the secret to hosting a great party?"

"Well, I'm sure I don't know." My host's modesty was unconvincing, and more becoming because of it. "I do have one rule, and that's mix it up. You can't only invite movie people. Too much shoptalk, too many jealousies you don't know about. You want to strike a balance. A few guests from the society pages, folks who have made a splash in other parts of the newspaper, even the odd rough-and-tumble type. That's a recipe for an evening. Variety is a necessity when you throw these little get-togethers two or three times a month."

Two or three times a month. An impressed coo seemed the only appropriate reaction, so I tried one on for size. "Our readers are familiar with the stars. Let's talk about some of the others in your mix, like Princess Natalie Szabo."

"Her life story's a picture in itself. A member of the Hungarian royal family now estranged from her fatherland. Or is it motherland? Cut off from her fortune, at any rate."

"We've heard tell she's considering a movie career."

"I could see her playing Garbo types, like in *Anna Karenina*. She has that dark and mysterious way about her. Very . . . European."

"Speaking of dark and mysterious, is it true the object of her passion is Armand Troncosa?"

"Aren't you well informed? I had the pleasure of meeting the princess through Armand. Has quite the yen for her."

"Does he?"

"Armand's a bit of a ladies' man. Something of a roué, I suppose you'd say. Different young lady on his arm every night. But once he met Natalie, he was transformed. He's escorted her here several times. You can tell he's beyond infatuated with her. Smitten. Besotted. All rather sweet, I thought."

"You mentioned rough-and-tumble types. That brings me to something I wanted to ask you about."

"Heavens. Sounds serious."

"I'd like to confirm you knew Ruby Carroll. The poor girl who was recently murdered. The one the newspapers call the Alley Angel."

Addison lowered his glass of iced tea. He stared intently at me for a long moment then shifted closer, scraping his chair on the terrazzo.

"My apologies, Lillian. I was debating whether to have something stronger brought to the table to toast your initiative. I've been waiting for someone to ask me about Ruby. Such a shame, what happened to her. Who thought *Modern Movie* would come to me before the police did? I applaud you."

The praise, as always, was a joy to receive. But it could blow up in my face should Gene arrive. "I'm sure they'll be here before you know it. It's only been a few days. Was Ruby a regular guest?"

"No. She attended a few parties some time ago. On the arm of a friend of a friend."

Then how did she have an invitation? "Does this friend of a friend have a name?"

"I'd rather not say. You understand."

"Of course." I added a few new teeth marks to the pencil's collection. "Was it Tommy Carpa?"

"By thunder! I'll be raising a toast to you yet." Addison traced a pattern into the condensation on his glass. "Carpa's a restaurateur and nightclub owner, they told me, sort of a Billy Wilkerson in the making. So I invited him. He brought lovely ladies along, and they're always a welcome addition."

"And one of those lovely ladies was Ruby Carroll."

"Yes. I chatted with her several times. Seemed an intelligent girl, and I told her so. Too smart to be involved with the likes of Mr. Carpa." He pronounced Tommy's surname as if he were trying to hold it away from his body.

"When did you last see Ruby?"

"About six months ago, when I also saw the last of Mr. Carpa. I banished him and his cohort from my parties."

"Why, may I ask?"

"Now, Lillian, that I can't answer. I really can't."

I set down my pencil. "Mr. Rice. Addison. You have my word nothing you tell me will appear in the pages of *Modern Movie*."

"I trust you. I do. But I feel damned awkward about it, and it was so long ago I'm sure it has nothing to do with what happened to Ruby. Now can I clear up this business about Wallace Beery that was in your magazine?"

I was trying to figure out how to inquire about the puzzle piece invitation in Ruby's belongings when Mrs. Somers waddled out in no small degree of consternation. "A Detective Morrow is here to see you, sir."

Addison heaved himself to his feet and rubbed his hands together. "Send him out! Remarkable. Simply remarkable. Stay right here, Lillian."

I assured Addison I wasn't about to go anywhere.

GENE MIRACULOUSLY MAINTAINED his sangfroid when Addison introduced me as "the noted correspondent for *Modern Movie* who scooped the LAPD." He even smiled as he shook my hand, grinding his teeth and a few of my bones in the process. "We don't subscribe to Miss Frost's publication at headquarters. If you wouldn't mind bringing us latecomers up to speed?"

"I almost feel Lillian should do the honors considering how she bested you." Addison laughed, and with my eyes I begged him to stop flattering me.

At the end of Addison's recitation, Gene asked, "Why'd you ban Carpa from your house, Mr. Rice?"

"I suppose I have to tell you, don't I? Lillian, you gave me your word, remember. This is off the record." Addison's body slumped as if he were starting to melt. "He had been, ah, engaging in illicit activities on the premises."

"Illicit activities such as?"

"Mr. Carpa supplied narcotics to several of my guests. It's also my understanding his lady friends . . . offered paid companionship. I never confirmed that. In any case, I'm certain Ruby wasn't involved."

How I longed to believe that.

"You didn't report these activities to the police?" Gene asked.

"I didn't want one man to spoil my parties. I felt the prudent course of action was to bar him from my home."

"Carpa couldn't have taken that well."

"No, but there wasn't much he could do about it. Before I spoke to him I made sure I had some, as they say in the pictures, backup." A grin surfaced on his face, at once embarrassed and mischievous. "I hire off-duty police officers to serve as security for my get-togethers. So everyone can feel comfortable, you understand. I had them on hand when I instructed Tommy to leave."

"And Ruby got the heave-ho at the same time?" I asked.

"Yes, all of Mr. Carpa's guests did. I took Ruby aside that evening and told her she could do better than a common hoodlum destined for jail. Even offered to help find her a job. I never heard from her again."

Gene placed the puzzle piece on the table. "This was among Miss Carroll's possessions. We have reason to believe it's an invitation to your most recent party."

"It most certainly is. Ruby had this? I can't fathom how. I had no way of contacting her, so I couldn't have invited her even if I'd wanted to."

"There's a date written on the back. December eleventh. Any significance to that?"

"No. I don't have a party planned then. Not yet, anyway." Addison signaled Mrs. Somers. "Gladys, I think we may have filled in the upper left quadrant."

"I believe you may be right. Shall we check?"

We decamped for what I assumed to be the game room, a deduction based solely on the pool table, chessboards, and pinball machines. An enormous jigsaw puzzle, incomplete and supported by several easels, depicted the very house we stood in. It looked equally gaudy in two dimensions. Mrs. Somers slotted the piece from Ruby's suitcase into position easily. She then consulted a nearby file. Her subsequent bulletin did not come as a surprise. "That invitation was sent to Princess Natalie Szabo."

"If Ruby had Natalie's invitation, that means Natalie didn't come to the party," Gene said.

"Yes. I was disappointed. It was the first time she would have attended on her own and not as Armand Troncosa's guest. He was traveling."

"Still is. We haven't been able to locate him." Gene pointedly turned to me. "And we've been trying."

"Forgive me for interrupting," Mrs. Somers murmured efficiently, "but a letter from the princess arrived in this morning's post. I have it here." She held an envelope aloft, which Addison waved into Gene's hands. I didn't intend to peer over his shoulder as he read. It simply happened. The stationery was from the Merriman Hotel in San Francisco. The letters sloped uphill as if marching double-time across the page.

November 6

Dearest Addy,

A quick note to beg your forgiveness for my absence from this evening's gaiety. An urgent matter called me north at the last minute. Crushed, crushed to miss all the fun. Don't hold my inexcusable lapse in manners against me when drafting your next guest list.

With all my affection,

Natalie

"Postmarked in San Francisco on Monday," Gene said with a glance at the Merriman Hotel's envelope.

"And I'd so looked forward to squiring Natalie around," Addison said. "Such a warm presence. Always talking about her charity work back in the old country. Orphanages, soup kitchens . . . or would that be goulash kitchens?" He paused, enjoying his joke. "Told me about her family in America. Has a cousin, down on her luck, who lives out here now. Trying to break into pictures."

The butterflies were back in my stomach, larger now. "Did the princess mention this cousin by name?"

"Yes, I believe she did. Rose? No. It was Roza."

I became light-headed so quickly I feared I would topple forward and undo everyone's efforts on the jigsaw puzzle.

"Roza Karolyi?" Gene kept his voice neutral.

"Yes! My apologies, Detective Morrow. Clearly you've been working on this matter diligently. Have you met Miss Karolyi?"

"No. But her name's come up." Gene reached out to steady me, the look in his eyes pulling me into an instant conspiracy. *Say nothing.*

"If you find her, do tell me. I'd love to help her out. For the life of me I can't figure out how Ruby acquired Natalie's invitation. They hardly moved in the same circles. Now, Miss Frost, can we get back to Wallace Beery and how he left a crack in my floor?"

He took me by the arm before I could reply and led me deeper into the house. Gene, trailing us, addressed Mrs. Somers. "Where did you send Princess Natalie's invitation?"

The woman with all the answers checked her records. "In care of the Hotel Normandie Park."

Gene did what a humble fake reporter couldn't get away with and requested a copy of the party's guest list. Addison dispatched Mrs. Somers to retrieve one.

We entered a dining room featuring a table for twenty. Addison stopped behind a chair and pointed to the floor. There it was, a hairline crack in the marble. "Behold, Mr. Beery's last stand. Your magazine said he did that falling off a chair."

"That wasn't the case?"

"Oh, no. He was on the table at the time." While we waited for Mrs. Somers to return, Addison and I went back and forth on the subject of movies. He made a strong case that Greta Garbo was a better actress than Marlene Dietrich while Gene sat stonily. I was mounting a halfhearted defense of *The Garden of Allah* when the secretary reappeared with the guest list.

"We'll finish this discussion another day," Addison said. "I can't remember the last time I spoke to someone who's seen as many pictures as I have."

"And her with a full-time job and everything," Gene said.

"A job many girls would envy, I'm sure."

"Huh?" I'd been having so much fun talking about pictures I'd forgotten my imaginary journalism career. "Oh, they do. All my friends want to be me."

Addison shook both our hands fervently. "What a day this has been. A reporter and a detective grilling me in my own home. This is giving me such ideas for my next party. A third-degree bash! I can see it now."

18

AS THE SPRAWLING estate of Addison Rice receded, I envisioned the kind of place I'd want for myself. I could only picture one of those sleek Manhattan apartments with a baby grand piano, a wet bar, and a view of the city's twinkling lights. Even with warm air against my skin and the scent of eucalyptus so strong it burst on my tongue, I maintained a New Yorker's idea of home.

I changed the baby grand to an upright French provincial, creating more space for entertaining. I had the luxury of rearranging my fantasy abode's furniture because Gene, in the driver's seat next to me, wasn't saying a word. He was busy exercising his jaw muscles, ratcheting the lower half of his face tight. I feared for his molars and my well-being.

I had just added a fainting couch when Gene finally acknowledged me. "So you're a reporter now."

"Technically a stringer affiliated with *Modern Movie*."

"Edith informed me it was all her idea. I'd like to see your notes."

I held up my steno pad. Gene glanced at the hieroglyphics inscribed thereon. "Can you decipher that?"

"Unfortunately, no. The conversation wasn't dull, but my pencil was."

"You realize I'll have to tell Rice who you really are when I interview him again. And who Roza Karolyi was."

"You mean Princess Roza of Hungary? With its fabled

goulash kitchens in both Buda and Pest, on the banks of the mighty Danube?"

"What picture did you learn that from? Ten to one Boris Karloff was in it."

"It was in Sister Luke's geography class. And you're thinking of Bela Lugosi."

"I'll take cues from anyone who can find Natalie."

"She doesn't want to be found. She wants to fade away."

"Yeah. About that. Consider the timetable. Ruby is killed and Natalie blows town. But she writes a letter from San Francisco on Saturday to stay on Rice's good side and guest list. That implies she plans on returning to Los Angeles. Come Monday morning, though, she's telephoning you with this 'fade away' jazz."

"You think she left town for a few days and decided to make it permanent?"

"I think Natalie's in trouble and may *be* trouble. We wired Ruby's family. The name Natalie Szabo means nothing to them."

"Maybe they have to keep their connection to the Szabos secret. For political reasons."

"Or maybe Ruby was pulling the wool over Natalie's eyes, taking advantage of her. They cross paths, they both speak Hungarian. A familiar tongue far from home? I don't need to tell you how comforting that can be."

"Sure. Whenever I hear George Raft it's like a warm blanket on a cold night."

"Ruby's ready to commiserate about life back home in . . . where was it again?"

"Buda and Pest."

"Could you see Ruby making hay out of that kind of connection?"

Could I. But I didn't want to. I wanted my version of events to be true, for Ruby and Natalie to be Roza and Natalya, related by blood and nobility. I wanted to be the one true friend to two players in a story of international intrigue and romance.

"As for Armand Troncosa," Gene said, "I spoke to that sidekick of his, Esteban Riordan. He says Troncosa went to Kentucky to see a man about a horse, an actual quadruped. He left Thursday—Ruby was killed that night—and is due back soon."

"Esteban's not a sidekick. He's a majordomo."

"Thanks for the clarification. I'd hate to rile up their union. Riordan also said he has no idea where Natalie is."

"May I ask a question?"

"Like the veteran newshound you are?"

"What about Tommy Carpa? You heard what Addison said. He's, he's a . . . procurer. And a peddler of drugs. And he dragged Ruby into what he was doing, and got her banned from Addison's house, and I knew all along he was rotten."

When I ran out of gas, Gene spoke calmly. "I did hear what Rice said. All it tells us is a fellow we knew was bad is actually worse."

"No," I insisted. "It means more than that. It has to."

"Rice banished him months ago. Why wait so long to act? Especially when Carpa's trying to go legitimate. Kept talking up some deal to open a new joint with straight investors when we brought him in the other day."

That's why, I thought. *To ensure his past stays in the past.*

"More interesting to me is Beckett," Gene went on. "He's been looking for Natalie from the start. Why? I'd ask him, but his girl says he left town to work another case, which seems awfully convenient." He threw a sidelong glance at me. "Did he say anything else to you?"

"Nothing but gossip and nonsense."

"Specifically what gossip and nonsense?"

My hand forced, I rehashed Beckett's yarn about Gene and his partner's widow in my best disinterested fashion.

When I finished, Gene grunted. "He's still foisting that chestnut on people?"

"If it helps, I didn't believe a word."

"You should have. Beckett got most of it right." Gene's windburned hands shifted on the steering wheel. "My partner Teddy Lomax and I were after a fella, robbed the California Republic Bank of twenty thousand dollars. We ran him down. He shot Teddy. I shot him. The money never turned up."

"And Teddy's wife?"

"Abigail grew up next door to me in Bunker Hill. I introduced her to Teddy. Her husband was dead. I was responsible."

"You weren't—"

"Don't tell me different, Lillian. Please. I know what's my fault and what isn't. So I look out for her. Stop by, visit. Take her to the pictures so she's not sitting in an empty house by herself. Probably saw one of those Sophie Lang movies with her for all I know. Let people talk. She enjoys the company. As do I. Company's all it is. She still loves Teddy. Always will."

I had nothing to say in response. I felt a shoddy, uncalled-for relief, with a chaser of guilt.

"And now," Gene said after a suitable interval, "I have a favor to ask."

"Anything."

"It won't entail your lying to me or anyone else. I hope that's not a problem." He handed me the guest list to Addison's party. "Tell me if any of these names are familiar. And I mean from your days with Ruby, not the pages of *Modern Movie*."

The clarification proved necessary. Plenty of names on Addison's register registered, including Mr. and Mrs. Bob Hope and Princess Natalie Szabo and guest. I drew in my breath as I spotted an entry for Mr. and Mrs. L. J. Minot. Diana and Laurence had undoubtedly filled in their piece of the puzzle. An act of God wouldn't stop them from making an appearance, Diana to see and be seen as stipulated in her Lodestar contract and Laurence to indulge his wandering eye.

"Here's one," I told Gene. "Another of Mrs. Lindros's former tenants. Diana Galway, formerly Diane O'Rourke. Listed here as Mrs. L. J. Minot, 'L' for Laurence. She lied to me about knowing Natalie and Armand."

"I'll talk to her. Keep going through the list. See if you can finish before we get to the Normandie Park."

"Is that where we're going?"

"It *is* on the way. Somebody there can tell us if and when Natalie checked out."

The rest of the roster held few surprises. "No more friends of Ruby I'm aware of, although every name on the list is familiar. Except one or two, like this one. Truck Hannah."

"Truck Hannah? Rice really does mix it up."

"Are you going to enlighten me?"

"He manages the Angels. The baseball team that plays out at Wrigley Field."

"C'mon. I'm no authority, but even *I* know Wrigley Field is in Chicago."

"There are two ballparks called Wrigley Field. Both named after the chewing gum magnate. You've got a lot to learn, young lady. About baseball and California." Gene proceeded to give me a brief education about the workings of the Pacific Coast League. I had never heard him say so many words at once.

THE BRASS SIGN that announced the Hotel Normandie Park gleamed beneath a fresh coat of polish. The rest of the building wasn't as vigorously maintained, looking shabby in the late afternoon light. The Normandie Park was a dowager among

Los Angeles hotels, flawless carriage still visible beneath a faded, outdated dress. It was exactly where a princess without portfolio would stay.

Gene's detective shield brought forth the hotel's manager, Mr. Leggett, a fussy beanpole with pomade troweling his hair into submission. "We're always happy to assist the police," he declared. "The Normandie Park is a world-class establishment. We housed a number of Olympic athletes during the 1932 Games. It was quite the honor. Gained us an international reputation."

"Didn't some lady shot-putters knock holes in your walls?" Gene asked.

Leggett wilted. "A few incidents blown out of proportion by the press."

Gene accompanied Leggett to the manager's office. I passed the time not playing hopscotch on the lobby's black and white marble tiles. Gene emerged ten minutes later and cocked his head toward the exit.

"The staff of the Hotel Normandie Park have never heard of Princess Natalya Szabo or just plain Natalie Szabo. They may not even be up on Hungary."

I stared at Gene, dumbfounded. "Leggett let me go through the file myself," he said. "No Natalie. I cast the net wider, looked for Troncosa, Carroll, Karolyi, any name that looked familiar or even vaguely Hungarian. Came up empty."

"If Natalie was never registered here, how did she get her invitation?"

"Simple. Somebody's lying." Apparently I pulled a face at Gene's comment. "Chin up, Lillian. When people start lying, it's a sign you're onto something. It's looking more likely Ruby and Natalie were up to no good together. Possibly trying to dupe Troncosa. He's the only person in this scenario with money. Which they're both in need of."

"I know." I sighed. "This doesn't look good, does it? Nuts. I was hoping for the fairy tale."

"Too late for that," Gene said. "Natalie's in hiding and Ruby's dead."

He started the car and steered back along the tree-lined drive toward Wilshire Boulevard. I felt a brood coming on. "I don't understand. We found out so much yet I feel like we don't know anything."

"Par for the course in my line."

"I think I'd find your job very frustrating."

"All the more reason for you to stop trying to do it. Can I ask something that's been bothering me for days?"

His somber tone scissored through my mood. "Of course."

"Would you really wear a getup like that one in Miss Head's office to the fights?"

"I'd take any excuse to wear an outfit like that. I've never actually been to a prizefight. Sometimes I'd catch a glimpse of one at Queensboro Arena from the Ditmars El train. Should I go? Do you like the fights?"

"Sure. Two guys bashing away at each other, the world reduced to the foot and a half in front of their faces, and one of them always loses. What's not to like?"

"Sounds like it parallels your job in some ways."

"Boxing parallels a lot of things. That's why people like it. You should come to a bout. Dressed however you'd like."

I had no idea if Gene had just asked me out. But it gave me something more pleasant to ponder on the ride home.

19

A FEW HOURS into my shift, I wasn't sure which part of me hurt most. My toes throbbed, jammed as they were into a pair of midnight-blue stacked heel Mary Janes as fetching as they were unforgiving. My cheeks ached from smiling at Los Angeles matrons as I girded their loins with vulcanized rubber. My back was stiff thanks to my holding it flagpole-straight around Mr. Valentine.

Yet my ears weren't burning. No word from Gene since he'd dropped me off the night before. Not that I'd been thinking about him and what I might wear to the fights.

At lunchtime I made short work of a bowl of noodle soup with occasional chicken and beat a path to a phone booth. Edith took my call, saying hello through clenched teeth as if barely holding her rage in check.

"Is everything all right?" I asked.

"One moment." After a pause, she sounded like her usual self. "Sorry, dear. I had pins in my mouth."

Edith's efficiency had rubbed off on me; I'd rehearsed my report while waiting on customers and kept her questions to a minimum. "Addison is another lead Gene only has because of you."

"I ran into Preston Sturges—the writer you met?—this morning. Preston cuts quite the broad social swath, so I asked about Princess Natalie. As it happens, she's dined at his café Snyder's. She was with several people including Armand Troncosa. She possesses a true regal presence, says Preston. He should know, considering he was practically raised in Europe."

"I wonder if Ruby was one of the people with her."

"Wearing a costume I designed, for a picture Preston wrote! What madness that would be. Hold on again, would you?" I could hear her issuing instructions. "No, the tulle ruffle is for the ball gown. Is she here now?" Edith returned. "Duty calls, as it must for you."

"Oh, it does. I just don't feel like answering."

"Come now, Lillian. Opportunity is effort's reward."

I emerged from the booth as Mr. Valentine bustled past in a lather. "An entire busload of women from San Bernardino has arrived," he said. "I need every salesgirl I can get."

Edith's counsel ringing in my ears, I pasted on a grin. My cheeks squeaked but held. "Point me toward them, sir."

I DEVOTED THE afternoon to the Inland Empire Beautification Campaign, Petticoats and Peignoirs Division. Dizzy with purpose, I wheeled to wait on my next customer.

"They certainly keep you busy around here," Gene said.

My brain sputtered once or twice before it finally turned over. "I'm dealing with the whole San Berdoo Junior League single-handed."

"And I was hoping for a minute of your time. Can you spare one?"

I scanned the sales floor's far horizon and spied Mr. Valentine doing his Flying Dutchman act by Purses. "Let's talk where it's quiet. There's a lull in Robes and Negligees."

Gene fidgeted with his hat. "Try to stick to Robes."

I positioned myself before a display of my favorites, darling rayon twill models featuring floral prints, and pretended to showcase various features to Gene. "What's the latest?"

"I spent the day talking to guests of Addison Rice who met Natalie. Several said they called on her at the Normandie Park. Only no two people identified the same room as Natalie's. She'd be in the penthouse one day, the Trieste suite the next. Whichever one happened to be vacant."

"You were right. Someone at the hotel is covering for her."

"Not many princesses require a desk man as an accomplice. She's looking more and more like a bad egg, given the timing of her disappearance. I've got Hansen trying to scare up a photograph of her." He idly opened one of the robes on the display rack to inspect the lining. "Natalie's shaping up to be the key to this entire business, and right now you're the last person who spoke to her."

I didn't need to be reminded of that fact. "Was Diana Galway one of the guests you interviewed?"

"The very first, out on the Lodestar lot. You were right. She claims not to know either Natalie or Armand Troncosa."

"Something her husband immediately contradicted."

"I remember. Which is why Laurence Minot was stop number two. Only he told me he'd never heard of them."

"That's a lie. First Diana lies to me, then Laurence lies to you. On the record."

"So it would seem. What do you think of this, Frost? Seems nice." He gestured at the robe.

"It is. Nice enough to be out of my price range. Why would Laurence change his story?"

Gene lifted a blue robe from the rack and held it up to me. "I have an idea. Minot was in San Francisco last Friday, the day after Ruby was killed. 'Visiting friends,' he says. 'Hearst's people. On the prowl for material for pictures.' He barely made it back for Rice's party. He stayed at the Merriman Hotel."

Where Natalie's letter to Addison came from.

Gene replaced the robe and considered a purple one. "I

called and confirmed Minot was a guest. Natalie's name wasn't on the register."

"It wouldn't be if she was staying with him. Is that what you think? Laurence and Natalie are having an affair?"

"As reasons to lie go, infidelity is always a good one. So you'd recommend this robe?"

"Absolutely, sir. It's one of our finest. Looks like hand-painted satin but is completely washable. Available in Dusty Rose, Arctic Blue, and Lazy Day Lavender." I dropped my voice to a whisper. "What happens now?"

Gene stared at me and whispered in kind. "Now, Frost? Now I buy the robe."

"You—you're actually going to buy it? I thought this was a dodge."

"It started as one. But you sold me."

If only I'd unleashed my powers of persuasion in the fur salon. Already I was imagining a lazy day suitable for lounging in lavender.

"And Abigail mentioned she could use a new robe," Gene said.

Wasn't that the height of folly, assuming I'd be the beneficiary of Gene's largesse. "Let me show you some others that might be more to her liking. Are you going to ask Laurence about his trip to San Francisco?"

"Not right away. Lodestar security sat in on our interview."

"Why?"

"Because Barney Groff wanted them there. The studios look out for each other. None of them wants a scandal with business booming again. A black eye for Lodestar is a black eye for Paramount and Hollywood in general. Meaning I can't press Laurence about that black eye he recently had." Gene chuckled without a trace of amusement. "Not yet, anyway."

"How about this one?" I presented another robe.

"Abigail's not really a fan of stripes. Or flannel. And isn't it kind of . . . masculine?"

"The trim cut makes it unique. And it buttons down the front so it won't fly open."

Gene shook his head. "What I need is independent verification Laurence knows Natalie. Beckett might provide it. Natalie definitely could. And the only individual they've both seen fit to contact, Frost, is you. That's mainly why I'm here. You hear from either of them again, send up a flare at once. Understood?"

So much for any romantic fantasy he'd come to the store to bask in my presence. I swallowed hard, hung the flannel job back up, and nodded. "Understood. Let me get you that robe. What color would you like?"

"Pink's fine."

"Dusty Rose it is. Oh, wait. You need to know the recipient's bust size." All wasn't lost. There was no way he could have been entrusted with that particular number.

"Thirty-six."

Damn.

GENE HAD SCARCELY departed with his haphazardly wrapped gift when Mr. Valentine materialized at my counter, crimson handkerchief in full flower. "About that last sale, Miss Frost."

"Yes, sir. I convinced the gentleman to spring for the imitation satin model."

"I fully expect it to be returned. The 'gentleman' was quite obviously the detective who's been here before. May I ask the purpose of your little charade? I was under the impression you'd recommitted to work."

I was scrambling for a rebuttal when the unlikeliest ally hove into view at Mr. Valentine's elbow. Edith Head cleared her throat to gain his attention, then faced me. "You're right, young lady, those are excellent pieces. Thank you for suggesting I look at them." Now a glance at Mr. Valentine. "Would you be the manager, sir?"

"Yes. May I be of some assistance?"

"I hope to assist you. Permit me to introduce myself." With a white-gloved hand she offered her card, which he accepted with reverent grace. "Paramount is arranging shopping expeditions for several actresses we have under contract. Marsha Hunt, Frances Farmer. We want to bring them to department stores and allow them their choice of what real women are wearing."

"A splendid notion. Tremayne's would be honored to participate."

"Wonderful. I'll inform my superiors. That handkerchief is a marvelous color, incidentally. Such a refreshingly bold choice. If I could finish speaking with your salesgirl?"

Mr. Valentine bowed and strode away like a figurehead on the prow of a ship, his pocket square a beacon in the night.

"Thank you," I gushed to Edith. "Were you serious about the shopping trips?"

"Absolutely. They're slated for Bullock's, but I'll see what I can do. On to more important matters. That card I gave you with the writing on the puzzle piece."

I emptied my handbag's contents onto the counter, finding the card in question. Edith inspected it. "December eleventh, seven thirty," she said. "Only that's not what it says, is it? Merely our interpretation of it."

"I don't understand."

"Twelve eleven was the actual notation. It occurred to me this afternoon when I was speaking with another of our writers, Billy Wilder. Brilliant man, so funny. From Vienna originally.

He has a script in production with Mr. Lubitsch. Travis has outdone himself with his costumes for Miss Colbert. At any rate, Billy wrote down a date. And as I looked at it—"

"Oh, Lord," I said, a memory coming back to me.

He'd come into Tremayne's several months ago, an older fellow in a Tyrolean hat with accent to match. Once I'd deciphered it, we got along like a house on fire as I helped him select some items for his frau back in Deutschland. Mr. Valentine and I watched as he pulled out his checkbook and wrote the date as twelve-slash-six. I gave Mr. V the high sign, branding Siegfried a swindler trying to postdate his check. But Mr. Valentine smoothly asked the Germanic gent to correct his date from the European to the American style. The customer happily tore up his check and started over.

"The date's written backward," I said.

"Not backward, dear. Differently. A definite possibility if the writing, like the invitation, is not Ruby's but *Natalie's*."

"So it's not December eleventh but November twelfth." I flipped calendar pages in my head. "Today."

"Which means the princess's appointment is in about ninety minutes. The question is where?"

"The Hotel Normandie Park would be my guess. That's where Natalie received visitors."

"An excellent thought. I tried calling Detective Morrow but haven't been able to reach him. Having overheard your boss, I know why. He was here. I don't suppose he said where he was off to next? That's unfortunate. I'd venture to the hotel myself but Travis . . . requires my assistance this evening."

From her careful phrasing, it was clear Edith was again covering for the genius of glamour. But she was right. This opportunity couldn't slip through our fingers. It was time for a daring move, and only I was dumb enough to make it.

"I'm off the clock in ten minutes. I'll go straight to the

Normandie Park. You tell Gene. And before you say it, I won't do anything foolish."

"I was going to ask if you had anything to wear over that." Edith pointed at my dress, the color that of an egg yolk from a particularly contented hen. "It's lovely but a touch . . . vivid for early evening."

I vowed to borrow a cardigan from one of the girls. Perhaps yellow wasn't ideal for meeting royalty. But I didn't have time to change. And with luck they had the saying in Hungary, too. *Any friend of Ruby's . . .*

20

THE LOBBY OF the Normandie Park had been primped for the evening. The floor tiles and the doorman were buffed to a high shine. Care had been taken to groom the nap of the grass-green carpet on which herds of couches and low-slung tables contentedly grazed. I lassoed a settee with a view of the reception desk, where a lissome blonde stood watch. *It's an acting exercise,* I told myself. *I am rich and on vacation, not poor and on a wild-goose chase. The chancellor shall hear of your impertinence.*

When an elderly man spoke to the clerk, the futility of my plan hit me. How would I know if anyone was asking for Natalie? I couldn't hear anything. The lady herself could glide past and I wouldn't recognize her unless she carried a scepter to dinner.

I'd stepped toward the blonde when the elevator disgorged a clown car's worth of activity. A pair of barking dogs dragged a surly man in a chauffeur's cap. Two screaming children followed, twin boys running like they'd bolted out of the gate at Aqueduct Racetrack. A nanny strained to impose order while the preoccupied parents angled toward the desk. I scanned the room for crowned heads while waiting my turn.

The revolving door gave out with a gust and blew in an elegant figure. Olive of skin and nimble of step, black hair gleaming, mustache perfectly manicured. His pearl-gray suit draped like it had been fitted on him an instant before. He carried a bouquet of red roses. His eyes settled briefly on every woman in the lobby. Each of us enjoyed exclusive access to his small, formal smile for a moment before he moved on to the next. I flushed slightly, as if he'd just twirled me around a dance floor.

As the family caravan barked and shushed their way into the night, the new arrival addressed the statuesque clerk. I inched closer.

"You are, I fear, mistaken." His speech bore a distinct Latin flavor and an agitated quality.

"I've looked, sir, but we don't have a guest by that name."

"Only last week I escorted her to her suite. No. I must insist you look again." He punctuated his polite but forceful request with a tap on the counter.

The flustered clerk danced to his tune. "I'm sorry, sir. No Natalie Szabo."

He had to be Armand Troncosa. I knew from the moment he'd entered the lobby. I felt a surge of pride, followed by a tidal wave of panic. *What now?*

"Most distressing. Bring forth your manager, my dear. At once." The would-be suitor laid the roses on the desk. The clerk reached for the phone. I seized my chance.

"Pardon me, sir."

With some subtle adjustments, he transformed his expression from dissatisfied customer to that of a man happy to chat with a woman. Any woman. "Yes, miss. How might I assist you?"

"Don't think me rude, but I couldn't help overhearing—"

"Lil?"

I hadn't imagined that chill wind at my back. It was the revolving door again, admitting Esteban Riordan. Troncosa's man Friday looked dapper despite the suspicion in his eyes.

"Hello, Esteban. It's actually Lillian. Lillian Frost."

Esteban positioned himself between me and his employer. I was viewed as a threat. "This is the woman I told you about."

"Never. This cannot be the scatterbrained visitor you described." Troncosa took my hand as if he held the deed to it and pressed his lips to my skin. I was dealing with an Olympic-caliber

Lothario. "Lillian, not Lil, I am Armand Troncosa. You already know Esteban. And Natalie, too, I believe."

"It's a pleasure to meet you. I regret I haven't met the princess."

"No? Yet you use her name to try gaining entry to my home." Troncosa glanced at Esteban, who nodded in confirmation.

"If I could explain?"

After a moment's consideration, Troncosa dispatched the hotel clerk with an arched eyebrow and proceeded to a settee. Esteban remained standing and vigilant. "Very well, Lillian," Troncosa said. "You may explain."

"Natalie and I have a mutual acquaintance. Ruby Carroll."

"This other woman both you and the police mentioned to Esteban. Sadly, the name is unfamiliar to me."

"Ruby Carroll was what she called herself professionally. Her right name was Roza Karolyi."

Comprehension illuminated Troncosa's face as Esteban's head snapped around. "Natalya's cousin!" Troncosa spoke to Esteban as much as me. "I have not yet had the pleasure."

"Natalie has spoken of her. The actress," Esteban said.

"Then you are friends with my Natalya's family." Troncosa started to smile, buoyed by this prospect. Then his face gave way to grief. "But Esteban tells me this Ruby has been in the newspapers. She is dead?"

I nodded. "She was murdered."

Troncosa clenched his fists and made a keening sound, like a coyote's mournful cry. Esteban knelt by his side. "*¡Que tragedia!*" Troncosa said. "Then Natalya has suffered a great loss. My sympathies to you as well, Lillian. You wish to convey this sad news to Natalya?"

"She knows. I spoke to her by telephone a few days ago."

"You did?" Troncosa said a few words in Spanish to Esteban, one of them being *policía*. "Please. I offer my total assistance. Avail yourself of me. What can I do?"

"You could tell me how you and Natalie met."

Troncosa couldn't help grinning, already warming to the tale. "A chance encounter in a hotel bar. The unplanned stop that changed the course of my life. Natalya was there, alone, her beauty drawing the eye. Also her sadness. She joined our party. Slowly she revealed the story of what brought her to America. It is unfortunately a story we've heard too often in these troubled times. Conspiracies of hoodlums taking over the old regimes in Europe. Brigands masquerading as statesmen. Her family under threat, she fled with a few items of sentimental value and vowed to help her country from afar."

"Did she speak much of her family in America?"

"Briefly. She did not wish to burden me with her troubles. I only know of Roza because I heard her recounting the poor girl's plight to a friend."

"Addison Rice?"

"Yes! Is that why you seem familiar, my dear? Do you know Addison?"

"I've enjoyed his hospitality once or twice." Okay, once. But I enjoyed it immensely.

"A splendid man, Addison. A captain of industry and true connoisseur of character. Natalya tried to flee his party when I first took her there, certain she would find it a bore. But she and Addison became fast friends. Unlike me, Addison is able to appreciate beauty from afar."

He took my hand and rested it on the burgundy brocade of the couch between us. "You do not know me, Miss Frost. I am aware some view me as nothing more than a wastrel. A . . . Latin lover, as the films made in your fine city say. For too long a time, that is exactly what I was."

His eyes took on a faraway cast as Esteban bowed his head in shared shame. I waited for my scoffing instinct to kick in and was astonished when it didn't. Troncosa seemed completely ridiculous and utterly sincere at the same time. Los Angeles, I was learning, was thick with such people.

"I do not exaggerate when I say meeting Natalya altered me to my core. Troncosa, who would have one rendezvous at lunch, another at dinner, a third before the sun rose. Who vowed never to become serious about any woman! I dedicated myself to Natalya. An old soul, a melancholy spirit, a refugee. I like to think each time we meet, Natalya feels stronger, more able to carry on. She not only showed me my life needed purpose, she provided it as well. When I am in the presence of Natalya, all other women disappear." He released my hand and looked me square in the eye. "This is why she must become my wife."

I required a moment to capture my breath. "You and Natalie are to be married?"

"It is my deepest wish, and the reason I am here with you now. We arranged to meet at seven thirty tonight. I hope to hear Natalya formally accept my marriage proposal. My second, I should say. The first occurred within days of our meeting and was an impulse, a surprise even to myself. Natalya knew this and gracefully held me at bay. But her discretion only strengthened my resolve. Before my trip I asked Natalya for her hand again. She already had much on her mind. She has been approached about a film career and is toying with the notion even though the business, for all the pleasure it gives, is filled with jackals and scoundrels. She told me she would visit friends in San Francisco, consider her future, and give me her answer upon my return. I rushed here at once to receive her reply." Hence the date on the puzzle piece. Troncosa glanced around the lobby for Natalie but there was only the clerk, her face turned away.

It was a sad story. Bringing red roses to a cold hotel lobby anticipating a princess only to wind up on a sofa with a girl who sold garters for a living.

"Natalie sent Addison a letter from San Francisco," I said.

"But no one has seen or heard from her since she called me a few nights ago. The police haven't been able to find her."

"Surely they do not harbor suspicions that Natalya might be involved in her cousin's fate." Troncosa's voice carried the sound of a glove slap across the face. His ferocity unnerved me into silence. All at once he was on his feet, stalking the slick tiles, unleashing great torrents of Spanish. Esteban responded in kind, his body language serving as translation. *Stay calm. Everything is fine.*

I finally regained my voice. "I'm not the police. All I know is they want to talk to her. I don't suppose you have a photograph of Natalie? That would be a great help."

"Of course. I could not possibly travel without a reminder of her." He removed a slender ostrich billfold from his jacket. "My Natalya," he said, handing me a three-by-five photograph.

It had been taken candidly in a nightclub, the subject caught off guard but willing to play along. The regal bearing I'd heard about registered on film, the eyes beneath the dark hair swept forward in a sophisticated style projecting both haughtiness and an impish amusement. She wore a silver lamé gown that captured the flashbulb's light and saucily threw it back.

I'd seen the gown before, in Ruby's suitcase. I'd seen the regal bearing before. I'd seen the princess before.

There are moments when time stands still and you notice the world more sharply, in minute detail. I looked up from the photo and the lobby seemed brighter, more solid than it had before. Troncosa's eyes shone with greater intensity and I discerned the individual hairs of his mustache quivering as his lips parted to pose a question.

"Is she not beautiful?"

Not only was she beautiful, she was Ruby.

I answered with all honesty. "She is."

21

WHEN GENE STRODE into the Normandie Park I extricated myself from conversation with Troncosa and Esteban, the photograph of Troncosa's beloved still in my hand. It took an inordinate amount of time to traverse the lobby thanks to the give in my knees and a sudden trepidation about the universe in general. Reality had been turned so inside out that I half expected gravity to be on banker's hours. Once safely across the floor, I pulled Gene behind a grove of potted palm trees.

"This better be good. Edith Head is sending me on more calls than Central Dispatch. Something about European numbers? I recognize Esteban Riordan, so I'm guessing that's Troncosa finally showing his face. Tell me you didn't spill what little we've learned."

"I've had more important things to keep from him." I presented the photograph to Gene.

"This is Ruby, isn't it?"

"It's also the photo of Princess Natalie that Troncosa has been carrying next to his heart."

Gene stared at me, then angled the photo toward the light as if it might yield new secrets. "Damn it. Goddamnit."

"I can't get my head around any of this. Who called me pretending to be Natalie? Who sent that letter to Addison?"

"Rice has some explaining to do: Guzzling iced tea, yapping about Ruby *and* Natalie. Lying the whole damn time."

"You think he was lying?"

A charitable word for Gene's look was incredulous. "Frost, he talked about them like they were separate people."

"I'm afraid he thinks they were."

"You honestly believe he was hoodwinked?"

"Yes. I do. Because what he's saying is so absurd. If Addison was going to lie, why admit he knew Ruby in the first place? He didn't have to volunteer that."

Gene frowned. "You're saying genius inventor duped by starstruck kid from Ohio? Sorry, I'm not buying it."

"You've got it backwards. *Addison* is the starstruck one. He's the perfect audience. That's how Ruby got away with it. That, a new hair color, and six months' distance."

"Then did Ruby set out to bamboozle Rice? Was he the turkey in this shoot?"

"No idea. I only know Addison's going to be mortified."

"One millionaire at a time. What did you tell Troncosa when you saw the photograph?"

"Nothing. I've been in shock. Troncosa's been talking about polo. Is the word 'chukkers' or 'chukkas'?"

"How should I know?" Gene peered through the trees like he was on safari. His game huddled close, Esteban's head low, Troncosa's eyes tracking every motion in the room in hope of sighting Natalie rushing toward him. I felt unwell.

"Shall I introduce you?" I asked Gene.

"You'd better. This is going to get uncomfortable in a hurry, so we should get started."

TRONCOSA SUGGESTED A table at the Normandie Park's bar, assuring us it poured a serviceable Sidecar. Gene countered with the police station, and Troncosa consented at once. "Official business demands an official setting."

After dispatching Esteban on an errand unknown, he got

into Gene's car, surrendering the rear seat to me. Whether out of gallantry or a need to feel he wasn't under arrest, I couldn't say.

A quiet ride ended at a quiet squad room, the four detectives on duty eyeing each other over penny ante poker hands. Gene planted me in a chair near his desk then whisked Troncosa to an interview room, to shatter his heart in privacy.

I snagged a newspaper off a nearby desk. Mrs. Roosevelt made a valiant attempt to interest me with her column but her visit to an experimental sawmill couldn't hold my attention. I was about to ask to be dealt into the card game—Uncle Danny had taught me a few tricks—when Esteban arrived carrying a manila envelope.

"Lillian. I'm pleased we have this opportunity to speak." His voice implored me for forgiveness. "You understand it was not my place to tell you anything about Armand and Natalie when you came to the house the other day."

"I'm sorry I tried to deceive you."

He hoisted the envelope. "Another photograph of the princess. Armand asked me to retrieve it for the detective."

The photo showed a smiling Ruby—correction, Natalie—snuggled under Troncosa's arm in a different nightclub. She was in the white Sophie Lang gown, the one she would die in. My only thought was that she must have hated wearing it a second time.

"They look so happy," I said.

"But of course. They are in love."

They are in love. I had to remind myself that as far as Esteban knew, the affair continued. He had no inkling that Natalie had perished the same night as Ruby.

"How long have they been seeing each other?"

"Almost eight weeks."

"That's pretty fast for a marriage proposal."

"Two, as Armand told you. For him, eight weeks is an eternity."

"Is he really that much of a ladies' man?"

"He was until he met the princess. He was quite bereft when she spurned his first offer of marriage."

"But Armand got right back up on the horse."

"Which horse?" Esteban blinked at me, then his face brightened. "Ah, yes. Not the one in Kentucky he intended to purchase. Armand regards rejection as a temporary condition. He vowed to win her hand."

"Is there competition for it? Does Natalie have other suitors?"

"Not as such." Esteban licked his lips nervously. "As you might imagine, Natalie has met many people in the business of making motion pictures. She is entertaining the notion of becoming an actress as a means of supporting herself. Some of those suggesting the idea are more aggressive than others. Armand has heard that Natalie is seeing one of these men. She spoke of going to San Francisco to consider Armand's second proposal. Armand feared she would travel there with that man."

"Who is he?"

"A motion picture director named Minot. You perhaps know him?"

"Our paths have crossed." I decided to test a theory. "He looked like he'd crossed more than someone's path recently. I think he exchanged blows with someone. Someone who can defend himself."

Esteban's gaze wandered across the room, where poker chips rattled. "Armand is a passionate man. He saw Minot outside a club last week with a woman. Not Natalie, but also not Minot's wife, an actress whose name eludes me. Armand made a statement to Minot that could be considered impolite. Minot took offense."

"And Armand settled his hash."

A quizzical smile alighted on Esteban's face, making him look like a young boy. "I do not know what you mean, yet I do. Yes. Hash was most definitely settled. Apparently Minot told Natalie about the fight and warned her Armand was a madman. Armand, for his part, went to Natalie and said the contretemps had convinced him to ask for her hand again. His rash behavior, I believe, is why she requested time to reflect. He is quite certain she will accept this time." Esteban rose. "Would you care for some water? I see a cooler in the back."

A moment later he handed me a paper cup and stood solicitously by while I drank it. "Armand didn't require a majordomo on his trip?"

"He had me stay behind to make preparations for an engagement party. And his hosts at the Airmont Stables tend to his every need. I had no objections. I'm not particularly fond of airplane travel."

"Armand traveled by plane?" That shortened the trip considerably, meaning he could have been in Los Angeles when Ruby was killed.

"He wanted to complete his business quickly, the sooner to hear Natalie's answer. I collected him at the airport and drove directly to their rendezvous."

"He must have put on a fresh suit first. The one he's wearing still has chalk marks from the tailors."

"Armand changed his wardrobe upon arrival. He also had his barber meet him at the terminal. On such an auspicious evening, Armand insists on looking his best."

"I notice you don't call him Señor Troncosa."

He grinned, deep-set eyes almost disappearing under unruly brows. "I would in a more formal setting. But we've known each other too long for that. Armand's father hired mine for his skills as a horseman. Armand and I were thrown together as boys.

Alas, I did not inherit my father's gifts—my brother did—so another trade was fated for me. Actually several. Whatever Armand requires. Do you believe he will receive, as you say, a fair shake from the police?"

"Naturally. Why wouldn't he?"

"His . . . democratic nature. Armand has friends high and low. For a man who has never wanted for anything in life, he conducts himself in every venue with great ease. He never makes himself the center of attention, but does not lack for people who treat him as such."

"I had a friend like that." I couldn't help glancing at the photograph in Esteban's hands, of Ruby in full Natalie mufti. "We'd walk into a party and everyone would gravitate to her. I'd feel like the moon orbiting the earth."

"Seen only by reflected light." Esteban's laugh was a rich, manly sound, gold coins tumbling in a leather bag. "Still, better to be seen, is it not? To be closer to the fire than to the darkness? And may I say, Miss Frost, you would be seen regardless of circumstance. You provide your own illumination."

Before I could blush, the interview room door opened. Troncosa emerged, his spirit diminished. Even his once-crisp suit seemed drab, jacket gaping open, shoulders at half-mast. Esteban stepped forward, but Gene intercepted him.

"Mr. Riordan, a word?" Esteban glanced at Troncosa for permission then trailed Gene into the room.

Troncosa took both of my hands, the grip under his faintly scented skin firm. "I thank you, Lillian."

"For what?"

"Had you not come to the hotel, I would still not know about Natalya. You brought the truth to me earlier than it might have come, and for that I am in your debt."

"I'm sorry I had to play a role in delivering such terrible news."

"What is worse is I have lost Natalya twice. My princess did not exist, a mere shadow. And now even that shadow has disappeared." He slumped against Gene's desk, face ashen, gaze aimed at the floor as if willing it to drop away beneath him.

When Esteban exited the interview room, he went to Troncosa and embraced him. Friends now, not majordomo and employer. Gene continued over to me.

"They're taking this hard," I said.

"Troncosa seemed blindsided, all right, but there's plenty to look into. Like this trip of his. Says he was in Kentucky to meet with an Arabian prince about a Russian racehorse."

"Bet you never heard that one before."

"And he's got a motive. Suppose he learned his true love was making a monkey out of him?" Gene pressed a palm to his face. "You realize what Ruby's playacting does."

"It puts you back at square one."

"Is there a square zero? Customarily in a murder investigation, you at least identify the victim correctly. All this legwork thinking Ruby was the target—"

"And it may have been Natalie the whole time."

"This case will be my career. A new man couldn't tell the players *with* a scorecard. I'll be working it until I keel over, my son left to pick up my notebook and carry on." The smile on his face added a thousand years to his age. "Who am I kidding? I'll never have time to sire a son. We'll have to talk to everyone again before word of this farce makes the papers. Somebody had to be aware of Ruby's little stunt."

"I'd say that clears Addison Rice."

"You're that convinced the old boy hadn't figured it out?"

"I'm certain of it. You have to let him know now. He can't read about this in the papers. He'll be humiliated. All he did was try to help. Giving advice to Ruby, inviting a refugee into his home."

"I get it. The man's a living saint."

"I just don't think he deserves to be made a laughingstock in print."

"You Catholic girls. Always with the sob stories."

I heard footsteps and saw Esteban making a return trip to the water cooler.

"Round two with Troncosa," Gene said. "You wait in the lobby. I'll arrange for someone to take you home."

AT THE FRONT desk, two women were vociferously protesting their prostitution arrests. Their fashion crimes were more troubling and I devoutly wished Edith could serve as their counsel. One of them took in my canary-yellow dress and chalked me up as a member of the sisterhood. I assumed Gene would break up the poker game and dispatch the winner to drive me as penance. Instead, Esteban appeared.

"Armand heard you needed a ride and instructed me to oblige." Brooking no argument—as if I were about to pose one—he waved me toward the doors and then to the Pierce-Arrow brougham, its blue finish gleaming under a streetlamp. He opened the rear door for me.

"I couldn't sit in the back. Not after tonight." Esteban held my arm as I slid into the passenger seat. Off we went, engine purring like a freshly sated puma.

The evening's events lulled us into silence. When Esteban spoke, it was with eyes fixed straight ahead. "What did she call herself, your friend?"

"Ruby."

"Ruby. She did not seem like a Ruby." Another awkward pause. "She was attempting to trick Armand, then. She sought his money."

"I honestly don't know. Maybe at first. But that could have changed."

"What other reason could she have for this treachery?" His fingers twitched against the wheel. "I should have sensed it. I should have seen through her pretense."

"Why? No one did."

Esteban glanced over at me. "Armand had strong feelings for your friend. This was unlike his usual flirtations. He may seem frivolous, but he is a man in love with life."

"Ruby was the same way," I said. "Probably why they got along so well."

OUTSIDE MRS. QUIGLEY'S, Esteban asked me to wait. He took a black velvet box from his jacket. "Armand also wishes to present you with a token of his appreciation."

"That's not necessary. The ride was enough."

"On his behalf, I insist." He rested the box in the palm of my hand. Not opening it, I decided, would seem rude.

Inside was a thin chain of gold. At thc end of it dangled a small pendant of green stone.

"This is an emerald," I said, more for confirmation than anything else.

"I realize it may seem excessive. But generosity is Armand's nature. This particular stone is a product of the mines owned by the Troncosa family. To him, they are commonplace. He gives them away regularly."

"It's beautiful. But surely this is too much. I haven't done anything."

"On the contrary. Without your intervention Armand would have believed he had been rejected by his true love. You did him a great service."

"I suppose I did." *Attagirl, mermaid. Take whatever lavish gifts you can lay your mitts on.* I set the pendant in the box, the chain puddling around it.

"Good night, Miss Frost. Meeting you has been a rare pleasure." Esteban paused, looking into my eyes. For a moment I hoped he might buss my cheek in the continental fashion. Instead he clambered out of the car and held the door for me, not getting behind the wheel again until I was safely inside.

Upstairs I collapsed onto the bed, exhausted. I held the necklace up to the light and watched the stone sparkle. It was a wholly unwarranted gift, and it felt improper to keep it. But I could always return it the next day.

Or perhaps the day after that.

In the meantime, I pondered a question. If I were the recipient of such a prize simply for being the bearer of bad tidings, then Natalie must have amassed a trove of similar gewgaws.

So where were they?

22

EDITH'S FRIEND AND confidant Bill Ihnen flagged me down outside the Paramount Wardrobe building, the brown paper bag he waved anointing the breeze with cinnamon. "Doughnuts scavenged from the commissary. This time of day, they're just thrown out."

"Then you have prevented a tragedy. I've been at work all day and only ate half a bologna sandwich. Keep wagging those in front of me and I'll follow you clear to Pasadena."

"No need to go that far. Edo's on one of the soundstages. Shall we take a stroll?"

We kept to the shade, the studio's industrious energy coursing around us. "I'm up to date on your endeavors," Bill said. "Let me congratulate you on achieving the impossible. You got Edith to venture off the lot. The woman makes grindstones nervous. Paramount's most dedicated employee. Soul of the place since 1924."

"She's been here that long? She looks so young."

"Nobody knows how old Edo is. Have to cut her open and count the rings. I hope this Ruby business sorts itself out soon. Edith's struggling to keep her footing in the job with Travis's contract due for renewal. She'd be lost without work. I can't picture her at home with Charlie. Heard you two met."

"And I said something unforgivably foolish."

Bill patted my shoulder. "I doubt you said anything Edith doesn't already know. She knows just about everything."

We made our way into a building the size of an airplane hangar. The warning light by the elephant door was off, the sign beneath identifying the production as COLLEGE SWING. Inside, a rakish man with an eye patch held court next to a motion picture camera, his body language indicating an off-color story was in progress. The camera's dozing eye faced thirty square feet of bogus grass and cramped foliage, bushes jostling for space like straphangers in a subway car. A section of ivy-covered wall with a *Romeo and Juliet*–type balcony overlooked the fray.

Through the scrum of electricians and assorted assistants I spotted a petite dervish in a gray shirtwaist. "There's Edith. Standing by—who is *that*?"

Edith supervised a pixie-faced wardrobe girl who whirled around a dark-haired man with legs so long he had to sit on a stool so she could work her magic. Wings sprouted from his back. Cupid's wings, judging from the crossbow partly hidden behind his muscular thigh. One glimpse of his exposed sock garters and the blood in my head had elsewhere to be.

"John Payne, the star of *Love on Toast.* A B picture I worked on, out next month. I'd invite you to the premiere but we're not having one. No fault of John's. He's a fine singer, too."

Edith saw us and waved. John Payne turned in our direction, grimaced slightly, then threw in a good-sport wave of his own.

"Actors amaze me. I couldn't be so calm and collected sitting in my shorts with all these people around," Bill said.

"He's not wearing pants? I hadn't noticed."

"WON'T PRESTON STURGES be surprised?" A puckish gleam flashed behind Edith's eyeglasses. "Him insisting Princess Natalie was the essence of royalty."

"You must remember this is Hollywood." Bill chuckled. "Where everyone believes stories for a living and deem themselves worthy of a princess's company. Ruby came up with the perfect ploy."

I'd been dragged away from a partially clad John Payne with only Bill's salvaged sinkers as compensation. We'd retired to Edith's office. Sketch pads and fabric swatches cluttered the glass-topped coffee table, me sprinkling cinnamon dust over them like some ravenous fairy.

"You realize Ruby had the ideal accomplice," I told Edith. "You. Ruby was a good actress. I read lines with her enough to know. But your clothes made Natalie real. Not just to everyone else, but to Ruby. She'd put on an exquisitely tailored suit or a satin gown, say she was a highborn head of Hungary, and make the world believe it. Her acting, her accent, those were finishing touches. Your costumes did the heavy lifting. To the extent Gene still doesn't know who the intended victim was, Ruby or Natalie. It's entirely possible the killer murdered someone who doesn't exist."

"Lillian's right," Bill said. "It's the highest compliment that can be paid to your designs. You helped a fictional creation take root in the real world."

"I hadn't thought of it like that." Edith clutched her shoulders, her features abruptly drawn. For the first time since we'd met, she was shaken. She seemed not only tiny, but vulnerable. "If my designs contributed to Ruby's masquerade, they contributed to her murder. I pick up a sketch pad and it ends with a poor girl lying in an alley dead."

Bill took her hand. "Steady there, old girl. None of this is your fault. Ruby made her own bed."

"Oh, I know you're right. But I can't help feeling a sense of responsibility. An obligation to Ruby. I wish I'd acted on my doubts about Princess Natalie more quickly."

"You had doubts?" I asked. "Since when?"

"Since you received that phone call purportedly from her. Her dialogue seemed, well, familiar. Then it dawned on me. It actually *was* dialogue. Lines I'd heard before. Women being creatures of the heart, her saying now that she'd learned how Hollywood expected her to behave, she liked it here and intended to stay."

"Don't tell me that's from a movie, too."

"*The Scarlet Empress*. I screened it again to confirm it."

Bill shook his head as he dove into the bag for another doughnut. "Where else to learn how royalty should talk than a picture about royalty? How'd it hold up, by the way?"

"It's Travis's masterpiece. Those gowns! We won't see such lavishness again. I still remember his arguments with Marlene over her fur hat. Too much like Garbo's in *Queen Christina*, he said. But Marlene insisted, and she was right. Then of course there's the letter."

"From Marlene?" I asked.

"No, dear, from Natalie ostensibly to Mr. Rice. I haven't seen it myself, but I'd be curious whether the date was written in the European style. That's how Ruby, as Natalie, wrote it on the puzzle piece. As opposed to November sixth, the way an impostor would write it."

"But Natalie herself was an impostor," Bill pointed out.

"Yes. It does become confusing." Edith had kicked off her black pumps to curl up on the couch. Now she stepped back into them. "Which is why I choose to view events solely from Ruby's perspective. She invents a character, Princess Natalie. Gives her a history doubtless drawn from her own family. Steals an appropriate wardrobe. Thinks of her creation as a separate entity, a second self, if you will. 'Natalie is the most elegant woman. Natalie will get me my big break.'"

"She wrote herself a role," Bill said.

"And took it on the road." Edith began to pace the floor. "Starting at a hotel bar, then with Mr. Troncosa and his circle of friends. Next came her first real review. Addison Rice."

"Troncosa said that Ruby—sorry, Natalie," I corrected, "tried to flee Addison's house when he brought her to a party."

"Because Ruby was afraid of being recognized. She'd been careful to avoid people she knew. Suddenly she finds herself face-to-face with Mr. Rice, who'd met her several times. And he sees not the young actress he'd banished from his home, but a beguiling Hungarian princess. The encounter could only have galvanized her. Encouraged her to continue the masquerade."

I pictured Ruby at Addison's party, realizing there was no way to avoid meeting her host, knowing she'd have to sink or swim. The Ruby I knew would have hurled herself into Natalie's persona with abandon. She would have strode across the foyer, offering her hand for Addison to kiss, smothering any skepticism with the force of her charisma. That night, Ruby had triumphed beyond her wildest dreams. She'd not only fooled Addison. She'd fooled herself.

"She picked a terrible time for a bravura performance," Bill said. "If Rice had exposed the phony princess, Ruby would be alive today. What about Laurence Minot? Didn't he also know Ruby and Natalie and not see what was in front of him?"

"Much as it pains me," I said, "I have to give Laurence a pass. He'd only met Ruby once, at his wedding reception when they'd both had a few. He basically knew Natalie and Natalie alone. I'm rather jealous of him, actually. I'd give anything to have seen Ruby in action as Natalie."

"And that's what is key here," Edith said. "Natalie is a *character,* created by Ruby. One to which she was so committed she even wrote the date differently when essaying the part. But the telephone call and the letter are instances of someone else playing Natalie, without Ruby's dedication."

I joined Edith in pacing, partly to show off my outfit. I'd replaced the black belt on my taupe knit dress with a cherry-red scarf. A fetching addition, I thought, but Edith hadn't noticed it. Or worse, she had and didn't find it worthy of comment.

"But who would do that?" I asked. "And why?"

"It's not my place to speculate. What does Detective Morrow think?"

"He thinks he needs some time off. He's also keen to talk to Laurence Minot again."

A crisp shake of the head from Edith. "Detective Morrow is allowing Mr. Minot's amorous entanglement with Natalie and donnybrook with Mr. Troncosa to cloud his judgment. Mr. Minot would hardly send Addison Rice a letter implicating himself."

"Edo," Bill announced, "it's time for you to speculate."

She sighed, accepting his wisdom. "The party responsible for the letter and the phone call can only be that unsavory private investigator, Mr. Beckett."

"Because he strong-armed that photographer into stealing clothes for Ruby," Bill said.

"Because he orchestrated this from the outset. We now know why he resorted to that odious deception with your friend, Lillian, to acquire a picture of Ruby. The point being it was an older photograph in which Ruby was blond and didn't superficially resemble Natalie. Having it appear in the newspapers delayed any connection between the two women."

"Beckett wanted the investigation to spin its wheels."

"He then took additional steps to maintain the fiction Ruby and Natalie were different people." Edith faced me. "I fear you won't like this next notion one bit."

"I don't like any of it so far." Marching around the room wasn't winning plaudits for my fashion acumen, so I perched on Adele's stool.

"Remember it was Mr. Beckett who asked *you* about Natalie, giving you her surname. He then turned up after Natalie's supposed telephone call to reinforce her importance. In order to sustain the illusion Natalie was still alive, he needed help. Unwitting accomplices to corroborate Natalie's continued existence. I believe he used you as a cat's-paw."

My voice quavered. "But why me?"

"Because you were already involved in the investigation. A call from Natalie to the police might have been ignored. But if she telephoned you . . ."

"I'd run to Gene and spill everything. How very clever of Mr. Beckett."

Bill passed me the bag containing the last doughnut. "What lovely shoes," Edith said of my red patent leather pumps. Both the pastry and the compliment had been extended out of pity. That didn't prevent me from accepting them.

"Then Beckett killed Ruby." Bill's words split the difference between statement and question.

"Entirely possible, not yet certain. Too much remains unknown. For instance, why would Ruby still pretend to be Natalie with the risk of exposure increasing and multiple suitors vying for her hand?"

"To land one of those suitors as a rich husband," Bill suggested.

"Then she would have accepted Mr. Troncosa's first proposal. She certainly wouldn't have left him guessing about her response to his second. And what explains her protracted dalliance with Mr. Minot?"

"Spite," I said. "Ruby was jealous of Diana. Stealing her husband was a way to get back at her."

"You don't honestly believe that." Edith pointed at me like a district attorney. "Would Ruby have engaged in a deception like this for criminal gain?"

The concentration on her face daunted me. I thought about Ruby, the small-town girl who craved only stardom. "No. She wanted attention. But she wouldn't have hurt anyone."

"Then the agenda wasn't hers, but Mr. Beckett's. He forced Ruby to continue stringing along the various parties who knew her as Natalie to some undetermined end."

"Natalie's jewelry," I said. "Troncosa must have showered her with gifts, but we haven't found any."

"That would be one possibility," Edith allowed.

"So Beckett tumbled to Ruby's racket, playing at being a princess for fun and champagne." Bill diagrammed furiously on his mental chalkboard. "He made her keep up the act so he could turn a profit on it. We don't know *how* he found out."

"Come now, Bill. Mr. Beckett is a private investigator. He was hired to follow either Ruby or Natalie. In the course of doing his job, he stumbled upon the other identity."

"Put like that, it's obvious." He seemed delighted at being bettered by her—and Edith, I realized, relied on him as a sounding board. "Then we just have to figure out which one Beckett was following, and who hired him to follow her."

"I have some ideas about that," I said.

Edith nodded. "I thought you might."

After a soft knock, the office door opened. A gangly youth with the disinterested air of some executive's nephew fidgeted in the corridor. "Sorry to interrupt, Miss Head, but Mr. Archainbaud needs you on set immediately."

"What's wrong?"

"Dorothy Lamour's costume is . . ." The young man's hair was so fair I could see his scalp blush along with his cheeks. "Her sarong wrap, it's, um, unwrapping."

Edith had a bag in hand as she pushed the errand boy aside. "For goodness's sake. When will they listen? I told George we had to sew her into it."

"Unwrapping, huh?" Bill turned to me with a grin. "If you'll excuse me, I think I'd like to see this."

23

I WANTED THE office to be shabby. I wanted Winton Beckett to be operating out of a hovel. But the Loomis Building, off Broadway near Pershing Square, was reputable if tired. Every tenant of the sober gray brick structure from the See-Mack Duplicator Company to Allied Asbestos Pad was doing their best to get by. The elevator operator wished me a pleasant day as he deposited me on the fourth floor.

Beckett's office was at the end of a narrow corridor reeking of Dutch cleanser. Movement was visible through the door's pebbled glass. The brunette at the reception desk scarcely glanced up from the emery board she dragged across her fingernails. "Mr. Beckett isn't in. I can take a message or notarize a document if that's why you're here."

I'd known Beckett wouldn't be there. I was interested in his girl, the one Gene mentioned. She wore a maroon dress with a black bow and matching buttons on the puffed sleeves. She was pretty in an indistinct way, like a wax figure fashioned to resemble a famous person you couldn't identify. Even bored, her voice sounded familiar. I imagined it with an accent, Slavic by way of von Sternberg.

"What's your name?" I asked.

The emery board stopped moving. "Mavis Kreutzer. Who's asking?"

"Someone who needs a document notarized. I should see if you're any good at it."

I snatched a piece of paper off her desk. It was a shopping list: *oleo, coffee, evaporated milk.* The items written in the same sloping script on Natalie's letter to Addison.

As I returned the list, I noticed the hastily packed boxes behind her desk. "Big Marlene Dietrich fan, are you, Mavis?"

Her eyes sparked, recognizing that the game was up. "I couldn't give a Spanish fig for her. I don't go to pictures to look at women. You're Lillian."

"And you're 'Natalie.'"

"Command performances only." The emery board scraped her nails again.

I nudged one of the boxes with my foot. "This looks like Beckett will be gone for a while."

"I'm pretty sure the son of a bitch is gone for good. But the rent's paid up, so I'm using the space myself. Kreutzer Typing and Notary Services. I like your shoes."

"Thanks. Do you know where the son of a bitch is? Maybe back in San Francisco?"

"Unlikely. San Francisco was just a daylong affair. Win whisked me up there, had me write a letter and spread a little green, then sent me back to the grind. Not even a trip to Chinatown for some good chow mein. The stuff here is the pits."

"Did you meet the real Natalie?"

"Nope. Win told me about her, though, gave me pointers on what to say. The Dietrich was my idea. Did you like?"

"I liked." Her blasé attitude was discomfiting; she'd worked with Beckett too long to bother concealing her mercenary instincts. "Why was your boss forcing Natalie to jump through hoops?"

"Why does anybody do anything? Money."

"What form did this money take?"

The question provoked a chilly smile. "You've seen the rocks, then. Gorgeous, aren't they? Natalie picked up a new sparkler every time she stepped out. Win plucked 'em right off her. He'd loan her one or two whenever she saw Mr. South of the Border. I'd hear Win on the phone, coordinating her ensemble. He always wanted her to look nice."

"Too bad he couldn't take his own advice. That jacket of his is atrocious."

She abruptly flipped the emery board into the trash. I'd struck a nerve. Maybe the jacket had been her Christmas gift to him several lifetimes ago, when both believed in peace on earth and goodwill to men.

"I imagine this caper was supposed to run until Natalie got herself hitched. Shame she got herself killed instead. Do you think Beckett did it?"

"Do you think I'd ask?"

"No, Mavis, I don't think you would. Not when good chow mein's in the offing."

She stood up, opened a closet door, and kicked one of the boxes toward it.

"What's Win's plan now the money's stopped rolling in?"

"Oh, honey." Her contempt was the least synthetic emotion she'd shown so far, and still there was something off-the-shelf about it. "Money keeps rolling in. Thing about Win, by the time he gets involved, there's already plenty of wrongdoing going on."

"So he's blackmailing people. Let me guess. Diana Galway's sin is she stooped to being your boss's client. With Laurence Minot, it's photos of him and Natalie."

Mavis's expression would shame the sphinx. "The photos are only the start. Win's holding something bigger on Minot. Don't ask. I don't know what it is."

Proof of murder was the obvious thought—provided, of course, that Beckett hadn't killed Ruby himself. It became vitally important for me to leave, to get away from Mavis Kreutzer at once. I'd paid her a compliment by comparing her to a wax figure. Wax figures at least have a core. Mavis was a husk, hollowed out by years of disappointment. She was what Ruby had been on her way to becoming, and I fleetingly entertained the loathsome notion that perhaps Ruby was better off.

"You must be pretty positive Beckett's not coming back to tell me all this."

"He promised me one of those pieces of Natalie's. A diamond ring I'd picked out. Should've stashed it in a coffee can when I had the chance. I'll never see it again, so to hell with him." She pushed the box into the closet and shut the door. "You must meet people at Tremayne's who need secretarial services. Pass along my name, would you? I do good work, and I'm always open for business."

SWEET-TALKING MY WAY onto the Lodestar lot wasn't difficult with the end of workday exodus underway. But the soundstage hosting *Hearts in Spring*, directed by Laurence Minot and featuring Diana Galway in the role of Susie, still teemed with activity. As I approached I was engulfed by a sea of blondes dressed like dolls. Short gingham skirts over mountains of petticoats, hair in pigtails, circles of rouge on their cheeks. I washed ashore by a wall as they rolled past for a smoke break, tap shoes clicking.

No Raggedy Ann getup for the picture's third female lead. Diana sat in a corner of the set, a robe draped over her lacy peignoir. Waves of chestnut hair framed her face as she pored over the latest *Photoplay* the way Father Costigan used to study the *Daily Racing Form*.

"I thought those magazines were only for us fans."

She started as if I'd woken her. "My photo spread is inside."

"Did you smile for the birdie?"

"Four hours in the broiling sun at the Riviera Country Club and they only use two lousy pictures." She tossed the magazine to the floor. I marveled at the speed with which she'd acquired that essential accessory to Hollywood success, a permanent sense of dissatisfaction. "I won't ask if you've heard. Detective Morrow was here this morning and told us you're in this up to your ears. We know about Ruby pretending to be a princess."

"Give her some credit. She delivered the performance of a lifetime as Natalie. Got great notices including a marriage proposal."

Diana tensed. Let her wonder from whom the proposal had come. We were both acting now, and while Diana had the training I had the motivation.

"She overplayed it, I'll bet, knowing Ruby," Diana said. "Loads of grand gestures."

"But an authentic Hungarian accent. You said Gene told *us*."

"Yes, well, apparently, Laurence did know Natalie in a professional capacity. Remember I said she wanted to be an actress."

"Meaning he lied to the police before."

"No, he simply forgot he'd been introduced to her at the studio. In a *professional capacity*."

All the theatrics were making me tired. Maybe that was why I'd washed out as an actress. I lacked the stamina for it.

"I doubt a *professional capacity* is what got your husband punched in the face. Or why you hired a private investigator to follow him."

Diana's transformation was jarring. First the tears, hot and sudden. Then her face collapsed, revealing the emotions roiling beneath. The raw materials of her trade laid bare. "It wasn't supposed to turn out this way. Laurence had become so distant. And Ruby was too busy to talk to me about him. I was alone. Of course I'd heard of Princess Natalie. Everyone was talking about her, even Laurence. Then he started spending more time away from home. I knew Natalie was his type. An aristocrat. Everything I'm not. I never thought—" Her voice caught, and she began weeping even harder. "Did Ruby hate me? Is that why she'd go to all this trouble? Because she hated me that much?"

There was no calculation to her show of neediness, no technique. It was like watching a world-class jockey lose control of a thoroughbred, and I wanted the spectacle to end before someone got hurt. "This wasn't about you," I said. "You knew Ruby. She never planned anything."

"I'd try to get a look at this princess at parties," Diana said. "But she was always on the other side of the room, or had just left. I got it in my head she was avoiding me."

"She was. You two couldn't meet face-to-face. You'd have queered Ruby's disguise."

"I know that now. But at the time it only confirmed my suspicion Laurence was seeing this Natalie behind my back. I had to *know,* don't you understand?"

"I understand. So you hired Winton Beckett."

Her nod was accompanied by a shuddering sob. Tracks of mascara bracketed her nose, but somehow she was still gorgeous and somehow I still felt sorry for her. The world was a truly unjust place. "He followed Laurence for two weeks and told me I had nothing to worry about."

I wondered if Beckett had ever formulated a sentence containing even a kernel of truth. "And what did he tell you late last night or this morning, once he knew the truth about Natalie was out?"

"How . . . how did you know?"

"I used to read tea leaves."

"Beckett called this morning before Detective Morrow arrived. He told me he had photographs of Laurence and Ruby together. He wanted money to hush them up. I asked why *I* should pay since I'm the wronged party. He said the photos only existed because I suspected my husband of having an affair. Worse, he *was* having an affair, and the woman in question was murdered. He's right. The scandal would ruin me."

"You told Gene this?"

"No. I didn't. I couldn't."

"You will. Your career isn't the most important thing on God's green earth."

"Lillian!"

"Listen to me. If Beckett didn't kill Ruby, he knows who did. You have to tell Gene. Or I will."

"You're right. I was only . . . it's been a terrible day, you see." She flashed a life-will-go-on smile as she palmed the tears from her cheeks. "It's not often you learn your late best friend seduced your husband under a false identity and now you're being blackmailed because of it. I'll call Detective Morrow once we finish filming. I will." She caught sight of herself in a mirror and yelped. "Good Lord, I look a fright! I need to get to Makeup at once!"

With a flutter of robe, she was gone. Her performance machinery was clanking back into place, but wasn't fully oiled yet. I didn't believe for an instant she'd call Gene.

THE FIRST TWO phones I encountered were props. I was going for the hat trick when a voice said, "Hey, don't I know you?"

A tall man studied me with puzzlement. His jug ears did seem familiar. "You an actress or something?"

"I tend toward something."

Behind him the gingham dollies trooped back to the set, arranging themselves in concentric circles. "Cripes, I remember! I was at your screen test."

My heart fell to my shoes and continued on toward Peking. "You remember that? It was ages ago."

"Oh, but sister, you were the worst." He shook his head and started to walk away. "Maybe ever."

"At least I made an impression," I hollered after him. It wasn't much consolation. Especially when I was shushed by five people.

A preoccupied Laurence Minot leaned forward in his director's chair. With his call of "Action," the set filled with music and tapping. Relentless, implacable tapping.

The dancers had surrounded an oversized canopy bed. Diana feigned sleep while a dream sprang to life around her. The girls tapped like their lives depended on it, the machine-gun clatter echoing. The lead dancer's feet were a blur while her face held a frozen grin. I feared she could lose her footing or her sanity at any moment. The music climaxed as two burly men just out of frame mercifully hoisted her before the camera for her close-up.

Laurence issued an unimpressed "Cut." He spoke a few words to an assistant at his side, then lit a cigarette. My phone call could wait.

"Not now, I'm thinking." Laurence waved his hand to dismiss me and almost ignited my sleeve.

"I don't work for you."

He turned quickly toward me, then retreated as much as the canvas chair would allow. "I'm beginning to wonder if you work for anyone, considering how often you're underfoot. Here to commiserate with my lovely wife?"

"I already have. We were talking about Natalie Szabo."

"A bolt from the blue, that. Diana's old pal pulling a fast one on everybody."

"Including you."

He shrugged. "No sense denying it now."

"Not everybody had met Ruby before. You had."

"Along with three hundred other people at my wedding. Ruby was Diana's friend, not mine."

"If I put on a wig and some of Claudette Colbert's togs, would you recognize me?"

"You're a sight taller than Claudette. And I could shoot you from both sides."

"Touché. When you two became involved, did you know Natalie was practically engaged to Armand Troncosa?"

Laurence flinched, to my immense pleasure. "I was only involved with Natalie professionally. And I never want to hear that greasy rat bastard's name again."

"Did you two cross swords?"

"We exchanged words."

"On what subject? Horseflesh? Tweed prices?"

"He objected to my interest in Natalie. Or Ruby. I explained the facts in plainest English, then made the mistake of turning my back on that perfumed pretty boy. He sucker-punched me."

"That doesn't seem like Armand's style. I'm picturing you taking a wild swing and him hitting back. Accurately."

"Think what you want. I've got more pressing problems."

"And one of them is named Beckett."

He hurtled out of his chair. "How do you know that? You didn't hear it from Diana because I haven't told her."

"Great. Beckett's blackmailing the pair of you and neither one's told the other or the police. What does he have on you?"

"Some photographs that could be easily misconstrued in light of Ruby's death."

"Sure. It looks like you're canoodling when you're actually discussing Ibsen. That's the only hold Beckett has on you?"

"It's all the hold he needs." Laurence gazed in disgust at the neon meringue that was his set. "Fighting to save my job when it's been reduced to this. I directed *Journey's End* on stage, you know. Brothers in arms, mankind at his best. That was something real. But this gossamer nonsense?"

"It looks like a wonderful dream."

"You'd say that. You're a woman. All you want is a happy ending."

"What's wrong with a happy ending?"

"Name a single soul in line for one."

The jug-eared fellow told Laurence the next setup was ready. I left to continue my quest for a phone. I didn't trust either of the Minots to do the right thing.

I trudged across the Lodestar lot as the sun set and starlets fanned out through the city for highballs and merriment. Ahead for me was the meatloaf at the corner diner. If I timed my entrance right, I could claim the thick slice at the heel. It wasn't much of a happy ending. But I'd settle for it.

24

ON THE SEVENTH day, I did not rest. The usual Sunday horde of marcelled Visigoths laid waste to Tremayne's, and I did my level best to help them sack and pillage. I'd told Gene all I'd learned and hoped for an update without expecting or receiving one. That night I ate stew with Mrs. Quigley and Miss Sarah, listened to Jack Benny, and turned in feeling as giddy as I once did on Christmas Eve, certain my dreams would be fulfilled come morning.

But Monday's newspapers brought only coal for my stocking. They contained no mention of Princess Natalie's true identity, the absence giving rise to many a dark surmise: that Barney Groff was again abroad in the land; and that Diana and Laurence were conspiring together, jointly stonewalling Gene about Beckett's blackmail.

Late in the afternoon I held out a parcel to a well-preserved older lady but she made no move to receive it, transfixed by a sight over my shoulder. Her voice was an ardent whisper. "Good Lord. Isn't that Ramon Novarro?"

I threw a look behind me. "No, ma'am. Ramon is shorter." The woman accepted her purchases and reluctantly walked away.

Only then did Armand Troncosa approach the counter, his chalk-stripe suit as black as his mood. His aubergine shirt and purple-and-white necktie made me realize I knew what "resplendent" meant. "Lillian. I trust it is not an imposition to visit you at your place of employment."

"It's perfectly fine. How are you?"

"I am en route to see your Detective Morrow. He has requested a list of every gift I gave to Natalya. He wishes to search for them in . . ." He faltered, either out of distaste for or unfamiliarity with the next phrase. "Pawnbroker shops."

Gene was turning over rocks hunting for Winton Beckett, following up on what Mavis Kreutzer had told me. I wondered if he'd bearded her in her borrowed den, and found myself hoping he hadn't.

"Imagine if Natalya and I had wed." Troncosa's voice had lost its silky tone. "What a fool I would have been."

"I think Ruby tried to spare you that fate."

"Spare me? It was her plan all along to gain my fortune."

"You said yourself she was reluctant to become engaged. Perhaps marriage wasn't part of her plan. Perhaps by refusing your proposal, she had your best interests in mind."

"Perhaps you defend her because she was your friend."

The accusatory edge of his words drove me back a step. At the same time an obscure loyalty asserted itself, not so much to Ruby as to Natalie. Ruby's greatest performance, one I'd never have the opportunity to witness firsthand.

"Truth be told," I said, "Ruby wasn't much of a friend. But you should know she didn't intend you any harm."

"I know no such thing. I know nothing about Ruby, other than she scattered my tokens of affection to the four winds for a pittance."

"Ruby didn't do that," I blurted out. "That was someone else."

"So she had a partner in her deceit? Hardly an endorsement of her character."

I kept silent, having already said too much. That gave

Troncosa time to turn my words over and come up with a more accurate interpretation.

"Unless . . . Ruby was forced into this charade. Is that what you suggest, Lillian? Was she manipulated into deceiving me?" Troncosa reached across the counter and seized my wrist. Not forcefully; he might not even have been aware of his action. But I was finding it impossible to ignore. "If that is so, you must tell me. I demand the name of this Svengali."

Something brutish and, worse, wounded lurked behind Troncosa's eyes. I recalled Kay's dire speculation that he was in exile after killing a man in Argentina and found it all too easy to swallow. As for the physical act of swallowing, that had suddenly become difficult.

"Is there a problem?" Mr. Valentine's voice boomed across the floor, his shoes clicking briskly against the linoleum. Never was I so happy to see a chartreuse pocket square.

By the time he reached us, Troncosa was staring at his hand and wondering who had wrapped it around mine. "No," he said. "My apologies." With a bow he struck off toward the elevators.

My boss watched him go, then looked at me. "Miss Frost?"

"It's an extremely long story," I finally said.

"I see. Heaven forfend we detain you unnecessarily." He pinched the bridge of his nose. "Your shift is almost over. I suggest we discuss this in the morning."

I COLLECTED MY purse and my thoughts, then started for the employees' entrance. When I saw Esteban Riordan battling through shoppers toward me, I almost turned tail and ran. Only the concern on his face made me stand my ground. He raised his hands, leery of spooking me.

"Lillian. Armand is beside himself. He wishes to make amends."

"I don't care to see him right now."

Esteban lowered his eyes. "I understand. But you of all people can appreciate Armand is under tremendous strain. He has said and perhaps done things he regrets. He still owes you a great deal, and will not be at ease until he apologizes. Please, I know how much this means to him. And I will be present when he speaks with you."

Saying the last sentence pained him. What choice did I have? "Very well. But outside the store."

Esteban moved to touch my arm, only to reconsider.

The Pierce-Arrow looked vivid in the glow of the display window, Tremayne's latest fall fashions arranged on a family of mannequins seated around a Thanksgiving dinner complete with papier-mâché turkey. Troncosa climbed out of the car as we neared. Esteban smoothly positioned himself between us, a protective gesture that only made me feel more defenseless. Troncosa also didn't cotton to it, if the snap of his head was any indication.

"Lillian. My behavior was inexcusable, yet I beg your forgiveness. To put you in such a position at work is unconscionable. Shall I speak to someone in authority at the store?"

"Better we should forget it."

"As you wish. Allow me to escort you home."

"You don't have to do that."

"But I do. And it will permit us to have the conversation I came to have with you. You must tell me about Ruby. Tell me about the woman I loved but did not know. Tell me something to make her real to me."

She was a hard-eyed dreamer who kept company with Tommy Carpa and pilfered family treasures from unsuspecting roommates. I didn't think that would go over well in Troncosa's current state of mind. And if I let him work on me, I might slip up and give him Beckett's name.

I shook my head. "That would be a mistake."

"Please. Your cup overflows with memories while mine is empty. You cannot share?"

It was a cheap ploy, and my almost falling for it doomed his chances. "No, I'm sorry."

The conversation wasn't going as he'd expected. Troncosa's savage side peered out at me again then darted away. "You surprise me, Lillian. You would prefer to leave me thinking the worst of Ruby?"

"I can't help what you think." I glanced toward the employees' door but my sole potential agent of deliverance was Horace, the ancient security guard armed only with the overpowering aroma of the homemade liniment he used on his rheumatic joints. "I have to catch the streetcar."

Troncosa, not to be denied, slipped around Esteban. Who in turn shadowed him and started to speak. The blast of a taxi's horn drowned out his words. A reckless driver took the corner too fast, tires screeching. Before I could turn toward the commotion I heard a sharp crack, and the plate glass display window behind me shattered.

Esteban yelled "Get down!" and hurled himself at Troncosa. I dove to the concrete as a second, then third gunshot blasted the display. Mannequins toppled.

The car, a black sedan, never stopped moving. It sped down the street, a fusillade of horns in its wake.

Esteban helped me to my feet as Troncosa brushed himself off. Most of the window had fallen into the display but shards of glass littered the sidewalk.

"Are you all right?" Esteban asked.

"I think so." I looked at my shaking hands, spotting a few scrapes on my palms and one or two on my knees. "I may not be a little later."

A policeman sprinted over and demanded details. Troncosa provided them in a steady voice, so composed you'd have thought he'd been shot at before. Maybe he had. The officer jotted down the particulars. "Stay here while I call this in."

"Raise Detective Morrow in Robbery Homicide. Tell him it's Miss Frost." The officer eyed me skeptically, but my hands were trembling more now and demanded my full attention. Esteban wrapped his arm around me. I left it where it was.

Horace the security guard, invigorated by the action, stood a post before the remains of the window. Within moments every Tremayne's employee and customer had shown up to rubberneck the damage. I wanted to tell Georgie the stock boy to fetch a broom and start sweeping. The street was a mess.

When Gene arrived, he noted Esteban's arm on my shoulders without comment and asked after my well-being. Hansen snubbed me, climbing up into the ruined display and poking among the broken glass. "And here I thought I was the only one ever wanted to open up on a family dinner."

"Mr. Troncosa, I was expecting you downtown," Gene said. "Someone want to walk me through what happened?"

This time I took the lead, Troncosa and Esteban confirming and elaborating. Yes, it was a black car. No, we hadn't seen the driver. No, none of us noticed the license plate.

Gene drummed the cover of his notebook with his pen. "Now for Professor Quiz's main question. Who was the unknown person in the dark car aiming at?"

Hansen held up the carcass of the papier-mâché turkey. "It probably wasn't old Tom here."

"It was obviously me." Troncosa shouldered forward to brave some phantom firing squad. "Who else could it be?"

"Possibly Miss Frost, given she works at Tremayne's. Did anyone know you were coming to the store, Mr. Troncosa?"

"No. But we could have easily been followed. Perhaps it's best I leave this city if I'm being used as target practice on public streets."

"If it's all the same to you, I'd prefer nobody go anywhere just yet."

"I hope that doesn't include me," I said, "because these stockings are a lost cause. I'm going to replace them. A lady likes to look her best even at times of adversity." I stepped toward the employees' door, knees and palms burning. I hadn't hit the pavement that hard since grammar school recess, when gangly limbs meant jumping rope qualified me for hazard pay.

Gene pulled me close, concern in his eyes and spearmint on his breath. He pointedly placed his hand where Esteban's had been on my shoulder. I felt a reassuring squeeze. "You sure you're all right?"

"If I'm worrying about my clothes, I'm probably okay."

"I understand Troncosa visited you in the store and came on kind of strong."

"Yes," I said, omitting *to the extent he seems capable of a crime of passion, like killing the woman who gulled him*. "You don't really think someone could have been shooting at me."

"Right now my only thought is I'll take you home whenever you're ready. You just say the word."

As he walked away I spotted Mr. Valentine in the display window, shaking his head at the fallen mannequins like he was going to have bury them all personally, turkey included. Tomorrow morning could take its sweet time coming.

25

IN MY DREAM the display window dummies had risen from the debris of their ruined Thanksgiving and were chasing me up Broadway, the mother brandishing a horn of plenty like a blunderbuss. Their footsteps sounded hollow, like rapping on wood. It took me a moment to realize I'd awakened and someone was knocking on my door. My relief was tempered by the fact I had a visitor at five past midnight. I rousted an umbrella, my version of a Louisville Slugger, and inquired as to my caller's identity.

"It's Vi."

We hadn't spoken since our dustup over Tommy Carpa and the purloined comb. "How'd you get into the building?"

"I waited outside and followed one of your neighbors in. Can you open up? I think he's watching me."

Not Mr. Pendergast, I hoped, foreseeing with crystal-ball clarity six months of him buttonholing me in the hall to ask when Blondie would come by again.

"Are you alone? Or do you have Tommy in tow?"

"It's just me. I swear."

I took her at her word. Vi was wearing her waitress uniform, the glare of the overhead light giving the short black dress a dull sheen.

"What's so urgent?"

"Tommy wants to talk to you."

"Not on your life. Wait, you know where he is?"

"For the next little while, anyway. He's only staying there

until I bring you to him. He heard what happened at Tremayne's. He wants you to know he didn't have anything to do with it."

"The smart play is for you to call the police and tell them where Tommy's holed up."

"I can't do that, Lillian. I promised."

"Aren't you taking this infatuation too far? I know you think you're in love with Tommy. What's worse is you seem to think he's in love with you."

She shook her head once, the sweep as deliberate as a searchlight's. "Not anymore. Not the way he's acting. He's swooning over a dead girl. I know that now."

"So why help him?"

"Because it might help you, too. You've got no reason to trust me after how I acted, but I would never lead you into trouble. Honest. Tommy only wants to talk."

She raised three fingers, the Girl Scout sign testament to her sincerity. Maybe Vi really was over the palooka. I raided my closet wondering what Edith would advise me to wear to a wee hour rendezvous in an undisclosed location. Black seemed right.

VI FIRED UP Tommy's green Packard and pointed it toward West Hollywood. Anyone still awake was there. I stared out at the stumpy palm trees lining Sunset Boulevard, watching swells swan in and out of nightclubs swaddled in furs that suited the calendar if not the climate.

One block off the main drag, the action became markedly more furtive. Dark figures in shadowy doorways, their clothes still flashy but their faces turned away from the street. The Packard pulled up outside a brick bunker with curtains shrouding gun-slit windows. The faded sign over the door announced ELMO'S with a shrug.

The interior didn't nudge the needle on the charm meter.

We navigated a maze of tables occupied by couples who'd clearly made poor choices long before setting foot in Elmo's. Vi reached a thickset man holding up the wall on the far side of the room.

"Hey, Hazel," he said to Vi. "Can you sing? Our regular girl came down with something."

"A case of better judgment?" I offered to no reply.

"Sorry, Harry. I'm tone-deaf." Vi gestured at the wall. "We've got to go up."

Harry stepped aside. The door behind him, flush with the wall and so low I had to duck under the frame, was almost unnoticeable. It gave onto a rickety flight of stairs.

"Since when are you tone-deaf? And Hazel?"

"Like I'd sing or use my right name in this dump." The secondhand defiance in her voice made sweet little Vi sound, once again, like Ruby.

One of the doors on the next floor led into a dingy storeroom. Vi knocked softly on the other.

"Took long enough," Tommy grumbled as he let us into a dank office crowded with cast-off furniture. An open fifth of rye kept company on the scarred desktop with the remains of a barbecue pork sandwich.

"Be nice to Vi," I said. "I'm only here because she asked."

"Thanks, kid." He said it as pleasantly as he could. Vi left us alone, closing the door behind her.

"See? I can be cordial." Tommy shoveled his hair back, leaving it standing up in wild thickets. The room was stifling and reeked of desperation, some of it vintage. "Place used to be a speakeasy. Did a lot of business in this neighborhood once upon a time."

The hour was late for a history lesson. "Vi says you have something to tell me."

He snuffed out a cigarette and promptly sparked another,

pacing all the while. "You were there when someone took a shot at Troncosa today."

Interesting he had no compunction about naming Troncosa the target. "I saw the whole thing. What there was to see."

"You didn't see me."

"I also didn't see Vice President Garner or Rin Tin Tin."

"That's because none of us had anything to do with it. Innocent parties to a man and dog." He kept moving, changing course abruptly, trailing smoke like an engine on the Rock Island Line. "I wanted you to know that. And to relay that fact to John Law."

"I don't know it's a fact. And it would sound better coming from you. Could you light somewhere a minute? I'm getting dizzy tracking you around the room."

He perched almost daintily on the edge of an armchair. "I know how lazy cops are. They're going to figure I took a run at Troncosa. I need you to convince them otherwise."

"You haven't convinced me yet. You have reasons to want Troncosa dead. Maybe you think he had something to do with Ruby's murder. Maybe you hate him because he had Ruby and you didn't, even if he thought she was a princess named Natalie."

"That spic didn't have her. He's got geetus I couldn't make if I ran every legit joint in California, but he never had Ruby."

"How do you know that?"

"She told me."

"She told you what, exactly? And when?"

He leaned forward and looked me in the eye. I stared right back. I was mad. After all, I'd been asleep in my cozy bed.

"You ask a lot of questions," he said.

"And you're asking for favors."

"If I tell you, you'll talk to your buddy Morrow?"

"If your story makes sense."

"It makes sense all right." He stood up. Time for more laps. "Ruby dumped me after we got in trouble at a big house in the hills a while back."

"When Addison Rice banned you?"

"Christ. Who told you?"

"Addison. He mentioned narcotics and prostitution."

"Ruby was never part of that." Tommy jabbed two fingers at me, throttling his cigarette. "I took her there to enjoy herself. And she did. So did Addison's friends. Until he caught wise, made a lot of noise. I laughed it off. Plenty of parties up there looking for the entertainments I can provide. But Ruby wasn't happy about it. She finally figured out I wasn't enough of a gentleman for her. Said she could do better than me. Hell, I'd been telling her that from the start." He stopped walking the floor and smoothed his hair. This time it behaved. "About three weeks ago, she shows up at the club. Needs to talk. First time I saw her with dark hair. I preferred her as a blonde. Suited her personality. She fills me in on what she's been up to, playing at being a princess. I was kinda proud of her. I'd seen this Natalie's name in the papers, thought about inviting her to my club."

"But Ruby wasn't there to brag."

Tommy spit away a fleck of tobacco. "Yeah. Turns out some private detective name of Beckett found out what she was doing. She'd gotten her hooks into Troncosa as well as a picture director called Minot. Beckett was strong-arming her into taking them and anyone else for all she could lay her hands on."

"What did she want you to do?"

"Exert some pressure of my own. Lean on Beckett, let him know Ruby had friends. Who know how to deal with blackmailers."

"What went wrong?"

Tommy's brow beetled. "Fucking Beckett."

"Pardon your French."

"Fucking Beckett did his legwork. He was ready for me. He knew the cops Rice had acting as muscle when he read me the riot act. Beckett had them primed to talk at his say so. Would've loused up my plans to expand into legitimate areas. A certain shadiness most people don't mind. Ask your pal Addison. But drugs? Girls? That's low class. And I've got a deal for a new place cooking. With some Rotarians, for Christ's sake."

"Ruby must not have taken the news you weren't going to lift a finger for her very well."

The burning end of his cigarette swung in my direction. "I lifted a finger. I'd have lifted my whole goddamned hand if she asked. I told her I'd say to hell with the Rotarians. Pansies, the lot of them. She said she had another way."

"Did she say what it was?"

"Yeah, and I told her it'd never fly. Minot was wrapped around her finger. She was banking on him getting her in at his studio. Minot was going to direct her in a screen test—as Princess Natalie. She'd wow 'em, sign a contract, and let Lodestar security handle Beckett."

It didn't sound like such a harebrained scheme to me. It would have given Ruby leverage with Beckett, and it explained why she'd strung Laurence along. Malice against Diana had nothing to do with it; Edith had been right yet again. "That test would have been something to see," I said. "I wish she'd pulled it off."

"I don't. She'd have been Natalie for good. Like Ruby never existed." A silence overtook Tommy. He stared at a stain on the wall the exact size and shape of a T-bone steak hurled in anger. "But Minot wasn't interested in her talents. Not her acting talents, anyway. If he only knew she was running a sandy on him. He's another mug I'd like to get my hands on."

It was no idle threat; the air around Tommy crackled with violence. I groped behind me for the doorknob.

"I should have beaten Beckett to death when I had the

chance." Tommy said it ruefully, the way I'd regret not buying a discounted dress. "Solved everyone's problems at once."

"Do you think Beckett killed Ruby?"

"If Ruby tried to put one over on him, he'd pop her and leave her with the trash. Tell Morrow that."

"I'll give him your side of the story. Whether he believes it is up to him."

"Don't bother telling where you saw me. I'll be shoving off a second after you leave."

"Sticking close?"

"For a spell. But Mexico's a hop, skip, and a jump away. Caliente's nice this time of year."

"I hear it's nice any time of year."

"Ruby always liked it. You could have come along on one of our trips if you'd been nicer to me."

VI SAID NOTHING as she drove me home, giving me time to absorb Tommy's story. I couldn't dislodge Gene's words from my mind: anybody who knew Ruby and Natalie were one and the same fell under greater suspicion. Tommy had made that knowledge the centerpiece of his tale. In trying to clear his name, he'd only dug himself in deeper.

Outside Mrs. Quigley's, Vi turned to me. "I told you he loved her."

"You were listening at the door."

"I couldn't listen to that singer they found." She gnawed on her lower lip. "I may not be seeing you again. It's time for me to head back to Seattle. I'm not cut out for life down here."

I opened the car door. "If you're tough enough to see Tommy for who he is, you're tough enough to wait out these fools in casting. Do me a favor, Hazel. Don't head north just yet. Opportunity is effort's reward."

26

I'D ABOUT READIED myself for my return to Tremayne's when Mrs. Quigley beat a tattoo brimming with brio on my door. I soon saw why. In each hand she held an ultramarine glass globe overflowing with pink and white petunias.

"Two bouquets!" she bubbled. "But only one card."

Lillian,

Thinking of you after your ordeal. Give the second arrangement to your boss as a peace offering.

EH

It was a lovely gesture as well as a shrewd one. Typical of Edith. But I didn't see why I should inconvenience myself ferrying flowers on the streetcar to a man who *hadn't* been shot at, so on my windowsills both vases remained. My flat never looked so homey.

A team of glaziers coaxed Tremayne's new display window into its frame. I took their labors as a sign that life goes on, new days dawn, and other such optimistic hokum. The era of good feeling lasted three full minutes, until Mr. Valentine beckoned me to his ersatz office. The thought struck me: *I should have brought the petunias.*

He was wedged behind his desk in the stock room, mask of tragedy face in place. Actors aren't the only ones who have performances to repeat. As he delivered lines clearly familiar to him, my internal elevator began its downward plunge.

"We need to talk."

I smiled, hoping he'd respond in kind. He did not. The elevator's brakes failed to catch, the car continuing its plummet to the bottom of the shaft.

"Mrs. Tremayne spoke with me last evening. I'm sure you know how supportive she is of her employees. The elocution lessons, the tearoom discount, that's all her doing."

A last-ditch lunge at the emergency brake. "She's very generous. It's one of the reasons I love working here."

"Even her generosity has its limits. Those limits have been reached." He semaphored his distress with his handkerchief, a shock of tangerine. "I'm afraid we're letting you go, Lillian."

The cable snapped. Just like that, I'd failed at two careers.

"Because of the window?"

"The window was merely the last straw. Other recent incidents contributed, like your frequent absences. I explained to Mrs. Tremayne that you were a promising employee, but the decision wasn't mine."

"You couldn't have fired me over the phone and saved me streetcar fare?" I aimed for a joking tone but could hear the anger in my voice when my words hit the air. I'd traveled thousands of miles alone, realized I was unsuited to be an actress, and found a niche for myself at Tremayne's. Now I was out on my ear with zero prospects. Worse, I was venting my frustration on Mr. Valentine, who'd at least pled my case to the gorgon whose name hung over the door.

My now-former boss, unflappable to the last, reached into his pocket and retrieved a quarter. "For the streetcar. When you land on your feet, Lillian, I hope you'll continue to shop at Tremayne's."

I took the coin. From now on, every cent counted.

• • •

I RETURNED TO Ladies' Foundations for a valedictory tour. A stack of slips had been knocked askew. I made no move to straighten it. It was no longer my responsibility. Instead I called Gene, determined to accomplish *something* this morning.

"Thank God," he said. "When there were no messages waiting, I feared the worst."

"I figured what Tommy Carpa told me last night would keep." I heard Gene's chair squeak as he leaned forward. My story didn't take long to relay. "Tommy made it plain he wasn't about to stay where he was, so don't give me grief about not telephoning right away."

"I wasn't going to. Is everything all right? You sound tense."

"Being fired will do that to you."

"What? That's a hell of a thing. Does Tremayne's think you shot out that window yourself? I'm sorry, Lillian. I truly am. What will you do now?"

"The very question I'm pondering. You know any department stores that need a salesgirl?"

"Let me ask around."

"You're serious?"

"I don't have department store connections, but I know other people. I'll honestly be able to tell them what a hard worker you are by the effort you put into doing my job. I'll do whatever I can for you."

I was touched. "That would be swell. Thank you."

On my way to bid adieu to the salesladies, I straightened the stack of slips. Once a Catholic girl, always a Catholic girl. God and Mrs. Tremayne were watching.

"WHAT BRINGS YOU hither in the middle of the day?" Kay had a pencil behind her ear.

"Explaining will take several minutes."

She ushered me into a *Modern Movie* office empty of people but full of trophies. Golf, tennis, you name it. "Welcome to the inner sanctum of Max Bittner. He's worried being an editor at a fan magazine is a feminine occupation and wants to show he's all man. As if pinching the secretaries wasn't enough. He's never touched me, I've noticed. Your timing is impeccable. Guess what I just found out?"

Her mile-wide grin told me her news was happier than mine. "Gable's getting divorced?"

"Better than that. I've been assigned my first story. A feature, no less. With a byline."

"That's fantastic!" I gave her a hug. "A year of checking punctuation and they finally realized what a great writer you are. What's the story?"

"You're going to love this. Your pal Addison Rice. I suggested we do the piece you ran past him. America's number-one movie fan, host to the stars. *Modern Movie* and Addison both went for it! No mention of Tommy and Ruby, of course. But here's the kicker. I've been invited to his next party!"

My smile, sincere though it was, became a pain to hold in place. "Consider me officially jealous. What's the theme? Do you have to dress like Thomas Jefferson and go on a scavenger hunt?"

"Oh, it's worse than that. It's a 'come as you are' party. Addison sent photographers with the invitations. Your picture's snapped as you get the envelope, and that's how you have to show up. They caught me yesterday with this lousy pencil behind my ear. Now nobody will let me take it out. At least I had on a nice dress. That paprika one, with the brown collar and belt? That's what I'll be wearing come Saturday night."

"You're lucky. If they'd gone to Mrs. Lindros's you could have been wearing an apron with flour all over your hands."

"I feel queasy just contemplating that. Now what are you doing here?"

My tale of woe made it Kay's turn to hug me. "And here I am gloating. I feel like a heel. What are you going to do?"

"Cry in my tap water then read the help wanted ads."

"The want ads are for saps. I'll get word to Ready and send up some smoke signals of my own."

Ruby had tipped me to the fact months ago. *In this town, mermaid, it's who you know.*

"What about Edith Head?" Kay asked. "She could get you into Paramount easy."

"Doing what? I can't draw a lick."

"They have other departments. It's a movie studio, you know. They make pictures there. Use her ready ear to promote yourself a position."

It was a savvy suggestion, one I'd file away for future reference. "First Edith would probably like to hear about last night's run-in with Tommy Carpa."

Kay planted herself behind Max Bittner's desk. Aside from the portion of her face obscured by a loving cup won at a La Monica Ballroom dance contest, she looked very editorial. "You've been holding out. Dish."

ON THE WAY home I picked up the afternoon papers, the brutal execution of Tremayne's display window on every front page. Kay may have lacked faith in the want ads, but a girl had to start somewhere. Mrs. Quigley, sweeping the front steps with more élan than elbow grease, nodded at the bundle under my arm. "Sending news of your exploits to the folks?"

"That's right." No sense alarming her about my ability to pay the rent yet.

Inside I changed into a faded green housedress, hem drooping in despondency, and an old gray sweatshirt. The knock came halfway through the first HELP WANTED—FEMALE column. Vi burst into the apartment. "They're out of their minds at that store, letting you go."

I shut the door behind her. "Hush. I don't want Mrs. Quigley to know. How'd you find out?"

"I'd been thinking about last night, so I phoned Tremayne's hoping we could have lunch. Some stuffy fellow told me 'Miss Frost is no longer in Tremayne's employ.'"

"Yes, I'm a lady of leisure now, reading the want ads and realizing I have no skills that will land me a job."

"I know a nightclub that needs a new waitress."

"You quit? Good for you!"

"Tommy won't agree. But nuts to him, anyway."

"Then we should both be checking the paper."

"Find me a nice secretarial position. The kind where the boss marries me within a year."

"I circled one of those earlier."

"What pretty flowers! Hey, you've got two!"

"Want one? I was supposed to give one away." And should have. Currying favor with Mr. Valentine might not have warded off the ax, but it wouldn't have hurt. In Edith I had the equivalent of a fairy godmother, yet I had shunned her guidance.

As Vi lifted a vase, the strap on her green jumper slipped. She tugged it back over the sleeve of her blouse. "This never fit. I shouldn't have bought the darn thing."

"It's adorable. Your problem is your bosom is too big."

"Too big? First time I ever heard that." She adjusted the opposite strap before it tumbled.

"If you moved the buttons down that wouldn't happen."

"You're one to be giving fashion advice. You look like something the cat wouldn't bother to drag in."

We started perusing the ads, the situations situation so dire

I was overjoyed when another knock heralded the next visitor to darken my doorstep. He was a short man who looked like he'd been forced into semi-decent seersucker at gunpoint. A sheen of exertion glowed on his broad forehead.

"Lillian Frost?" When I confirmed, he exhaled in relief. "You're a tough one to track down."

"Why are you looking for me?"

Up snapped his arm with Prussian precision, an envelope in his hand. "To deliver this."

He stepped back at the same time. I trailed him into the corridor without thinking about it. "What is it?"

"Open it and see."

Another strategic retreat accompanied the instruction, and still I kept following. I heard Vi charging across the floor as I took the envelope. The deliveryman's eyes shifted toward the stairs. I sensed motion there an instant too late.

The world went white as Vi reached me. Only the feel of creamy vellum paper kept me anchored to the earth.

"What's happening?" That was Vi.

"You're pulling my leg." Another voice, not the deliveryman's but somehow familiar.

The light from the flashbulb faded by degrees. The first thing I saw was the writing on the card, which my fingers had automatically extracted from the envelope. Across the top were two words. *Say cheese.* Underneath, an address I recognized.

My next thoughts were twinned. *I am being invited to Addison Rice's party. And I look like hell.*

Vi snatched the card from my fingertips. The world continued to reassert itself. I hadn't been hallucinating. The stairwell shutterbug not only sounded like Ken Nolan, he looked like him, too.

"You're back," I said to him. "Have you seen Beckett?"

"No. And whatever you do, don't let on you saw me."

The deliveryman turned to Ken. "You know this one?"

"She got me eighty-sixed from Paramount. She's the reason I had to take this cockamamie job."

"Don't blame me," I said. "You're the one who got mixed up in Ruby's shenanigans."

"And don't knock the job, either." The deliveryman gripped his lapels. "Money is money."

"Can somebody tell me what's going on?" Vi studied the card she'd taken from me. "You're being invited to a party?"

"That's right, girlie," Addison's postman said. "Only proviso is you come as you are right this minute."

"But I'm a mess." I held my arms out from my sides.

Ken snorted as he reached into his camera bag. "Serves you right for answering the door dressed like Ma Kettle."

"And we've got the picture to prove it," the deliveryman said. "If you're not wearing what you've got on now, back down the hill you'll go."

"Am I in the picture, too?" Vi asked. "I didn't see the flashbulb pop, so I was probably looking the wrong way."

Ken's hand snaked out of the bag toward his camera. I glimpsed the bulb concealed in his fingers and realized what he was up to. I pulled Vi back inside my apartment and slammed the door as Ken leaped forward.

"Vi *is* in the photo, isn't she?" I hollered through the closed door.

"I am? Does that mean I get to go to the party, too?"

Ken and his partner held a whispered conference in the hall as Vi began bouncing in excitement, sending both of her jumper straps sagging.

"Tell me the truth, Ken. Can you even see what I'm wearing? Is that why you were trying to take another photo?"

His sigh carried through reasonably solid oak. "I won't know until I print it. But Blondie was all over you."

"Look, miss, we're going to need another photo," the deliveryman wheedled. "Won't take a minute."

"Nothing doing." Vi stood with her hands on her hips, spoiling for a fight, buxom flyweight division. "We've got the invite. You've got the photo. We're coming as we are and taking our chances."

Another hushed squabble in the hall, ended by Kenneth's associate. "We don't have time to argue. We got too many of these damn envelopes to deliver."

"Is the name Minot on your list?" I yelled.

"We hit that pile yesterday." The deliveryman cackled. "That'll be some picture. The wife mad as a hornet in her gardening clothes, the husband laughing his ass off while ogling the neighbor lady."

27

BARNEY GROFF EMERGED from Edith Head's office like a sword from a scabbard, steely and ready to inflict damage. He puffed on an excessively fragrant cigar and glowered at me, trying to remember why he'd chosen to forget my name.

Edith followed him out, features as always imperturbable. The square neckline of her black dress showcased a loop of gold supporting a large amber stone. As Groff stalked off, Edith apologized for making me wait. It wasn't like I had anywhere else to be. Besides, I needed time to figure out how to slip my ulterior motive into the conversation.

Once Vi and I had been certain that Ken and his cohort were gone, we'd emptied my closet of its contents and laid the pickings on the bed. All things considered, my best option would be wrapping myself in the duvet.

Vi held up an ash-blue rayon gown with shirred sleeves and a tie back sash. I'd worn it to my first nightclub, and every formal event since. "Is this your only gown?"

"It was the latest thing three years ago."

She patted my arm. "It's had a swell run. But three years is a long time."

"I have to look my best for Addison's party. A Gimbels special circa 1934 won't cut it." That's when I got the bright idea to pick Edith's brain for fashion advice, provided I could find a way to broach the subject.

Edith waved me into a chair. "First things first. Did you really throw yourself in front of a bullet for Armand Troncosa?"

"Hardly. I threw myself on the ground and let the bullets fall where they may."

"Smart girl."

Edith had been tracking the scant developments in the papers. I passed along the tidbits I'd gleaned from Gene: both Winton Beckett and Tommy Carpa still unpresent and unaccounted for; inconsistencies in Armand Troncosa's itinerary making it conceivable he was in Los Angeles when Ruby was killed; Diana and Laurence denying any knowledge of Beckett.

"So an abundance of suspects," Edith said. "Marvelous."

"Maybe Gene was right to focus on Laurence if Beckett has the goods on him."

"That doesn't mean Mr. Minot killed Ruby. There's another possibility. Ruby was likely pressuring him to film her screen test if she viewed it as her escape hatch." Edith polished her glasses. "Suppose her imprecations succeeded."

"You—you think Laurence *already* shot the test?"

"Wasn't that his play when he attempted to sway you? He boasted he could arrange your test with one phone call. Wouldn't he do likewise for a woman he was involved with intimately? If such footage exists, it would expose Mr. Minot as a fool—and link him conclusively to a murdered girl."

"Could Beckett have the test in his possession?"

"No, the footage—again, if it exists—is at Lodestar Pictures. Where no one understands its significance because the actress featured is identified as Natalie Szabo, not Ruby Carroll. But knowledge of its existence would be sufficient for Mr. Beckett to blackmail Mr. Minot."

Edith was not merely theorizing a ticking time bomb that could destroy Laurence's career. She was suggesting that in a vault off Western Avenue lay a few feet of celluloid representing

Ruby's final screen appearance—and my sole chance to meet Natalie. I knew I'd do anything to clap eyes on it, the prospect propelling me from my seat. "You've got to tell Gene."

"I'm afraid I can do nothing of the sort. You saw Mr. Groff's histrionic exit. He none too subtly informed me the studios are monitoring Detective Morrow's investigation. If word were to get out about police interest in the test, some unscrupulous employee at Lodestar might dispose of it to spare them the publicity."

"That can't happen!" I didn't realize I'd yelled until Edith gripped my hand to console me.

"It won't. I'll try to confirm the test exists. Quietly. That may take time, though, and my concern is Mr. Minot will become desperate and attempt to destroy the footage himself. If only we could keep an eye on him."

I seized the segue. "I have a chance to see Laurence this weekend." I told her about Addison's invitation and my resultant dilemma.

"I don't see the problem. If your clothes can't be seen in the photo, your options are endless."

"There's the rub. Nothing I own suits the occasion."

Edith peered at me in disappointment, having no truck with transparent self-pity. "You're completely wrong. It's not a debutante ball, for goodness sake. It's a Hollywood party. Calling attention to yourself is the last thing you want to do."

"So I don't have to wear a fabulous gown?"

"I forbid you to."

"Right. Dungarees and a halter top it is."

"Don't be ludicrous. All day long actresses are forced into the frippery people like me design for them." She pulled out her sketchbook and paged to a drawing of an elaborate Elizabethan gown. "A laced corset, hoops, and five pounds of skirts. After wearing something like that for hours, the emphasis is on comfort while still looking good. Understatement, that's the order of the evening."

She removed her glasses and inspected me. "Turn around." After I'd executed my three-sixty, she nodded. "Slacks. Definitely."

"To a party?"

"High-waisted linen slacks, a gold or silver belt, a silk blouse, a low-heeled shoe. You'll blend in perfectly."

I pictured myself so attired. Cocktail in one hand, the other poised to accept the offer of a dance with a handsome stranger. Then reality intruded.

"Too bad I don't have any high-waisted linen slacks. Only these old cotton ones. And I don't remember seeing a silk blouse in my closet." I flopped back into the chair, throwing my legs over the side.

"Enough moping." Edith then uttered words I never dreamed she'd say. "Perhaps we could take a page from Ruby's book."

TWENTY MINUTES LATER I stood before the mirror in Travis Banton's salon, posing in a white silk button-down blouse as light as an angel's kiss and dark brown linen slacks that gave me the appearance of a lower order Vanderbilt.

Edith prowled around, making minute adjustments. "A girl your height, you're lucky we found something to work with. You'll see Bill at this soiree with his latest conquest. He's already asked me what color tie he should wear and what corsage would complement it. You two will have to fill me in on what everyone else wore." She couldn't mask the wistful note in her voice.

"You must be invited to events like these constantly."

"No, never. I'm too busy to attend anyway." She stepped back to appraise her efforts. "You could give Garbo a run for her money."

"I prefer Dietrich."

"Ah, Marlene. I adore working with her. She understands the power of wardrobe. The last time she was here she brought Travis a kugel she'd baked herself. Can you imagine?"

"Is that how I stay on your good side, Edie? Bake you a kugel? Maybe you'd settle for a pound cake."

I turned to discover Barbara Stanwyck behind me. No longer the temptress of *Baby Face,* sleeping her way to the top of the Gotham Trust building and scandalizing the theaterful of jaded New Yorkers around me, the actress was rectitude personified in a tan bouclé suit with black trim and matching oversized buttons. Her long auburn hair was pulled back and she wore no makeup save lipstick, which made her look younger than she did onscreen. I somehow remained upright on the pedestal, a signature accomplishment in my life.

"Barbara, you're welcome with or without a gift," Edith said. "You're not here for a fitting."

"Just dropped by to say hello. No Travis?"

"Not today."

"He doesn't see me as a clotheshorse anyway. Is he . . . being a good boy?"

"He's doing his best," Edith said with a knowing look. I'd just been made privy to some confidence. I didn't know what, exactly, but something.

Remembering to breathe, I stepped down from the pedestal. Up close Barbara Stanwyck seemed small yet hardy, a piece of jetsam stripped to its strengths by its travels. She smiled, but her eyes retained a faint, permanent unease. Not the standard Hollywood stripe but the deeper variety of one who'd known turmoil and expected more of the same. "Pleased to meet you. I'm Barbara."

Her accent was more pronounced in person, and in it I heard the clink of subway tokens. "Lillian. I'm from New York, too."

"You're not trying to take my place in pictures, are you?" Her throaty laugh was exactly as I'd heard it at the movies. "I'll put up a fight."

"Oh, no. I'm not an actress," I said, no doubt to her overwhelming relief.

"Lillian wanted to know what I thought of this outfit for Addison Rice's party this weekend," Edith said.

"Will you be there, Lillian? We'll have to have a drink. Whatever Edie's advice is, take it. She found a way to give the suits they always put me in some flair so I don't look like I'm out collecting for the Salvation Army. If she says wear hip waders and an Indian headdress, don't argue. You'll be the most fashionable girl there."

"What do you think of this?" Edith lifted a hand in my direction. "Casual, but just so."

"It's lovely. Beats my getup. Thanks to Addison's antics, I'll be looking like a fugitive from a circus tent."

"What will you be wearing?" I asked.

"You'll see on Saturday. I'll be hard to miss." She shook her head. "'Come as you are.' Oh, brother."

I WAS BEHIND the Japanese screen changing back into a pumpkin when I heard the door open. Peeking around the corner I saw Adele Balkan in earnest conversation with Edith.

Dressed, I stepped out from behind the screen as Edith said, "Tell Howard I'll take care of it. Again."

She looked to me as Adele hurried from the room. "When are you due at Tremayne's?"

"That's a long story."

"I don't like the sound of that. May I impose upon you to come with me? I could use your help."

"Of course. Where are we going?"

"That's another long story. Why don't we take turns enlightening each other in my car?"

I had barely settled myself when she pointed her sedan at Gower and let fly. "What's our secret mission?"

"To locate Travis. Adele received a call from Howard Greer. He ran the department before Travis and hired me on. Howard has his own salon in Hollywood. He and Travis enjoy a few drinks now and again."

"And sometimes more than a few?"

"Precisely. That's where the trouble starts. They were out all night. Howard offered Travis a ride home, but Travis said he'd rather take the streetcar. Last month we found him shuttling to Santa Monica and back. Having a lovely time, he said. Never mind I was sick with worry."

"Riding the streetcar with a snootful doesn't sound so bad."

"Travis's reputation has suffered enough. The studio's already weary of his cavalier behavior. This will be another black mark against his name, unless we find him first and pour several gallons of hot coffee into him."

"You want to protect him."

"Travis is the best designer in pictures, perhaps ever. I've learned more from him than I could ever hope to repay." She glanced over at me. "I take it you've heard otherwise about our relationship."

"Just gossip. But if Travis were let go, wouldn't you be top choice to replace him?"

"Unlikely." She set her jaw and kept her eyes on the road. "Lead designer is a role to be cast like any other, and the thinking is I lack the star power. I'm a woman and I came up through the ranks. I don't have the requisite status, the pedigree. Howard began with Lady Duff Gordon. I grew up in a Nevada mining camp, tying scarves on burros that happened by. Travis had his own studio in New York, designing for Ziegfeld and society women. Mary Pickford married Douglas Fairbanks in a Banton original. My career began dressing elephants in *The Wanderer*. I used real fruit and flowers in the garlands. The beasts ate them all before the cameras started rolling."

I couldn't help it. I laughed. Edith mustered a tight smile as the car continued rocketing forward.

"The studio is already auditioning replacements for Travis and they're holding true to form. They've brought Ernest Dryden out from New York. He's designing Bing Crosby's next picture." She chuckled darkly. "Ernest made his reputation on *The Garden of Allah*, but those are all Travis's gowns. Dietrich loathed Ernest's designs and insisted Travis take over. Travis did Ernest's best work, and Ernest may well end up replacing him."

"Maybe you can stay on with Mr. Dryden."

"No. New brooms sweep clean. I'm too associated with Travis. I'll go where he goes, provided he'll have me. And if he doesn't, well, I can always dust off my teaching credential and go back to giving French lessons." She didn't sound enthused by the idea. "I do wish Travis would stay here. If only he'd settle down."

Edith squinted through the windshield. "There's a streetcar ahead. Keep your eyes peeled. If he's not on this one we'll wait at the Santa Monica turnaround and pray he didn't switch to another line."

The streetcar rattled past, hissing. I couldn't pick Travis Banton out of a lineup but doubted he resembled the only male passenger aboard, a burly man in coveralls with a bag of tools under his arm.

Edith glanced up, too, and quickly corrected our drift into the next lane in response to my ladylike yelp of terror. "We weren't even close to hitting that truck. On to Santa Monica it is. Tell me about Tremayne's. Did the flowers help?"

"Tremayne's and I are past flowers." When I finished my story, Edith shook her head in something miles from sympathy.

"I must say I'm surprised, Lillian, coming in downcast over not having anything to wear to this party when loss of steady income is of substantially more import."

"I know, but—" Any excuse would wither under Edith's scrutiny. "The party is Saturday night."

"We've solved that problem. Now, about your career. Are you considering positions outside of retail?"

"I'm up for anything from rodeo clown to fan dancer."

"What do you think about working in Wardrobe? Securing you a position could be one of my last acts at Paramount. No special treatment, mind you. You'd be picking up pins off the floor like everyone else. It's a good way to learn the business."

"But I can't draw. Or sew."

"It's not talent that matters in this work but drive. And you're not lacking in that. I offer myself as a case in point. I would ask you to keep this incident under your hat as I'm not exactly proud of it. I was a student when Howard Greer placed an ad for sketch artists. I knew he prized versatility, so I brought along plenty of sketches and was hired on the spot."

"That's wonderful. But as I said, I can't draw."

"If I might finish . . . not all the sketches were mine. I borrowed some from my classmates—"

"And passed them off as your own? You *lied* your way into Paramount?"

Her look would have sent a charging bull up a tree. "No, I did not. I explicitly told Mr. Greer, 'This is what we're doing at school.' And it was. Once I'd gotten the job, I worked harder than anyone else. What matters is I created the opportunity."

It was impossible to contemplate a job offer at breakneck speed. "Let me think about it," I said.

"Thinking about it is a luxury you can't afford. The world

says no on a regular basis. It's up to you to say yes. Here's another streetcar."

We stopped at a traffic light with the streetcar on our left. I clambered into the backseat. A dapper man sat with his arm on the window ledge as if he were grand marshal in a parade. He waggled his fingers at me then touched the brim of his straw boater. "Good morning!" he called.

"We may be in luck," I told Edith.

The gent's gaze shifted to her. "I'll be damned. Edie, is that you?"

"Travis!" Edith replied. "Stay right there."

Horn blaring, she scissored across the right lane and pulled into a parking space. We bailed out and sprinted to the next streetcar stop. Panting, I pulled myself aboard.

Travis Banton rose, the picture of pickled dignity in a gray suit with a blue striped tie, both slightly withered after a night's revelry. He had a puggish nose and full lips that unfurled in a smile. "What a lovely surprise." He snatched a handrail as the streetcar started forward again. "Will you ladies accompany me on my excursion?"

"We'll sit awhile, Travis." Edith wiped off her spectacles.

"It's a beautiful run. Busy streets yielding to the quiet of the beach, serenity only a few stops away. We'll finish with a swim. The very thing on such a day." He took a nip from a silver flask then held it out to me.

"Not until the sun passes the yardarm," I said.

Knowing not to offer any to Edith, Banton downed another slug then stowed the flask. "I don't believe I've had the pleasure of making your acquaintance."

"This is Lillian Frost. Why don't I drive us all back to the studio?"

"This conveyance is smoother. I've ridden with you before. And what about our day at the beach?"

"Right now we should get you back to work. A line of actresses awaits your singular magic." The flattery sounded forced in Edith's delivery.

"Along with spying eyes, reporting my every false move. It's no life for us artistic types. And you could take care of those temperamental ladies with one hand behind your back."

"They don't want me, Travis. They want you."

Banton stared intently at Edith, as if trying to gaze through her glasses into her soul. But the lenses were too thick. He abandoned that enterprise and grinned at me.

"What say you, Miss Frost? Shall I return to the studio, home to ceaseless toil and friends like faithful Edith? Or carry on with my poor man's holiday?"

"The Pacific isn't going anywhere," I said.

"Miss Frost, you are as wise as you are tall." He stood with the grandeur of a surrendering general and pulled the bell cord. "Driver! We shall disembark here. This world will not glamorize itself."

28

"STOP FIDGETING. YOU'RE making me carsick."

"I'm not fidgeting, Vi. I'm preventing wear on these clothes." I adjusted the gold chain belt adorning my Paramount-issued slacks. We were doubled up in the backseat of Ready's car en route to Addison Rice's soiree. I'd been to parties before. I wasn't fidgeting. Honest.

Kay swiveled in her forward perch, pencil in position behind her ear. "I'm warning you two. I'm staying 'til the bitter end, so if you get bored find your own way home."

"Bored? I don't plan on being bored," Vi said.

"She's in the Prince Charming market," I added.

"Too bad I'm dressed like Cinderella before the ball."

The straps on Vi's jumper were down for the night. The extra glimpse of peaches and cream skin would hopefully prevent anyone from noticing she'd relocated the garment's troublesome buttons. "Oh, knock it off," I said. "You look lovely."

"But am I de-lovely? Say, didn't Bob Hope introduce that song on Broadway? Think he'll be here tonight?" With her clear soprano, Vi trilled the chorus of Cole Porter's hit.

Kay cut her off. "Can you hyenas keep it down? I need to prepare."

"Sorry, Mother."

Anticipation mounted along with Ready's car as we scaled the hillside. Once through the gates of Addison's estate fairy lights twinkled in the trees like celestial escorts guiding us heavenward.

"Reckon you could fire a cannon in Hollywood tonight and not nick anyone's ride." Ready eased us out of a long queue of cars waiting to discharge their passengers and expertly maneuvered into a tight squeeze of a parking spot.

"And I thought horses were your specialty," I said.

"Most fellers who hire on for parking detail don't know squat about motor vehicles. And we don't have time to wait. Kay has work to do. Don't you, honey?"

A slamming door was her response. Ready loped after her. Vi and I indulged in some last second preening, then joined the guests streaming through the massive front door into the foyer.

"I'd better not be the most ridiculously dressed person here tonight," Vi fumed.

One glance at the reception room walls, papered with the candid photographs snapped by Ken and his associates, indicated Vi would be spared that indignity. It was quite the gallery, luminaries with startled mugs looking like they'd been served a subpoena rather than an invitation. In the distance I spotted a monumental top hat straight out of Lewis Carroll, garnished with a deep purple ribbon. Addison, naturally, was underneath it. He greeted each of his guests warmly and then, with a sotto voce pointer from Mrs. Somers, steered them either left or right to compare their current attire to that in the photograph. I wondered if he'd dare send anyone scurrying home for not matching their two-dimensional selves, and decided he would. Addison took his frivolity seriously.

He slapped a tall man in tennis whites on the back. Before I could confirm it was Cary Grant, it was our turn.

"The guest of honor!" Addison cried. "Survivor of the Battle of Tremayne's Gulch." He twiddled his fingers on the brim of his hat. "Like the topper? Easiest way for folks to find me in the forest of folderol."

"I love it. Thank you for inviting me even though I lied to you about being a reporter."

"Nonsense. Your stunt put me in mind of Torchy Blane. Glenda Farrell is sensational in those pictures. She's here somewhere." He drew me aside so we could speak in confidence. "The invitation is my way of thanking you. Detective Morrow explained you advocated on my behalf and helped keep my name out of the papers."

"I was happy to do it."

"I only wish you didn't have to. As God is my witness, I believed Ruby and Natalie were two different girls. Maybe I should come out of retirement. All this leisure is making my brain go to pot along with my belly." He patted his ample midsection. "After all you've been through it would be criminal to deny you entry. But rules are rules."

With a pained smile from the swollen Mrs. Somers, he led us to the photo Ken had taken and inspected it with a mock stern expression. The image depicted an ungainly scrum of two bodies, my eyes huge with confusion as Vi vaulted to my aid. I was baffled, Vi eager; Ken had admirably captured us in our natural states. Part of my bare calf was visible, as was a hint of coarse gray sweatshirt sleeve.

Addison tutted. "Your comely friend looks the same, but I don't believe that's your blouse peeking out from behind her."

"Oh, I can vouch for her," Vi said. "Lillian always wears silk at home. She positively lounges in it."

Addison rubbed each of his chins in sequence. "Given the inconclusive evidence, the court has no choice but to decide on your behalf. Go in and enjoy yourselves! Lillian, we'll discuss your adventure at length once you have a few drinks in you."

The reception room opened onto the vast slate patio where I'd sipped iced tea with Addison. Two well-stocked bars now stood sentry at either end. A few steps down the swimming pool, lit from beneath, didn't yet have any takers while four tentlike cabanas stood empty, their canvas sides pulled back with ties. To the right of the pool a dance floor had been laid over the grass. A swing band played while a couple dressed for golf made a valiant effort at a rumba, cleats clicking on parquetry. My eyes skimmed the crowd, illuminated by the occasional burst of a flashbulb courtesy of a roving band of photographers. Everywhere I looked there were beautiful people in bathrobes, shower caps and—

"There's a gorilla here," Vi said.

"It's someone in a suit. Either that or the poor brute was trained to guzzle martinis. He must have horned in on someone's snapshot, like you."

A flame-haired beauty passed us, the barely there towel around her held in place by a diamond brooch the size of salad plate. Famous faces and white-jacketed waiters alike brazenly studied her walk. She was such an eye-catcher even I ogled her, not noticing that Bill Ihnen had stopped by my side.

"Now *that*," he said, "is a safety pin."

"I bet she feels safer with it on."

"And I bet she takes it off before the night is over."

"Is it going to be that kind of party?" Vi asked.

"Would that bother you?"

"Are you kidding? That's why we're here."

Bill waved over a blonde on a chaise longue whose lavender orchid corsage, I noted, perfectly complemented Bill's tie. He'd taken Edith's advice. The blonde shook her head and pointed blame at her shoes. "My date," Bill said. "I don't think she's getting out of that chair. On her feet all day, dancing in Laurence Minot's latest inanity at Lodestar."

"The director of *Hearts in Spring* is on the guest list, along with his wife."

"Then I can tell him to stop being handsy with the chorines." He left with a wink and a promise to find us later.

"It's no fair," Vi said. "Besides that knockout in the towel, I've seen two girls in swimsuits and one in a nightie. But the men are covered up. Where are the physiques?"

"I see what you mean. Not a torso in sight." I nodded toward a broad back in a linen jacket. "How come he couldn't have been lying poolside when his invite showed up?"

"You've already seen him with his shirt off. It's Johnny Weissmuller. You know, Tarzan."

"That explains the gorilla."

We retrieved some martinis, already drunk on the atmosphere. The warm night air and paper lanterns lent a dreamlike aspect to the proceedings. By the time we circled the dance floor it had filled up nicely. A man with shaving cream on half his face fox-trotted carefully with a woman in pajamas. Bill had even persuaded his date to rise from her sick chair. She was a wonderful dancer—and so, to my surprise, was Bill.

"Excuse me, weren't you in the papers?"

I turned to see who'd addressed me and a blinding flash was my reward. At least this time I knew who it was.

As my eyes recovered, Ken Nolan lowered his camera but not his guard. "Hello, Frost. I see you and your friend made it past Cerberus at the door."

"Addison has a soft spot for me. Do you work for him now?"

"Tonight I do. Photographers at a party. I don't get it. Now everyone will be on their best behavior." He copped a coupe of champagne from a passing tray and downed it in one.

"None for me, thanks," I said.

"I have to keep my strength up. At least you two look like you're enjoying yourselves. Unlike those Gloomy Gusses yonder." He nodded across the dance floor. Armand Troncosa and Esteban Riordan stood side by side like they were at the rail at Santa Anita and had lost sight of the nag they'd gambled their bankroll on.

"Saw that cowboy friend of yours. Maybe I'll stalk him for a while." Ken drifted patioward, then about-faced and eyeballed my clothes with alarm. "Hang on. Where'd you get those duds?"

"There's Ready." I pointed. Ken turned. I snagged Vi's elbow and ran.

We worked our way back around the floor. Troncosa was dressed in a full riding habit while Esteban wore surprisingly dingy sweat clothes and a pained expression. Troncosa kissed my hand then Vi's once I introduced her. "I am pleased to see you out after the unpleasantness at the store," he said.

"Likewise. Where did Addison's army catch you?"

"I was about to participate in my usual polo match at the Vista Del Mar Athletic Club while Esteban did his pentathlon training. I must confess Addison's sense of humor eludes me. To be at such a function without a cravat . . ." He trailed off, mourning a bygone age. Esteban, meanwhile, looked ready to dig himself a hole and lie in it.

"You're not concerned someone may take another shot at you?"

"My sole concern, again, is should that unlikely event occur I will not be wearing a necktie. I must show my enemies a Troncosa is not easily cowed." He flashed his pearly whites at the night and then exclusively at Vi. "In my country, the best way to do that is to dance. Shall we?"

Vi made a noise at the back of her throat like a kitten being offered a plate of cream. As Troncosa took her hand, he turned to Esteban. "I'm afraid that much as I hate carrying it in the pocket of these trousers, I will require my cigarette case. Retrieve it from the car, would you?"

They spun onto the floor. Esteban seemed to shrink into his clothes. "Would that I were not guarding Armand so closely when that photographer arrived. I look and feel a fool. Ever since our polo triumph at the Berlin Olympiad, Armand has been pushing for Argentina's involvement in every sport. The pentathlon is mine. I would gladly fare worse in all five events if it meant not being in this ridiculous garb in front of you."

"You won't be saying that in Tokyo come 1940."

"Armand is clearly under great strain, because he neglected to compliment you. Permit me to do so. You look radiant. Would it be forward of me to ask in advance for a dance? I won't be running errands all evening."

"I would like that."

Another smile and he took his leave. I felt my cheeks redden. I wondered how rusty my tango steps were, then why I thought I knew any to get rusty in the first place.

A WAITER BEGGED me to relieve him of some of his burden of stuffed shrimp. Scarfing down sustenance, I spotted Diana and Laurence making a fashionably late entrance. Lodestar's ingénue was indeed outfitted in gardening togs—faded blue blouse, denim pants, thick gloves. The pièce de résistance was the floppy hat tied under her chin. Bleached from the sun and fraying at the edges, it was a chapeau no self-respecting scarecrow would deign to don. The only favor it did Diana was hiding the scowl directed at her husband. I watched the two of them squabble in pantomime until she caught me staring and nodded in recognition. I had no interest in interrupting them, so I smiled back and veered away.

A roar erupted from the crowd as the bandleader beckoned a woman forward. I couldn't make her out but didn't need to once she reached the microphone. Martha Raye, the radio star famed for her large mouth and offbeat song stylings, started bellowing her way through "Love in Bloom."

I would have gone down to enjoy the show were it not for a frantic blur of movement to my right. A dressed-for-the-links Bob Hope was signaling me with his fingers, his eyebrows, the tip of his nose—and the fact he'd stepped away from his handsome wife, Dolores, to do so gave me the impression he was trying to arrange an amorous assignation. I responded with a flurry of nonsensical gestures, indicating either to steal third base or meet me at the boathouse—Addison presumably had a boathouse—then beat a hasty retreat to the left.

That's when I spotted her. A wraithlike figure in the shadows at the side of the house, the pale white of her gown adding to her spectral presence. I only saw her from behind. Her hair was lighter than it had been the last time I'd laid eyes on her, but not as blond as when we'd shared a room.

Ruby.

The breath halted in my throat. I was happy I'd listened to Edith and worn slacks, otherwise my gooseflesh would have been visible.

The woman took another step, and the darkness spilling onto the lawn from the house claimed her. I sprinted in pursuit, swerving around a waiter and a cackling pair of drunkards.

I rounded the corner. The woman—it wasn't Ruby, it couldn't be—had paused by a window. Her back still to me, right hand on her hip as she gazed up at the night sky as if to curse it. I willed myself to inch forward, found my voice in its hiding spot near the base of my spine.

"H-hello?"

The first hint of the woman's profile shattered the spell, her nose too sharp. By the time I could see the entirety of her vulpine features, made bleary by drink, I understood how I had been fooled.

Gertrude Michael, the actress who portrayed Sophie Lang and whose clothes Ruby had stolen, peered at me. Her eyes gleamed dully like pennies fished out of the bottom of the bowl. A tumbler dangled from her fingers.

"Excuse me," I said. "I thought you were someone else."

The smile came to her lips too easily, the consonants with too much effort. "That's the trouble. I'm always me. Some party, isn't it? Don't know a soul here." She shook her glass, the ice rattling like disinterred bones. "Could you freshen this up for me, sweetie?"

I nodded, left her where she was, and flagged down a waiter for directions to the powder room. As I walked up to the door a woman exited, mascara streaked halfway to her chin.

Good Lord, I thought. *I'm finding nothing but winners tonight.* I played Samaritan and asked if she was all right.

"Just ducky." Her smile was as broad as Park Avenue. "I was crying when Addison's boys handed me the invitation. I'm not crying anymore." She kissed me on the lips and plunged back into the party.

Ah, Hollywood.

AFTER A FEW moments at a sink large enough to wash a Great Dane in, I ventured outside again. I made a slow perambulation of the house's perimeter, hearing occasional whispers from lovers who had slipped away for a few moments of solitude. The party had become a living thing, sprawling across Addison's property, the occasional pop of a flashbulb like a nerve firing. One of them burst some distance ahead, its light scarcely illuminating the figure skulking in the shadows a few yards from me. If it weren't for his haystack hair and vulgar suit I might have missed him entirely.

Give this to Winton Beckett. He'd shown up at a come-as-you-are party as a low-rent private eye, albeit one without an invitation judging from how he shied away from the guests. He angled with purpose toward the cabanas surrounding the pool.

I did the only thing I could think of. I followed him.

29

THE CABANAS WERE finally being put to use. The ties holding back the sides of the one Beckett approached had been undone. He listened outside the canvas walls a moment then entered, the fabric falling into place behind him.

I maintained a suitable distance. As if I had any inkling what a suitable distance was. With every step I glanced around in search of a friendly face. Some of the burly gents in suits were undoubtedly off-duty police officers hired by Addison to provide security, but none of them noticed me in my hour of need. Maybe if I'd been wearing a towel.

No sound escaped the cabana, not that I could hear anything over the band's raucous rendition of "Little Brown Jug." I edged over to an eye-level gap where two fabric flaps came together.

A voice boomed in my ear. "*Ooh*, do you have to pay a nickel for a peep?"

I almost leaped into the arms of Martha Raye. She stood next to me, teeth gleaming as if each had its own spotlight. Her number with the band finished, she'd apparently decided to instigate heart attacks in random guests. Anyone in the cabana had to have heard her.

Sure enough, Beckett slipped out of the pool side of the tent and back toward the house. I turned to Martha Raye—"You were terrific!"—and then, discretion shot to hell, hoisted a flap in time to see one on the opposite side of the cabana fluttering. I ran through and peered out.

Nothing but backlit figures on and around the dance floor. The band was cooking and everyone was in motion. I was missing one hell of a bash.

I sprinted back the way I'd come. Martha Raye had wandered off to startle some other unsuspecting soul. Beckett climbed the slight rise toward Addison's house. He'd affected an exaggerated drunken gait to avoid other revelers. It worked; the people at the lip of the patio gave him and his hideous jacket a wide berth. I ventured up to the partygoers, seeking allies.

And, to my relief, spotted Kay. She was speaking with a woman who carried herself with the hauteur of a queen despite being dressed in the couture of a farmer's wife. I signaled Kay frantically.

She, in turn, flashed a buzz-off look and turned to eliminate eye contact. Some friend.

The few seconds cost me. Beckett had disappeared, possibly into the house. I darted to the closest set of open French doors and glimpsed something on the tile that I hadn't seen in the darkness outside.

A spattering of blood drops, leading toward the reception room. Beckett wasn't feigning drunkenness. He was genuinely staggering. I started running flat out.

The noise level in the house had increased with the partygoers now multiple sheets to the wind. I was elbowed and jostled repeatedly. The only thing keeping me from screaming in frustration was the knowledge that Beckett was facing the same treatment while being considerably worse for wear. Where was his jacket? Why couldn't I see his god-awful—

The next person to bump into me at least had the decency to apologize. I wheeled and stared into Bill Ihnen's eyes, his dancer on his arm.

"Lillian, you two weren't introduced. This is—"

"Bill, Beckett's here! Find Addison! Tell him no one can leave!"

Bill asked no questions, striking off with his girl in tow. The rich red oval of her agape mouth seemed to hang in the air for a moment after he'd tugged her aside.

Deploying years of subway skills I battered my way through the house and onto Addison's canted drive. Again Beckett's sad sartorial sense came to my aid; I saw his jacket as he reeled through the jumble of cars parked to the right of the front door. He glanced into one, then another. A beat later, a black sedan lurched away from the lawn. He'd been hunting for any vehicle with keys in it.

I could do the same, but there'd be no point. I didn't know how to drive. And by the time Red Car tracks had been laid to Addison's neck of the woods, Winton Beckett would be in Tierra del Fuego.

Lights washed over me. A low-slung convertible purred up the drive. Without thinking I waved my arms and charged the car. Brakes squealed as the roadster came to a stop.

"Okay, kid, I see you."

My laughter was involuntary. Barbara Stanwyck was at the wheel, her hair in curlers and pink cold cream slathered on her face.

"I don't suppose you'd want to follow a car."

The actress grinned. "Hop in. I didn't want to go to Addy's party looking like this anyway." She spun the steering wheel and we pulled out.

"Lillian, wasn't it? I don't suppose you'd have a handkerchief handy?"

I did and surrendered it gladly. Barbara proved an adept driver, negotiating the downhill curves with aplomb as she wiped cold cream from her face. "It's not this color in the photograph. What I had on when those fellas showed up was white.

But pink is funnier. If I had to walk around like this, I was going for the laugh."

She was wearing the twin of the quilted peach bathrobe that hung in my aunt Joyce's closet. "Addison certainly caught you off guard," I said.

"I *would* answer the door on the maid's night off. If you ask me, Addison planned it. He's got everyone buffaloed with that roly-poly favorite uncle dodge. The man's sharper than a drawer of steak knives. Mind if I ask who we're following?"

"A private detective, blackmailer, and possibly worse."

"And all my rifles back at the ranch. Addison likes to spread the invitations around."

"This guy wasn't invited. And I think he regrets crashing."

"Do you know this character?"

"Not that well. But he knew my friend Ruby."

"Ruby," Barbara said. "You don't say."

The road's grade eased and we spotted the sedan's taillights ahead. Barbara tried to match Beckett's speed. "He'll crash again at this rate."

"He may be hurrying to a doctor. Just keep him in sight if you can."

It should have been a pleasant drive. The scent of laurel trees abundant, scintillating company. Instead I gripped the dashboard as we hurtled down the hillside. We flew past the shuttered gates of Addison's neighbors, few lights on in the faux chalets and castles.

We rounded another bend and both gasped for breath. The sedan had slowed considerably. It was mere yards ahead of us now, weaving between lanes. Barbara hit the brakes.

"There's something the matter with him," she said. "Anyone on their way up will plow into that car." She coasted behind the sedan and blasted her horn. Beckett continued to swerve across the road.

"Can you cut him off before he hurts himself or somebody else?"

"I'm no stunt driver." Barbara glanced down at the speedometer, now indicating ten miles an hour, and a daredevil spark ignited in her eyes. "But it can't hurt to try."

At the first opportunity she drew ahead of the sedan. Beckett was slumped forward, not even looking at the road. Barbara cranked the wheel and brought her car to a sideways halt.

The lights from the sedan hit us. Beckett was conscious enough to spot the convertible blocking his path. He overcorrected, veering onto the shoulder and into a palm tree at a caterpillar's speed. The sound of the collision was a hollow metallic *thunk* right out of a cartoon. The sedan settled with a hiss, engine grumbling.

Barbara swung her car behind the sedan while I gibbered praise for her driving acumen.

"Thanks, but what do we do now?"

"I'm going to check on him. Could you phone for help?"

"And leave you alone out here? Are you sure that's a good idea?"

"No. But I don't have a better one." To stop myself from considering the implications, I got out of the convertible and walked toward the sedan.

The car's exhaust hung in the air in a foul cloud. I reached in and switched the ignition off. Beckett gripped the steering wheel as if it were all that was keeping him alive. Maybe it was. I forced myself to concentrate on his jacket. It made a prettier sight than the bloodstain spreading across the shirt beneath it.

"Gotta see Doc Satterlee. Echo Park." He groaned in pain.

I placed my hand on his shoulder. "Help's on the way."

"Satterlee's the man. Sawbones owes me. He'll patch me up." Beckett made the gruesome noise twice before I recognized it as laughter. For an instant his eyes regained their usual grim mirth. "Nobody's putting one over on me. Gotta make this meal ticket pay off. I'll cut you a slice, kitten. Echo Park."

"Okay. Next stop, Echo Park."

"Good girl." He closed his eyes. I could have asked him any of the thousand questions whirling around my head. Instead, I left my hand where it was. It seemed the more important thing to do.

30

WHEN ONE OF the many police officers trekking to Addison Rice's manse dropped me at the door, a rumpled Gene was there to greet me. The sight of him allowed me to breathe easy for the first time in what felt like days but had been little more than an hour. Applying the most delicate of viselike grips to my elbow, Gene steered me around the house without a word. Which was fine by me. I wasn't in the mood for talking.

"We'll stay outside," Gene said evenly. "Barney Groff is here and making repeated demands for your head. He thinks you jeopardized the life of one of the studio's assets."

"How is she? Barbara Stanwyck. She came back up while another detective talked to me."

"I spoke to her. She's fine." Gene released my arm and we walked companionably through one of Addison's gardens, night-blooming flowers perfuming the air.

I hadn't broken down after Beckett died. I didn't when Barbara Stanwyck returned from a nearby house telling me she'd telephoned the police. "You should sit down, dear," she said, pointing to the shoulder of the road.

"I can't get these clothes dirty. They don't belong to me." With that, I'd burst into tears. Barbara walked me to her convertible and patted my hand while I bawled my eyes out. Not for Beckett, but for Ruby and everything that happened to both of us since we'd come west.

All right, maybe a little for Beckett.

At some point a battalion of squad cars started uphill. Barbara joined them while I spewed a mile-a-minute statement to a baffled detective named Yocum. At some point he realized only Gene would make head or tail of it, so he flagged down a car to take me to the summit. Where, to my amazement, the party was still going strong. Every inch of dance floor was occupied. The atmosphere was equal parts danger and relief, a siege mentality merging with the desperate celebration of a farewell blowout.

"Rice closed the gates after you lit out with Miss Stanwyck," Gene told me. "No one in or out until we arrived. I'll hand it to you, that helped."

"Then the liquor is still here."

Gene's well-trained eyebrows barely budged. "You know where the bars are. I'll find you in a bit."

En route to the libations line I spotted familiar silhouettes on a bench, framed by the light from the pool. Vi and Armand Troncosa were not quite cuddling, his arm around her shoulder more a shelter against the chill. Esteban left his vigil over them when he saw me, arms stretched wide for an embrace. I wasn't prepared to reciprocate, and he kept them open awkwardly. "Are you all right? Everyone is talking about you." He scowled. "You should not take such foolish risks."

Vi hurled herself at me. "I was so worried! I heard you bolted out of here with Claudette Colbert! Are you okay?"

"Not really, no."

Troncosa took charge. "I am happy to see you, Lillian. Yet unhappy no one has thought to secure you a drink after your ordeal. Would you care for one?"

"Oh, God, yes. Something tall and cool."

"A refreshment much like yourself, then." The silver-tongued devil. He turned to Vi. "And you, my dear? Or is your nose still ticklish?" Vi nodded, almost bashful. An eloquent movement of

Troncosa's shoulders said *Let's amscray* to Esteban. The two men left to queue up in our stead at the nearest bar.

"Don't go thinking I've fallen for Armand," Vi said. "We're just having fun."

"Of course you are. Everybody in the joint's having fun but me. Have you two been together all night?"

"I told you, don't worry about me."

"I know, but I'm wondering. Did Armand sneak away before the gates closed or did you two dance every dance?"

"With the same fortunate man . . ." Vi's singing trailed off. "Wait. You don't think he—" She instantly become serious, straining to remember. "Esteban brought Armand's cigarette case and they talked for a minute. In Spanish, so I didn't get a word. Then Armand went for drinks after Martha Raye finished. Did you see her? What a panic!"

"Panic's one word for it. What did you have to drink?"

"Champagne. That's why Armand made that crack about my nose before. I'm not really used to it."

I nodded. "Champagne. Not a cocktail. So he could have snagged glasses from any passing waiter."

"Yes. I suppose he could." The prospect of what I was suggesting both depressed and excited her.

While we waited, Vi rattled off a list of the celebrities she'd seen. Troncosa finally returned bearing a tray liberated from the help. A Tom Collins for me, more nose-tickling champagne for him and Vi. Esteban brought up the rear with a glass of something dark.

"A toast," Troncosa said. "To unexpected adventures."

We clinked glasses. I could feel their questions coming and knew I wasn't up to them. "I should find Detective Morrow. Would you excuse me?"

Troncosa took Vi's arm and they strolled toward the house. Esteban lingered. "I trust we will dance another evening." He seized my hand and kissed it before taking his leave, his lips barely grazing my skin. Poor Esteban. He had Troncosa's moves but none of his panache.

I walked to the pool. The gorilla chased girls around it, the furry head of his costume now floating in the shallow end. The flame-haired woman I'd glimpsed earlier swam over to it and tossed it out of the water. I didn't see her towel anywhere. I sat in a cushioned chair at a glass-topped table with my drink, letting the pool's cool blue light wash over me.

"The story making the rounds," Bill Ihnen said as he took a seat, "is that you and James Cagney sped down the hill with pistols in each hand shooting at a truckload of gangsters."

"I'd see that picture. But it's not even close to the truth."

"Then I should probably stop telling it that way."

"Where's your date?"

He nodded toward the dance floor. "Tripping the light with a new friend. She found it odd I was taking orders from you."

"Sorry about that."

"Don't be. I'm always happy to have something to do at these things."

"You said before you were going to protect her from Laurence Minot. Did you happen to see him around the time of my big exit?"

"His wife's been easier to keep track of, thanks to that ridiculous hat. I saw them a while ago, having a quarrel. Very public. Almost staged, I thought. But it was after you'd left."

Gene collapsed into a chair, aggravation etched deeply into his face. He introduced himself to Bill, then turned to me. "I can't hold Groff at bay much longer. He insists on talking to you."

"Then you'll need another drink, along with something to eat. Allow me." Bill was off before I could thank him or place an order.

"What exactly happened to Beckett?" I asked.

"He was shot. Twice, at close range. You didn't hear it?"

"No. But the band was playing and Martha Raye was foghorning in my ear. That must have covered up the sound."

"Particularly if we're talking about a small-caliber weapon."

"Like the one that killed Ruby?"

Gene nodded. I set to work on my Tom Collins. I had another one on the way, after all. "Why do you think Beckett was here?"

"To put the touch on someone. Minot. Diana. Possibly both. Maybe Troncosa or the bandleader. He confronts his victims in public, forces them to ante up in a hurry. Only drawback to the plan is there's enough of a racket here that a suitably prepared individual could shoot him and no one would notice." He glanced over my shoulder. "Batten down the hatches, Frost. Storm's about to hit."

I became aware of a peculiar aura I'd only experienced when standing next to a train engine, of tremendous power barely contained. Barney Groff slammed Bill's chair into the table with such force the resulting clang made me wince. His hoarse whisper yearned to be a roar. "Who the hell do you think you are?"

"Easy." Gene breathed the word.

"I've waited long enough. I'd imagine with so many off-duty personnel present at a murder scene, the LAPD has a budding scandal all its own to occupy your time." Groff bent at the waist, vulturelike, to address me. "You put Miss Stanwyck's life in danger. I'll have you arrested for kidnapping."

"How could it be kidnapping if she was driving?"

"You forced her to participate in a high-speed chase."

"She wanted to do it."

"You had no idea what was happening when you roped her into this misadventure. I also understand a member of the press, a Miss Dambach, is at this party because of you."

"You consider Kay a member of the press? Could you tell her that? Because she'd love to hear it."

"I'll be having words with Miss Dambach, if only to keep tonight's mayhem under wraps." Groff stepped back from the table and smiled at me. For the first time in the conversation, I was afraid. "Those are lovely clothes. Where did you get them? Or could Miss Head tell me when I speak to her yet again?"

"Are Miss Frost's clothes relevant?" Gene asked.

"Maybe not to you. But they're important to Paramount Pictures. As is the well-being of our players. Rest assured we will prosecute this to the fullest extent of the law. We . . ."

Never had I seen anyone go so white so quickly. I was turning to see what had put the fear of God or Joseph Breen into Groff when Barbara Stanwyck laid a hand on my shoulder. She'd taken the curlers out of her hair and removed her bathrobe to reveal a simple navy blue sheath. In other words, she looked every inch a movie star.

"Oh, for Pete's sake, Barney. It wasn't kidnapping. It was more like hitchhiking."

Groff arranged his features into their most patronizing formation. It was a poor choice, because Barbara gave him both barrels. "And need I remind you I'm not on the Paramount payroll. I look after myself in this town, picking and choosing who I do pictures for, and there's nothing to stop me from calling Zeppo and saying I'm not interested in doing business with Paramount again. If I want to take a joyride with a friend, neither of us has to answer to the studio about it."

Beet-red at being shown up, Groff ratcheted up the smarm. "All true, Miss Stanwyck. But surely you acknowledge we only have your best interests at heart."

"I know you do, Barney. And I appreciate it. But you also have to know when to give two ladies room to blow off steam.

Now let Lillian alone. She's had enough commotion for one night."

Groff dusted off his we're-all-friends-here grin, which hadn't seen action since his soda shop days. "Of course. Detective Morrow, a word?" With that, he vanished into the shadows like Dwight Frye. Gene rolled his eyes and went with him.

"That was a fair bit of acting there," Barbara said. "He managed to slink away without it looking like he was slinking. I should ask how he did that."

"Thank you for defending me."

"Think nothing of it, dear. Those studio bullyboys, making like they're worried about me. All they're concerned about is the shooting schedule."

"Still, I hope I didn't ruin your evening."

She laughed, a warm, wonderful sound. "Are you kidding? No one had to see me in curlers and cold cream. I'm having a marvelous time. And it's about to get better. Would you excuse me?" She stepped away from the table and into the arms of a saturnine dreamboat with dark wavy hair and a sexy widow's peak who'd materialized out of the ether. Robert Taylor smiled at me then led his best girl to the dance floor. Vi spotted them and whispered giddily to Troncosa. He spun her closer to them.

Bill returned with a reserve Tom Collins and the thickest ham sandwich on record. "I raided the kitchen. I heard Barbara giving Groff what for. Edith adores her."

"I can see why. What did she mean about calling Zeppo?"

"Zeppo Marx. Herb. He's her agent. What'd I miss? Edith will expect a full report."

GRADUALLY THE CROWD trickled out, each guest giving their name to the police and their congratulations to Addison. Troncosa escorted Vi to a late supper, Esteban whisking them both away. Barbara Stanwyck said good-bye before she and Robert Taylor left so she could fix him eggs. I'd lost track of Diana and Laurence, but according to Bill everyone else had heard their contentious departure.

The band was breaking up when I spotted Kay for the first time in ages. "There you are," I said. "I was about to go inside and pick a room for the night. Let me know if we can leave before my birthday."

"Where's your detective?"

"Detecting, presumably. And he's hardly my detective."

"Oh, sure. He gives carte blanche in an investigation to any idly interested citizen of Los Angeles. Very forward thinking, our Gene."

I wasn't willing to dissect the nature of my relationship with Gene just then, especially with Kay. Not that I had the answers anyway. "Why are you looking for him?"

I would have called Kay's expression smug if I hadn't been her friend. "Everyone who had a grudge against Beckett was at this party, right?"

"That's a long list, but just about. Tommy Carpa was the only one not here."

Yes, that expression was definitely smug, now tinged with maniacal triumph. "Except he was."

A FEW MINUTES later, Gene and I stood at the end of Addison's driveway, contemplating Tommy Carpa's nearly new green Packard parked all by its lonesome.

"Kay didn't notice it until the cars thinned out," I said.

"And where is Kay?"

"In conversation with Barney Groff. He seemed particularly eager to speak to her."

"It's not just the gates of Paramount swinging wide for her

tonight." Gene aimed a flashlight at the registration on the Packard's steering column. "So Carpa was here. He had to leave in a hurry, saw his car was boxed in and took off without it."

"He could still be here, hiding in one of the rooms. The house is big enough."

"Good thought, but I had officers sweep the place first thing. They're doing it again now, but it's more likely he hoofed it down to the boulevard or caught a ride with someone else. We'll put a bulletin out for him."

"Why would Tommy be here?"

"My guess is he was trailing Beckett, although it could have been the other way around. Unfortunately Tommy's the only one in a position to say."

"That still doesn't tell us who the one being followed was here to meet."

"Nobody can verify where they were when Beckett was shot. Laurence Minot swears his wife was fastened to him like a limpet all night. She backed him up on that, but there's a redhead in a towel says Minot propositioned her. Which means Diana was solo for part of the evening as well. Troncosa at least admitted he couldn't account for his every minute. Still, they were invited to the party. Carpa's the one who crashed."

"That doesn't mean he did anything."

"No, but it makes him more likely to." Gene eyed Tommy's car with malice. "Just when I was thinking I'd be out of here before dawn."

"I'm going to see if I can't get a cup of coffee. Want me to send one out?" Gene nodded absently. I hiked up the drive.

Addison stood by the front door, sending off stragglers. He doffed his gigantic hat to me. "You've made this party the event of the year, my dear. How can I ever repay you?" Pointing me toward the java, I told him, would be a propitious start.

Ready and Ken Nolan lolled in the kitchen, smoking

cigarettes. Ready sprang to his feet when he saw me. Ken snickered, the jerk.

"Have you seen Kay?" Ready asked.

"She's talking to her future. Could be a while."

Ken stood and whispered in Ready's ear. I'd have bet Kay's cowboy was incapable of blushing. I'd have lost. It truly was a night full of surprises.

31

THE ROBBERY HOMICIDE bureau had a thready pulse in the wee hours, a handful of detectives minting fresh paperwork, a stoop-backed janitor collecting the old. He nodded gallantly as he passed, reassuring me that no matter the time of night someone was on the job.

I gave a stop-and-start rendition of the evening's events, Gene periodically consulting with assorted solemn figures who summoned him with flicks of their mighty gray heads. Hansen cruised in during one of these absences, my biggest fan saying nothing to me, instead whistling "You Can't Pull the Wool Over My Eyes" off-key.

Gene returned looking only slightly defeated and greeted Hansen. "Any word on Carpa?"

"Trees were shaken, producing neither hide nor hair. He's being alibied left and right, though. Stories don't match at all."

"Meaning Tommy's not around to coordinate. Maybe he *is* lamming." Gene took a sip of coffee black enough to be accessorized by diamonds and pressed the heels of his hands to his face. "That's enough for now. We'll talk more in the morning. Later in the morning, because it's morning now."

"Cucumber slices over the eyes will keep you looking springtime fresh," I told him.

"I'll get a few out of the icebox. Your ride's downstairs."

As I gathered my things, Hansen said, "She's been a pest

since this started, but she's right about the cucumber business. The wife does that."

IN THE STAIRWELL I passed Mavis Kreutzer, in the company of a policeman. Beckett's secretary looked calm, like she kept a mourning dress and a makeup bag by the telephone for just such occasions. On the landing, she flashed me an inappropriately winsome smile.

"Told you I should have made use of that coffee can," she said, and I knew in my bones she had other post-midnight trips to the police station in her future.

Two vagrants and a woman in a crimson dress with sadly optimistic ruffles sat in the corners of the station lobby as if blown there by a breeze. Edith Head stood in the center of the room in a black suit accented by pink stripes, cataloging her surroundings with interest. I suspected the others had scattered to escape her gaze.

"Edith! What are you doing here?"

"I thought you could use a friendly face and a ride home. Shall we?" As she turned, her eyes fell on the lady of the evening in the corner. "That's a lovely color for you, but a terribly cheap fabric. Remember, you get what you pay for."

The night air didn't do much to revivify me or dispel my amazement. Edith led the way to her roadster. I hesitated, leery about getting into her car again with light at a premium.

"Don't loiter, Lillian. You might be arrested this time."

If I was going to meet my maker, at least I was dressed for it. Edith, sensitive to my unease, pulled onto the street with care. "Bill telephoned me. As did Barney Groff."

"I'm afraid he might have recognized these clothes."

"If so, it was a fortunate guess. I don't believe Mr. Groff sees any Paramount pictures. Or even likes the picture business."

She took her eyes off the road briefly to size me up. "I must compliment you. For all the evening's trials, those garments look pristine."

"The whole time I was terrified of being shot. Not because I'd be injured, but because the clothes would be ruined."

"My wardrobe girls could have fixed them had the worst occurred. Let's be thankful their skills weren't put to the test." She spotted a stop sign at the last minute and stood on the brakes. I mewled decorously.

"I imagine the story will be all over the papers tomorrow."

"Various stories will appear in various papers tomorrow. The *Times* will report Addison Rice's latest bash grew so boisterous the police were summoned. Some of the officers were mistaken for costumed revelers and pulled onto the dance floor by Constance and Joan Bennett. The *Telegraph*, meanwhile, will feature an amusing item about a couple who found Barbara Stanwyck on their doorstep in the dead of night, asking to use their telephone to call her mechanic."

"Nothing about a murder?"

"Or the alleged kidnapping of Miss Stanwyck." Another sidelong glance from Edith. "I cannot wait for our next fitting. I want to hear her version of this yarn."

"What would Groff say if he knew you were giving aid and comfort to Lillian Frost, the notorious kidnapper?"

"Putative notorious kidnapper. Don't you worry. I can hold my own with Mr. Groff. It never hurts to be underestimated. Can you bear telling the evening's saga again?"

She got the full version, complete with newsreel and cartoon. Edith's interruptions were limited to grunts directed at motorists and other nocturnal creatures foolish enough to venture into her car's path.

"How did Laurence Minot seem to you? Any signs of distress?"

"He's such a cold fish I don't know if distress would register."

"Typical of directors."

"I've come to learn you don't do anything without a reason. Why do you ask about Laurence in particular?"

"His name came up in conversation today. I had a fitting with an actress this afternoon. The studio recently loaned her out to Lodestar."

"And this fitting was coincidentally scheduled for today?"

It's a good thing Edith's smiles were so tight, or I'd have glimpsed the canary feathers. "I *did* have to see her at some point. She's the chatty sort, this actress. I had to leave in the middle of the fitting to chase after Adele and I don't think she stopped talking while I was gone. At any rate, I asked her how she enjoyed working at Lodestar. Mr. Minot was mentioned."

"Quite casually, of course."

"Quite. Mr. Minot has been talking up his latest discovery all over the lot. Minor European royalty he had, it's said, fallen for. According to this actress, Mr. Minot did indeed put Natalie on film. No one's seen the test yet. Mr. Minot is angling for a private screening with the head of the studio."

My heart ached for Ruby all over again. She'd come so close to getting away with it.

"Now we know why Winton Beckett risked turning up at Addison's party."

"And we have a new problem. With Mr. Beckett dead, Mr. Minot may feel emboldened to eliminate the final threat to him."

"He'll try to dispose of the screen test now. It proves he and Natalie were involved."

"I've already told Detective Morrow. On to more pressing business. Tell me what everyone at the party wore. Leave out no detail. The details are *essential*."

Somehow Edith managed to coax minutiae about the guests' attire out of me I had no idea I'd retained. I still had more ground to cover when we reached Mrs. Quigley's.

"You can finish your report when you return the clothes."

"Thanks again for everything. What now? Back to bed, then a huge Sunday breakfast?"

Edith looked scandalized. "Heavens, no! I'm off to Travis's house to make sure he's intact, then I'll drive us both to the studio. I do it most mornings. He could stand to put in the extra time."

MISS SARAH PROWLED the porch as I dug for my keys. At least someone was awake to greet me. "Lying in wait for the milkman?"

The regal feline strutted around my legs in reply, rubbing herself against the linen of my slacks.

"Watch it. These aren't mine. Time to come inside."

I stooped to pick her up and heard a loud noise. A few splinters of doorjamb rained down on Miss Sarah's dusky fur. She was so startled she darted right into my hands.

I told myself it wasn't a gunshot. I told myself again as I hit the deck. The house keys were in my hand, one of them jabbing Miss Sarah in the belly. But I couldn't open the door without stepping into the glow of the porch light, and I wasn't certain where the shot—why deny it?—had come from. I lay there, heart drumming against the knees mashed against my bosom, toe of my left shoe wedged into a mouse hole in the baseboard. Miss Sarah, at least, remained perfectly still in my arms. She could stay forever as far as I was concerned, the fussy Burmese the only reason I was still breathing. I glanced down and spotted a smear of dirt on the leg of my slacks. My borrowed slacks. My borrowed Paramount slacks that I'd taken such good care of. I'd kept them flawless while chasing after a dying man alongside the star of *Night Nurse* only to sully them at my own front door.

The angry sigh escaped my lips before I could stop it. The oleander bush at the end of the porch rustled, as if someone were peering through it.

Followed by the most beautiful sound in the world—lurid laughter on the other side of the front door.

"Really, Frederick, you must leave. Some of my tenants get up early. Even on Sunday."

The door creaked open, casting yellow light on my hiding place. My eyes snapped to the oleander, but in the shifting shadows I couldn't tell if the branches were moving.

"Turn out the lights!" I croaked.

"What? Who—?" Mrs. Quigley, bless her, leaned out to gawp at me at the same time she flicked the switches by her hand. Both the porch and entry lights were doused. I rolled to the porch railing holding my savior Miss Sarah aloft. As I moved, I thought I heard footsteps retreating from the building. But I couldn't be sure, because Mrs. Quigley was already making with the questions.

"Lillian, what is this foolishness? Did you drink too much at that party?" She shooed someone into her apartment, undoubtedly lamenting she couldn't pretend it was the cat nestled in my arms.

"No, just dropped something." Before my assailant could fire again, I rose to a Bronko Nagurski squat with Miss Sarah playing pigskin and charged the door. Mrs. Quigley slammed it behind me. I glanced into her front parlor and glimpsed Frederick. Her gentleman caller was a heavy-set fellow in a threadbare salesman's suit, fascinated by the assortment of doilies on her sofa.

I handed Mrs. Quigley her heroic cat.

"Sorry I woke you. I didn't mean to make so much noise. Good night." On I went upstairs, leaving Mrs. Quigley to soothe her bewildered swain.

GENE HAD LEFT the police station—whether for the night or the nonce, the sergeant didn't know—so my message said I could be reached at Mrs. Lindros's place. No way I was staying by myself on this night.

Of course, that meant telephoning Mrs. Lindros's place after three in the morning. I dialed with crossed fingers. Vi picked up immediately, her voice muffled by a mouthful of food and a strange clattering in the background.

"Thank God you answered," I said.

"I'm staying up as late as I can. I don't want tonight to end."

Would that I felt the same way. "Is Ready still around?"

"Hat in hand and heading for the door. Shall I send him to your place?"

He arrived scant moments later. Having been briefed by me, he'd circled the block before pulling up outside and observed nothing untoward. He ushered me to the car and drove straight to Mrs. Lindros's.

Vi was in her pj's, which in turn wore a fine layer of coffee cake crumbs. The clattering was explained by the sight of Kay, hunched over a typewriter in the kitchen with not one but two pencils in her hair.

"Hiya, doll," she said without raising her eyes from the paper scrolling past the cylinder. "What's cooking?"

"The usual. Someone took a shot at me."

That warranted a look, but only a brief one. "Sure, I can see it. Beckett's dying words might have been his killer's name. Were they?"

"No."

"There we are, then. Any more coffee, Vi?"

Vi, who had run over to hug me, scampered to fetch the pot. She refilled Kay's mug and spoke over the top of her head as if she weren't there. "Kay's typing up her impressions of the party while they're fresh. She's going to write something for one of the big newspapers!"

"Congratulations. Did Barney Groff set this up, perchance?"

"You know, kids, it'd be easier for mama to make her deadline if you took the chatter outside. Vi, coffee?"

"Check your cup, Louella." We left the room and passed a redfaced Ready at the front door.

"Sorry if Kay was a mite curt with you. She's had a big day."

"We all have." I gave Ready a kiss good night. He gazed fearfully into the kitchen as Vi and I climbed to her room.

"You're staying with me tonight," Vi said. "I won't hear any arguments."

"I'm not hearing any, either."

On her bed lay a box. Small. Black velvet. Another of Armand Troncosa's exceedingly generous gifts. Vi danced over to it, prying open the top with care. I saw a familiar glint of green.

"Isn't this divine?"

"It's something. From Armand?"

"Yes! His friend Esteban gave it to me when he drove me home. We went to Armand's house after the party for a light supper and a final glass of champagne. Armand said we needed one. Can you imagine that, *needing* a glass of champagne?" She giggled, her nose still ticklish.

"When did you leave his place?"

"About an hour and a half ago, I think. I can't really remember." Another peal of angelic laughter as she lifted the necklace from the box and held the emerald against her neck. "A token of Armand's admiration. I've never gotten a token of anyone's anything before."

I felt awkward, afraid I'd have to disabuse Vi of any notion the trinket warming itself against her skin represented a pledging of Armand's troth.

"Listen, Vi," I started.

"Don't worry. I'm not expecting anything from Armand."

"You're not?"

"We spent the night talking about Ruby. He wanted to know what she was like. It was Tommy all over again, only with better cologne. At least I got something out of it this time. This will really go with that copper-colored dress I bought."

"It will. You'll look great. So tell me about Armand's house. Leave out no detail. The details are *essential*."

32

MY SCHEME TO sneak out of Mrs. Lindros's house without talking to anyone was scuppered when I realized I had nothing to wear. My party clothes were draped on a chair next to Vi's bed so I couldn't see the stain on the slacks. I wasn't about to push my luck by donning Paramount's wardrobe again.

That meant finding something else to put on. I roused Vi. She leaped out of bed eager to help. In two shakes she'd procured a navy blue housedress printed with white anchors.

"Where's the little sailor hat that goes with it?"

"Ever hear that line about beggars and choosers?"

"Point taken. Where'd you scare this up?"

"A new girl. Lorraine, from Kansas. She wants to be a comedienne."

Her best bet if she was my height. The dress billowed a bit, so I tied it around my waist with a belt. Not an Edith Head original, but it would do.

My agenda went further awry downstairs, where I was blackjacked by the scent of bacon. Kay worked multiple burners like an irritatingly fresh-faced fry cook. "Morning, gals! Help yourselves to some eats." Vi required no additional prompting, grabbing a chair as Kay fetched hash browns at their apex of crispness. "Sorry I was curt with you last night."

"You were working. So you're going to write for one of the papers? Give Lorna Whitcomb a run for her money?"

"Mr. Groff dangled the prospect. It remains to be seen if I can snatch it off the hook. In any case, I'm bound to get more assignments at *Modern Movie* thanks to you."

She set down a plate—bacon, potatoes, pancakes fluffier than the pillows upstairs—on a buttermilk biscuit–adjacent stretch of table. "Dig in. Do you want eggs? Barbara Stanwyck gave me her recipe."

My eyes and stomach vaulted to the food, but my legs stayed put. Stupid legs. I'd never questioned Kay's motives before, but I did so now.

She busied herself at the stove again, apparently expecting lumberjacks. "I feel awful about not listening to what happened after the party. Somebody shot at you?"

I nodded as Vi poached a slice of my bacon.

"My God." Kay studied me with practiced concern. "Any idea who it was?"

The scale of the treachery unfolding on the tablecloth dawned on me. "Kay? Are you pumping me for information? And using breakfast to do it?"

"Can't I fix a friend a meal after a trying experience?"

"Not on a Sunday morning," Vi said, suspicion not dulling her appetite. "You never cook Sunday mornings."

"Oh, hush," Kay said, but it was too late. She was hoping to ferret out more material she could use in bargaining with Groff, and knew me well enough to serve her attack on a chipped blue plate with maple syrup at the ready. The betrayal was like a knife in my heart, the blade dripping with fresh butter.

Canning the charade, Kay said, "Can't blame a girl for working every angle she's got."

"I'm an angle now? I thought we were friends."

"We *are* friends, sweetheart. That's why I don't exactly tumble to your attitude here. Edith Head gets to use you but your friends don't?"

One woman looking to save her job, the other fighting to forge a career of her own. I could understand how Kay thought of Edith and herself as cut from the same cloth, and I couldn't begin to articulate the many ways she was wrong. Not even to myself.

"Enjoy your breakfast," I said. I retrieved my party clothes and headed for the door, resisting Kay's importuning to stay. The aroma of bacon was harder to ignore, but I managed.

THE GOUGE IN the doorjamb where the bullet had been removed was a stubbornly unblinking eye gazing back at me, answering my question about whether the police had visited Mrs. Quigley's. I stared at it like Scrooge's door knocker, praying it would resolve into some otherworldly sign. No such luck. It remained an irregular hole in the wood.

Mrs. Quigley bustled into the lobby as soon as I entered. Normally we'd talk in her parlor, but she seemed determined to pretend the room had been excised from the building now that I'd seen Frederick. "The police were here at the crack of dawn. They ruined my door frame and didn't so much as apologize. You're to telephone them at once. You also received a call from the actress Diana Galway! With an invitation to Sunday brunch! My land, you're going everywhere these days." She smiled at me. I smiled back. All four of our eyes strayed to the empty parlor. And we ended the conversation there.

Gene, again, wasn't at the police station. The desk officer I spoke to, however, had been issued clear instructions. I could practically hear him ticking off the boxes on a sheet of paper. "You are to remain exactly where you are and wait for Detective Morrow. You are to go nowhere else. You are to stay put. Is all of this clear to you?"

"One more time would help."

"I am to ignore your smart-aleck comment and ask where you are right now."

I mouthed apologies to all the saints I could think of. "At the home of Diana Galway. Let me give you the address."

After confirming with Diana and arranging a cab, I turned to find Miss Sarah behind me. The pitiless look in her eyes said *I own you*. Even more than it usually did.

THE HOUSEMAID LED me into Castle Minot shortly after eleven. I'd showered and changed into a shirtwaist dress and pumps. No-nonsense attire. I had business to attend to.

As we stepped into the backyard Diana scampered to a table in response to an unspoken call of *Places!* Laurence was already on his mark, seated and paging through the *Times*. A pool sparkled a few feet away. *Another one*, I thought, and realized I'd become blasé at the prospect of owning a swimming pool. Perhaps I'd already been in Los Angeles too long.

Husband and wife smiled hugely at me. I gave as good as I got. I wasn't walking into this matinee cold. I had lines of my own.

"Lillian, I'm so glad you could make it." Diana's lounging outfit—wide-legged slacks and blouse that tied around her midriff—overcompensated for the previous evening's party togs. Her straw hat was a world away from her gardening one, which I assumed she'd set ablaze upon arriving home. Laurence, meanwhile, had gone full lord of the manor with a smoking jacket and ascot.

"I'm thrilled you invited me."

"I'm thrilled you're here."

"We're all thrilled," Laurence said, Diana laughing as if he'd tossed off a bon mot worthy of Noël Coward. He waved at an iced pitcher of crimson liquid on the table. "Aperitif? It's Campari. All the Italians are drinking it."

I nodded, and Laurence prepared a glass with ice and a spray of soda. I took a sip and pursed my lips.

"Bitter," Laurence said, "but you get used to it."

"Just like Hollywood."

Diana laughed again, favoring me with a clap as well. "Darling, let's get Lillian fixed up with a plate."

The creamed finnan haddie wasn't a patch on Kay's breakfast bribe. I wondered how rude it would be to ask the maid if any bacon was lying around, and if it would be too much bother to fry it up. Laurence was right about the Campari, though; it was growing on me. We passed a lively hour in the jacaranda-scented breeze discussing events at Addison's. Diana and Laurence had set aside their differences to present a unified front, punctuating their conversation with loving glances and hand-holding. All of it transparently designed to get me to give up whatever I'd learned that hadn't made its way into the papers.

But I knew better. I didn't say a word about the attempted William Tell scene on my porch or ask Laurence about Natalie's screen test. When Gene arrived, I'd flip over my cards. Until then I'd commiserate, turn their questions around, play dumb. At last, a role suited to my talents.

Laurence wearied of my act. He pushed away from the table and flicked his napkin in surrender. "If you'll excuse me, I'll leave you ladies to it."

"Where are you off to?" I asked.

"The studio. No rest for the wicked."

"On a Sunday?"

"Quietest day on the lot. Good chance to get ahead."

Also, I feared, the perfect time for him to dispose of the footage of Ruby. I couldn't let him leave until Gene had talked to him. "You know, Laurence, there's something I've been meaning to ask you about picture making."

"He would know," Diana trilled, beaming at her man.

Laurence seemed far less intrigued. "And what's that?"

A good question. Excellent, in fact. I reached for the Campari as a delaying tactic. And spotted an unannounced guest over Laurence's shoulder.

Tommy Carpa forced his way through a hedge at the yard's boundary. The scratches his passage had left on his face along with the stray leaves in his hair and on his tattered suit should have lent him a comical appearance. But coupled with the wild, up-all-night look in his eyes—and the gun in his hand—they only made him come across as deranged. I set the pitcher down as he ran across the lawn, moving so quickly I began to think I was dreaming.

Then Diana shrieked. At least I knew I was awake.

Laurence wheeled toward the source of his wife's distress as Tommy clouted him across the head with the gun. The move spared him the worst of the blow, which still gashed open his temple. Laurence braced himself against the table, then tore the ascot from his throat and pressed it to the wound. It was, so help me, one of the most dashing things I'd ever witnessed.

Tommy loomed over him, breathing heavily. Not from physical exertion but the effort of holding himself in check. He wanted to kill Laurence, this second. "Tell it, Minot."

"Tell what, old man?"

"The story of you and Ruby. Although you'll probably louse it up. I seen your pictures. Story ain't your strength."

The comment wounded Laurence more than the blow to the head. "I don't know what you mean."

The last ember of logic died in Tommy's eyes as he jabbed Laurence's shoulder with the gun. "I loved her. *Loved* her. And you didn't even know who she was."

Another poke with the pistol, harder this time. Laurence

huffed out a breath in pain. I had to say something before Tommy became unhinged.

"Tommy, calm down. The police are looking for you. They found your car at Addison Rice's house."

"I'll tell them why I was there. I was shadowing this bum. Have been since I heard about his little movie with Natalie."

"Movie?" Diana whispered.

"The screen test you had her do. The one she pinned her hopes on. The one that meant everything to her." Tommy hunkered down next to Laurence, pressing the gun into his ribs. "How was she?"

"She was good." Laurence cocked his head. "Wonderful, actually."

"You're goddamned right she was wonderful. You know how I know? Because she was acting *every second* she was with you." Tears welled in Tommy's eyes but never sounded in his voice. "You didn't need to put my girl in front of a camera. She *lived* her screen test."

Diana wept silently into her napkin.

"You're right," Laurence said. "I've got much to atone for. I treated her shabbily. But I swear to you, I didn't kill her."

"She fooled you. It was on camera that she fooled you, and that would end you. Is that what you and Beckett talked about last night?"

Laurence stiffened. "I never said a word to him."

"I saw you. Moving like a bat out of hell to get away from him."

"Exactly." Laurence shifted in his seat and, for some reason, began making his case to me. "I spotted Beckett at the party. So I went to find Addison."

"Beckett knew everything." Tommy's voice had no life in it, like a recording that was winding down. "He knew you'd shot the screen test. Knew you'd killed Ruby."

"I'm telling you, I didn't."

"It all leads back to you, showman. Your catting around with her. Your harpy of a wife here hiring Beckett to follow you. Beckett pushed Ruby to the brink. But he's out of the picture now. You're the only one I've got left."

Left? Had Tommy just confessed to killing Beckett? Was he about to do the same to Laurence? Laurence clearly had the same thought, because he dropped the ascot and threw himself on Tommy's mercy.

"I'm sorry. For everything I've done. But I didn't kill anyone."

"You heard him, Tommy," I said in my most soothing tone. "Maybe you have the wrong man."

Tommy turned to me. Which allowed Diana to rise from her seat and point at her spouse. "You bastard! You lying bastard!" She slapped at Laurence's head. Tommy spun back to the two of them. I exercised my only option. I tossed my glass onto the tiles surrounding the swimming pool. It shattered, the last of the Campari looking like a splash of blood.

Tommy pivoted toward the sound. Laurence kicked a chair into his legs. Exhaustion had frayed Tommy's nerves and his reflexes. He stumbled into the table, the pistol slipping from his hand and skidding toward the blue water of the pool.

Diana's high-heeled shoe stomped on it. She snatched up the gun and leveled it between Tommy and Laurence, and uncomfortably close to me. I tried to decide if it was better to have the gun in the hands of a vengeful gangster or a betrayed actress. An answer never came to me.

"Baby, listen," Laurence foolishly started, and it all went downhill from there.

The gun swung toward him. Tommy tensed, ready to lunge for it. Diana backed toward the house so she could keep an eye on everyone. "Don't either of you move!"

"Diana, this is silly. Give me the gun." Laurence used the fait accompli voice I'd heard him deploy on set. Away from the cameras, it didn't pack the same punch.

"You've cheated on me every day since our wedding, haven't you?"

"Yes. As you knew I would."

"But with Ruby? My friend?"

"I didn't know she was Ruby. I honestly didn't. She certainly wasn't your friend."

His words were only strengthening Diana's resolve to pull the trigger. "Give me one reason why I shouldn't shoot you in the heart right now," she said.

The world-weariness in Laurence's reply was breathtaking. "Because it's too small a target, my dear. You're not that good a shot."

"I've got a reason," I said. "Anybody want to hear it?"

No? No takers? Too bad. I was going to say it anyway.

"Shooting someone in front of the police is a bad idea."

Diana looked at me with contempt, as well she should have. The trick had whiskers on it. Good thing it wasn't a trick.

Gene had dispatched two uniformed officers to the house's side door to prevent Tommy from escaping. That meant Gene could devote all his attention to Diana. Knowing her, it was the smart approach. He stepped out of the house, arms wide. "Miss Galway. Put down the gun."

Diana hesitated, mainly to extend her big moment. The woman knew how to take direction. She set Tommy's pistol on the table then collapsed in her chair with a sob.

Tommy, to my amazement, allowed the cops to slap handcuffs on him without protest. Eyes now clear, he looked at Gene imploringly. "Talk to Minot. He was about to give it up. He killed my girl."

"Hardly," Laurence said. "He confessed to killing Beckett himself."

Gene nodded at the uniforms, and they manhandled Tommy into the house. Tommy spoke over his shoulder with a chilling calm. "He's the one you want, Morrow. Ask his wife."

There followed a moment of silence, broken only by the song of birds who'd skipped rehearsal and didn't know their cues. Gene finally spoke. "I'm so glad we arranged to meet here, Miss Frost. I suggest we attend to Mr. Minot's injury. Then someone can explain what in the hell is going on around here."

"Better call Publicity at Lodestar," I told Diana as I pushed in my chair. "You apprehended a fugitive and only lost a highball glass. That definitely deserves a spread in *Photoplay*."

33

BRIGHT AND EARLY Monday morning—all right, several cups of coffee into Monday afternoon—I walked into Edith's office with a brown paper parcel under my arm. "Laundry service for Miss Head."

"It didn't take you long to find a position that exploits your many talents." Edith was a duotone symphony in a black dress with patch pockets, black and white buttons down the front, and a wide white belt. She opened the package and inspected the clothes I'd borrowed for the party, folded to the best of my ability.

"I'd planned on delivering those anyway, so I was surprised to get your telephone call. What's up?"

"We should wait for Detective Morrow so I won't have to go through this twice. Have you recovered from your weekend?"

"Just about. A benefit to being temporarily without visible means of support is I slept well into this morning."

I angled toward an armchair. Edith rescued a slim leather-bound volume before I sat on it. "François Villon," she said with her presumably flawless French accent.

"And who's he when he's at home?"

"A French poet of the fifteenth century. Surely you studied him in school."

"Nuns, as a rule, aren't wild about French poetry. François merits a motion picture, I take it."

"He's already had one, with William Farnum. Before your time, I should think. He's getting a second. Preston is writing it. Why they're wasting him on swordsmen and pageantry is beyond me. The man's a born comic."

I laid the book atop a foot-high stack of similar tomes. "Are these about Villon, too?"

"Histories of the period. To provide a feel for what ladies of the era were wearing."

I tested my biceps by hoisting one of the volumes into my lap. "How are you going to talk an actress into wearing one of these headpieces? They're like deer antlers swaddled in linen."

The corners of Edith's mouth briefly migrated upward. "I have the book open when the actress arrives for her fitting. We gush and coo over the design of the distant past. I lament that the studio won't let me embrace that look for fear modern audiences will reject actresses in such garb. Invariably the actress will screw up her face, turn to me and say—"

"'They'll believe *me* in it.' I'm starting to think you're an evil genius. At least you don't have to worry about anyone stealing a headdress to wear to Don the Beachcomber."

There was a knock at the door. Edith and I turned expecting Gene and instead found a heavy-lidded man with a broad forehead and an intense continental bearing. He resembled a dapper Peter Lorre, down to the slightly protruding eyes. "Forgive me, Edith," he said, his precise diction severing the "H" from her name. "I don't wish to intrude."

"It's fine, Ernest. Can I help you?"

The man—obviously Ernest Dryden, the designer Edith pegged as the heir apparent at Paramount—shrugged helplessly. "I'm looking for Travis."

"Have you tried the workroom? He has so many pieces to keep track of these days. Quite the full plate."

"Yes. An excellent suggestion." Dryden smiled vacantly,

bulging eyes looking through me to take in the walls of Edith's office. Already plotting his use of the space when he claimed the throne. With a Prussian bow, he exited. I was disappointed he didn't leave a visiting card.

Edith, rattled by the encounter with Dryden, calmed herself by refolding the clothes I'd returned to her. "How goes the job hunt?"

"Slow out of the blocks. Rumor has it Bullock's is hiring for their children's department. Wrestling sticky little darlings into velvet Christmas dresses. I've said one novena I get the job and two I don't."

"The offer of a position here still stands. And the clock, as Mr. Dryden's appearance portends, is ticking. Why you insist on looking this gift horse in the mouth is beyond me."

It was beyond me, too. "Can I ask . . . why do you want me to work here? Why are you being so kind to me?"

"Ah. So at last you figured it out. Saw through all my plotting to the trap I've been laying for you." Edith set the clothes aside and playfully swatted me. "There's no mystery to it, Lillian. No hidden motive. We've been through a lot together these last few days, and you've proven yourself time and again. Plus I know something about how difficult it can be for a clear-eyed young woman to find a place in this city and this industry. You're at a loose end and I'd like to help, that's all. I don't expect you to follow in my footsteps and turn wardrobe into your life's work. I'm offering a job, so you can keep body and soul together until a situation more to your liking presents itself." A barb of annoyance rose in her voice. "Honestly, you'd think you didn't want to work for me. I cannot fathom why you haven't said yes already."

And like that, I knew why I hadn't said yes—and why I would say no. We *had* been through a lot together, Edith and I, and after that whirlwind I didn't want to be one of dozens of underlings vying for crumbs of her attention. I wanted to be Edith's peer, not her pin girl. To achieve that I'd need to create my own opportunities, the way she had when she'd braved the Bronson Gate in 1924 with a fistful of other people's sketches.

I was fumbling for an explanation, a means of saying I wanted to lasso my own future, when Gene let himself into the office. He looked surprisingly well rested and I told him so.

"Cucumber slices on the eyes, like you suggested. All right, Miss Head. What have you unearthed that requires my presence and Miss Frost's, apparently?"

"Yes. Well." Edith smoothed the patch pockets on her dress. "I've come into possession of Ruby Carroll's screen test."

Any lingering traces of skepticism were wiped clean from Gene's face. He looked like a young boy seeing his first pony. "The one directed by Laurence Minot?"

"Yes. As soon as I confirmed the test's existence, I contacted a friend at Lodestar and invented a reason to view it. I had to call in more than a few favors. But it seemed to me if the police and not a rival studio requested the footage, the film would never see the light of a projector. Particularly now that Mr. Minot may face legal difficulty." She lowered her head. "Excessive on my part, I know. I apologize if I've overstepped my bounds."

After staring at her a moment, Gene raised a hand in benediction. "Considering your scheme worked, I'll forgive your zeal. Have you watched the footage?"

"Yes. Not much of use in it, but I thought you'd want to see it for yourself. And I assumed Lillian would be interested for personal reasons. I've taken the liberty of reserving a screening room."

"Of course you have," Gene said, with a hint of admiration.

• • •

THE AIR IN the screening room was still redolent of the cigars and dreams snuffed out by the previous occupants. Edith stepped into the projection booth, leaving Gene and me to chat.

"Anybody fold under questioning?" I asked.

"Not yet. Carpa's clammed up while Minot won't stop talking. Wants to do a picture on how the police actually work. 'A tough story about real men, what?' I asked where the dancing numbers would go. He insists he's innocent, like Tommy when he was still talking."

"Then who do you think did it?"

"Carpa. Straight down the line. He killed Ruby in a jealous rage. Beckett held it over his head until Carpa got the drop on him. I can tell from your face you don't agree."

"No, it's not that. I just don't understand why Tommy would then want to kill Laurence."

Gene didn't squirm. He was a real man, after all. "He blames Minot for Ruby's situation. Carpa genuinely loved the girl and harbors a lot of guilt over what he did."

The explanation seemed a bit . . . *psychological,* for both Tommy and Gene. Far be it from me to poke holes in it when I was more concerned about somebody poking holes in me. "Then you think Tommy took that shot outside my place?"

"Stands to reason. You were the last person to talk to Beckett before he died. He could have named his killer." Gene smiled. "But with Tommy in custody, you can ride the streetcars freely to your many job interviews."

"Gee, thanks."

Edith returned to the screening room. "All set. Shall we?" As the lights went down, she squeezed my hand.

THE FILM LEADER blitzed past, a hazy countdown of numbers. Then a glimpse of the clapperboard with its chalk code, shadows of assorted technicians . . . and standing in the midst of the chaos, Ruby. Never more alive. Knowing all this activity was about her. Feeding on it. Her huge brown eyes open wide and peering to her left, listening to someone with the faintest of smiles on her Cupid's bow lips. Conspiring from the first shot. Her eyebrows were full, to compete with the pile of dark hair atop her head.

I would never get used to Ruby as a brunette. She'd always be a blonde to me. But then I wasn't looking at Ruby. It was Natalie wearing a black beaded gown, the Lodestar wardrobe department's hasty concession to period dress. She nodded and the stone at her throat bobbed. She placed a hand over it self-consciously, addressing an off-screen interlocutor.

"No, it's my own piece," she said of the necklace. "For good luck. I hope this is acceptable." Natalie's voice was Ruby's but huskier, a Slavic accent creeping in around the consonants, flattening the vowels. It seemed effortless and unforced, a manner of speech she'd grown up hearing and could replicate without thinking.

Goddamned if she didn't look and sound like a princess. No wonder half the town fell for her.

A whiskey-thick laugh from off-camera. Laurence Minot, his own voice muffled. "Not a problem, my dear. It suits our character. Do you think you'll need luck? Have you been in front of a camera before?"

"I am only alive in front of them." Her eyes flicked to the lens, and for a moment I couldn't move, think, or breathe.

Hey there, mermaid. Good to see you again.

Nice to see you, too, Ruby.

AN ABRUPT CUT and Ruby was downstage, slinking toward the camera. Laurence offered encouragement and threw out questions to put his leading lady at ease. *What do you like most about America? Ice cream. What do you miss about your homeland? Dreaming of coming to this country. And goulash. I put paprika in your Irish stew, but it is not the same.* Once she forgot a word and chided herself in Hungarian. Laurence roared, clearly dazzled by her.

So was I. I couldn't see Ruby anymore. I could only see Natalie. An exotic presence both more distant and far warmer than Ruby had ever been. Had I made her acquaintance onscreen, I would have gladly followed her anywhere.

"Very well, Miss Szabo." Laurence sounded louder; I could picture him leaning forward, straining to get closer. "Are you ready?"

Another cut, and now Ruby was in the dead center of the frame, gaze leveled at a point to the right of the camera's lens. The shot showcased her good side. Never had she looked more beautiful.

"You think simply because you are a member of the court you may speak to me in this fashion. You believe by virtue of being born of the right parents you are free to move through this world however you see fit. But there are other laws a man must obey, Monsieur LeFevre. Rules a true gentleman need not be taught."

I knew the lines. *I knew them.* Ruby had been given the same dreadful dialogue foisted on me during my Lodestar screen test, back when we had first met. I'd interpreted the material in a superficial way, alternating between rage and tears. But Ruby played it coyly, amused by the effrontery of the young nobleman in the scene. She paused and moved her eyes up and down this phantom partner, undressing him as she dressed him down.

"As a lady, I am limited in how I can respond. The chancellor shall hear of your impertinence. When we meet again, perhaps you will understand your station—and mine—somewhat better." She flicked open an invisible fan and turned away, waving at someone on the other side of an imagined ballroom.

Laurence yelled "Cut!" and Natalie cackled. It was an earthy laugh, Ruby's laugh, and she pointed toward the camera about to give some technician hell.

Then the screen went black and the lights came up.

Gene pinched the crown of his hat. "She was good."

"They didn't dress her well," Edith said. "At Paramount, we'd have given her a gown she could truly move in."

I nodded at them both. "Could we watch that again?"

GENE TOOK THE reel of film with him when he left. Edith walked me back to her office and fixed afternoon tea. She said nothing more about the test, bubbling on about the challenges posed by the Villon picture. Her words washed over me like a warm bath.

From the hallway came singing, a full-throated rendition of "Goody Goody" that made up in spirit what it lacked in style. Edith huffed to the door as Adele, still warbling, entered with another armful of French histories.

"I do wish you'd stop carrying on like that," Edith said. "It's inappropriate workplace behavior."

"You're not teaching at the Hollywood School for Girls anymore." Adele said hello to me. "Say, that's a lovely necklace."

Edith leaned in for an inspection of her own. "Yes. I'd noticed it, too. A striking stone."

That morning I'd toiled like a coal miner to dig something out of my closet smart enough to wear to Paramount. I'd livened up a brown print dress with an orange belt and rust-colored French-heeled pumps. But the outfit needed a final grace note. Then I spied the velvet box atop my bureau. I was reluctant to wear Armand Troncosa's gift, particularly after Vi had received one, too. But once I tried it on my resolve crumbled. Edith's praise absolved me of any residual guilt.

"My only fear is running into every other girl in town who has one." Off Edith's puzzlement I added, "It's from Armand Troncosa. He hands them out like candy at a carnival."

"Does he? May I?" She already had the stone pinched between her fingers and angled toward the closest lamp.

"What carnivals do you go to?" Adele asked. "I've never gotten free candy."

A tug on the chain pulled the necklace taut and I stumbled toward Edith. Her eyes blazed with concentration. I fumbled for the clasp. "Did you want me to take it off?"

"That won't be necessary." She placed the stone gently against my dress. It felt cold through the fabric, changed somehow. "If you wouldn't object to delaying your job hunt, I can think of a more productive way for us to spend some time."

34

IT WAS EASILY the cleanest diner I'd ever been in, as well as the largest and currently the emptiest. Nary a coffee ring on the countertop, seating clear to the horizon. The decor, though, left something to be desired. Enormous cardboard cutouts of athletes affixed to checked wallpaper, wildly out of place French doors, columns and trellises erupting from the floor.

"I don't understand," I said to Edith. "Where's the kitchen supposed to be?"

"It's a set, dear."

"I know, but a nod to reality would help the illusion. If this were an actual diner, your food would be cold by the time it got to you. I see an order window by the—is that a bandstand?"

"It's for the number with Betty Grable and Skinnay Ennis. We're dressing the girls in very contemporary coed fashions. Knit skirts, sweater sets, some darling crocheted caps."

"You'd need one to keep warm while waiting for your lunch."

Adjourning to the set of *College Swing* had been Edith's idea. Even Travis Banton's office couldn't accommodate the number of guests we were expecting, so she'd arranged to use a Paramount soundstage—with help from on high in the person of Barney Groff. I was supposed to be pushing several tables together but kept being distracted by the production designer's notion of campus life. Anything that seemed vaguely collegiate had been included, coherence be damned.

"Bill would hate this set. And the Alden College hangout is called 'The Hangout'? Who wrote this?"

"Preston Sturges contributed a few jokes. The funny ones, I imagine he'd say. Would you mind finishing with the furniture before your critique?"

I completed my assignment as Gene walked in, using the diner's door even though one entire wall was missing. Judging from his expression he was past second and onto third thoughts about Edith's plan. He surveyed our makeshift assembly room and then Edith warily. "You're sure about this?"

"Not even remotely, Detective. I *am* sure you and your men are more than capable of handling whatever might result from this gambit."

Hansen escorted Tommy Carpa onto the soundstage. Tommy's hands were in shackles, his wrists folded demurely so the metal was almost invisible. Hansen shoved him in the back, but his heart wasn't in it. Tommy dropped into a chair at the table. Hansen turned to Gene. "Ought to book you a room at the booby hatch for going along with this." Then he looked at Edith and me. "For the record, this is the dumbest idea I ever heard of."

"Duly noted, Detective. I thank you for your cooperation."

"You wouldn't have it if it was up to me. This kind of burlesque is strictly for the Follies Theater. I'd have put the kibosh on it myself, but one word from your man and it's on with the baggy pants for us."

I longed to argue with him, to point out Hansen hadn't kicked when Groff was calling the tune earlier, but Edith wisely chose another path. "Your forbearance is appreciated. Did you know Betty Grable will be performing on that bandstand later this week?" Hansen feigned indifference, but was quick to accept Edith's offer of a tour of the set.

Tommy seemed strangely at peace, a man who'd accepted his fate. I had to resist the impulse to sweep the ever-present forelock of hair out of his eyes myself. He glanced around the set and grunted. "Floor plan of this joint is terrible. Where's the kitchen supposed to be?"

The Mirthless Minots were next. The not-so-happily married couple might as well have shown up separately. Laurence breezed in, spotted the docile Tommy, and bolted to Gene in protest. Diana clutched a long tweed coat tightly around herself. White satin accented with lace peeked out from beneath the hem, the color and fabric familiar. "Isn't that from the lullaby number?" I asked. "I thought you'd wrapped that."

"We did. But that bastard insists on reshooting it." She glared at her husband, now settling himself as far from Tommy as he could. "He's determined to make my life a living hell no matter the cost to the studio. Do you know what he said to me in front of the entire company?"

I would never find out, because I had to greet our final guests. Armand Troncosa forced a watery smile. Esteban trailed after him, so concerned about Troncosa he scarcely registered my presence. With them was an unexpected hanger-on. Addison Rice barreled over, taking both my hands and pumping them like he was drilling for oil.

"I hope it's okay I tagged along. I was bidding bon voyage to Armand when you called him. He mentioned he was coming to see you and Miss Head, and . . . I've never been on a movie lot before, can you imagine that? Who's in this picture again?"

I was hung up on one of Addison's earlier statements. "Armand is leaving?"

"Packed up his kit bag this morning. Heading home. Can't say I blame him. How did he put it? 'The sunshine of one's native land is the greatest balm for a broken heart.' Sounded better with his accent."

I excused myself and approached Esteban, watching his employer converse with Gene. Troncosa was speaking emphatically and enumerating points on his fingers. There were going to be more than five of them. The weariness on Esteban's face made it plain he had been up late and then far too early.

"I'm so glad Armand could come," I told him. "Not too much of an inconvenience, I hope."

Esteban's eyes never left Troncosa. "Armand doesn't understand the point of this gathering. He attended only at your request."

"I hear he's returning to Argentina. Tell me it's just a short trip."

"Alas, no. Home is the place for him now."

"I'm sorry to hear that. And doubly glad you're here, too, so we can say good-bye."

Esteban finally looked at me. At that moment Gene backed away from Troncosa with his arms raised in a placating gesture. He glanced at Edith, his eyes suggesting that now would be a good time to get the show on the road.

With a clap of her hands, Edith called the motley crew to order. We arranged ourselves around the table, Edith at its head, Tommy slumped at the center of one side, Hansen next to him, Gene directly behind him. Laurence and Troncosa glowered stylishly at one another.

Edith introduced herself. "I'd like to thank everyone for indulging me today. Miss Galway, may I say what a lovely coat that is. Señor Riordan, please, join us."

After a lordly wave of Troncosa's hand, Esteban nodded at Edith and sat next to his employer.

Before Edith could continue, Laurence spoke up. "I'll repeat to you, Miss Head, what I told Detective Morris. I would never have come had I known this maniac"—an accusatory finger aimed at Tommy, who replied with a lazy smile—"would be here. He assaulted me in my own home."

"He'll behave," Gene said. "And my name is Morrow."

"Come now, Minot." Troncosa tossed the words across the table like poisoned darts. "You assaulted me, yet I don't object to your presence."

The spark of a lighter in the recesses of the soundstage drew my eye. The flame briefly illuminated Barney Groff's face before darkness again consumed him. I wasn't surprised he'd opted to observe our conclave. He'd pulled strings to make it happen at Edith's request and now wanted to see if, as she claimed, she could bring the whole grisly affair to a conclusion.

Aware she was under his watchful eye, she swiftly asserted control over the situation. "Gentlemen, at the risk of stirring up further bad blood, I asked you here to confirm the sequence of events involving Ruby Carroll, also known as Princess Natalie Szabo."

A sharp bark of laughter from Diana, who then stroked the surface of her coat.

Edith was unruffled. "Señor Troncosa. Princess Natalie requested time to consider your second proposal of marriage and would be taking a trip in your absence, is that correct?"

"To San Francisco," Troncosa said. "In the company of Mr. Minot."

"We never traveled together." Laurence spoke with the bravery that only comes from having a table between you and the man who'd cleaned your clock. Diana shook her head in disgust.

Edith turned to Esteban. "Señor Riordan, is that consistent with your understanding of the facts?"

Esteban's jaw clenched as if trying to keep prisoner any words that might be used against Troncosa. I had no doubt if given the opportunity, Esteban would have chosen to perish quietly under the table rather than say anything. He nodded once.

"With that established . . ." From the deep pockets of her dress Edith removed a pair of drawstring velvet pouches. She opened each in turn and extracted two identical necklaces, twinned emeralds dangling from fine gold chains. She handed one to me. I mimicked her presentation as we turned toward Troncosa like a pair of mannequins in Tremayne's.

"Señor Troncosa. Would you be so kind as to identify these pieces of jewelry?"

Troncosa leaned forward, his interest reluctantly piqued. He eyed each piece, then Edith herself, sensing a trap. He rose from his seat to inspect the one draped over my fingers, smiling winningly at me first. Then he sat down.

"They would appear," he said slowly, "to be Troncosa stones. From mines in which my family has an interest."

Now Edith faced me. "Lillian? You brought them in. Would you do the honors?"

I raised the necklace in my hand aloft. "This one is mine. A gift from Armand. The other belongs to my friend Violet. Also given to her by Armand."

"A lovely girl, Miss Webb," Troncosa said.

Hansen's eyes were tiny and hard. "You get these by the gross and hand 'em out to your girlfriends?"

"I occasionally make presents of my family's assets to foster goodwill among friends."

"Listen to him," Laurence said. "Like he's with the League of Nations."

Troncosa drew himself up. "Is generosity frowned upon in this country?"

"Not at all." Edith pressed on. "Another quality shared by both of these pieces—"

"The stones are phonies," Diana said. "I can tell from here."

Edith bristled at having her thunder stolen, but only for a moment. "Miss Galway is correct. Paramount's own jewelry expert confirmed it. Uncommonly good forgeries."

Her last sentence was drowned out by the uproar from the table. Assorted gasps, shocked laughter, the crash of Troncosa's chair hitting the floor as he seized my hand to examine the necklace more closely. Esteban gaped at his employer in amazement.

"This is slanderous, Miss Head. What you suggest sullies my good name, and I will not permit—"

He couldn't continue, not with Laurence's braying laughter bouncing off the high ceiling. "Unbelievable. Another jumped-up little fraud. I should have known."

Even Tommy showed signs of animation. "I don't get it. You mean this guy's a hustler like me?"

Troncosa withstood their mockery with the slow-burning wrath of the true aristocrat. "The name Troncosa is known throughout South America. I am most assuredly not, as Mr. Carpa would have it, a hustler. I can only presume various officials have decided the most suitable person to blame for this late unpleasantness is the foreigner, and the rest of you have consented to go along with this travesty of justice to ease your own passages. But I will not submit to this. Esteban, contact my attorney."

Edith stayed Esteban with her hand. "Señor Troncosa, I have no intention of impugning your integrity. I only state an incontrovertible fact. The stones in these necklaces are fakes."

Mollified, Troncosa again considered the necklace I held. "This truly is your necklace, Lillian?"

"Yes. The one Esteban gave me."

Troncosa turned to his majordomo. "Your explanation?"

"I have none, Armand. I simply present the pieces given to me at your direction."

"Pieces, I should add," Edith said, "that our expert estimates would cost in the vicinity of four to five hundred dollars each."

"And you're giving 'em away like Cracker Jack prizes." Hansen was impressed. "So where are the real stones?"

"I have no idea," Troncosa said. "I accept both my friends Esteban and Lillian at their word, so the explanation lies elsewhere. The stones have far to travel before they reach me. The substitution could have been made any number of places."

Laurence hooted at that theory. Addison's expression was rapt. He had a front-row seat for the kind of spectacle that typically cost two bits in the picture house, and he wanted to catch every syllable.

Edith cleared her throat. The gathering fell silent. How this tiny woman was able to hold sway over us all I would never understand. "It might be instructive to compare these counterfeits to the genuine article. Detective Morrow?"

Gene was already quick-stepping to the soundstage door. He held it open and pointed at someone waiting.

Into the building came two uniformed police officers. They moved in ungainly fashion, carrying a metal box between them. The officers deposited it on a table with a heavy *thud*. Addison leaned forward in anticipation. Everyone else, I couldn't help noticing, reared back, as if fearing what might lie within.

Gene opened the box, the lid giving out with a theatrical creak. With tremendous care he extracted a necklace, larger and more ornate than the ones Vi and I had been given, the emerald easily triple the size. It danced at the end of its filigreed chain, setting off a gorgeous play of verdant color. It didn't need light to dazzle, providing its own. There was something primal about this jewel, a wildfire distilled into its essence and made eternal. Mine, by comparison, was an anemic little sister with no spark, no radiance.

But the surest proof of the larger necklace's worth was

Diana's gasp, at once awestruck and avaricious. Try as they might, her eyes couldn't out-glitter what they beheld.

Troncosa also stared at the necklace, stripped of his aplomb. "Where . . . where did you get this?"

"You recognize this piece, perhaps, Señor Troncosa? I thought you might." Edith walked over to one of the officers.

Then she snatched the hat off his head and put it on her own at a jaunty angle. Only Tommy got a kick out of it.

Edith took the second officer's hat and tossed it to Troncosa. He caught it out of instinct. By this time I had maneuvered behind him so I could see what he saw: the slightly faded label inside the hat reading PROPERTY PARAMOUNT PICTURES.

"The necklace is real," Edith said. "The officers are fake. Actors outfitted by the studio's costume department. Which is also where I found the necklace."

She removed the hat and took a moment to smooth her hair, allowing the revelation to sink in.

"I owe poor Ruby an apology," she said. "When I learned she was stealing clothes, wearing paste, playing a role, I assumed everything about her characterization of Natalie was false. It didn't occur to me that perhaps one thing about her performance was authentic. You gave Natalie this necklace, did you not, Señor Troncosa?"

The answer came in a tightly controlled whisper. "*Sí.*"

"When was this?"

"When I asked for her hand the first time. I fear the extravagance of the gesture frightened her, so when I proposed again I restrained myself."

"Miss Frost found this necklace in a suitcase along with the clothes Ruby needed to carry out her ruse of being Princess Natalie. All of these items were returned to the studio. I regret I didn't give the necklace the consideration it deserved at the time. It was placed quickly, too quickly, into storage. Dismissed as an imitation, part of a costume, like everything else in the suitcase."

Only I caught the pointed glance Edith threw in Barney Groff's direction, and Groff's sullen look at the soundstage floor.

"And there it might have stayed," Edith continued. "But I noticed it around Natalie's neck in the screen test directed by Mr. Minot. She wore it for good luck, Señor Troncosa, a fact I hope brings you some small degree of comfort."

A grave nod from Troncosa indicated that this was so.

"Then Lillian wore a piece that matched it—almost. A piece that was clearly a forgery, one she'd received as a gift. At that point, the answer was obvious."

"Not to me," Diana said.

"Ruby's necklace is real because you gave it to her, Señor Troncosa. You handed it to her yourself, before Mr. Beckett discovered her ruse and took possession of your other gifts to her. While these two necklaces were delivered by someone else."

Esteban met Edith's eyes. "By me. Are you making an accusation?"

"Again, Señor Riordan, I am only stating facts. The stones in these two necklaces are counterfeit. The counterfeits were delivered by you. You cannot deny either statement."

"No, but from them it can be inferred that I am somehow responsible. That I am a thief. And that, I deny." He turned to Troncosa. "It is as you said. They are placing blame on the foreigner. Why would I take advantage of you, Armand? How long have we known each other?"

"Some time." The note of suspicion in Troncosa's voice sounded like a door closing.

Esteban next threw himself on my mercy. "Lillian. Surely you can't believe I had any part in deceiving you?"

I had no answer for him. Fortunately, Gene intervened. He had returned the necklace to the metal box. Now he spoke with unmistakable authority while Edith stepped away from the table, the transfer of power choreographed. "How many of these . . . trinkets would you authorize Esteban to give away, Mr. Troncosa?"

"I couldn't begin to guess."

"Which means it's a few. Each worth several hundred dollars, as Miss Head has pointed out. Be a nice way to feather your nest, Mr. Riordan, selling the real stones, switching in phonies, no one the wiser. Not the girls, not your employer."

"Everyone happy," I said, not a little wistfully.

"Then Mr. Troncosa falls for a princess. You must have been relieved when Natalie turned down his proposal. Then he asked again, and you understood this was different. This was love. Natalie wanted time to consider. You didn't know she was in trouble and desperately searching for a way out. You thought she was taking the proposal seriously. If she said yes, there'd be no more trinkets to give to lovely women. There went all that money. Maybe your job, too. You started to think your gravy train was making its final stop."

Esteban shook his head. Looked to Troncosa beseechingly.

"You did what you felt you had to do," Edith said softly. "You killed a false princess to protect real jewels."

"Only Beckett saw you do it, because he was following Natalie. Beckett saw what you did and held it over you." Gene's voice was as flat as the Great Plains and every bit as barren of sanctuary. "He told you where to leave the body so she'd be identified as Ruby, not Natalie. He told you how to play it when first Lillian and then I showed up at Troncosa's house. He made it look like Natalie was still alive. All the while blackmailing everyone he could. Minot. Miss Galway. You."

"I tell you, I do not know any Beckett!"

"When Troncosa came back to Los Angeles and there was no sign of Natalie, you were to encourage him to return to Argentina. Unfortunately for you, Miss Frost was there to make the connection between Ruby and Natalie. At that point, you improvised. You arranged for someone to shoot at Troncosa. Not to hit him, but to *miss*. A tricky piece of business, except you and several colleagues are in training for the Olympic pentathlon. One of the events in that sport is target shooting. We're already talking to your friends at the Vista Del Mar Athletic Club. Beckett figured out you were behind the shooting at Tremayne's. He ambushed you at Rice's party. And you took your chance to get out from under his thumb."

"This is lunacy. You can't prove any of this!"

Edith spoke up. "Unless the other necklaces you distributed on Señor Troncosa's behalf are also counterfeit."

The prospect brought Esteban up short. Again he lobbied Troncosa. "Armand. You must believe me."

Troncosa folded his arms across his chest. "I find I don't know what to believe."

Esteban snorted, a lifetime of contempt in the sound. "Of course. What should I expect from a man who does not know true quality? Who cannot recognize the stones from his own family's mines? Who mistakes for a princess that confidence woman? That cheap, tawdry . . . whore?"

At that perfectly timed last word, Troncosa sprang at him. Esteban propelled himself away from the table. Hansen grabbed Troncosa's arms and forced him back into his seat. Diana instinctively darted to Laurence, who held her close. I had my own problem to deal with. Namely the barrel of Esteban's .22, jabbed into my side. He'd played Troncosa flawlessly, goading him to cover pulling the gun from his jacket.

Esteban gripped my arm, his fingers digging to the bone. "Miss Frost has graciously agreed to accompany me. If you would excuse us?"

He began walking backward, jerking me roughly toward the door. Gene and Hansen fanned out on either side of us, their hands empty but their jackets wide.

"You won't get off the lot," Gene said. "There are officers at every door."

"Like the ones who brought in the necklace? I am willing to take my chances." He took another step.

"Careful of that cable," Edith said.

Esteban glanced down. I lifted the heel of my clearance rack pumps and delivered all of my weight to his instep. He roared and pushed me away. Unfortunately I slammed into Gene. Hansen shifted toward us for an instant, allowing Esteban to regain his footing and stagger toward the door.

A thunderous clatter arose behind me. The sound of one of the tables overturning. Tommy Carpa, his face a mask of grief, had flipped it over when he leaped out of his seat. Bellowing, he charged at Esteban, hands still shackled, a human missile.

Esteban fired a single panicked shot. Tommy never wavered, still rushing forward.

He plowed into Esteban, the two of them going down in a roiling tangle of legs. Tommy snarled as he butted his head against Esteban's chest and arms. Gene and Hansen sprinted over to separate them, Esteban looking almost relieved as Gene hauled him to his feet. Hansen, meanwhile, dragged Tommy onto his backside. Too Much Tommy's unruly hair framed eyes that had gone completely blank.

"You killed her," he said. "You killed the only woman I ever loved and didn't even know it was her."

Every soundstage door banged open, blue uniforms bulling

their way in, overflowing the Hangout. Gene held Esteban toward them like laundry he wanted carted away.

"They're real," he said. "Want to check their hats?"

I lost sight of them as Edith fussed over me for a moment, making sure I hadn't been hurt.

"I didn't even damage my shoe," I said. "They make sturdy heels at the May Company."

The tide of blue washed out of the soundstage, bearing Esteban, Tommy, and Hansen away. Gene, after checking on me, asked a shaken Troncosa to come with him. He agreed, pausing to give an unsteady wave at the stage door. Diana was weeping next to it, Laurence holding her close and cooing in her ear.

Barney Groff had walked over to the bandstand. He crouched by the bass drum and probed a hole in its head. Edith and I guardedly joined him.

"Yon gunman's shot went wide. Bullet pierced this drum. Studio property damaged on your watch, Miss Head."

"I'm terribly sorry, Mr. Groff."

"I wouldn't worry about it. That's why we have skilled craftsmen on the payroll, to attend to this sort of thing." He stood up and dusted off his hands. He gave Edith a nod and then, to my disbelief, turned to me. "Miss Frost," he said. That was all I was going to get. He strolled toward Diana and Laurence.

Addison bounced over to us, ecstatic. "What a show! Better than the last few Philo Vance pictures combined! I insist we go out to celebrate. My treat."

"A gracious offer, Mr. Rice, but I'm afraid I must decline. Too much to accomplish today. Perhaps you'll invite me to your next party. And Lillian, aren't you off to Bullock's to see about a job?" Edith peered over her spectacles at me then, with another of her standard compressed smiles, marched away. I watched her small black-clad frame hurry through the outer door.

"What a professional. Who could work after such excitement?" Addison grinned at me like a naughty schoolboy. "What do you say, Lillian? Would you like a ride to Bullock's or can I persuade you to play hooky?"

I thought it over for all of two seconds, then slipped my arm in his. "No persuasion necessary. I've got an idea. Let's go to the movies."

35

HOLLYWOOD'S BRIGHTEST STARS surrounded us when Edith and I lunched a week later. They weren't in the Paramount commissary, alas; they gazed out from the movie posters gracing the walls.

We'd said our hellos when Preston Sturges stopped by our table. The rakish writer was wearing a cocoa-brown suit with a pale green tie and matching pocket square so abundant Edith could have wrapped it around Dorothy Lamour.

"Did you ladies peruse Lorna Whitcomb's column this morning?" he asked. Before either of us could answer he'd pulled up a chair, smoothed his mustache and signaled a waitress in one seamless movement.

"I won't read one word that woman writes." Next to the natty Sturges, Edith looked like a convent runaway in one of her deceptively plain dresses. This one was midnight blue with intricate black embroidery at the collar and cuffs, a reward for close attention.

"I've been getting my news from the radio," I said. "It's cheaper."

"Lorna relayed the latest glad tidings for Laurence Minot and Diana Galway. New Lodestar contracts for both, a lovers' getaway in the cards."

"That's crazy. They were making nice last time I saw them, but I was convinced Diana was going to drop Laurence from a height. I wanted to watch."

Sturges paused to appreciate the waitress standing before us, from the freckles on her button nose to the name etched on the tag at her pert bosom. "Dearest Eve. We must have coffee, gallons of it, post haste."

Edith and I ordered lunch, then Sturges held forth. "Hollywood marriages, Lillian, aren't about love. They're more like mutual-aid societies. Diana's smart enough to see she needs Minot. For now, anyway. While Laurence has to prove he can be well behaved. Lorna says they're embarking on a cruise. Pity the hands setting sail on that vessel." He hoisted his java in their honor, as did we all.

Sturges then fixed his gaze on me. "Now. I demand to know everything about this nefarious business. I won't tell a soul other than anyone in my general vicinity when I'm clutching a highball glass."

His word was good enough for me. Esteban's arrest for Ruby's murder—not Natalie's—had been duly reported in the newspapers, any details that might embarrass Hollywood's hierarchy artfully suppressed by Barney Groff and his ilk. But whispers could never be silenced. The curious case of Princess Natalya had entered the ranks of show business open secrets.

"It turns out Esteban had been padding Armand Troncosa's books for years. Not just the jewels, but every household expense he could think of. He was robbing Armand blind."

"The perfect payment for blind trust," Edith said. "Mr. Troncosa has the curse of thinking everyone likes him."

"No wonder he felt at home here," Sturges said. "And you figured all this out by getting an eyeful of some emeralds?"

Edith fussed with her just-arrived plate. "This story is entirely too sad. A man murders a woman who didn't exist, but poor Ruby dies."

"What it needs is a happy ending. The story, I mean." As he spoke, Sturges's eyes focused on a point behind my head. I doubted it was the poster for *The Squaw Man* entrancing him. "Romance triumphs, our girl falls into a fortune, the whole kit and caboodle. There's a comedy in there somewhere. Beautiful con woman, a rich man who sees through the eyes of love, which makes him blind to . . . hmm." He stood up and remembered his manners. "Enjoy your lunch, ladies. Must dash." Sturges walked away, patting his mustache and muttering to himself.

"We won't be seeing him for a while," Edith said.

"Unless we go to his restaurant. If it's still open."

As we ate, Edith described her Thanksgiving—naturally, she'd worked through the holiday—and Travis Banton's fortunes. Before she could object I ordered two slices of apple pie for dessert. "It's on me. I'm celebrating."

I received one of the designer's skeptical looks. She had fifty-seven varieties of them, this one friendlier than most. "What's the occasion?"

"I'm starting a new job tomorrow."

"Wonderful! Child wrangler at Bullock's?"

"No. Addison Rice's social secretary."

"That's marvelous!" She broke off a tiny morsel of pie with her fork. "How did it happen?"

"After the excitement here I couldn't bear to go to Bullock's. Instead Addison and I saw a double feature at the Rialto then went out for a prime rib dinner. I told him about getting fired and he got this gleam in his eye. Mrs. Somers had been pushing him to hire her replacement so she could train the new girl before her baby came. He offered me the job, pending Mrs. Somers's seal of approval."

"I assume the position will entail more than watching movies."

"And how. I met with Mrs. Somers yesterday and she walked me through the duties. Correspondence, organizing the parties, keeping Addison out of trouble. She asked me approximately one million questions. Addison said I passed the interview with flying colors."

"I'm not surprised. I recognized your resourcefulness the day we met."

"I'd better be resourceful for what he's paying me. It's more than I'd have gotten with two promotions at Tremayne's."

"You asked for a clothing allowance, of course."

I lowered my coffee cup. "Should I have?"

"Naturally. There will be numerous occasions you'll have to dress for. That navy suit of yours will only go so far."

I brushed a chunk of pie crust off Old Reliable. Then another. "I love this suit."

"As you should. It's quite flattering. And may I say you've accessorized it beautifully."

My fingers strayed to the brooch on my lapel. Two intertwined gold circles set with garnets. It was high time my mother's legacy got some California sunshine.

"You need a host of such suits in neutral colors. Light gray, tan." Edith looked me over, and for an instant I felt more like a project than a person. "We'll work within your new salary. If you can secure a clothing allowance in the meantime, so much the better."

On the walk back to the Wardrobe building we passed the *College Swing* soundstage. The joyful noise of the band rehearsing the title tune barreled through the open doors. Not that I could enjoy it with Edith listing the bounty of clothes I'd need to serve as Addison's secretary.

"Gowns for parties, dresses for afternoon teas, lighter clothes for trips to his desert home. People never know how to dress for the heat. You're lucky that I do. Perhaps a riding habit. A man of his status must keep horses."

My head was spinning, so I was relieved to see Bill Ihnen bounding toward us from the soundstage, jacket open and tie askew. "Heard the music and stopped for a listen. The lyrics are Greek to me." He gave Edith a peck on the cheek, then me. "Good thing I ran into you, Edo. If my date's going to be in pale blue satin, do I wear—"

"No offense, buster, but wait your turn."

Edith reared back in mock surprise. "You expect Bill to hold off until we've dealt with your work wardrobe? He doesn't have that kind of time."

"I need your advice on what to wear on a date, too. And I'm more in the dark than he is."

Bill bowed in my direction, yielding Edith's attention to me. "Would it be with Detective Morrow?" she asked.

"Yes. Gene's taking me to the fights this weekend."

"How many bouts are on the card? Will you be going to dinner as well? Before or after the fights? And where?"

"He didn't offer me a contract, Edith. He just asked if I wanted to go."

"You should have found that out first. Still, there are a few items I can show you that will double for the new job and your weekend plans. You can pick up something similar at Tremayne's when you share your good news. As for you, Bill . . . I'm sorry. You're on your own."

Magnanimous in victory, I blew Bill a Bronx cheer. Edith had already resumed her fast-paced stride back to Wardrobe. I scrambled after her, rummaging in my handbag for a notepad as I ran. I couldn't afford to miss a word.

Turn the page for a sneak peek at
the next Lillian Frost & Edith Head mystery

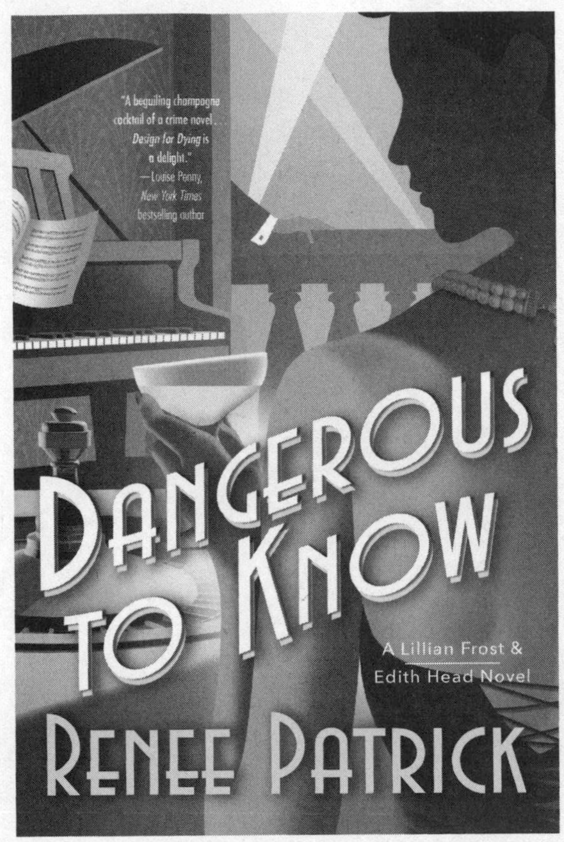

Available April 2017

Los Angeles Register *December 2, 1938*

LORNA WHITCOMB'S EYES ON HOLLYWOOD

Ah, December in Los Angeles, the season when our starlets simmer with jealousy contemplating their East Coast cousins. What sets them off? The furriers' shopwindows full of mink and silver fox. Pity the poor sweltering sirens whose sole chill is the cold shoulder from producers; the only snowflakes they see are made of soap, strewn on soundstages to turn Culver City into Chamonix . . . Overheard on the Warners lot from a fluttery female watching George Brent walk by: "Now I know what started those forest fires!" . . . Does Gotham's high-society smuggling case have tentacles reaching all the way to the movie colony? Albert Chaperau, self-styled producer and diplomat, stands accused of helping Park Avenue plutocrats evade Customs duties on gowns and jewels freighted in from Europe. Comes word local luminaries may also have benefitted from his extra-legal largesse. We hear the brouhaha began at a diamond-encrusted Manhattan dinner party in October, but whoever has the skinny on that swanky soiree isn't talking.

1

"THE FOOD WAS too rich, for one thing. So were the guests. The dinner party was a dud long before the Nazis got involved."

I looked over at Edith Head, a blur of motion behind her sketch pad. "But you've heard my Chaperau saga before. More than once."

"True, dear, but your account is so entertaining."

"You can't buffalo me. This is about Lorna Whitcomb's column this morning. Are Paramount stars involved?"

"One hears rumors, so one seeks facts. You were there, eyewitness to history. Humor me. Don't mind my sketching. I can draw and listen at the same time. It's the essence of the job."

A trace of paint fumes perfumed Edith's office in the Wardrobe department at Paramount Pictures, olfactory proof she had finally arrived. The suite had formerly been home to Edith's mentor Travis Banton. She had assumed Banton's responsibilities in March when the studio opted not to renew the brilliant but bibulous costume designer's contract. Paramount hadn't been in a hurry to bestow his title or office on Edith, though, the formal announcement coming after she'd been doing his job for months. Her first official act as Paramount's lead designer had been to have her new domain repainted, the walls now a soft gray. "Like a French salon," she'd said. "A muted palette places the focus on the actress, where it should be. Besides, if I don't change something in here no one will take me seriously."

Edith's personal transformation was more dramatic. She'd

abandoned her bobbed hairstyle in favor of bangs with a chignon at the back. The new coiffure was a touch severe when paired with Edith's owlish spectacles, but it suited her businesslike demeanor perfectly. I'd complimented her on it when I'd entered the office that morning. She'd waved me off. "Copied from Anna May Wong. A new look for the new position. With my unfortunate forehead, I'm afraid the options are rather limited. Then I remembered how striking Miss Wong's hair looked when she returned to the studio to make *Dangerous to Know*. I haven't decided if I'm going to keep it."

I owed my presence at the infamous dinner party, along with a bounty of other opportunities, to my friendship with Edith. If she wanted to hear the story again, then she'd get the full roadshow rendition. My goal: uncork a spellbinder to make her set aside her sketch pad.

"The entire trip happened at the last minute. That's how it is with Addison." Meaning Addison Rice, the retired industrialist who had inexplicably seen fit to give me a job. "His wife Maude was about to sail for Europe with a companion, but the grim news from the Continent was giving her second thoughts. Addison decided to see her off in New York, and asked me to come along."

"Because it's your hometown," Edith said.

"I think it was more he wanted company on the trip back. It was a whirlwind jaunt. We waved our handkerchiefs at the *Queen Mary*, leaving me enough time to race out to Flushing and visit my uncle Danny and aunt Joyce."

"How are they?"

"Dying to meet you. I gave you some buildup. While we were in Gasparino's Luncheonette, Addison ran into a familiar face on Fifth Avenue."

"Albert Chaperau. The producer."

"Who'd been haunting Addison's parties, looking to meet people. So thrilled was he to see his bosom pal that he finagled us invites to a Park Avenue dinner. Instead of going to a picture at Radio City Music Hall, Addison and I turned up like foundlings at the home of a state supreme court justice."

I described our hosts. Judge Edgar Lauer, a bluff man in his late sixties, wore the authoritative air of someone who handed down verdicts even when he wasn't on the bench. His fiftyish wife Elma made a more vivid impression, thanks to the wardrobe she'd chosen for the occasion. "That gown," I whispered, still thunderstruck lo these six weeks later.

Edith looked up from her sketch pad, but her pencil kept moving. I hadn't won her over yet.

"Picture a floor-length sheath of white silk jersey," I said. "With a gargantuan royal-blue bow covering most of the bodice. The points of which unfortunately emphasized Mrs. Lauer's sagging jawline."

"It sounds quite audacious."

"That's one word for it. It wasn't designed for a matron entertaining at home. It was meant to be worn in some Parisian boîte by a woman half her age."

"Someone like you?" Edith said with one of her patented closed-lipped smiles. "I don't believe you ever told me what you wore that evening."

"I made do."

"With what, exactly?"

"You've seen the dress. Ice-blue satin with a square neckline and short matching jacket."

"For a formal dinner?" Edith raised an eyebrow. Now I prayed she'd continue sketching, not wanting to earn her undivided attention this way.

"Didn't I say it was a whirlwind jaunt? That was the best outfit I brought."

"You are the social secretary for one of the most prominent men in Los Angeles, and you weren't prepared for the possibility of a formal dinner? A floor-length dress, evening shoes, and a wrap would have taken the same amount of space."

"Not the way I pack." It didn't seem the time to point out how far I'd come in the year since I'd been a failed actress turned shopgirl without a pair of evening shoes to my name. "It's not as if Addison had a tuxedo. He wore blue serge!"

Edith closed her eyes with tremendous forbearance. "Go on."

"The Lauers throw more sedate affairs than Addison's. Their guests hail from politics, industry, and the *Social Register.* Albert Chaperau was completely out of place. You've seen his picture in the newspapers? Heavyset fellow, head like a salt block? All these staid sorts and there's Chaperau, filling the air with ideas like so many soap bubbles, not caring virtually all of them were destined to pop and leave only slickness behind."

"A taste of Los Angeles," Edith said.

"Truth be told, I enjoyed having him there for that very reason. He was just back from Europe and had a whole slate of projects he'd discussed abroad, including an American version of his film *Mayerling.*"

"I know it was a huge success, considering it's in French," Edith said. "But how does he propose to get that ending out of the Breen Office alive?"

"That was my first question. Actually, my first question was, 'Can Charles Boyer star in it again?' Chaperau said the murder-suicide of Crown Prince Rudolf and his young love was a matter of Austrian history, and any American retelling would be true to the record."

Edith clucked dubiously, just as I had.

"Dinner was served," I went on, "the first course a deathly white cream of mushroom soup. I was seated next to Serge Rubinstein, a financier who'd cornered the market in coarseness. Addison mentioned he'd just sent his wife off on a tour of the Continent. Chaperau asked where she was visiting. 'I wouldn't put faith in maps much longer,' he says. 'Those poor souls in the Sudetenland didn't think they were in Germany.' Everyone at the table had recently been in Europe and had a dire report to contribute. Judge Lauer believed the Austrian Anschluss and the Sudeten crisis had only whetted Hitler's aggression. Mrs. Lauer said their summer shopping had been spoiled by the mood of despair. All the while Addison is turning paler than his soup."

"The poor man," Edith said. "He must have thought he'd dispatched his wife into near-certain doom."

"For his sake I wanted the war talk to stop, so I went to my can't-miss subject. Who should play Scarlett O'Hara in *Gone with the Wind?*

"Still stumping for Joan Bennett?"

"She's only the perfect choice. Admit it. But sadly, no one took the bait, because Chaperau insisted on polishing his credentials. He announced he was recently named attaché for the government of Nicaragua. Which came as a surprise, because I thought he was French. Rubinstein asked what a banana republic needed with a picture maker, and Chaperau held forth on films as a universal export, shaping ideas around the globe. He claimed Hitler himself knew this, and it was why the exodus of talent from the UFA studios in Berlin distressed him. Then Judge Lauer weighed in. 'Hitler's a madman who must be stopped. We're fooling ourselves if we think otherwise.'"

Edith made a quiet sound of satisfaction. Whether at the judge's politics or her own still-in-progress sketch, I couldn't tell. Time for bold methods. Time for me to *act*.

I stood and began staggering around the room. "Throughout the conversation, Rosa the maid had been refilling glasses. Now she stops and slams her tray onto the sideboard." I performed the scene, reeling into Edith's desk. My Rosa had a clubfoot, my hammy instincts getting the better of me. "Mrs. Lauer asked if she was all right. But Rosa, her face bright red, was not." I gave my next words a Teutonic twist. "'I am happy to work in your home, Mrs. Lauer. But first and foremost, I am a true German. I love Adolf Hitler. And I will not abide anyone speaking this way about the Führer. If these insults do not cease at once, I will stop serving. The choice is yours.'"

Edith finally put down her pencil and gaped at me. I had her captivated at last. Game, set, and match, Frost.

"It was so quiet after Rosa's outburst, I was certain everyone in the dining room could hear my heart racing. Then Rubinstein asks, 'Is Park Avenue part of the Sudetenland, too?' Judge Lauer, an old hand at pronouncing sentences, stands up. 'Then you may go at once, Rosa.' The maid storms out one door, Mrs. Lauer scurries out another in tears. I went after her. She was still apologizing to me when Rosa appeared, wearing a coat as black as a nun's habit. She looked at Mrs. Lauer and said, 'Madam. There remains the matter of references.'"

Edith hooted with laughter. "Rosa certainly has her nerve. Marvelous accent, by the way. You sound like Marlene Dietrich."

"Addison's is even better. We've been telling this story a lot. Rosa's request hit Mrs. Lauer like a bracer. She drew herself up and asked Rosa if her sister still worked as a retainer for the former Grand Duchess Marie of Russia. 'Not only will I *not* provide you with a reference,' she proclaimed, 'but perhaps I will telephone the grand duchess and let her know what kind of blood runs in your family.' To which Rosa replied, 'Only good German blood, madam, something the grand duchess already knows. Much as you know there are telephone calls I, too, can make.' With that, Rosa moved past us and out into the night. Mrs. Lauer and I linked arms and returned to our soup."

"Remarkable," Edith said. "But of course it wasn't over."

"Oh, no. Throwing Manhattan's most awkward dinner party since the Gilded Age wasn't enough. The next day, Addison and I belatedly made it to Radio City to see *The Mad Miss Manton*."

"Ah, Stanwyck." Edith sighed, with me happily taking a second chorus. Barbara Stanwyck was one of our favorite people.

"While the picture played, the Lauers' world collapsed. Rosa Weber, freshly unemployed, marched into the U.S. Customs offices and spilled every bean in her possession. The Lauers, she told the authorities, were guilty of smuggling, along with Albert Chaperau. It seems Mrs. Lauer cleaned out various ateliers on her summer excursion to Paris. Chaperau then transported her purchases in his luggage, which bypassed customs inspection owing to his dubious diplomatic status as a representative of Nicaragua. Consequently, Mrs. Lauer avoided paying import duties on the clothes. A few days later, Albert Chaperau—right name Shapiro—was taken into custody at his suite at the Pierre. He was in white tie and tails at the time, having been at the Stork Club until four in the morning. I say if you have to be arrested, that's the way to do it."

Edith nodded in agreement.

"Customs men also raided the Lauers' apartment, hauling cases of couture away. By then Addison and I were back in Los Angeles. A Customs agent, gruff man name of Higgins, drove out to ask us about the dinner party. He said last year the Lauers hadn't declared a load of fancy clothes and jewelry, costing them more than ten thousand dollars in duties and fines. Agent Higgins made it clear the Customs Service was not in the second-chance business. He also said Mrs. Lauer had hied herself to a sanitarium. I felt for her. She didn't strike me as particularly black-hearted or criminal. Just another rich woman insulated from the real world. Plus she agreed Joan Bennett would make a splendid Scarlett O'Hara."

"I almost sympathize with Mrs. Lauer for going along with Mr. Chaperau's proposal," Edith said. "I had no idea I was supposed to pay import duties on the gowns I purchased when the studio sent me to Paris this summer. There I am on the dock, suddenly owing a fortune! A man from the New York office had to come down and set matters right. Mrs. Lauer's outré dinner party gown had been smuggled in by Mr. Chaperau, I take it."

"It's now being held as evidence. Your turn to spin a yarn, Edith. What have you heard about Chaperau's West Coast operations?"

"Only that he appears to have made his services available to at least one figure at Paramount. The place is in an uproar. An encore of your account of the dinner seemed in order."

Typical Edith, gathering intelligence on behalf of the studio where she spent every waking moment. I pressed her for the suspect star's name knowing she'd keep mum. Such was her loyalty. Were Paramount under siege, tiny Edith would hoist a pike and defend the Bronson Gate.

Bested, I asked, "What were you sketching away madly on?"

"Dorothy Lamour's costumes for the new Jack Benny picture."

"Speaking of Jack—"

Edith huffed out a sigh. "I haven't forgotten my promise to get you into an early screening of *Artists and Models Abroad*." In addition to starring my favorite comedian, Jack Benny, and my personal Scarlett O'Hara, Joan Bennett, *Artists and Models Abroad* boasted a fashion show sequence already being touted in fan magazines: a parade of gowns from the finest designers in Paris. Schiaparelli and Lanvin, Maggy Rouff and Alix. I was champing at the bit for an advance look, and my eagerness undoubtedly chafed Edith given her costumes were being upstaged by the haute couture.

Edith's receptionist knocked on the door. "Pardon me, Miss Head, your next appointment is here."

Marlene Dietrich coasted into the office, crooked smile first. She wore a pale green daytime suit with a subtle checkered pattern and slightly flared skirt. The matching emerald veil on her low-crowned hat did extraordinary favors for eyes that required no help.

Edith and Dietrich embraced, the actress bending to kiss the diminutive designer on both cheeks. Edith introduced me, my knees knocking at the prospect that Dietrich had somehow heard my cut-rate imitation of her. "But Lillian and I have already met," Dietrich said, her accent an ermine wrap around every syllable. I sounded nothing like her. "At a party hosted by your lovely employer Mr. Rice. Perhaps you remember?"

"How could I forget? You played the musical saw." The image of Dietrich flicking her dress to one side, tucking the handle of the blade between those impossible legs, remained a high point of my Hollywood sojourn.

Dietrich crossed those legs now as she sat down and took immediate possession of the room. I rose, preparing to leave the ladies alone.

"Thank you for arranging this opportunity to consult with your esteemed guest," Dietrich said.

I cocked an expectant eye toward the door only to discover that Dietrich gaze again aimed squarely at me. Apparently, *I* was the esteemed guest.

What had Edith walked me into?

About the Authors

RENEE PATRICK is the pseudonym for married authors Rosemarie and Vince Keenan. Rosemarie is a research administrator and a poet. Vince is a screenwriter and a journalist. Both native New Yorkers, they currently live in Seattle, Washington.